INFERNO

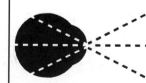

This Large Print Book carries the
Seal of Approval of N.A.V.H.

INFERNO

KAREN HARPER

WHEELER PUBLISHING
An imprint of Thomson Gale, a part of The Thomson Corporation

THOMSON
™
GALE

Detroit • New York • San Francisco • New Haven, Conn. • Waterville, Maine • London

THOMSON
GALE

LIBRARY OF CONGRESS CATALOGING-IN-PUBLICATION DATA

Harper, Karen (Karen S.)
  Inferno / by Karen Harper.
    p. cm. — (Wheeler Publishing large print romance)
  ISBN-13: 978-1-59722-549-6 (hardcover : alk. paper)
  ISBN-10: 1-59722-549-5 (hardcover : alk. paper)
  1. Bush pilots — Montana — Fiction. 2. Widows — Fiction. 3.
Government investigators — Fiction. 4. Arsonists — Fiction. 5. Montana —
Fiction. 6. Large type books. I. Title.
PS3558.A624792I54 2007
813'.54—dc22
                                              2007011036

Published in 2007 by arrangement with Harlequin Books, S.A.

Printed in the United States of America on permanent paper
10 9 8 7 6 5 4 3 2 1

To all our fellow travelers on the Ohio State Alumni Rocky Mountain trip, especially Marilyn and Jack, Debbie and Nadine.

And as ever, to my fellow traveler through life, Don, for all the help and support.

PROLOGUE

August 29, 2005
The sound of sirens always soothed his soul. In the pitch-black night, the throbbing lights of the fire engines and cop cars did not make his pulse pound, but rather made it slow and steady itself. As ever, he was completely in control.

Curtain up! Showtime! Evan Durand lay flat against the porch roof across the street, four houses down from the conflagration. He had a front-row seat in the balcony to watch the actors in the grand pageant. For he was both director and producer of the chaos he had created with such care and cleverness.

They would never catch him, never pin the multistate string of arsons on him. *In Like A Ghost, Out Like A Ghost* — that was the name of this epic drama, Evan thought as he twisted his mother's onyx ring around his little finger with his thumb.

Both the wildfire in the woodlot 6.4 miles away and this blaze in a house a stone's throw from a suburban fire station were in his script. He was the genius in the Durand family, not his father. Let the hotshot FBI Serial Arson Team think they could identify him by his M.O. That's what they were desperate to do. He was so proud his work was getting national reviews now, not just local ones! Finally, the morons had figured out that his successes were linked, were from the same brilliant brain.

The cops shouted at the growing crowd of onlookers to get back. An EMS vehicle and two more fire engines screeched up, much too late. They'd been pulled away by his smaller decoy fire. Firefighters piled from the ladder truck. It reminded him of a circus act where the clowns spilled out, and he shook with laughter. Some carried axes; some dragged hoses. They were fighting a smoke-belching fire less than a third of a mile from their station house, yet they'd been suckered in again. Evan Durand — rave reviews and standing room only; America's firefighters — a one-night stand. And the FBI team — beneath contempt.

On his belly, Evan inched away from the edge of the porch roof, closer to the house. He'd been hiding in the bushes when a young couple ran out to watch, and he'd used the woodpile they had stacked close to their house to get up on the porch roof. Man, if he'd chosen them instead of Jane Stinchcomb, he wouldn't have had to do much more than throw a low-grade liquid accelerant here, then toss a match. The pile, the porch and the entire wooden frame would be ablaze in minutes.

But Evan always chose the house of a woman living alone. That had made the fire-fighters and local arson investigators in Helena, Mission Viejo, Boulder, Seattle, Salt Lake, Reno, Lake Tahoe and Boise blame themselves even more when they failed. And now that the FBI had been called in, this would make them feel like the fools they were, he thought, and gave his ring another hard twist. A little woodlot fire made them late for their big entrance.

For the first time, Evan heard the woman's screams from the burning house. Rising action! At least the protagonist had great voice projection.

He'd jimmied her front window and heaved the jar of liquid white phosphorus where it would ignite the bottom of the staircase and trap her upstairs. WP or Willy Pete, his source had called the volatile stuff when he'd sold it to him. And all the research Evan had done on it was absolutely on target. He could smell its garlic-like stench; its flames were as yellow as the glare of a spotlight. Its dense white smoke was a curtain ready to go up.

Had the doomed heroine of the tragedy been sleeping through all the noise and flames and smoke before this moment? Had she missed the sound of shattering glass? She was probably so used to hearing sirens that she didn't react at first, not even when they came close. People living near fire stations, much like firefighters themselves — especially those cocky crews battling wildfires — were way too certain they were safe. He'd proved that.

Evan watched four firefighters charge inside while one climbed a ladder. Incandescent, canary-colored flames waved merrily from the blown-out lower windows, even as the hoses poured in water. Sand smothered WP better than water, but this would work eventually. Meanwhile, the cops kept the growing cluster of neighbors and fire junkies back from the belching heat.

And then he saw something that made his pulse pound. An unmarked black car pulled up and three men and a woman jumped out. They showed the cops something in their hands — no doubt their badges — and charged right through the yellow-tape perimeter.

One of the men was broad shouldered and blond, while another was gray-haired. The third, a heavyset man, limped badly. He could tell that the woman was fairly young and had long, brown hair. It had to be the vaunted FBI arson team.

Now they would realize that their so-called Boy Next Door Arsonist had brought his operation to their own backyard. This fire was just nine miles from their FBI office in downtown Denver, where they tried to track him with all their forensic evidence and wild profiling theories. Evan had a good notion to drive right over to their office and start a fire there.

The thought made him laugh so hard he felt the shingles vibrate under him. He tried to make out the faces of the new arrivals, but they didn't turn his way. Besides, it was difficult to see through the smoke screen created by the WP.

A crick in his neck suddenly pained him, so he rotated his head to ease it. And then he saw the old woman. Her face lit by dancing flames, she was staring out a second-story window of this house. How long had she been there? And had she glimpsed his face? Evan longed to savor this Dante's

Inferno — no, *Durand's* Inferno — but knew he had to get the hell out of Denver. Yet not before he left some sort of insulting message for the government crew. The sobriquet Boy Next Door Arsonist was all wrong. He was not a boy, but thirty years old. Besides, he wanted to be called something worthy, like the Fire Phantom or Smoke Ghost. Speaking of which, he had to disappear now, and fast.

Evan pulled his baseball cap down over his forehead and belly-crawled away from the woman's window to the edge of the roof. What if she phoned the cops? He had a mind to bust in her window and shut her up for good, but that was not the way he operated. Peons worked with brute strength, not with the finesse and intellect that were his calling cards.

Evan scooted to the side of the porch, scraping his stomach right through his black T-shirt, and then dangled his legs until his feet found the top of the woodpile. When he let go, he snagged his ring, yanking his knuckle. At least the ring didn't pull off.

Fortunately none of the cops at the scene so much as looked his direction as he walked calmly away between two houses. After about a hundred yards, he began to run. He hoped that old lady wasn't a glitch in his master plan. Maybe, with this pièce de résistance tonight, it was time for a break, another change of scenery. Back to the wilds for a while, like that little California working vacation two years ago. Only this time he'd go somewhere he knew, somewhere farther out so he could get lost — really lost.

And he knew just the place.

1

September 5, 2005

Lauren Taylor left the Lost Lake area and flew her white Cessna 206 combination wheeled-pontoon plane over the crest of Salish Range and down into the Flathead Valley. The county seat of Kalispell lay beneath her as she followed the Flathead River and Route 93 south. Though she'd made many instrument approaches to the city airport south of town during rain or snow storms, it was great to be able to just fly by the landmarks today. That always made her feel more in command of her life, which had spun badly out of control.

The firs, pines and spruces lining the lake and Bigfork Bay looked green from this height, but it hadn't rained in weeks and all of northwest Montana was bone dry. At least this weather made for an easy trip, thought Lauren, though she had no fear of flying, even in the mountains. In fact, she loved it. Up there, surrounded by massive granite peaks, or soaring over vast snow-fields and glaciers, she found an escape from her great loss.

The monumental tragedy of her thirty years was losing her husband Ross when he fought a wildfire two summers ago. He'd left her with a log house on the edge of a small town, this plane and their son, Nicky, now six years old.

Thank heavens Ross had taught her to fly this trusty old warhorse. They had nick-named the plane *Silver,* after the Lone Ranger's pure white steed in the old cowboy stories. *Silver* was her and Nicky's livelihood and her lifeline to the outside. Their mountain-sheltered town of Vermillion was miles from any populated areas and could be reached on the ground only by twisting roads, which rockslides or winter avalanches sometimes cut off completely. Still, as far as Lauren was concerned, after once seeing the jade green, glacial-melt Lost Lake, its alpine meadows and protective ring of mountains, nothing else compared.

Silver and six other pontoon or ice-runner aircraft flew everything — from mail and food, to hikers and skiers — between Ver-million and Kalispell. Her plane could seat up to six, but Lauren usually took out the back four seats for cargo. Today she was picking up newspapers, mail and cartons of dairy products for the general store, plus one passenger, a hiker named Rocky Marston who had contacted her via her Web site.

From Kalispell it was an hour's flight to Vermillion and Lost Lake. At three hundred dollars an hour per passenger, she figured this Marston guy must really like solo hiking. There were fewer passengers in the summer than in the winter when the ski lodge was open. If Marston had bargained with her, she might have come down in price, but he'd e-mailed her only once from Phoenix. She was grateful for the money. Nicky's birthday was coming up, and she wanted to buy him a beginner's mountain bike.

"Cessna Niner One Zulu," came the crackling voice on her radio, answering her earlier call for permission to land. "Cleared for approach into Kalispell. Welcome back to the big city, Lauren."

"Good morning, Jim. Cessna Niner One Zulu out of Vermillion, following clearance into the airport."

Jim Kline, the chief air traffic controller, wasn't kidding. Kalispell, with a population around fourteen thousand, was the big city to a girl from Vermillion, which boasted six hundred and eighteen year-round residents. And to Nicky, who came along with her sometimes to hit a restaurant, movie or the stores, this place was about as exciting as seeing New York or London.

This summer she'd brought him, her friend Dee Cobern and Dee's grandson, Larson, to Woodland Park, where they used the water slides and floated on inner tubes in the lazy river. Another time, the four of them had gone swimming in Foy's Lake, which warmed up in the summer, unlike Lost Lake. And another great memory — Ross had proposed to her in Lawrence Park's picnic area in the gazebo.

Over the intersection of Routes 2 and 93, Lauren started her descent. As usual, *Silver's* landing gear came down with a clunk. Lauren backed off the power and drifted down, lowering the flaps to coast in. She landed the plane gently; Ross would have been proud. She taxied down the single northwest to southeast runway toward the only refrigerated storage shed. After locking the parking brake, she shut down the engine at the tie-down on the east side of the tarmac.

She waved to Stan Jensen, the guy who helped load cargoes. He was all smiles, no doubt because he was headed for a month's vacation camping in Canada. Then she noted a dark-haired man in new-looking, brown-green camouflage heading across the tarmac toward the plane. He carried a big backpack and some other gear. Sunglasses and unruly, blowing hair obscured his face, but he reminded her of one of the First Nation men in the area who had Blackfeet or Crow blood. He was probably her charter.

As she opened the door to get out, she whispered to herself, "Calm down, mister, 'cause you're going to have to wait 'til Vermillion's milk and mail gets loaded."

She jumped down, surprised to feel the warmth on the tarmac this early in the morning, but the temperatures had been above average all summer. Striding to meet the man, she held out her hand to shake his. She noted he had pristine-looking gear and new hiking boots.

"Rocky Marston?"

"Yes, ma'am. Figured it was you by the timing and the picture of your plane on the Web site."

"You must be a real veteran hiker to head up into the hills around Lost Lake alone."

"I'm a veteran, at least. Done my time in Iraq and want some peace and quiet for a while."

So, she thought, the fatigues were not just for effect or camouflage in the forest; he was used to them. His big, expensive back-pack did make him look like a guy who could take care of himself. It had the kind with aluminum supports, which often indicated a pup tent.

"Where did you come in from?" she asked.

"Flew into the Glacier Park airport from Arizona. Love the mountains."

"Ever been to the Lost Lake area before?"

"Nope. Look, I don't mean to take up your time talking."

She took the hint. Besides, she wanted to be back soon after Nicky got out of school. "We'll be airborne as soon as I load up and refuel," she told him, glancing toward Stan, who was already pushing a dolly of cartons toward the plane. "Would you like to ride up front? Or I can set up a seat for you behind the cockpit."

"Definitely in front," he said, twisting a surprisingly dainty onyx ring on his small finger with the thumb of the same hand. "Flying's not my thing, so that way, I'll feel more in control."

"I can't believe we must have been near the bastard, but we're no closer to stopping him," Brad Hale told his boss, Mike Edwards. The other three members of the FBI Serial Arson Team nodded.

19

"Despite this insulting letter, I think we're at a dead end 'til our 'Boy Next Door' torches something — or someone — else," Mike admitted. "Even the report from our Behavior Analysis Unit says we don't have the typical torch here." Swearing under his breath, he dropped the FBI profiling report on the table along with the letter they'd received from the arsonist.

Brad, age thirty-four, the newest member of the team with only two years under his belt, had been staring at the gruesome photos of the latest arson scene; now he glared at the letter, too. The national FBI database had sent it and its envelope back, claiming they were clean — no prints, not even saliva on the flap to test for DNA. The paper was standard, its handler must have used gloves; and the printer was a commonly used laser type. So what if they'd deduced the arsonist was right-handed from the burn marks left by flammable liquid splashed at several of the arson scenes? The majority of people were right-handed. They had next to nothing.

And VICAP, the FBI's Violent Criminal Apprehension Program, was no help. The arsonist had used different accelerants in every fire and left behind nothing but sanitized crime scenes. And now, to add insult to injury, the bastard was trying to call the shots in this letter.

But what really infuriated Brad was that his research into the accelerant used this time — white phosphorus — had turned up next to nothing. The minute his eyes had begun to burn and he'd smelled the sulfur stench at the fire scene, he'd guessed what the BND, as they called the Boy Next Door arsonist, had used. Then, sifting through the charred ruins the next day, his guess had been verified.

But even knowing BND had used liquid white phosphorus had not helped the team trace him.

The military had employed that highly volatile compound since World War II, and as recently as last year's Battle for Fallujah, but military supplies of WP were closely guarded. And though WP was also a common product in the manufacturing of soft drinks and toothpaste, Brad's calls to businesses that used white phosphorus had turned up no reports of any missing. Besides, the stuff was extremely volatile to transport. It was like the guy had spirited it in. No wonder BND thought he deserved to be called phantom or ghost.

Though he was listening to Mike, Brad stared so hard at the photos of this latest

BND arson scene that his eyeballs ached. The woman's house was a blackened shell, her body badly burned. Though the fire-fighters had gotten her out without losing any of their own this time, Jane Stinchcomb had died of second- and third-degree burns in the hospital the next day. That brought the deaths caused by the string of ten arsons in seven western states to four — three women living alone and a firefighter.

"Now I get why they called in the FBI," Clay Smith, another old hand at this, said. "And I don't mean because anyone thinks we can solve this mess. If this is allowed to turn into a cold case, we take the heat — 'scuse the scrambled metaphors."

Usually arsons were handled by local investigators, but this case had been given to the FBI team not only because it concerned interstate crime, but because it fell under the new antiterrorism laws. Though he was only thirty-four, Brad had worked for years to get on this team. He'd been trained as both a firefighter and an FBI agent, then gone to the National Fire Academy at Emmetsburg, Maryland. It was pure chance he was currently working in his hometown of Denver. The FBI team was sent all over, but the field office here was fairly central to the scattered arsons.

It wasn't only that Brad was on a mission to stop such heinous crimes or that he wanted to make good on his old home turf. He was driven to atone for a family tragedy. This case was the worst he'd seen, and he'd do anything to solve it.

"Not only is the press on our backs, but now the torch himself!" Jen Connors, the only woman on the team, said in her usual sardonic tone. She kept playing with her empty coffee cup; they'd all drunk enough java lately, they could have taken a bath in it. She suddenly slammed both fists on the table, which was cluttered with maps, photos and more than one psychological profile of typical torches.

"Give me a break!" she went on, gesturing at the letter. "The perp doesn't want to be called the Boy Next Door because it's 'too cute and common.' He demands we call him the Fire Phantom or at least the Smoke Ghost? Maybe he should just do our press releases for us!"

"Hell," Mike muttered, "maybe he *is* a ghost."

"I think he's a gamer," Brad said. "He's having the time of his life with all this. But how does he support himself with all the moving around he does?"

"And," Jen put in, raking her fingers

through her long brown hair, "why does he hate firefighters so much?"

"Listen up," Mike said. "I haven't earned these gray hairs for nothing. Let's go another round with theories on that, however far out or old hat. Go! Brad?"

"Okay," he said, tearing his gaze away from the photos. "Someone BND loved was killed in a fire, and he blames the fire department for not getting there in time."

Jen said, "Or how about he wanted more than anything to be a firefighter, but was turned down for the job. Then his girl left or betrayed him, and he's out to get both single women and firefighters."

"But he's a smart guy," Brad insisted. "He could surely pass the tests to get to join a fire department. If he can pull our strings, he could play the system to get in."

"Unless he bombed out on the psych part of it during interviews," Mike said. "Still, some screeners don't pick up on wackos who are fascinated by fires for the wrong reasons. Hell, too many torches turn out to be volunteer or even pro firefighters."

"But don't you have the feeling BND's been passing as a normal guy?" Clay asked, leaning back in his chair and clasping his hands behind his head. "I know he moves around a lot, but we've had media articles out on him, and *America's Most Wanted* usually turns up some kind of lead. We don't have a face to go with the crimes, but he's evidently passing for Joe Schmo — Mr. Nice."

"Not exactly a Joe Schmo, because he's bright and proud of it," Jen added. "It's a typical arsonist profile in that respect — above-average intelligence but still some sort of a failure."

Brad noted that Clay's hands were shaking. Clay had been trying to quit smoking, but the pressure was about ready to suck him into the habit again. He got up to pace, despite the fact he was out of shape and limped badly. They seemed to be going in circles — and they were starting to get on each other's nerves.

"Other theories?" Mike prompted, rapping his knuckles on the table. "Even if we've hashed them over a hundred times before, let's hear it."

Brad said, "Though a lot of arsonists are adrenaline junkies, he's an attention junkie. He loves looking at the fire and saying, 'I made that,' but he wants others to be impressed, too. 'I am smarter than the cops, than the fire guys, than the FBI.' He wants media coverage and wants to manage it by naming himself. He wants to control others' lives — and deaths. He's having a real good time playing God."

Though he had more to say, his voice drifted off. The three of them were staring bleary-eyed at him. It was only midmorning, but since they'd gotten the taunting note from BND, they'd hardly slept. Yet Brad knew that wasn't why their attention was riveted on him right now.

They thought he was speaking about his own father, who'd been an eco-arsonist here in Denver and was now serving eighteen years in the federal prison system for torching luxury homes built on the fringes of a nature preserve. The shock and shame had killed his mother — the doctors had called it sudden cardiac infarction — and disillusioned and humiliated Brad. But somehow, when he was trying to stop other arsonists, his own anger and pain receded — at least, for a little while.

Mike cleared his throat in the tense silence. "Now listen up. I'm going to the Stinchcomb funeral this afternoon to see if I can spot any smoke ghosts or fire phantoms. Maybe the perp's so pleased with himself he'll drop by or hang around the burial site. Not that likely, but frankly, I'm grasping at straws. Brad, man the office 'til I get back. You other two get some shut-eye so you can pull the all-nighter. Until we get a break, we'll work this in shifts round the clock, 'cause we're all so damn tired we can't see straight."

Lauren hoped Rocky Marston didn't mind that she kept talking, because a wave of exhaustion had washed over her just after they took off. Ever since losing Ross, she hardly ever slept straight for more than a couple of hours at night. But she could hardly tell a guy whose life was in her hands as they soared toward jagged mountain peaks that she was sleepy. She knew, if she'd just get through a couple more minutes, that her exhaustion would pass. Yet Rocky Marston had hardly said a word, even as she'd pointed out interesting sites in Flathead Valley.

"So what did you do in Iraq?" she asked.

"Tried to stay alive."

"I mean security, engineering, supplies? My husband was armored division in Desert Storm — tanks."

"Actually, I guarded the big brass. Black-ops stuff I can't talk about."

"Oh." She started to feel impressed, but she wasn't sure if she believed him. He might just be trying to shut her up.

"You should be aware of bears and mountain lions, especially if you hike alone," she said, trying another subject. "Black bears will stay out of your way, but the brown bears and grizzlies can be aggressive. The mountain lions are sneaky and dangerous but are seldom seen. They're called the ghosts of the Rockies."

"Yeah? I like that name."

He got quiet again. Maybe the guy just wanted to enjoy the stunning scenery. An occasional glacier field glittered in the sun. Snow still clung to the highest peaks while snowmelt streams slammed down cliff faces in silver torrents, however dry the weather had been.

After a while, as if he'd read her mind, he said, "You're in a drought around here, right?" He was twisting his ring again.

"A long one, so please watch your campfires."

"Oh, I sure will."

Brad could have danced around the table when he took the call from one of Jane Stinchcomb's neighbors. The FBI's hotline number — which he had wanted to call something else but was overruled — had been printed in the local papers.

"You probably think it's strange that we're not at the funeral," Peter Lockwood went on as Brad pressed the phone to his ear, "but we didn't know Ms. Stinchcomb that well. My mother's been living with us until we can get her into a good assisted-living program. She doesn't have Alzheimer's, but her memory comes and goes."

"And she saw something the night of the fire that might help?" Brad prompted when the man hesitated. "I promise you, we protect our sources."

"Yeah, she saw something all right. Susan and I went out to watch close up, but my mother stayed in her room because she could see the fire from there. It's been a week since the fire, but today she told us that she had seen a strange man dressed in black, lying flat on our porch roof right under her bedroom window, also watching the fire. When he saw her, he took off. We both talked to her, Agent Hale, and we think she's telling the truth. I mean, unless the guy was trying to hide, why not just join the crowd watching the blaze?"

Brad's heartbeat kicked up. "And could your mother describe this man? We could have her work with an FBI sketch artist."

"Like I said, sometimes we're not sure stuff she says is legit, but she insists she can describe him, what he was wearing and especially his profile."

Brad gripped the phone hard and threw his head back in relief. It was something. It was a start.

"Quite a view," Rocky Marston said as Lauren banked the plane. Finally the guy had offered something. His silence and brusque nature had made her nervous.

"That it is. People who see it from above or below never forget it."

"That's the ski lodge there?" he asked, pointing.

"Yep," she said. "The Lost Lake Ski Resort, a tiny town unto itself, at least in the winter months. There's always big competition for sports tourists in the Rockies, but the Vermillion City Council is also trying to build up tourism during the off-season."

"Hey, you never know," he said, becoming animated for once. "Something really big could put this little place on the map someday."

"Advertising costs big bucks and people here are torn about needing tourists yet not wanting this area overrun with them. We don't even have cell-phone service yet, though we have plans to build a couple of towers — one down at the far end of the lake."

She could tell he was looking at her now, not staring out the window for once. "You born and bred here?" he asked.

Lauren shook her head. "Grew up in the little town of Fostoria, Ohio. I spent one year of college at Ohio State in Columbus, not sure what I wanted to do. I came here to work one winter at the lodge, met my husband and never left. He used to be a fire warden for the district. Would you believe his first office was in that old wooden smoke-spotting tower, there on the hillside at four o'clock?"

"That thing isn't still staffed, is it? I heard Montana's got choppers, air tankers to drop water or retardants, spotting planes and all that. You or your husband ever fly this plane for smoke spotting?"

"My husband used to, but I stick to commercial flying. Ross got separated from his hotshot crew and was trapped with a friend in a wildfire in California in 2003. A government investigation ruled it a freak accident."

"Oh, sorry." He looked quickly away, as if to hide tears.

"Yeah, me, too. He was very smart about fires, so it's hard to understand how he and another guy got caught by flames — and on an upslope, too — when he knew better. It wasn't even a fire Mother Nature set —

lightning, I mean. Not arson, either. The so-called experts were thinning and sculpting the forests around a populated area for safety. The blaze got out of control in a place called Coyote Canyon."

"Morons! It just shows you can't trust anyone."

She sniffed hard. Marston cleared his throat as if he couldn't find other words, but then neither could she. The worst of her waking nightmares pressed hard on her heart. Again she saw in her mind's eye what had only been described to her, scenes she had read about in official reports and newspapers.

Her husband's death haunted her as if she'd been there with him. Ross and his friend Kyle separated from their crew and squad boss. Ross in the blast of superheated air and flame. Ross without his lifesaving, body-hugging fiberglass shelter that could have saved his life. Ross trapped and burned beyond recognition, beyond all sanity.

She jerked out of the horror but still hit the water a bit too hard. The pontoons bounced, skipped, hit again. Beside her, Marston braced himself against the control panel and swore.

"That's why my son and I call this plane *Silver*," she told him, trying to sound normal, even light. "You know, like 'Hi, Ho, Silver — away?'"

She figured he'd make a comment about women drivers, but he said, "Yeah, like 'Who was that masked man, because I wanted to thank him.' My dad used to watch that show on TV years ago. I heard it all the time from him, just like all the other trivial crap he knew and thought everyone else should, too. He was a real hog for attention and glory."

As Lauren steered the plane toward the dock at the west end of the town, she was relieved Marston didn't seem angry with her but with his father. After all, he'd only agreed to pay her half the three hundred dollars until she got him safely here.

2

By the time Lauren had stashed the rest of her passenger's fee in her purse — all cash again, three fifties — and had overseen the unloading of her cargo, Rocky Marston had simply disappeared.

Unlike most of her charters, he hadn't asked her where to buy supplies or anything about the town. But maybe for a guy who'd just finished a grueling tour in Iraq, wilderness hiking was nothing that needed concern or preparation. Besides, the general store was labeled just that, so anybody could find it.

Lauren made certain *Silver* was locked and tethered to its small space of dock, one big, winged bird among the small flock huddled there. The dock also sat on pontoons and was hauled out of the water in early November, when the lake began to ice over and they put sled-type runners on their planes.

Thinking about supplies for hiking reminded her that she had to pick up a few things and drop off the mail; the grocery store served as the post office, too. Then she'd pick up Nicky at her friend Dee's. Anytime Lauren couldn't meet her son after school, which was at the other end of town, Dee walked her grandson, Larson, and Nicky to her own house until Lauren could pick him up.

Lauren got into her old SUV and headed into town. Her house was located in what locals jokingly called the "burbs" of the tiny town. As she paid for her groceries, she asked Fran, the checkout worker, postmistress and cousin of the store's owner, "Did a hiker dressed in fatigues stop here for some supplies? I just brought in a new guy who's determined to hike solo, so I'm sure he needed to stock up."

"Haven't seen anyone but the same old same olds," Fran said and popped her gum. The smell of banana-strawberry emanated from her as she went back to sorting mail for the array of post office boxes lining the back wall of the store. Vermillion had no postal carriers, and like many residents, Fran held a variety of jobs to make ends meet.

"Well, he did have a large backpack," Lauren went on. "He probably came prepared."

"You tell him to watch out for bears?"

"Sure did, but after fighting terrorists, that probably sounded pretty tame to him."

"He comes in here, I'll give him ten percent off," Fran said as she cracked her gum again. "It's Clyde's policy for somebody who puts his life on the line to protect our freedoms, and all that. Here, you want to take your mail and Dee's?" she asked and handed over two packets as well as Dee's day-old *USA Today.* After losing Ross, Lauren had canceled her newspapers and magazines — and not just to save money. She did much better if she just shut out the world's woes.

Lauren arrived at Dee's as the boys were eating cookies and milk and playing a game of war with an old deck of cards. Despite their whooping and hollering, Nicky gave her a big hug around the waist as she stooped to ruffle his auburn hair and kiss the top of his head. The boy was a blend of her and Ross — her red hair and green eyes, his broad forehead and quick movements.

"And how was first grade today, gentlemen?" Lauren asked.

"Mom, we learned all about how you should call Indian tribes First Nations or Native Americans!" Nicky cried, his freckled face turned up to hers with his milk-mustache smile. "And never call them red men or redskins or nothing like that. And we're going to learn all about the Blackfeet who lived right around here. Did they really have black feet?"

"I'm not sure how they got that name, hon," she admitted, "but I just bet Mrs. Gates will teach you all about it."

Lauren reveled in the fact that her son was so open and affectionate today instead of distracted and moody. Maybe this new interest in local Indians would replace his obsession with superheroes like Batman and Spiderman. Since last Christmas he'd gone around the house with a towel pinned to his shirt for a cape and insisted on wearing his Batman pajamas all day when they didn't have to go out. He'd had more than one imaginary friend since Ross died, usually some powerful hero from a book or video. At least the Blackfeet really existed, and he'd be learning local history and respect for other people.

"And," Larson piped up from his place at the table, his mouth so full of cookie he spewed crumbs, "a Blackfeet chief named White Calf had to make a treat."

"Make a treaty," Nicky corrected, heading back to their card game as Dee gave Lauren a little smile and wave from the kitchen door. "A treaty means the tribe had to give up their land in change for peace. That's what Mrs. Gates said, 'member?"

"Land that is now Glacier National Park and all around Lost Lake, too," Larson said, his eyes huge through his glasses. The two of them were like a tag team now, picking up on each other's news. The fact that the classes were sometimes grouped put the younger students in with some older kids, and Lauren had noticed that this accelerated Nicky's vocabulary and learning speed.

"And when they lost their land to the U.S.," Nicky plunged on, "Chief White Calf said even if he died, he'd live in the mountains forever, like — um, 'The mountains are my last refrig,' so it must have been warm weather then, just like now."

Lauren bit her lip to keep from laughing. Behind the boys, Dee shook her head, threw up her hands and said, "I hope their fridges were big enough to keep a lot of buffalo meat cold all summer if they had weather like this."

"I've read what Chief White Calf said," Lauren told the boys, "and I think he said 'my last *refuge*,' meaning his last place to go, his safe shelter."

"I'll ask Mrs. Gates," Nicky said, as if his

teacher was the be-all and end-all of wisdom. Lauren was so glad he was excited about school this year. For the last two years, he had suffered from separation anxiety anytime she so much as went into another room.

"Hey, come in here a sec while I work on this casserole and let them finish their game," Dee said. Lauren joined Dee in her cozy, pine-paneled kitchen. Dee handed her a large sugar cookie, then went back to chopping onions.

Like most of the houses in town, the Cobern place sat slightly above Vermillion's single paved street on a rise of ground that slanted up toward the alpine meadow at the skirts of Mount Jefferson. Just beneath this chalet-style house lay Dee's small fashion and ski shop, Just Fur You, which, like the other shops and stores, faced the lake. Dee's place, like several specialty stores, was open limited hours in the off-skiing season. During the warm-weather months, she helped care for her only grandchild so her daughter, Suze, a local wildlife artist, could paint in peace, while her son-in-law worked at the lumber camp on the other side of Mount Jefferson.

As warm and wonderful as Dee had managed to make this home, it felt strange now, hollow, compared to when Dee's husband, Chuck, had lived here too. Despite the Coberns being almost twenty years their seniors, Chuck and Dee had been the Taylors' best friends, and they'd helped her survive these terrible last two years. But having lost Ross so tragically and permanently, Lauren couldn't fathom why Dee hadn't either forgiven or divorced her husband by now.

After Dee had learned that Chuck cheated on her with his old high-school sweetheart in Kalispell, he'd been living in a rented room at the ski lodge — for five months. Chuck was not only the town sheriff, but he headed the volunteer fire department, so he'd be sorely missed if he left the area — at least, by everyone but Dee.

It was Lauren who had flown Chuck into Kalispell and gone with him to the Regional Medical Center last week to get his shoulder set. And it was Lauren whom Dee had interrogated about whether Chuck had made any phone calls to unknowns or been out of Lauren's sight while he was there. Dee did care, so why didn't she show it to him?

"He's not ready to be forgiven yet," she'd said more than once, shaking her blond head while her blue eyes snapped. "Right now, it's out of my control."

Their breakup was the talk of the town. If little Vermillion had had a tabloid publication, their story would have been continual banner headlines to rival paparazzi coverage of a couple of feuding movie stars.

Now poor Chuck had broken his shoulder in a hiking accident. He couldn't drive, couldn't fish, couldn't do much but pop painkillers and try to rekindle his relationship with his wife over the phone. Still, Dee wouldn't take him back.

"I've heard all about the kids' day, but how are you doing?" Dee asked. "I saw you come into the dock."

"Did you see my passenger get off and walk uptown?" Lauren asked as she finished her cookie and started to chop a red pepper for the casserole. More often than not, Dee insisted she take half of a meal home for her and Nicky since Lauren had refused to let Dee pay her for their flights into Kalispell this summer.

"Nope. Didn't see hide nor hair of him, and it's a long dock. He probably stopped for a bite at the Bear's Den or hit the general store."

Lauren stopped chopping. "He didn't. I checked — the store, I mean."

"No big deal," Dee said, suddenly turning away to sort one-handed through her mail.

She flopped her newspaper she jokingly called *USA Yesterday* open on the counter between them as she started sautéing onions. "You think he dropped off the dock and drowned or something?" she teased. "Maybe he stopped at one of the B&Bs this end of town to get a room before he went into the wilds. So, was he weird or something?"

"Not exactly."

"Then I'll bet he was. Tell Dee."

"Not weird — just quiet."

"Man, he ought to blend right in around here. Except, that is, for the loudmouthed town sheriff who tried to talk me into letting him come back here in the afternoons — just when Larson's here, he said. Must be high on his pain meds. I told him he has plenty of places he can see his grandson — if you count his ski lodge digs, his office and the firehouse."

But Lauren had stopped listening. She stared at the secondary headline, which read, FBI Most Wanted: Boy Next Door Serial Arsonist/Murderer Finally Has a Face. And beneath it was a profile sketch that looked frighteningly familiar to her.

Her insides cartwheeled. It can't be, she thought as she leaned closer, then picked up the paper. It just can't be!

"What?" Dee's voice pierced her panic. "You look like you've seen a ghost."

"Don't say that. It says here this guy told the FBI he wants to be called the Fire Phantom or Smoke Ghost. And he's killed people — with fire."

"What?" Dee demanded, crowding close, putting her hands on Lauren's shoulder. "Lauren, you're just having one of your moments about losing Ross . . ."

"No, that's not it. He — this looks like my charter."

"Get a grip, girl! The guy just creeped you out. What are the chances that someone on the FBI's Most Wanted List would be here in Vermillion? When pigs fly."

"Or when arsonists do. Dee, I've got to call this national hotline number. And I should call Chuck, too."

"What's he going to do?" she said. "You're the one who told me he's not supposed to move around with that shoulder, and he's obviously completely out of it on narcotics, even if they are legal."

"I have to do something, just so I can sleep at night."

"As if you're doing that now. All right, go use my bedroom phone. But speaking as someone who used to love the local sheriff, let me warn you not to get everyone around here panicked."

"I know, I know," she conceded, heading for Dee's bedroom. "It can't be him. Like you said, not here in Vermillion. Don't worry, I'm keeping calm."

"It's not even a very detailed sketch," Dee called after her. "And did you read here, the information came from an elderly woman who saw him in the dead of night? Not exactly a solid source. Might be the FBI's grasping at straws and you probably are, too."

But that didn't help. Nothing did. Some of the things Rocky Marston had said . . . She wasn't actually keeping calm at all, because her heart was trying to pound right out of her chest.

"I wish we had an Indian story, but David and Goliath is a pretty good one," Nicky said, his voice slowing as he stretched and yawned in his bed. "Mostly 'cause the bad guy gets kilt with just a little stone."

"I think the idea behind the story is that even little people — like you and me — can fight back against something bad."

Sitting on the edge of her son's bed, Lauren thought again of the call she'd made to the FBI today in Denver. Was she crazy? Or could Rocky Marston be the serial arsonist and murderer they sought? It suddenly seemed so impossible and unreal, especially since no one else had seen him. He'd more or less disappeared into thin air.

"Indians could have stones like David threw," Nicky went on, his one-track mind riding the rails of his latest obsession. "There's stones everywhere round here, more than feathers birds have lost. Mom, Chief White Calf could fight back with stones to keep his land. He was a good guy, wasn't he? Some kids at school said the Indians were bad."

"I think White Calf had every right to want to keep his land here, just the way you and I want to keep Vermillion and Lost Lake beautiful — and safe."

"Could our house be on the land that was his?"

"I don't think the Indian tribes believed in owning land the way we do today, but it's possible he could have camped around here. The settlers back then wanted to live here too. They said the tribes should go to stay on reservations — places of their own, like we still have here in Montana. Remember when we went to see their powwow with the dancing?"

"I 'member only the pictures, when I was standing between you and Dad. Maybe I was too little then. I try to 'member lots of stuff we did when Dad was with us, but sometimes I can't."

"Then I'll take you to see a powwow again next summer. Listen, hon, let's talk about all this tomorrow, okay? You need to go to sleep so you can be wide awake for school."

"Yeah, 'cause Mrs. Gates is going to tell us more about how the Blackfeet lived. Mom, I have black feet, too, when I run around without shoes, so maybe that's where they got their name — if they didn't wear moc'sins . . ."

His voice faded and his eyelids drooped. After he said his prayers — always asking God to say hi to his dad — Lauren brushed his bangs back from his face and kissed his forehead. His little arms came tight around her neck, and she hugged him hard. She longed to rock him and cling to him, but she didn't want him to know how shaken she was. They let go; he sighed and snuggled into his Batman sheets.

"Be safe, Mom," he whispered their parting mantra. That was the farewell often spoken by those who fought wildfires in the West, a saying Ross had taught them both. They were the last words Lauren and her husband had ever said to each other.

"I love you. Be safe, my Nicky."

As she snapped off his bedside lamp, she thought how small he looked in his bed in this peaked-roof loft that used to be her and Ross's master bedroom. The top part of the A-frame second story of the house, it had sliding doors to a balcony with a great view of the mountains, but she almost never went out there anymore.

In the half darkness — Nicky insisted on a night-light in the adjoining bathroom — Lauren gazed out at purple shadows crouching in the trees and shrouding the mountains. Realizing she still held the book she'd read from, she leaned over to replace it on the shelf. Nicky often wanted her to read from this *Children's Book of Bible Stories* that had once been his father's. Before Ross died, the boy's favorite had been the creation story, with its drawings of all the animals in the garden, but now it was any sort of tale with "bad guys."

Though Lauren never closed the curtains, she suddenly yanked them shut. The familiar view seemed not protective but oppressive. She hurried downstairs to close the other curtains and recheck her window latches and door locks. Dear God in heaven, what if she'd brought a snake into this Eden?

47

The FBI team kept at it, renewed by calls pouring in about the BND arsonist. Mike and Brad were working the day shifts, Jen and Clay at night. They'd borrowed two secretaries from the field office here and were trying to follow up on any tips or intel that seemed credible.

Just as Brad got ready to go home at 9:00 p.m., Mike called him into his office and told him about a possible sighting in rural Montana, which didn't fit the perp's M.O. at all.

"Yet it makes a crazy kind of sense," Brad insisted when Mike relayed the phone call received from a female pilot living in a tiny town in northwest Montana. "He knows he could possibly be I.D.'d now. We've splashed his picture everywhere in the last couple of days. So he takes off for a while to podunk. I say we check this woman out, at least interview her so we can get an idea what her passenger was like — and even what she's like. We sure could use another eyewitness besides an old lady who doesn't know what year it is and saw him in the dark by firelight."

" 'In the dark by firelight.' Sounds almost

romantic," Mike murmured, rubbing his eyes with his thumb and index finger. "Yeah, my sentiments exactly about our lady pilot, Ms. Taylor, so you're catching a plane first thing in the morning for Kalispell, Montana."

"Can't I fly clear into — What's the name of her town you mentioned? Vermillion?"

"I'm having her meet you at the Kalispell airport, though you'll be flying into big Glacier International. I have no idea if taxis exist to get you between airports, but you'll handle it. And do some background work on her before you leave here tonight. If you think she's squirrelly or not worth more time after you meet her, thank her and get the hell back here. If she seems credible, use your own judgment about flying to Vermillion with her to look around a bit — without stirring everyone up there so the guy disappears again. It may be a wild-goose chase, but it's probably almost goose-hunting season in Montana."

Just above Lauren Taylor's small spread of land, Evan Durand hunkered down in the line of shivering aspens. It was after dark but the three-quarter moon shed wan light. He'd never had a more picturesque place to live and work for a while. What a great vacation spot! It was more beautiful than he remembered, but then again, the other time was in the dead of winter.

He'd been watching her place for several hours, but he already had the area almost memorized. Above the aspens stretched an alpine meadow in late-summer bloom. Even in the darkness, the ring of mountains seemed to occupy the sky. He could still hear the crooked snowmelt stream in the small ravine that passed the house not far from her lot line. A row of blue spruce six feet tall marked her property boundary. He would not have been able to pick it out otherwise, since she had no neighbors in sight. She'd been home since about four-thirty with the boy, and no one had stopped or even driven by on the narrow gravel road.

Evan studied the silvered silhouette of the cozy log house, one and a half stories with steep roofs to shed snow. In daylight, the logs looked shellacked on the outside, like the ski-lodge cabins, which probably protected the wood from insect borers, snow and water damage. He had planned a respite from his work here, but this was pretty tempting. There was no fire hydrant in sight, though a hose could suck water out of the lake about twenty yards beyond her lot line. All these things he filed away in his infinite memory.

Since he couldn't ask anyone and didn't want to be seen — ghosts and phantoms were only seen by their chosen ones — it had taken him almost until dark to find out where she lived. When she'd left the dock, she'd driven off uptown. That had misled him at first, but then he'd seen her SUV go by with her and the boy in it. He could have asked her where she lived, but that might have made her nervous. He wanted to know everything about her, but from his own observation, his own homework, not what others, including her dead husband, had told him.

Yeah, the master actor, not the Phantom of the Opera but the Phantom of the Fires. Evan Durand was taking his act on the road. Like summer-stock theater, he told himself. New drama, act one! Light the lights!

So, first things first. Since he'd arrived, he'd been eyeing the large vegetable garden she had surrounded with a six-foot-high wire fence. Protection from marauding animals, but not the human kind. From here it looked as if she only grew root vegetables, but he believed in a healthy diet. Though he'd packed plenty of tuna and peanut butter, he fully intended to also live off the land, and that included people's gardens and castoffs. It was shameful what individuals, grocery stores and restaurants threw out these days.

A batting cage and a small soccer net were set up in the backyard, and her son had draped the soccer net with an old blue-and-gray-striped blanket. Earlier tonight, the kid had been playing Indian with a ribbon around his head and a feather stuck in it. When his mother had seen him out the window, she'd hustled him back inside. That meant to Evan, who had to admit he was a great student of character, that the boy was obedient but still had a mind of his own. And that his mother was too damn controlling.

He was a cute kid, though too short to be spotted easily through the cabin windows unless Evan went to higher ground. But then, he was too distant to see what was going on. The moment it got dark, Lauren Taylor had surprised him by closing her curtains.

That made him uneasy. There was nothing but wildlife — including himself, he thought, with a chuckle. And since she had seemed so at home here, he didn't take her for one who would be fearful. Her husband hadn't been a bit scared, only too nosy, too dangerous.

Evan had figured out who Lauren was the second he'd seen her Web site. Imagine stumbling on Ross Taylor's widow. Taylor had talked about her and the boy, but when Evan had chosen Vermillion for his little vacation, he'd never thought she'd be sticking it out on the edge of the frontier, living — almost — alone. On the other hand, her friend, whose mailbox read Cobern, evidently really did live alone.

Evan sighed. He'd surveil them both, get to know them better than they knew themselves, then decide. Or maybe he'd outdo himself in a blaze of glory — he smiled at another of his brilliant double entendres — with two women going up in flames instead of just one.

3

Lauren's stomach was more knotted than the macramé purse she had beside her in the restaurant booth. Under the table, she kept bouncing her foot; she was biting the inside of her lower lip. As high-strung as she got sometimes, she'd never felt this jittery.

She glanced at her watch again. Five 'til. At 2:00 p.m., just one day after she had phoned the FBI hotline listed in Dee's newspaper, she was to meet Special Agent Bradley Hale from Denver in the Western Wings Coffee Shop at the Kalispell City Airport. She was early and kept an eye on the front door, chatting with people when she had to and trying not to get too jazzed on caffeine.

When her insomnia started to get worse, she'd cut caffeine out completely for two weeks, but had quickly learned that wasn't to blame. Her grief, regrets and the nagging feeling she'd tried so hard to bury with Ross were the culprits. Official government report or not, something had been very wrong about the way he'd died.

And now she wanted help from the government, from one of their own, on a completely different matter, even though she'd told herself not to trust them. She sucked in a quick breath. That was surely him coming across the street. At least he hadn't shown up in a suit and tie. But his khakis looked pressed and he wore a jean jacket over a light blue shirt with a button-down collar, no less. Slung over one shoulder was a black duffel bag. Wearing opaque aviator sunglasses, he kept looking around as he crossed the street. Agent Hale reminded her of those no-nonsense Secret Service guys who protected the president. His boss, Agent Mike Edwards, had told her to keep this man's presence a secret for now. Except for telling Dee, she had.

As he came closer, Agent Hale both assured her — he looked so in charge — and distressed her, because he was a real hunk. She shifted on the hard wooden seat as he opened the door and stepped in, swiveling his head right and left as if he expected to be attacked. His face was angular, with a strong jaw, prominent brow and aquiline nose. His Nordic coloring made him look like a Viking. On the other hand, as he came in through a door in the middle of the mural with life-size painted figures of Lewis and Clark heading west through this area, he looked as if he belonged with those rough-hewn heroes. She might feel uneasy with this man, but Nicky would love him.

It was no miracle that he spotted her immediately, because she was the only woman in the place. Suddenly, Lauren wished she'd dressed less like a bush pilot and more like a businesswoman. She shoved her wayward red tresses behind both ears. Darn! She could feel her cheeks heat; she hardly ever blushed anymore.

"Lauren Taylor?"

Low voice, slightly raspy. He took off his shades to reveal clear blue, narrowed eyes, which seemed to take in every atom of her being. He extended his hand and she offered hers. His shake was warm and very firm. He was tall. She guessed he was about six feet, at least five inches taller than her, but maybe his broad shoulders made him seem even bigger.

"Agent Hale," she whispered, "thanks for coming. I'm sorry, though, I don't know where he is. I mean, he just disappeared after I flew him into the Lost Lake area."

"If it's him, he's good at disappearing. Can we talk here for a minute?" he asked, sliding into the other side of the booth across the narrow wooden table.

He was only going to stay a little while? He had come all this way for a few minutes?

"Oh, sure. Montanans are good at minding their own business — except for me, I guess. But I'm so worried." She clenched her hands in her lap where he couldn't see them. "I'd just die if my plane was the Trojan Horse that brought someone dangerous — deadly — into our town. And it's been tinder dry around here."

Lauren knew she sounded shaky. She hadn't meant to blurt out so much at once, but she was so glad to see him, to get some help on this. Dee had been right about Chuck. His injury made him pretty useless as a sheriff right now. And since his painkillers had him so doped up that he was delusional at times, she hadn't even tried to tell him about this.

"Ordinarily I sit with my eyes on the door, but you're the one who knows what this guy looks like," Brad Hale said, turning around once to glance at the entry. She could tell he noticed the Lewis and Clark mural, but he didn't remark on it.

"Coffee there? Menu or piece of pie?" the

café manager, Jerry, asked Agent Hale from behind the counter.

"Coffee, hold the rest," he told Jerry, then got up to get it himself from the counter before she could. He sat back down and slid what she thought was a wallet toward her. "You'd better start with that," he said, keeping his voice low. "Arsonists don't announce themselves, but special agents have to. These are my creds."

"Oh, right." She studied a gold badge pinned to a leather oval. It flaunted an eagle with arrows atop a shield that read: Federal Bureau of Investigation. U.S. Department of Justice. And under that was his photo; he looked so stern in it. Though she knew he was who he said, she skimmed the words with his photo: *Bradley Hale is a regularly appointed Special Agent of the Federal Bureau of Investigation and as such is charged with the duty of investigating violations of the laws of the United States in cases in which The United States is a party of interest.*

A party of interest, she thought. That was a strange way of saying it.

His knee bumped hers under the table. She sat back a bit, then turned the badge and slid it toward him. He was watching her like that golden eagle, his gaze as steel tipped as those arrows.

"Where should we start?" she asked.

His taut mouth tensed as he took a sip of steaming coffee. She was so close she could see his thick blond lashes and the slightest shadow of his beard. She was surprised she was so physically aware of him. Since Ross, she couldn't have cared less about another man.

"Did anyone else see this guy?"

Did he think she was making it up? She suddenly realized how Nicky must feel when she tried to talk him out of his bad-guys-hiding-in-the woods fixation.

"Stan Jensen. He works as a sort of porter here at the airport," she said. "But he left yesterday for a month's camping somewhere in Canada." At least that didn't seem to faze him; he only nodded.

"Besides the sketch of his profile you thought you recognized from the newspaper," he said, "give me the top three things this Rocky Marston said or did that made you suspicious."

"Fine," she said, wrapping her hands tight around her lukewarm coffee mug. "Besides the fact that he just disappeared into the woods without even buying supplies, he asked me if we were in a drought."

"Though that's pretty obvious," he countered, "and could pass for normal chitchat.

59

People always start with weather-type talk."

"He knew that Montana used choppers, air tankers and spotting planes to fight forest fires. Does this guy's résumé include forest fires?"

"Small ones, usually woodlots, but we think those are just to draw firefighters away so he can hit his real targets."

"Which are homes near fire stations?"

"Affirmative. Let me ask you this, Ms. Taylor —"

"Lauren is fine."

He nodded again. "Then I'm Brad. Please don't take this wrong, but I'm just wondering, considering your husband's occupation and his tragic loss, if you said anything leading to make Marston discuss firefighting?"

Her eyes widened and her lower lip dropped before she could hide her surprise. "Well, I guess I would expect you to do your homework on a potential witness. Yes, I did point out Lost Lake's old fire tower and mentioned that my husband was once a fire warden and that he'd died fighting a wildfire. You — do you know all that?"

Damn, damn, she thought. Maybe he believed she was just obsessed with fires since Ross died that way. Brad Hale wasn't going to help her.

"Sorry to bring that up," he added when

60

she hesitated. "Yes, I know all that."

"Agent Hale — Brad — I just feel that that man had a hidden agenda. There was something strange and — and wrong about him. I know that sounds like women's intuition, but I think he was seething with anger. I landed the plane a little rough on the lake and told him I'd named the plane *Silver,* as in the Lone Ranger, to calm him down, chitchat as you say."

Lauren sat forward now, leaning over the narrow table with her hands palm down on it. Her pulse pounded again; she knew her face was flushed but she didn't care. This man had to believe her. Ever since she'd brought Rocky Marston to Vermillion, she'd felt she was being watched, that Marston or whoever he really was had his eyes on her. Obsession, maybe. Paranoia, probably.

"Go on," he urged. "Angry about what? Could you tell?"

"Anger at or hatred for his father just spilled out of him. His tone got almost threatening when he told me his father flaunted a lot of 'trivia crap' that everyone had to know. And one more thing," she added, talking faster and faster. "He paid me all in cash when ninety-nine percent of my charters either pay the three-hundred-dollar fee by credit card or check."

She was actually winded. Realizing she was almost touching his hands, she sat back, folding her arms across her chest.

"The anger at his father may be significant," he admitted, nodding slightly. "It often fits an arsonist's profile — absent or superior father figure, weak or doting mother, who is also resented. Do you still have those bills he gave you?"

"I spent one, but I have the others at home."

"He didn't wear gloves?"

"No — and he grabbed his side of the control panel when I made that rough landing. I haven't cleaned that area."

"Since you've flown at least once since then, any prints may be gone from dust or even cold air. Still, now that I'm this far, Lauren, it's worth a try. I think the BND arsonist may have panicked when someone saw him at his last fire, so he took off for the hills — literally. Sad to say, we have him pegged as a very careful, bright guy, so it may be difficult to snag him. But I'd like you to write down everything physical about him you can remember, especially any distinguishing feature or unusual trait."

"I just remembered, he kept twisting a dainty onyx ring he wore on his right little finger. Things like that?"

"Anything. Anything that will help to nail this bastard," Brad gritted out through clenched teeth as he hit his fist on the table. Lauren sat up straighter; she wasn't the only one who was desperate here. This man was on a mission.

"Another thing," she added. "Marston said he just got back from duty in Iraq. When I asked him what he did there, he first said, 'Try to stay alive.' Then he told me he'd guarded the big brass, but that it was black-ops stuff he couldn't talk about. That could have been true, of course, but it struck me as phony."

"I'll check that out. If Marston's lying about a service record, even if it's so-called black-ops stuff, we should be able to discover that quickly."

"But you do believe it could be him?"

"Let's just say it's a big possibility. And since I have a fingerprint kit with me, I'd appreciate it if you'd show me your plane."

She felt relieved and much more at ease with him. That is, until he got up to pay the bill and she glimpsed a shoulder holster with a handgun under his jacket. But then, the arsonist was a killer, one who needed to be stopped with anything it took.

When her back doorbell rang, Dee threw

down her dish towel and went to answer it. Most folks in Vermillion didn't even lock their houses, but she had ever since she'd thrown Chuck out. If some of Dee's friends were here for a chat, they'd have to cut it short or else walk to the school with her to pick up Larson and Nicky, because the kids were out in fifteen minutes.

Chuck stood at the door, looking so like a specter of himself that she gave an involuntary moan deep in her throat. She hadn't seen him since his accident; now she looked at him without the red haze of her anger for the first time in five months.

He'd lost weight. His usually neatly clipped, silvering hair was scraggly — she'd always cut it for him — and his bronze complexion had faded. He wore a shoulder sling, with his arm resting on a pillow that was attached by Velcro to a wide band around his waist.

Her heart went out to him, but that's no doubt exactly what he wanted. In these tough times, why didn't he just go move in with Jidge McMahon, since he'd gone to her for the good times?

But Dee opened the door.

"I hope you didn't walk clear down here from the ski lodge," she told him, "but then I guess you can't drive."

He tried to force a jaunty grin that was more like a grimace. "Hello, sweetheart. Can't drive for maybe two months or so, the doc says. But I wanted to see Larson."

"You know he's not here yet. I have to go pick him and Nicky up. You — you look faint."

"Naw, just haven't done any exercise since this happened. Dee, truth is, I had to see *you.*"

She blinked back tears that prickled behind her eyelids. "You better come in before you fall down. You can stay to see Larson, then I'll drive you back to the lodge."

He didn't argue, didn't get riled as he had during their other few confrontations since a friend in Kalispell had told her she'd seen him and the newly divorced Jidge, his old high-school flame, going into the Best Western Hotel. At least he hadn't tried to deny what he'd done. But in a way, that made it worse.

"I don't want the boy — or you — to see me like this," he said, his usually robust voice sounding so shallow. "But I can't help it. Suze said to come stay with them, but I need to get back to work." Their daughter was trying to stay neutral in this family mess.

"To work?" Dee cried. "You can't work now — shouldn't even be out walking the streets!"

He half sat, half slumped onto a chair at the dining-room table, pulling it out first so he wouldn't bump his pillow support. He'd ripped the right sleeve of his shirt so he could drape it over the cast. She wondered how he managed to get dressed at all without help.

"I'm going off the meds," he announced. "They mess up my head."

"Lauren said the doctor told you that you'd need to take them for weeks. That even when you begin physical therapy, the pain will be severe, and —"

"Dee, damn it! My body pain's nothing next to how I feel about hurting you, about screwing — sorry, bad choice of words — messing up what we had."

"You didn't throw your meds away, did you?" she demanded, bending down to get right in his face. His eyes were bloodshot and unfocused; she was afraid he'd pass out. The stubble on his usually clean-shaven chin and cheeks made him look like one of those grungy rock stars. Thirty years of marriage and he was still a handsome man, damn him.

"Left my meds at the lodge," he muttered.

"Good, because when I take you back — drive you to the lodge, I mean — you're going to start on them again. Why don't you lie down here. I'll prepare Larson for what he's going to see and I'll tell the boys they can't be as noisy as usual. And after we all have something to eat, you're going back to bed at the lodge."

Grabbing her jacket off the peg by the back door, she left him where he was. Lauren had said he was strung out on the meds, but he was obviously in agony without them.

Dee went out and closed the door, then leaned against it, all strength gone from her legs for a moment.

Chuck had been the center of her life for more than thirty years. He was a man who became sheriff here — and fire chief — almost by default, for his real loves were leading camping-and-hunting trips, like his buddy Red Russert. But that was so iffy and seasonal around here. Chuck had taken the law enforcement job to support her and Suze because they loved life here, and she had thought he had loved her. It just showed you couldn't trust men, not even the ones you were willing to die for.

Brad Hale seemed to fill the interior of Lauren's plane in a way not even Ross had.

Brad was polite and businesslike, but he seemed a raw, huge presence in any size space.

"Under ordinary circumstances, do you touch this side of the control panel much?" he asked as he brushed graphite powder on the surfaces, then bent close to look at the results.

"No, and I keep it pretty spic and span in here. But he did grab it when I landed, right there below the oil-temp gauge."

"I see a few latent ones, and maybe this is a handprint," he said. "This *C.S.I.* stuff usually isn't my thing. And I'm going to have to print you so I can eliminate any of yours."

"Oh, sure. Besides, you could use them to check me out more than you already have."

"Standard procedure," he said, glancing up at her tart tone. "I'm sorry we had to background you. And I'm really sorry about the loss of your husband. I'm sure it's really impacted your boy, too."

She pressed her lips together and sighed hard through flared nostrils. "He's doing a little better, but he still has his own escape mechanisms, I guess you'd say. He has a terrific fantasy life."

"So do some grown men," he said, then added quickly, "but in some of them it's out of control. I'm theorizing that our arsonist thinks he's justified somehow, that he deserves to be king of the world."

"Rocky Marston seemed nervous, but he did say he liked to be in control."

Brad's head jerked up. "That really fits the profile. A lot of arsonists light fires because they feel inadequate and that helps them get their pain or failure out. It's like, 'Look at me, I am important, I am in control.' "

He got out another kit within that kit, then inked and rolled her fingers and thumbs.

"This seems old-fashioned," she said.

"It is, but we're not exactly in civilized territ— sorry, didn't mean it that way. I'm going to go express mail these to my team in Denver from that UPS drop box I saw back by the restaurant. Then I'd like you to fly me to Vermillion to look around, spend a night. Surely there's a motel."

"There's a ski lodge with rooms and cabins and several B&Bs."

"Sounds good. Are you game?"

"Anything to get that guy — if it's him."

Brad, who knew the beautiful mountains and towns around Denver well, was awed by the rugged beauty of the Salish Mountain Range and by the stunning woman who flew him over and through it. Lauren Taylor didn't wear a bit of makeup, but her shoulder-length, wild, strawberry-colored hair framed an animated, heart-shaped face highlighted by amazing green eyes. Her big, droopy sweater over snug jeans and scuffed western boots hid what must be a lithe, shapely body, but she got to him in a way no woman in a bikini ever would. Lauren seemed as natural and alluring as this territory over which they soared, cut off momentarily from the rest of the world.

"There's something I forgot to tell you but should have," she said, interrupting his thoughts.

"Shoot."

"Cell phones don't work well around Lost Lake, if at all."

"Yeah, you should have told me."

"I do carry a cell, but it only works when I'm not at Lost Lake. You can use my home phone anytime you want."

"I think we'll have to use our heads to locate this guy — and maybe some footwork, too. If he said he went hiking, maybe he did. Are you familiar with the back-country there? He's sure not intending to stay out a long time or pull some sort of escape over these mountains."

"Yes, I know the immediate area. But if we find him, won't he think something's fishy when he sees me?"

"If I can get someone else who knows the area, I will, but I don't want the word out right away about who I am or what we're doing. I don't want to induce panic among the locals or our suspect. And I'll be armed and ready. As for something fishy, everyone in town will think that of me if I don't get a cover story at least as good as the one Rocky Marston came up with. I'm thinking we'll put out the word — through you, too, if you're willing — that I'm a nature writer doing a story on the area for a travel magazine."

"You mean, tell no one the truth? My friend Dee Cobern already knows."

"We'll clue her in. She's the sheriff's wife, right, and your initial phone call to us was from her house?"

"Yes, but they're estranged right now, so he's living in a room at the ski lodge."

"Is there anything else I should know?" he asked and turned in his seat to put his hand on the back of her pilot's chair. Her hair, brushing against his inner wrist and palm, was as soft as it looked.

"Is there anything else *I* should know?" she countered.

In this bright light up here, even with his sunglasses, he could tell her slanted cheeks were coloring up. She'd blushed when he'd first sat down at her table at the airport too.

"You're still uneasy I backgrounded you?" he asked.

"Was it my entire bio? Including a Columbus, Ohio, speeding ticket when I was a freshman in college?"

"Okay, let's even the playing field. We're going to be partners in our hunt for Rocky Marston, after all, though I'll bet that name is bogus."

"So that evens the playing field — that you're telling me you suspect he used an alias?"

"No. I want you to know that I understand how hard it is to have something like your husband's loss hanging over you, always a part of you."

"You lost someone in a fire, too?"

"In a way. One of the reasons I'm so dedicated to my work is because my father was an arsonist."

Her eyes widened; she gripped the wheel hard, lifting and stiffening her arms.

"Everyone who works with me knows it," he went on, "so I have that always on my back, the invisible monkey clinging, making things I say and do be seen in that light. Yet it's a part of me that doesn't hold me back. It makes me better, more determined to stop others who use fire illegally and immorally for their own ends. And frankly, if that's the way you feel, too, so much the better to get this guy."

"Did your father's fires kill anyone?"

"No, thank God. He was what they call an eco-arsonist. He torched half-built luxury homes on a wildlife preserve outside Denver near our horse farm. I was in high school then. And despite being ashamed of him — and angry that we lost our business and our home and that it killed my mother — I missed him like hell. Still do. He's in prison and will be for years."

"I appreciate that you told me," she said as they descended into a cuplike valley with an amazing green glacier lake at its heart. He saw the little town along the western shoreline, looking like a toy village under a Christmas tree. Only this town was rimmed by meadows, deep, blue-green forests, and then the slate-gray mountains. It was so lovely that, for a moment, he forgot to breathe and even blinked back tears. What a sin — a sacrilege — if someone destroyed all this beauty with nature's precious, perilous gift of fire.

4

From above Lost Lake, where they landed at 6:00 p.m. that evening, Brad noticed the single block of false-facade, shoulder-to-shoulder commercial buildings and scattered houses that made Vermillion look like a Wild West movie set — minus the horses.

A sharp memory stabbed him. He'd loved horse packing in the backcountry around Denver with his parents. After his father was imprisoned and fined, they'd had to sell the stable of registered quarter horses they'd raised. Brad had been devastated to lose his big, sorrel gelding, Sam. He'd never forgotten the look in Sam's soft, doe eyes when his new owner led him away. All that had broken his mother's health and his heart.

"Anybody around here do backcountry horse packing?" he asked Lauren as she smoothly headed the plane toward the only dock on the lake. "You know, wilderness outfitters for camping trips?"

"If you're thinking of trying to track Marston on horses, it's probably not a good idea. A lot of the hiking trails are too narrow."

"No, I wasn't thinking of that."

"There are no local public stables. A few folks have a couple of horses they ride around the lake trail. I've borrowed two from the Fencer twins — teenage girls — before, just to get Nicky on a horse. We had a great time riding together."

"Give me a quick layout of the town," he said, anxious to change the subject. He'd told her enough about himself and only because he wanted her to trust him. No reason to get all emotional about his own losses. She didn't need to know that he hadn't been on horseback since he lost Sam, or that he could still bawl like a baby at the mere thought of the day everything he loved went up for auction — went up in smoke because of his father's fires. Brad made himself focus on Lauren's recital of places.

"Starting at this end of town, that's the only gas station," she said, pointing. "That first house belongs to one of the other pilots, Jim Hatfield, and his family. The other six regular pilots are all men. Anyone who wants to fly in or out checks in with Jim's wife, Carol, who keeps track of which plane is going into Kalispell and when. They use their living room as a sort of lobby."

That made Brad realize he needed to start thinking in terms of small-town America, at least from the last century if not before.

"And that large building anchoring the main street, the only paved street, is the general store," she went on.

"I was going to say Vermillion reminds me of a Wild West town, but that's exactly what it is — with a sheriff and, no doubt, a schoolmarm. And you and I are about to become the posse."

"Oh, yeah, it's wild all right. Nothing ever happens." She gave him the first smile he'd seen. It surprised him, lifting the tips of her green eyes and transforming her tired, worried look for a golden moment. Despite the cloud of anxiety that hung over her, he felt as if sunshine bathed him in warmth. He tore his gaze away.

"It's not a one-room schoolhouse," she was saying, "but it's all in one building, about a hundred and twenty-five kids, K through 8. The grades are grouped, and we have a total of five teachers, four women and one man, who is also the principal. Most families who have high-schoolers send them to boarding schools in Kalispell or Missoula, but a few homeschool. My son's a first-grader and loves his teacher — she's a real veteran. She actually taught my husband, too. But back to what you asked. Between the gas station and the school are shops for the ski season and the two restaurants. It's not a big choice in town, but during fall and winter the excellent ski-lodge restaurant is open, too. The two churches at the far end of town are Community Protestant, where Nicky and I attend — the one with the white steeple — and Saint Mark's Catholic, beyond that. A few homes you can't see are hidden by foliage or the uplands."

"And your home?"

"There," she said, pointing toward the shoreline quite a ways from the town as the plane cozied up to the dock. "You can just make out the peak of our A-frame roof. I can walk to town in about twelve minutes, but I usually drive."

"I checked on the roads in and out — or I should say, road."

"And that's sometimes blocked by rock slides or even avalanches in the winter. So my plane —"

"Heigh-ho, Silver!"

She nodded and smiled again. Though Brad was always hell-bent on chase and capture, he savored the light moment between them.

"*Silver* and these other pontoon planes," she went on, "are the stagecoaches that bring passengers and goods in and out in one hour instead of four on a scenic but tedious and sometimes dangerous, road. We are pretty isolated here, but that's part of the charm and beauty of the Lost Lake area. That is, unless a demented arsonist gets loose here."

Her smile tightened to pouted lips that trembled. Brad fought to keep his emotions in check, to stay rational, even as she gripped the wheel and blinked back tears. She was blushing again, with anger this time, he could tell. He was tempted to touch her, to reassure her, but he sat solemn and silent until she blurted, "You know the truth about what neither of us is saying! One smoking cigarette butt or spark from a campfire could mean an inferno with this drought. I want to help you find out if it's him and then find him!"

"We will," he said, annoyed his voice sounded rough with emotion. Unless they caught a break, it was going to be hardheaded, cold and calculating detail work that would capture Rocky Marston, or whoever he really was. "I'll do everything I can," he told her, "and the Bureau and I are grateful for your help."

After they stepped onto the floating dock, she tethered the plane, then led him ashore toward a gravel parking lot to an old black SUV that looked as if it had seen better days. They were heading first to pick up her son, where he planned to ask Dee Cobern to keep his identity a secret, except from her own husband.

"So Rocky Marston walked down this dock and just disappeared," he said, looking around and thinking the man must have hidden in the nearby trees or headed for the gas station restroom. "And no one else seems to have seen him. I'll have to ask around about him, say he's a friend of mine."

She bit her lower lip and narrowed those amazing green eyes, almost the color of the glacial-melt lake. He put his duffel bag in the back seat next to a Frisbee and soccer ball.

"You do believe me?" she asked as they closed their doors. "I mean, I realize people don't just vanish."

He turned to face her, close across the console. "Lauren, I believe you or I wouldn't be here." She looked exhausted, yet passion — even power — emanated from her. "Let's go, partner," he urged. "Like they say in the old western reruns, 'Time's a'wastin.' "

Dee Cobern used Lauren's oven to bake the chocolate-chip cookie dough she'd mixed at home. When she'd seen how happy Larson was to see his grandfather, she'd decided to bring Nicky home and let Chuck and Larson have some time together at her place — not that she was getting soft on Chuck's betrayal.

To keep the cookies large, round and uniform in size, she spooned up dough with a small ice-cream scoop. Most of them were for a bake sale at the school. Dee prided herself on neatness and perfection, at least in cooking, housekeeping and the layout of her shop. Her marriage, on the other hand . . . Heck, she'd once thought that was under control, too.

Peeking out the living-room window, Dee could see that Lauren's plane was at the dock, so it surely wouldn't take her long to learn that Nicky was already at home. When Lauren arrived, Dee would head back to her house, where her daughter might have already shown up, and send Chuck back to the ski lodge with Suze. Or even talk Chuck into going home with their daughter to be sure he got back on and stayed on those meds. She hoped Lauren hurried because she couldn't wait to hear what the FBI guy had said. More than likely, she thought, the whole thing was going to be a dead end.

Dee could see Nicky from the kitchen window that overlooked the backyard; he was playing Indian in a tent made from a blanket draped over his soccer net. He was in and out of it, looking for feathers, he'd said, but evidently collecting small stones that he piled just outside his doorway. Maybe he was making an imaginary campfire.

Evan Durand had just washed his hands in the snowmelt stream that rattled down the ravine next to Lauren Taylor's house when he looked up — and realized too late that he was facing her son about six feet away. The kid must have quietly and quickly come down the side of the ravine from his make-shift tent above. Evan had been watching him for a quarter hour as the boy scoured his backyard for small rocks.

What to do? Gag him and take him so he wouldn't tell his mother? But that would trigger a manhunt. That friend of hers who'd been watching the boy from the kitchen window could be down here in a flash.

But before he could either flee or grab the

kid, the boy blurted, "Are you real or are you an Indian ghost?"

"Me Indian ghost," he said in a low, singsong voice. He'd played Squanto in a Thanksgiving play once, the last performance his mother had allowed. He knew darn well that Indians didn't really talk like that, but maybe the kid had seen some of those old flicks that stereotyped them.

"Are you the ghost of Chief White Calf?" the boy asked, his eyes big as dinner plates.

Evan nodded. Was this kid serious?

"You're not dressed like pictures of the Blackfeet I seen," the boy accused, studying his green-and-brown camo outfit. "But I guess you have to be careful no one sees you."

Evan almost hooted a laugh at that. This was too good to be true. If he played his cards right here, this opened up all sorts of possibilities.

"That true," Evan said, frowning. He crossed his arms stiffly over his chest. "Chief White Calf of the Blackfeet not let enemy see him. Only chosen one can see him — that you, my friend."

"My name's Nicky Taylor, and we're learning all about what happened to your land in school. And that you said you'd live in the mountains forever. Did you fly in here from your sacred burial grounds in the Vermillion Valley?"

Evan nodded solemnly. "That all true. But you not tell anyone you have seen me. You alone can see me, my friend."

Evan squinted quickly up at the house. Even when he was standing, no one could spot him, unless they were on the balcony or roof.

"I want to be your friend," the boy vowed, crossing his heart. "I won't tell anyone, even my mom."

"And not any friends. Not the teacher tell you about my people. If you tell, White Calf disappear for good."

"I can keep a secret! Honestly, I can."

Evan hoped the woman in the house thought the boy was in his tent. He had to set this up quick and get the kid out of here, back in sight.

"You help feed White Calf?" Evan asked. What the hell? He'd been raiding the Dumpster behind the Bear's Den Restaurant and had taken carrots and radishes from the fenced-in Taylor garden, but he could smell something good baking out here. He'd love to supplement his canned tuna and peanut butter.

"Sure, but where will you be waiting?"

"You put food for White Calf in your

Indian tent. He get it at night."

"Well, okay, but be sure to get it early so it doesn't draw bears or 'coons. But you know all about that, right?"

"White Calf know all about mountain animals. We meet in this ravine again sometime, but you go out back of tent to come down here, so you not seen. No white man or woman but you, my friend, must see White Calf."

"I won't tell. I'll get you some stuff. Will you be watching for me?"

Evan nodded slowly and deliberately, trying to keep from smirking at how this had worked out. He actually believed the kid would keep the secret. And if he told someone, so what? They'd obviously take it with a huge grain of salt. Evan knew this type of child — sensitive, bright, imaginative. Maybe even brilliant.

"Remember," he told Nicky, "White Calf watching."

"Hi, Lauren." Suze, Dee and Chuck's twenty-five-year-old daughter, greeted Lauren and Brad at the door. "Come on in."

"This is Brad, a charter I just flew in," Lauren introduced them as briefly as she could. He had his black bag strapped over his shoulder. She wondered what was in it besides the fingerprint kit, since he seemed unwilling to let it out of his sight.

Suze and Brad shook hands. Suze wasn't pretty but she was striking with her huge mascaraed eyes and gypsy costumes. Not only did she draw stylized versions of local wildlife, but she seemed to be her own artistic production with flowing gestures and garments. Today she wore a full black skirt and magenta sweater over her boots, an orange silk scarf tied around her long tresses to hold them back from her vibrant face.

"Dad's here with Larson and me," Suze said to Lauren. "Mother took Nicky back to your place over an hour ago."

"Oh, okay. I'm glad Chuck's got a foot in the door anyway. Too bad she vacated."

Suze rolled her eyes. "She's not listening to anyone. I know Dad made a big mistake, but he's been eating crow for five months and needs his family right now."

She seemed to take Brad in for the first time, to really study him as if he was a subject for a drawing. He calmly studied her back.

"Brad's a nature writer," Lauren said. "He's here to do an article on this area."

"Man, I hope it helps attract off-ski-season buyers for local art," Suze said, pointing a thumb at herself that jangled her big bracelets. "Listen, I need to get going with Larson because I have to pick Steve up today. I'm going to leave Dad here so Mother has to deal with him — get him up to the lodge at least and back on his meds."

"Go ahead," Lauren urged. "I'll just see how he is, then I'll head home so I can free up your mom."

"Great. Thanks," Suze said, hugging Lauren lightly. "Larson, we've got to get going!" she called as she darted into the other room.

"Way to go," Brad told Lauren. "When she's gone, you can sound out Sheriff Cobern to see if I can parlay with him on this or not."

Suze came back through with Larson in tow. "Will you be staying long in Vermillion, Brad?"

"As long as it takes for me to get my work done."

"Have Lauren bring you to my studio — though in this weather, I usually draw outside."

"Suze, keep an eye out for wild animals and be careful," Lauren blurted.

Brad thought Chuck Cobern seemed to come to attention when he showed him his creds and introduced himself. But the guy looked like heck, and one glance made it obvious he'd be no good to him in searching for or arresting a possibly violent criminal.

"Most wanted?" Chuck repeated, sounding dazed. "Arson and murder?"

"We're still not certain that Rocky Marston is the Boy Next Door Arsonist," Brad admitted, "but I believe it's a valid lead. And right now, this is undercover work, except for what your wife knows from Lauren and what I'm telling you."

The sheriff winced each time he moved, even when he drew a deep breath. "Understood, Agent Hale, but if you get any proof this perp is here, we've got to spread the word to keep people safe." There was a long minute where Brad thought he might say something else, but he just stared off into space. "Will you keep me informed?" he added.

"Affirmative. And Lauren has agreed to give me some necessary information so I have an idea where to search."

"It's like you're after a wild animal — and in a way, you are." The sheriff had broken out into a sweat and was obviously having to concentrate on his thoughts. "I'm up at the ski lodge for now, if you need me. Or I can walk down to my office in town, even show you around the fire station. It's not much — one engine and one EMR vehicle, all volunteer help including me, the fire chief."

"Much appreciated," Brad said, realizing that last designation would make this man an automatic target of the BND arsonist, too — at least for humiliation. "I plan to look around the lodge ASAP. From the air, I thought some of the cabins looked pretty far-flung. If they stand empty this time of year, it might be a place the suspect could hide."

"He did show a lot of interest in the ski lodge," Lauren put in.

"I can check the cabins, save you time and effort," Chuck said and grimaced as he tried to gesture with his good arm.

"I'll handle that," Brad said. "I'm afraid you'd be at a disadvantage if you ran into him. First time I spot him, I'll call in help from the Bureau if I need to."

"Did Lauren tell you we have to call out by conventional phones? No cells, 'cept way up on the mountains or the fire tower."

"She told me," he said, though she hadn't mentioned a cell might work from the fire tower. It didn't look that far away. "I'd like to check that fire tower, too. It should provide a great view of the entire area."

"It does," Lauren said. "I've been up there, but not for — for over two years."

Her gaze met Brad's intense stare. He nodded, then glanced back at the sheriff. The guy looked as if he was about to keel over in his chair.

"I hope you'll be better soon, Sheriff Cobern," Brad told him. "Anything productive I learn, I'll keep you posted. I'm going to surveil the area and check around to see if anyone's seen Marston. I'll claim he's a friend who said he'd meet me here. If nothing turns up, we'll have to decide whether to warn and maybe protect some of your citizens. Or set some kind of trap."

"My wife gave me a photocopy of the newspaper article. Lauren can give you the list you'll be needing. But if it comes to that, I'll move in here and take care of Dee."

"Dee?" Lauren cried. "Why would Dee be in danger?"

"Because," Sheriff Cobern said, his voice shaky, "when you give Agent Hale a list of women living alone near Vermillion's fire station, she'll be on it, 'less she comes to her senses and lets me back in here. She told me once it would take Armageddon to make her take me back, but maybe this is it."

Evan thought the sunset over Mount Jefferson that evening was breathtaking, all smeared in red and orange, as if the sky itself was aflame. He lay on his back on his sleeping bag beneath the stand of aspens above Lauren Taylor's house, savoring the view and congratulating himself on how he'd handled her kid.

But it still annoyed the hell out of him that the Cobern woman had kept peeking out the window and had finally called the boy back inside, just the way his mother had henpecked her little chick. Just like his own mother . . .

He closed his eyes and let the red rage pour through him, though he stayed calm, completely in control. His hands clasped behind his head, he felt the pressure of the ring that he always wore, not because it bound him to his mother but because it freed him from her.

Evan, sweetie, you come on in right now! He heard her shrill voice from the depths of his soul. Years and years of that voice, even when he was no longer a child. *Time for your piano lesson! Be a good boy and come on now.*

The neighborhood kids had laughed at that for years. Some had even mimicked her voice, mocked how Evan had to get right home. They were playing touch football and poor little Evan had to go in to practice his musical scales, damn her.

And then when he'd tried out for the play at school, Agatha Christie's *Ten Little Indians,* no less, she'd said that was too arty, just a waste of time. He'd found his life's calling, but she said it would take too much time from his real studies and his piano practice — which he hated — and take too much time away from helping her at home while Dad was on the road so much. He hated them, too — *HATED THEM BOTH!* Couldn't they see how talented he was? Couldn't they let him run his own life? His senior year he didn't even try out but was asked to be in Shakespeare's *As You Like It* — and she didn't like that, either. No, he should major in science like his brilliant father.

Totally composed, he whispered,

" 'All the world's a stage,
And all the men and women merely play-
    ers.
They have their entrances and exits

And one man in his time plays many
parts.' "

Including, he thought, the part of the
ghost of Chief White Calf of the Blackfeet.
Including acting like a dutiful son while he
played his greatest part and planned his
mother's exit. And the colors of the fire that
had consumed her and left him with just
this ring were the very colors of the sunset
now fading through the trees, fading to the
cold ashes of death. . . .

Evan Durand sighed as he got up and
rolled his sleeping bag so it would be easier
to carry back to the ski-lodge lift-control
shed where he'd been staying. He knew the
small building inside out; he'd memorized
the mechanics of the lift the summer he'd
worked at the lodge, the summer he was
finally free from his mother and his dad was
off telling everyone in the universe how to
fight wildfires.

5

The last vestiges of a beautiful sunset lit the sky as Lauren waved goodbye to Dee and watched her drive away. "Mum's the word on everything I know about the Boy Next Door Arsonist," Dee had promised Brad. Lauren could tell she was shocked that an FBI agent had actually come to Vermillion — and that Rocky Marston could mean big trouble. "Since I'm not actually speaking to Chuck," Dee had added, "I have no one to discuss it with anyway."

Brad didn't comment as he carted his black bag into the house. Lauren intended to fix him and Nicky dinner, then call a friend's B&B to see if they could take him in on such short notice. Dee had said Nicky was in his room and that he'd fallen asleep, but she wanted to look in on him. He never took naps anymore, so she hoped he hadn't caught some bug at school.

"Make yourself at home while I check on

Nicky," Lauren told Brad, "then I'll fix us some food before I make you a diagram of who lives where, especially near the fire-house. You know, I was thinking —" She knew she was babbling as she led him into the living room and went over to draw the drapes. "Since Chuck is out of commission for this, Red Russert, our local hunting guide, might be a big help to you. He's a real veteran of the area, knows every nook and cranny for miles."

"Lauren," Brad said, turning her to face him before he let go of her arms, as if touching her had burned him, "you do not have to go one step with me outside this house. But I really do need your advice on where to look, who to ask if they've seen him."

"I want to help, even beyond these walls."

"Don't do it because you feel guilty for flying him in. If not your plane, it could have been one of the others. If he wants to hide out around here, it is not your fault. He would have come anyway."

Though she still had her jacket on and the day was warm, she suddenly felt chilled. She hugged herself. "I said I want to help and I mean it. Excuse me a sec. I'll just run upstairs to check on Nicky and tell him we have a guest. There's a bathroom right through there if you want to wash up," she added, turning toward the stairs that led to the loft. "I hope cheeseburgers are okay with you."

"Sounds great."

With a smile and a nod, she started upstairs. But she heard a noise from the kitchen below and went there first. Nicky was stuffing crackers, two big chocolate-chip cookies and an apple into a plastic sack.

"Dee said you were taking a nap, hon," she said. "Are you hungry? Packing your own lunch for school tomorrow?"

"Just getting some stuff for at night," he said, coming over to hug her. "Sometimes I wake up like you do and I feel hungry."

"Didn't you hear a man's voice? The charter I flew in today, Brad Hale, is going to eat with us before we drive him to Lacey's B&B."

"Does he have a reservation there? And is that why they call the place the Indians stay a reservation, like you can sleep there all night and get breakfast, too?" He looked guiltily down at the stuffed sack in his hands, then back up at her.

"I think it's because that was the land reserved for them," she said, opening the fridge to be sure she actually had defrosted the ground beef. "Brad's a writer, and I'm going to show him some places around here he can write about. And I'll just bet you can tell him some things about the Blackfeet."

"Oh, sure, even while you're fixing dinner."

"Come on and meet him then," she said and started for the living room. Brad was staring at the far wall, at a picture of Ross in full wildfire fighting gear, just above the pine bookshelf next to her desk.

On the shelf she still displayed several of his things: his Pulaski fire ax, his first set of Whites fire boots and his bright yellow, dog-eared copy of the federal handbook of firefighting, open to a page titled "How to Properly Refuse Risk." Why had she clung to those things? she wondered. Was she actually still angry with Ross that, at the last minute, he hadn't refused to risk his life?

Brad turned to her and said, "Big shoes to fill," before he surprised her by squatting to get to Nicky's height.

"I can see why your mother's so proud of you," Brad said when Lauren formally introduced the two of them. He offered the boy his hand and they shook, sizing each other up.

"If you're a writer," Nicky said, "you might want to do a story on the Blackfeet Indians. They used to be all around here.

But don't go out looking for any, 'cause there's bears and mountain lions, and it might be too dangerous."

"You know," Brad said, straightening to his full height, his eyes meeting hers over Nicky's head, "sometimes the only way to win is by doing something dangerous." He glanced at the yellow book, then back at her.

"Despite the odds," Lauren said, "wildfire fighters, like Nicky's father, always have a can-do spirit, and I like to live by that, too."

But it wasn't Ross now in her home, standing here strong and sure, asking Nicky about local Indians while she bolted back to the kitchen to fix supper. Soon she was going to put away that shrine she'd made to her husband. She had to get on with her life, and to do that, she had to help catch an arsonist.

If Brad turned his eyes, he could see Nicky, with a sparsely feathered headband on, watching a video while Lauren made a quick sketch of the town. The boy was engrossed in Disney's *Pocohontas,* though Lauren said he'd long outgrown the movie and hadn't asked to see it for a long time. He seemed as wrapped up in it as the striped blanket he'd tugged around his shoulders.

Nicky had easily accepted his mother's explanation that she was drawing the town for their guest so that he would be able to say who lived where when he wrote about it. Lauren Taylor was as good at well-worded half truths as anyone on the arson team, Brad thought.

He had used her phone to call the Denver office and talked to Jen, who was on the night shift with Clay. He filled her in and told them to watch for the express package with the fingerprints. He explained about the phone situation and gave them Lauren's number and the number of the B&B where he thought he'd be staying. He told them he was also planning to try to raise prints from three fifty-dollar bills Rocky Marston had given to Lauren, but wasn't sure when or how he'd get them out to them.

"Sounds like you're on Mars," Jen said, her voice sardonic. "So what's she like? Rough and ready?"

"Let's just say credible."

"Old, young, pretty, not?"

"I'm not saying this line's secure," he'd told her, frowning. "Read the dossier I e-mailed to Mike if you're so curious."

"Touchy. I thought this might give you a chance to get out of this rat trap and relax."

"This isn't some side trip to Disney, Jen."

"Not even Frontierland? Good luck, then. We'll process the prints the second they arrive and let you know pronto what turns up. And seriously, you know we can call in the cavalry if you need them — if this turns out to be anything."

"I'll check in tomorrow after I look around."

"Copy that. And I'm serious. Watch your back."

"Okay," Lauren announced when he hung up, "this is Vermillion, Montana and vicinity." She rotated the drawing toward him. She'd printed the names of who lived where and who owned what shops. She'd put a big X on the fire station, which also housed the tiny attached sheriff's office. "And," she went on as he bent over it, "the two women who best fit the possible target for Boy Next Door would be Dee — since she's been living alone lately — and Marilyn Gates."

"My teacher?" Nicky asked and hit the pause button. "What about Mrs. Gates?"

"I didn't know little pitchers had ears that big," Lauren murmured and twisted in her chair to look at her son. "Go back to your show, hon. I'm just telling Brad who lives where in town."

But he came closer, dragging his blanket.

"She moved from her house outside town 'cause it was too big for her after her husband died," Nicky said. He glanced at his mother's sketch. "She lives in a 'partment above the gift shop. Larson and I got to help her carry some things home from school once."

"I'll bet she's a good teacher," Brad said.

"The best. And she wears earplugs at night so if the sirens go off for a fire, she won't hear it as loud, but it doesn't happen much she told us."

"I'd like to meet her if your mom would set it up for me. I believe she's lived here a long time, so she might be able to help me with my writing."

"Oh, yeah, she can write really good. You should see the words she prints on the board, with no mistakes at all."

"With no mistakes at all," Lauren said as she straightened one of the new feathers in the boy's headdress and reached for her phone. "Now, wouldn't that be great?"

"She's the obvious choice for best teacher — and best possibility," Brad said. "So maybe you can ask if I could meet her tonight, when you take me into town."

"Sure, it's barely eight o'clock," Lauren said. "Unless she goes to bed early. She's no spring chicken."

"She's not chicken at all!" Nicky started to protest, but Brad rose from the table and gestured for the boy to follow him back to the sofa, away from the table where Lauren would make the call. He was pleased that Lauren got through to the woman at once, and he tried to keep her son occupied for a moment.

"If we stop to see Mrs. Gates tonight," Brad told the boy, "will you give me a little private time to talk to her about my project?"

"Sure."

"I can tell you really like to help your mother. You're getting to be a big boy. Would it be all right if I call you Nick?"

He looked surprised. "My dad used to call me that, but no one else does now."

"What do you think?"

"Yeah, it would be all right, just between us."

"It's all set," Lauren announced. "Turn off the TV, hon."

"She calls me hon, too," the boy whispered and clicked it off, then went back into the kitchen to look out the back window through the blinds as he'd done several times earlier. He was, Brad had guessed, keeping an eye on that makeshift Indian camp he'd made out back.

"You can vouch for this woman?" Brad asked Lauren as Nicky darted ahead of them to knock on his teacher's door. They had to walk up an enclosed staircase to get to her apartment, but Lauren had told Brad the view of the shoreline and lake from the second-story side porch was spectacular. And that there was a side entrance onto the porch.

"Vouch for her? You mean that she won't announce in class that there may be a deranged arsonist loose?" she whispered back. "I don't know how she'll take your news, but you might want to get her promise of secrecy first."

Suddenly looking grim, he nodded. Lauren was amazed — not only that Brad kept his black bag with him again, but that she was starting to read his mind. And she was surprised at how smoothly he orchestrated everything once they were inside. After a few minutes of conversation, he maneuvered Nicky into another room to look at a book with pictures of Blackfeet Indians, and the three of them huddled in the kitchenette where Marilyn Gates had just vowed she'd do anything to help the FBI.

But then, Lauren recalled, the woman had not one but two American flags in her classroom, and the kids always said the Pledge of Allegiance. She even had a blown-up photo of the Statue of Liberty over her fireplace, where one of those artificial logs burned easily and cleanly. The entire apartment looked absolutely spotless.

Marilyn Gates was in her mid-sixties but looked much younger, with her taut-skinned face, spry body and vivacious demeanor. She always joked that her white hair was from teaching two generations of Vermillion children, but she loved her work. A bit of a taskmaster, she was still filled with life and fun — which had not escaped the hawk eye of Russert, to whom, talk said, she'd given the cold shoulder. But as Marilyn Gates listened to Brad's calm, clipped explanation, Lauren noted that she looked neither lively nor amused.

"But that's dreadful," she said, wringing her hands when he explained the situation. "Most Wanted List for arson and murder? It's been bone dry around here all summer. If he burned this building, this entire block of the town could go up in flames."

"Yes, ma'am, I realize that."

"So you are warning me to keep a sharp eye out. Teachers have eyes in the back of their heads, you know."

"Yes, that's part of it. But because this arsonist has always set a perimeter blaze to draw firefighters away before he ignites a single woman's house near the station, I'm asking you to vacate this place immediately anytime you see or smell anything suspicious. Lauren says you have a second exit out the side. Is there anyplace nearby you could get to quickly to be safe?"

"Not many people live in this block, with all the shops," she said.

Lauren, realizing she might be treading on shaky ground, put in, "Red Russert lives over the Bear's Den Restaurant just two doors down on the other side of the firehouse."

"Unacceptable," she clipped out. "I can't be running to him for help, possibly in the middle of the night."

"But he's out on the trail so much in the summer," Lauren countered. Didn't this bright woman realize they were talking life and death here? "When he's away, he could at least leave you a key."

"I'll arrange something," Mrs. Gates said, her warm voice starting to ice over. Lauren could see now how this veteran teacher managed to keep kids in line with just a look or a word.

"And what does this firebug use to set his fires?" she asked Brad.

"Unlike most serial arsonists who are quite consistent, he amuses himself and tries to confuse authorities by using a variety of methods and accelerants."

"Such as?" Mrs. Gates quizzed the big, stern man in a way that surprised Lauren.

"He's used everything from an old-fashioned Molotov cocktail made of a gasoline-filled bottle with a cloth wick, to a new version of it with sugar, gasoline and potassium chlorate. He's employed 151 percent rum in one case, where the victim lived near a bar. In a house where the woman was a chain smoker, he used a smoldering cigarette with matches, cotton and a rope wick attached to a container of charcoal lighter fluid. We believe he even used potato chips because of their natural oil, but we're not certain because a fire started that way consumes all the evidence. Most recently, he used volatile white phosphorus at great risk to himself, but he may have chosen that because the woman who died in the fire once worked at a factory which used that chemical."

He stopped his recital; his intense gaze locked with Lauren's. Her stomach cartwheeled, partly from the intensity of his stare and partly because the devious intelligence of the man they were up against finally hit her with stunning impact.

"In short," Lauren said, exhaling hard, "he likes to research the place and victim he's chosen and use appropriate accelerants."

"Bingo," Brad said. "We can profile his basic method of operation, but he has no exact signature, such as one source of fuel we can use to trace him or lay a trap for him."

"But," Mrs. Gates put in, "speaking of profiles, didn't he come to Vermillion to keep a low profile? To hide out from your Most Wanted publicity Lauren saw in the newspaper? Which reminds me, Lauren," she said, turning to her. "Are you reading newspapers lately or watching the news? Because you've cut yourself off from the world that way, Nicky is woefully unaware of current events."

Lauren felt as if she'd been caught cheating during a test. "I just happened to see Dee's newspaper," she admitted. "I realize now that Nicky's older I need to change. It's just, after all that publicity over Ross's death, I needed to shut myself off some . . ."

"I know. I do know, my dear. Well, I certainly will heed your private, privileged warning, Agent Hale, and I thank you for it. Where can I reach you, should I notice something — or someone — awry?"

"You can call either Lacey's B&B or Lauren, and I'll check in with you on a regular basis," he told her. "Also, I'd like to have your phone numbers here and at the school."

He scribbled down what she recited in a small, black notebook he'd pulled from the inside of his jacket.

"Oh, you have a gun," Mrs. Gates said, clasping her hands together and pressing them to her pursed lips.

"Yes, ma'am. This man needs to be stopped, hopefully to stand trial, but stopped."

"My, all this seems so unreal," she marveled. "But I promise you I will keep my eyes peeled and my doors and windows locked. Nicky," she called, suddenly heading for the living room, "have you found any pictures of black feet on the Blackfeet Indians in that book?"

"Lauren," Brad said, touching her arm to hold her back as she started to follow, "I'm going to ask around first thing tomorrow if anyone's seen Marston. I'll describe him, not use the drawing. But I'm wondering if you'd have time to drive me to the fire tower at the other end of the lake about ten. Since you said Marston showed some interest in it, I'd like to take a close-up look and see if my cell phone works from there."

"We can't drive there. We'd have to walk, which would take a while, or use a boat or ride horses."

He frowned, looking suddenly very upset. He was just going to have to accept that this area was wilderness, she thought, and not what he was used to.

"Even if we took a boat, we'd have a hike after we got there, right?" he asked, shifting his weight from one foot to the other.

"Right. Horses are the best option. I could borrow two from the Fencer twins."

"Fine. I'll meet you at the dock at ten if you can get the horses. But what about your flying schedule?"

"I'll ask someone else to bring my cargo back tomorrow."

"Won't that put a dent in your pocketbook?"

"I told you I wanted to help and I meant it."

"There's a large reward for this guy, if your information leads to his arrest . . ."

"I don't care about any of that, nothing but getting that madman out of here before he hurts someone!"

"Mom, Mom!" Nicky cried as she and Brad joined him and his teacher. "I didn't learn if their feet were really black from this book, but see the red dirt in this picture? It's just like where our little stream goes into the lake. The Blackfeet visited places like that for sure!"

"That red soil is what the Blackfeet used to make ocher or bright red paint," Mrs. Gates explained. "That color is also called vermillion, and it's how our town was named. The tribe daubed vermillion paint on themselves for war, the color of a flaming sunset that signified death."

She stopped talking, then mouthed, "Sorry!" to Brad and Lauren. Brad just shrugged, but Lauren thought he looked more determined than ever. As for her, for the first time in two years, when she began to flashback to Ross's dreadful death, she stopped that violent vision before it could devour her. But that didn't stop the horror of her mounting terror that her little town could go up in an inferno of vermillion flames.

6

Lauren ran from the towering wall of orange flames, but her feet were like lead. The inferno reached for her. She was running scared, so scared. Was Ross with her? Surely this was her haunting nightmare where they ran together. She had to wake up — *wake up!* But, no, Brad Hale ran by her side, pulling her, helping her escape the devouring heat only to pull her into his arms where flames still licked at her . . .

Perspiring, Lauren sat up, wide awake, her covers churned to waves and wrapped around her. She groaned when she saw the bedside clock read 3:00 a.m.

She tried to snuggle down again, but when her mind began to replay the nightmare, then what had happened yesterday, she knew she was doomed. Better to get up and do something quiet, then try to sleep again.

She stuffed her feet into her terry-cloth slippers and padded to the window overlooking the backyard. Her bedroom was now on the first floor since she'd given Nicky the loft for his bedroom and playroom. Leaning her shoulder on the wall, she peered out through the curtains.

The three-quarter moon washed the area in wan light. She had always loved to sleep with the curtains, even the windows, open, to wake up and see the black silk sky, the moon and stars, to hear the breeze and night sounds through the trees and dream of dawn's new day. But on this warm latesummer night, she'd closed all the windows. No use being careless until Brad found what Rocky Marston was up to. Dear God, she prayed, don't let him be up to arson.

She went into the living room. In the dimness lit only by a night-light out in the kitchen, she took Ross's boots, his Pulaski firefighting ax and rule book off the shelf, then put them on the floor of the hall closet. Yes, she could admit now that she'd been angry with him for dying, for leaving her and Nicky alone. Ross had experience, and he knew the rules of fighting wildfires. How had he ever been trapped in that flaming canyon?

For a while after she'd buried him, she'd found herself imagining he was still alive, that someone else had been burned to death. Not Ross! Ross would come walking out of the forest behind the house someday to explain he'd had amnesia from a knock on the head or a fall, that the dental records she'd given the coroner had been someone else's.

She closed the closet door and sank to the floor, sitting cross-legged, and put her head in her hands. But she didn't cry. Nor, for once, did her brain replay scenes of her days with Ross. She pictured not her dead husband emerging from the moonlit darkness outside, but the arsonist, the Boy Next Door. And he looked just like dark-haired Rocky Marston.

She jumped up and made a circuit of the house, peeking out each window through the curtains. She went upstairs to listen to Nicky's deep, regular breathing, wondering where he'd put that sack of snacks he'd said he wanted at night. Again, she checked the lock to the balcony and peered out.

And gasped when she saw a bear move in the darkness. No, surely it was just shifting shadows in the breeze. Not only was this summer dry but it was windy. Besides, she made certain that her garbage can was always secure and nothing was left out to attract a bear. Thank God the grizzlies usually stayed higher in the mountains, but the smaller brown bears could be dangerous and the black bears were notorious marauders. There was no food outside but that in her garden. Though a bear could easily knock down her garden fence, it seemed to deter them. Still, she thought a raccoon might have gotten a few carrots or radishes the last two nights.

With her knees pulled up and her arms circling her shins, she sat in the beanbag chair in Nicky's room, thinking of places she could suggest Brad look for Marston around town, places she could take him besides the fire tower.

What if nothing — no one — ever turned up? What if no one else saw anything? That would be best, of course. But would Brad then wonder if, as she did with her son and his fantasy world, she'd imagined and embellished the whole thing? She suddenly wished this entire experience was just one long nightmare from which she would soon wake.

As good as her word, Lauren met Brad at the gas station with two saddled, old bay horses at 10:00 a.m. At least they weren't quarter horses, he thought, fighting to keep his mind on locating and trapping a possible criminal. He gave her a boost up, then easily mounted.

"That's right," she said, watching the way he took the reins and turned the horse, "you used to live on a horse farm. I think that would have been great fun. I can't recall who said, 'There is something about the outside of the horse that is good for the inside of the man.' What? What did I say?"

"Nothing," he told her as they headed north along the shore toward the fire tower. Lost Lake's narrow beaches were not soft sand but packed hard with small stones, so the horses' footing was good. "My memories of my horse-riding days are bittersweet, that's all."

She sobered instantly. "Because so much was lost when your father was convicted? I didn't mean to bring it up. But to even the playing field, as you put it yesterday, I feel the same way about the fire tower. When I first knew my husband, the winter I waited tables at the lodge, he was the fire warden there."

"We're a pair," he said, then wished he hadn't put it like that. No fraternizing with witnesses or suspects. But then again, he needed her help.

"Changing the subject," she said, riding beside him as they moved their mounts to a faster gait, "what kind of background does one need to be on the arson team, besides FBI training?"

"In my case, college major, criminology, University of Colorado at Boulder. Then Butte College Fire Academy in Chico, California. I worked in a fire department in Virginia, while applying repeatedly to the FBI Academy in Quantico. I think it took them a while to decide on me because of my father's incarceration. I never wavered about what I wanted to do, never looked back." He paused, then said, "But let's stay on track, in more ways than one. I checked at the gas station. The guys there did not see the man I described use their bathroom the day you flew him in — and their john has an inside entrance. Ditto for the stores and restaurant where I asked around and at the three B&Bs Mrs. Lacey called for me."

"It sounds as if Marston wants to earn those nicknames Fire Phantom or Smoke Ghost, except, thank God, he hasn't evidently lit so much as a candle here."

"Unless he's hiked out of town and lit campfires."

"You know, when I told him to watch his campfires in this drought, he said, 'I sure will.' Now, that sounds ominous."

"Have you remembered anything else he said?"

"Unfortunately one more thing. When I mentioned our area's competition for sports tourists, he said, 'Something really big could put this little place on the map someday.' Brad, I know he seems invisible, but I think he's the one. I just do. A huge fire could not only put Vermillion on the map, but erase it from the map, too!"

"Keep calm," he said. "The worse the situation, the better it is to keep calm." But they both urged their horses faster toward the old fire tower.

Evan heard a door slam nearby. It jolted him wide awake. He'd been out half the night foraging for food and for something better than his old drip torch to start a fire. He was burning the candle at both ends and felt as if he had a hangover.

He crawled out of his sleeping bag and peeked over the windowsill of the small building from which the ski lift was operated. It was less than a mile from the lodge itself, in the direction of the outlying cabins. Since this ten-by-ten shed hadn't been occupied for months, the windows were filthy, but he dared not wipe a spot clean. He looked, instead, through a glass darkly.

And saw a big man with a huge sling on his right arm lurching past toward the cabins. Evan had thought about sacking out in one of those but didn't want to break in — too obvious. Here he'd known where the extra key was hidden, just as it had been years ago. It almost made him wonder if Red Russert didn't still run the ski lift in season.

But what sobered him even more, that guy going by could be the sheriff. Last night Evan had overheard the cooks from the Bear's Den Restaurant when he'd had to hide behind their Dumpster. While they'd had their smokes out back, they'd talked about Sheriff Chuck Cobern and mentioned a huge sling with pillow support. When the cooks had said he'd been kicked out of his house by his wife, Evan had surmised that she was the one who had watched Nicky Taylor like a hawk. But if that was the sheriff, why was he here, and what — or who — was he looking for? Or was it standard practice in this backwoods place to check the lodge buildings off season?

And what if he looked in here?

Evan grabbed his sleeping bag and backpack and shoved them into the only corner from which they wouldn't be spotted if someone looked in the two windows. He hid behind the large wheel-and-cog mechanism that ran the lift as the man walked past on the path, his slow feet crunching gravel.

Still in control, Evan exhaled, then chuckled — chuckled at Chuck, if that's who it was. He'd really give the guy a shock if he started the lift from here; the loading platform with the cable of dangling double chairs was just a few yards away. Red Russert used to let him run the tramway from time to time, especially when he wanted a snort of whiskey from that little flask he always carried. Evan had loved running the massive machine, mostly because he imagined that the people riding it were on a spit to be roasted. If only he could have ignited those pine trees over which they were hauled up the mountain.

The returning sound of footsteps drew Evan from his reverie. Was the man heading back this way already?

A shadow dimmed the small shack as Sheriff Cobern peered in, lifting one hand to shade his eyes, then rubbing a circle of soil from the window. He moved away and rattled the door handle. What if he knew where the extra key was kept?

'Fraid so, Evan thought when he heard the key in the lock. Before the door could open, he darted behind it and grabbed a wrench from the pegboard on the wall, holding it over his head, poised in case the man came in instead of just looking.

A crystal-clear snapshot of hitting Ross Taylor over the head, then placing a rock near his prone body to make it look like he'd fallen and hit his head, flashed at him. How he detested *mano a mano* violence. Evan shook his head to clear it.

The door creaked. Looking really unsteady, lumbering like a big bear, the man stepped in.

When they reached the far end of the lake, Lauren and Brad followed a twisting forest path upward for ten minutes on horseback, then had to tether their mounts and hike the rest of the way. When they reached the concrete base of the fire tower, they climbed twenty sets of ten metal, very steep steps to the wooden-framed, tin-roofed structure. The view was both stunning and sobering, Lauren thought as she fumbled with the key that opened it, one she'd had to look for through all her old keys this morning.

Such a beautiful area, she thought, but so much to catch fire in this drought and wind.

"Quite a view," Brad said, gazing out over the panorama as they stepped inside, out of the breeze. She recalled that those were the very words Rocky Marston had used when she'd flown him into the area. Would she always be haunted by that hour with him? What else had she not recalled that he had said? At least she didn't feel Ross's presence here. She had thought she would, but Brad seemed to dominate the small area, despite its cinematic vistas.

"I don't see any signs that someone's been up here," he said, tearing his eyes away from the windows to look around on the floor. At first the place had the scent of dust, but with the door open, it quickly smelled fresh and new. Brad had her binoculars around his neck, but had only used them when they'd ridden past the ski lodge.

"I agree," she said. "Nothing but spiders and their webs."

"Tell me what I'm looking at out there and where a lone camper might have headed," he said as he gazed excitedly out the windows in one direction, then another, like a kid on Christmas morning who didn't know which package to open first.

"That's Mount Nizitopi at three o'clock," she said, pointing. He spun around to look out toward the west, lifting the binocs to his eyes. "Called, as I'm sure Nicky would tell you, for the Blackfeet name for themselves, meaning 'The Real People.' "

They were silent for a moment. Was he thinking Rocky Marston didn't seem real?

"The elevation is 3,363 meters or 11,033 feet," she went on. "Pilots have to know all that. It's the largest mountain, as you can see. Behind the town is Mount Jefferson —"

"Named for the president who sent Lewis and Clark west?" he asked, dipping the binocs to study her. When she nodded, he said, "I'm not as one-track-minded as I seem. Skip the stats, but tell me where the hiking trails go."

"They spread out all over from the lake, in almost every direction except due south," she said, pointing again. "The valley between Mount Nizitopi — there — and Mount Jefferson has trails. It's been called Vermillion Valley for years, but the Blackfeet used to call it the Piskun Valley, one of their sacred burial grounds. It's strange, isn't it, that the white settlers not only took native lands but renamed them? Wrong, too. But then again, I heard the word *piskun* means deep blood kettle, which sounds pretty scary, though I'm not sure what it is."

He nodded. "I'm sure your boy could fill me in on that."

"Here's hoping Mrs. Gates isn't teaching those kids *everything* about the Blackfeet, because they were fierce warriors. Anyway, that valley's very narrow and rocky, with a braided river and tiny lake, but there's no town in it or past it that Marston could have hiked to."

"Maybe he doesn't know that. It's pretty obvious he's not going high since there's still snow and even glaciers. And he's not heading around the mountain, because those waterfalls full of snowmelt would cut him off. If he's hiking out or is just camping in the area, he wouldn't go much higher than the tree line because of the cold. I don't know. I'm just thinking out loud. Are there any houses distant from town that we should check, just to be sure he isn't holed up there?" he asked, skimming the vista with the binocs again.

"Maybe even taken hostages, you mean?"

"That's not his M.O. I'll bet he's a guy who doesn't like hands-on violence, but you never know about someone when they're threatened or cornered. At least he's not going to feel trapped here with all this space. It may be partly why he picked the area. And even if he sees me, he can't possibly know who I am. Nor, probably, does he know who the sheriff is since Chuck is more or less out of commission. No, I'll bet — I hope — our Boy Next Door still feels things are completely under his control."

"I can call the families that live outside town and ask how things are in general. But let's just hope he doesn't know what single women live near the firehouse in town."

"That, unfortunately, I do not put past him."

"What about the big lumber camp on the other side of Mount Jefferson? Dee's son-in-law is a manager there. It has one of the oldest wooden flumes still in service. You know," she said, gesturing, "those huge wooden chutes on stilts that they fill with water to get the logs down from the slopes to the river and to trucks waiting farther down toward Kalispell. A lot of lumber operations use choppers for lifting logs now, but it's not cost effective here, with the distance and the price of fuel."

"I suppose if there are piles of wood there, an arsonist might be interested in a lumber camp. But it's just not him. Those are the ski slopes?" he asked, suddenly pointing. His hand accidentally bumped hers.

"Right, the bunny trails are the lowest below the first stop of the ski lift, then the serious slopes start up higher there and on the other side of the mountain. The Lost Lake Ski Lodge has twenty groomed runs, which are mostly alpine meadows right now, and almost three hundred inches of snow fall annually. I can take you up in the plane if you'd like a better view of the runs. The ski lift itself isn't in operation this time of year."

"It may come to that later. Let me see if my cell phone's going to connect from up here, as the sheriff mentioned."

He went outside and turned away to make the call, but she could see how animated he was and hear his deep voice lift when the call went through.

"Yeah, Mike, I found a place my cell would work besides an airplane around here, but it takes almost an hour by horse and foot to get to this spot, so I'll still be using Lauren Taylor's phone. . . . Not hide nor hair of him yet. . . . I know how busy it is there for you, but I still think I should stay at least another day."

Her hopes fell, not only that his boss might make him leave, but that they'd found no proof of the arsonist's presence yet. If Brad left, not only would she feel less secure, but wouldn't it mean that he — that the FBI — didn't believe her?

"No," Brad went on. "We're hardly ready to initiate a search and sweep here yet. You know how slippery he is. I don't want him bolting somewhere else, though there aren't many ways in or out of here. I'm trying to come up with a plan. . . ."

A plan, Lauren thought. She wondered if he'd share it with her, but she wouldn't ask, at least not directly, or he'd know she'd overheard. She turned away but listened intently.

"Copy that. So he was lying about any kind of service record, special ops or not, at least with the name he gave? Of course, he might be telling the truth about Iraq, but be using a false name. Still, none of that would prove he's our arsonist. Maybe he was just trying to impress a beautiful woman."

Lauren gasped. Brad thought she was a beautiful woman? That touched her. But if anything at that point, Marston had been trying to shut her up, not impress her.

"Since the prints from the airplane cockpit aren't back yet, I'll call you later today. . . . Hoping for a match from the Criminal Master File or the civilian ones stashed in the paper files . . . I took more prints from some money he touched. . . . Right, right, I've got that covered. . . ."

As he came back in, she was looking out over the lake. "It's awesome up here," he said, "but we've got to keep moving. I want to check the outer cabins of the lodge today, then get back into town. You okay so far, Lauren?"

She turned to him; their gazes met and held. "Okay up here, you mean, or trying to track down Marston?"

"Both. Up here, I guess."

"This danger to the area — and my bringing it in — has made me start to let some things go. The idea of a murderous arsonist loose is so potentially devastating that my troubles seem small by comparison. It helps me that you are letting me help."

"I'm sorry about your husband — and that he died fighting what he wanted to conquer."

Words burst from her like a broken dam. "The thing is, besides being skilled in fighting wildfires, he had lived through one catastrophe already, one they called a major rager. He knew how to avoid blowups, how to avoid backfires. He'd saved himself once already by what they call 'Keeping one foot in the black' — you know, standing or lying down on charred ground to let the flames race by. The government report said there was supposedly a black area he and his friend Kyle could have run to. As a matter of fact, it was what they call a big black, a decent-size area already burned. His salvation was just twenty yards away, and he knew it was better to run through the flames to that charred area than to run uphill!"

Brad put a big, heavy hand on her shoulder, gripping it hard. "I've read a lot about wildfires, but it's a whole different bag from the structural blazes I'm usually assigned. I really admire what wildfire fighters do, literally in the heat of things. My team usually goes in afterward to figure out the what, how and why — and the who."

"Yeah, the who. Let's get going," she said, pulling away before she clung to his arm. "We can check on how the sheriff's doing today, too, if he's at the lodge."

"Some news," he told her. "Marston was lying to you about serving in Iraq, let alone in black ops, but there's no fingerprint match yet."

"I hope you can come up with a plan to trap him."

"I need to look around more, learn more first."

When she locked the door and started down behind Brad, staring at the trees blowing below, at the closest waterfall crashing eternally down a cliff, Lauren had a strange moment of vertigo. For a pilot, that was disaster; she'd never felt like this before.

She gasped, grabbed the metal railing and clung to it. Why did these steps have to be so steep? It was almost like descending a ladder.

"Lauren? What is it?"

"Just dizzy for a sec. I'll be all right."

He scrambled back up behind her, his body pressing against her back to hold her safe against the metal steps. His knees strengthened her shaking legs, almost as if she was going to sit in his lap up here. His black bag, ever on his shoulder, blocked a bit of the kaleidoscope view that had made her feel tipsy.

His mouth was so close to the nape of her neck that she felt his warm breath even in the stiff breeze. "Tell me when it passes."

When it passes, she thought. When my old life with Ross passes is right now. I have to let him go, except for honoring his memory as Nicky's father. I have to go on, find the arsonist, safeguard this area, my home, my people. I have to get past my fear that there was foul play involved in Ross's death, and maybe even a government cover-up.

"Lauren, should we go back up where you can lie down for a few minutes?"

"No. It's passed."

"You didn't eat much at dinner last night. Did you sleep?"

"I'm an insomniac, but I got four hours straight, which is great for me."

"We're going down step by step, pretty much like this, with me just one step behind and under you."

"That will take forever. I'm all right. It was probably just low blood sugar. I've got a candy bar in my saddle pack."

"I'm sending you home."

"No, you're not. You need me at the lodge."

"An insomniac who gets dizzy flies planes?"

Meaning she wasn't to be trusted in the air — or on the ground? Damn, she was going to show this man he needed her, that she could help him find Rocky Marston. She'd get some more sleep tonight, she'd eat better. She'd been part of the problem and she would be part of the solution. There are no problems, her can-do husband used to say, only solutions, but he had been wrong.

They started down slowly, step by step almost in tandem.

"I'm just fine," she insisted.

"In general, I'd agree with that."

"Then let's go faster."

"Faster can be good sometimes. We've got a lot to do, but I'll keep it in mind."

7

At first Evan thought he'd just leave the sheriff on the floor with his head bleeding right next to the ski lift mechanism, as if he'd fallen there and knocked himself out. Totally believable, the state he was in. If the national park investigators had accepted that Ross Taylor tripped and hit his head, these rubes around here ought to assume this.

Evan patted the man down but found no gun on the guy. He probably couldn't draw one with his arm busted up like that anyway. Evan didn't like guns any more than he liked hitting someone over the head — much too violent — but he would have taken a revolver and buried it if he'd found one.

Evan did feel comfortable that no one would come looking for the sheriff right away. The lodge seemed almost deserted this time of year, except for an Asian guy who was maybe the janitor or grounds-keeper. Other people from town evidently came and went now and then to clean the place or tend the area, but Evan had spent most of his daylight hours near Lauren's house or watching the village, so he wasn't sure.

But then, looking toward the lodge, he saw Lauren Taylor ride in on horseback, as if his mere thoughts had conjured her up. She was with a tall man Evan hadn't seen before. They dismounted and went up the steps and into the lodge.

Evan took the sheriff's ring of keys and left him unconscious on the floor. Then he went out and hightailed it to the lodge and darted around to look in various windows. He finally located them inside, standing before the huge fireplace in the rustic, pine-wood lounge, speaking to the Asian guy, but he couldn't tell what they were saying.

He tried to read their body language. Was this man Lauren's friend, brother, boy-friend, lover? He was big and blond. Too clean-cut for Evan's tastes. Rough-hewn enough to fit in around here but not ragged or rangy-looking like most men in the area. But wait — Evan was pretty sure he'd seen that man go into the Cobern house with Lauren and her kid his second night in town. He now knew it was the sheriff's house, but since the two women were friends, it probably wasn't official business.

Maybe it was time to show everyone — the sheriff, Lauren, Mr. Clean-Cut here and this whole town that anything he wanted to do, he could. He would just think of this as a little warning, a subplot in the epic drama. He made the rules, he was in control.

As for the main plot, it was starting to look as if a fire at Lauren's house would be a good diversion for a bunch of local-yokel volunteer firefighters, though he was considering keeping Nicky safe. And then either the sheriff's very own home and wife or that of the older, single lady who lived next to the firehouse would provide the grand denouement of this drama — and provide his curtain call in Montana.

But he was also writing the script for a grand exit. To be or not to be a kidnapper? Should he force Lauren to fly him out by threatening her kid or let her go up in flames and coerce someone else to get him back to civilization after this little respite? Meanwhile, to illustrate who was in charge here, he wasn't just going to leave the sheriff on the floor. No, he was going to take him — all of them — for a real ride.

■ ■ ■ ■

Like all Lost Lake locals, Lauren was proud
of the lodge and not just because it poured
money and vitality into the little, isolated
community. It was a handsome, sprawling
building, rustic but state-of-the-art. The
central pine-and-cedar building was a
combination of hotel, restaurant and lounge.
The eight outer cabins, each with its own
fireplace, were for larger groups than the
rented rooms in the lodge. During the
season, a ski school and ski rental were
available outside. And the two-person-per-
chair ski lift skimmed over a skating rink
and took skiers up the mountain for ski
runs, cross-country trails, snowshoeing and
extreme snow sports. The place came alive
in the winter but seemed a ghost town now.

After she had introduced the lodge chef,
Peter Lee, to Brad, she once again admired
how her very own special agent questioned
someone, this time assuming the role of a
curious visitor and writer. Peter was an
ebony-haired man of Asian descent, who
had the disconcerting habit of rocking
slightly back and forth on his heels.

"Nothing much goes on in the summer,"
Peter assured Brad with his long-fingerec

hands clasped before his chest. "Still, we hoping to have music camp here next year, more hiking in the future. You come back, write about it and my cuisine in the winter, busy then, very busy, not only Asian food but fusion with good American winter food, venison, buffalo steaks, other wild game."

"I'll have to do that. Do you know if the sheriff is around right now? We might as well see him since we're here," Brad added. He'd evidently convinced himself Peter hadn't seen anyone unusual around.

"That's a good idea," Lauren chimed in, realizing she wasn't half as good at this kind of smooth duplicity.

"Saw him outside," Peter told them, rocking slightly forward. "Was going cabin to cabin, checking to be sure all is well. I tell him herbs and acupuncture instead of that strong medicine he take be good for his pain. He should take it easy, but will not. I fixing him food though. You stay for lunch, too?"

"If you'll let us be paying restaurant guests," Brad said, and Peter nodded his acquiescence. "Lauren, let's go enjoy the view outside and see if we can find the sheriff, then bring him back in here for some of Peter's fine cuisine — summer style."

"Still good," Peter promised. "Things always fresh and very good."

Outside, they didn't see "hide nor hair" of Chuck, as Lauren had overheard Brad tell his boss about Rocky Marston. Brad even yelled for him twice.

"He probably went back to his room in the lodge," she said. "I'm glad Peter's keeping an eye on him and feeding him."

"I want to get some food into you, too. That candy bar wasn't much after that incident on the tower steps. What's that cabin over there by the ski lift? It has a small circle of glass rubbed clean in all the dirt — like a little spy hole."

"I think that's the place that runs the ski lift — you know what I mean," she said and jogged after him as he headed toward it.

But something else snagged her attention. Just beyond the small building, the ski lift was running, the double chairs moving down and around through the empty loading ramp before being hoisted high into the blue, windy sky to climb the mountain. Of course, she realized someone could be here to work on it. Red Russert had run the lift for years, and a younger man, Greg Pierce, did it now.

Peering into the locked building, they could see it was empty. Brad kept looking inside, and Lauren, gazing out at the lift, saw no one.

No one, that is, except Chuck Cobern, fifty yards away, slumped in one of the chairs, being lifted farther out and up into the open air.

Evan had liked to run the ski lift, not to ride it, but he had no choice now. In addition to amusing himself by sending the sheriff out into the wild blue yonder, he needed a fast stage exit from this area and some sort of diversion. With his left arm, he held his sleeping bag and backpack on another ski-lift chair so they would not roll off. As soon as he made it to the top of the beginner slope, the safety bar would automatically disengage. Then he could jump off, hopefully control the lift from up there and make his escape through the trees just above the town.

He kept twisting around to look back. He'd dragged the unconscious sheriff and barely managed to heft him onto a two-person seat four chairs behind the one he had used to stash his gear. Then he sprinted to make it in time to his chair as they swung around the platform ramp.

Still unconscious, maybe dead, Cobern rode behind him. The only gamble Evan was taking here was that someone who knew how to stop the lift might get to the controls before he got to the first disembarkation point. Then he'd be dangling for anyone to see — or catch. But he was still just Rocky Marston. He'd say the sheriff was out of his head when he turned on the lift and got on, while Rocky had just been sitting in a lift chair, admiring the fabulous view.

"Brad!" Lauren screamed, seizing his arm and pointing. "Chuck Cobern's on the lift! Out there, look!"

"Slumped over, maybe unconscious. The binocs are in my saddle pack."

"There's a safety bar over him, but what if it doesn't work, especially when the chair swings around at the first stop?"

Brad ran back and rattled the door of the ski-lift control shed. "Locked," he muttered before he tried to use his shoulder like a battering ram. The door didn't budge. "Do you think Peter has a key or can work the lift?"

"I doubt it. Let's just break a window."

"If I can just get in there and reverse the thing, we can bring him right back to us."

He picked up a large rock and yelled at her, "Get away!"

She moved to the edge of the loading

ramp and heard the window shatter. She looked back and saw Brad get another rock to knock off the jagged pieces of glass that still framed the window. He couldn't reach the door by putting his arm through.

She could see the lift chairs going by. If Chuck fell off at the bunny ramp, he'd need help. Had he gone onto his meds and out of his head again? For his sake — and Dee's — she had to help him.

Yes, Lauren thought, for Dee, who loved and needed Chuck, though she was stubbornly, stupidly acting like she didn't.

Since Brad was almost inside, she could just wait here. But even from this distance, maybe twelve cars back, she could see Chuck leaning lower, lower . . . Safety bar or not, he could slip out and fall several hundred feet.

Before she knew she would move, Lauren jumped in front of the next moving double chair and let it take her. The safety bar came down over her lap and she held tight to it. With no one beside her, she listed slightly, just as Chuck's chair had.

She felt her chair give its usual little shudder as it lifted away from the platform, the same movement she recalled it would make when it went under each of the cross-arm pillars that kept the cables suspended high

138

above the valley.

She heard Brad's voice behind her, loud and angry. "Lauren, what the hell?"

She twisted around, cupped her hands and shouted, "He'll need help if he falls off at the first ramp — just above the town! Don't stop it until I get that far!"

But she didn't see Brad. He must have gone into the building through the jagged window. She looked ahead again, praying Chuck wouldn't fall off way up here.

The changing view seemed to rotate under her, around her. Too late, she realized it was worse than on the fire tower steps, but she fought to keep control of herself. A collage of colors from late wildflowers carpeted the slant of meadow, the area that would be the bunny slope and powder bowl when the first snows fell. Seemingly marching downward beneath her, the tops of parched blue-green spruce and tall lodgepole pine gave way to other alpine conifers reaching up above their canopy of dried, brown needles on the ground. The jagged mountain peaks came closer, shutting out the sky.

She held tightly to the safety railing, hoping she wouldn't have another dizzy spell. Lost Lake looked so small from here. . . . She felt lost in the whirling vortex of space, one little leaf blown about in the vastness.

But she kept hold of herself. She'd come to help Chuck and wanted desperately to help Brad. She had to stay strong.

Then, as she squinted far ahead at the chairs strung out like toys on a wire, she saw something else and gasped. Several cars ahead of Chuck's, someone else was in a chair, someone with a big blue backpack on the seat beside him, someone who had almost reached the first disembarkation platform to which Chuck and Lauren were now headed.

Panicked and furious, Brad made a quick study of the levers and moving parts of the ski-lift mechanism, then tried to move the largest lever backward.

It didn't budge.

Forward.

Nothing.

But why not? Was there a lock on this thing?

He tried to move two other, smaller levers. Nothing shifted, so there must be a lock release somewhere. Had Chuck set this thing in motion? But why?

The noise he and Lauren had made — or the maddening, steady hum of the lift motor — evidently drew Peter out of the lodge. He stuck his head in the door, gaped at the broken glass on the floor, then frowned at Brad.

"Why the lift going?" he demanded. "You break window? You not to touch that machine!"

"Somehow the sheriff started the lift, got on and blacked out. Lauren's jumped on to help him. Do you know how to work this thing? The levers won't budge."

"I only king of the kitchen. That not been on all summer. But maybe it got overriding from one of the terminals."

"What?" Brad demanded, glaring at the man while still trying to unjam the controls.

"It not have to be worked from here but can be worked from the first platform — or way at top," he said, pointing at the ceiling of the small shed. "Up at the bunny slope or the one where the best skiers go. You know, override."

"You mean these controls can be overridden by controls above?"

"That it," Peter said, nodding, "if you know how to do it. I can go to the lodge and phone Red Russert. He used to work on it. Can't call Greg Pierce since he gone to Helena to see his mother. Or maybe I can call Mrs. Cobern, tell her sheriff coming home a new way."

"Yeah, you call Mrs. Cobern and tell her

to get up here right now, in case I can get him back," Brad muttered and turned to the mazelike machine again. "And call Red Russert if you can get him!"

Lauren knew Brad would like to kill her. She was no doubt done as his partner. But in that split instant where she had seen Chuck needed help, she had just reacted. She only hoped that someone else didn't try to kill her before Brad got to her.

Because as the chairs ahead of her climbed toward the top of the intermediate and advanced ski runs, she saw that the third person must have gotten off. Would he be waiting there for Chuck's and her arrivals, or was he fleeing? And after all this looking high and low, could that big blue backpack mean it was Rocky Marston?

She breathed a sigh of relief as the chairs came to a swinging stop. Brad must have figured out the controls. Perhaps he could get the chairs to stop at a place where Chuck could get out on the platform, if he was able. But unless Brad had her binoculars or superhuman vision, how could he see this far to stop Chuck's chair at the upper platform? Maybe he was going to reverse their direction and return them to the lodge.

Lauren tried looking back down the slope,

but the chairs behind blocked her view of the lodge terminal. She squinted upward into the bright midday sun. Both the first rider and Chuck had disappeared over the rim of the platform above her while she dangled here, the chairs and her booted feet swaying slightly in the increasing breeze, high above the ground.

Then the lift shuddered. It jerked. Reversed the direction of the chairs, then slammed forward into motion again.

Lauren screamed, let go of the safety bar across her lap and grabbed for the side handholds to stay in her rocking chair. Ahead of her, the empty chairs shook violently. Brad didn't know what he was doing. Or the mechanism was malfunctioning. She almost dry heaved from fear.

The chairs started forward again, stopped, then advanced.

She recalled that the lift could be controlled by someone at any of the terminals, despite the fact that it was usually run by an operator down at the lodge.

As the ski lift began taking her up toward the platform she could not yet see, she wished Brad were here, or at least his gun. Despite living in the wilds, she and Ross had never owned a gun like most of the townspeople did. Some would have called

Ross a tree hugger, some a greeny, because of his stand on the environment. Had Brad's father been like that, she thought, and fought back with fire?

A jumble of emotions and jagged thoughts consumed her. Frenzy, frustration, regret and fear raced through her as her chair jerked and rocked again. Nicky. She should have put her own safety ahead of Chuck's because of Nicky. She had no immediate family left. If something happened to her, would Dee or Suze take him in? She needed to make out a will. She should have stopped mourning Ross long enough to take better care of herself and Nicky, too.

In awe and terror, she forced herself to watch the double chairs ahead of her as they climbed higher toward the top platform. Would she see Chuck or that other man? Or had they both disembarked on the bunny slope platform?

As she cleared the tops of the last of the spruces, she crouched in her seat, holding on tightly, bracing herself against some sort of attack.

She could see the platform now. Only Chuck was in sight. But he was sprawled on the ground — and he looked dead.

Dee was in Just Fur You, checking inventory for the coming season, when the phone rang. Grabbing the receiver, she heard Peter on the other end. Instantly she knew something was wrong with Chuck. Her heartbeat accelerated and she repeatedly punched a stack of down-filled parkas as she listened to him.

"He what?" she asked. "Slow down. He went for a ride on what?"

She squeezed her eyes shut to concentrate on what Peter was saying. The sheriff had gone on a ride on the ski lift, and Mrs. Taylor went after him. The travel writer had said to call Dee and tell her to come to the lodge. All Dee could think was that Chuck was back on his meds and had overdosed on them.

"Never mind about the override!" she interrupted Peter as he rattled on. "You tell Brad Hale I'll be there as fast as I can."

She left the parkas and sweaters where they'd dropped and was halfway out the door when she remembered that she'd told Lauren she'd pick up the boys again today so she could take Brad around. No doubt that's why they were at the lodge. Why hadn't they kept a better eye on Chuck? Lauren had gone after him. On horseback, or on the lift?

She dialed the Fencer twins, who babysat

for a lot of kids in town. Eighteen this year, Ginny and Gerri weren't sure what they wanted to do with their lives, but Dee had promised them winter jobs at the shop. She prayed they'd be home.

"Hi, Dee! We can tell it's you because we just got caller ID," a young voice said.

Dee didn't even take the time to think how pointless that was here in Vermillion, nor did she ask which girl she was talking to. Trying to keep her voice steady, she asked them to pick up Larson and Nicky at school, but to go into the office first to get permission. She asked one of them to take Larson to her house — the door would be open — and the other to take Nicky home. He knew where the extra key was.

Dee slammed the shop door on her way out, not bothering to lock it. Within two minutes she was in Chuck's truck and on her way out of town toward the lodge.

She should have kept Chuck at home, she scolded herself as she sped up after passing the school. Maybe not forgiven him, but taken him in while he was hurt. Why in heaven's name had he taken the ski lift up the mountain? At this time of year, there were rocky precipices up there with no snow to pad a fall.

"Oh, please, Chuck, don't do anything

desperate."

The moment Lauren's safety bar lifted from her lap, she jumped from her chair and stumbled away from the next ones as they rotated past on the platform. Her legs shook; her pulse pounded.

Just off the pavement, Chuck lay, his bloodied face up. His broken arm was still in its sling, but at a strange angle. His other arm was splayed straight out, palm down, as if he were bracing himself. He did not move. He might not even be breathing.

Lauren looked around and saw no one else. Could Marston be hiding in the trees and bushes about ten yards away?

"Chuck? Chuck!" she cried, gripping his good shoulder and shaking him slightly. Trembling, she knelt beside him and felt for his pulse. She couldn't tell if it was fast or slow, but it was there, so he was alive. Chuck Cobern had always been one tough cookie with everyone, except his own wife.

The wound on his head looked as if it had stopped bleeding. Had he hit it against the chair? No, the wound was starting to scab, so it wasn't completely fresh. Maybe he'd fallen and hit his head, then had no clue what he was doing. Or maybe Rocky Marston had knocked him out.

Lauren knew she'd never be able to heft him onto one of the moving chairs and make it in herself to steady him while they rode down the slope. Since the lift kept going smoothly now, maybe Brad would ride up here to help her. She'd just try to keep Chuck comfortable until help came.

Scowling again at the bushes, she prayed Marston had fled. Yet she wished she'd catch a glimpse of him, so she could be sure of what she'd seen — that he was real. Of course he was real, she scolded herself. If only Brad had seen him!

Lauren sat down with her back against one of the pillars supporting the cables and chairs. The metal was warm from the sun, and she could feel the hum of the cables running through it. Help would surely be here soon.

She patted down Chuck's lightweight jacket and came up with nothing. No gun, no holster. Nothing. He'd probably disarmed himself when he got so woozy from the meds.

She heard a rustle in the leaves and a snort. Turning, she expected to see Rocky Marston emerge from the foliage. Instead, a huge brown bear cocked its head and stared at her, as if to size her up.

8

"Mrs. Cobern, this way, this way!" Dee heard a shout and saw Peter windmilling his arm over by the ski lift.

Dee ran toward him, wondering where Brad was.

"He is there!" Peter said, as if he'd read her mind. He pointed out over the valley. "He say you stay here. He bring them back, and I keep the lift going."

"What happened?" she cried, shading her eyes and staring at the back of Brad's ski-lift chair. He hadn't gone far, maybe not out of earshot. It would be nearly ten minutes more before he'd reach the top of the bunny-hill runs.

"Sheriff must have started the lift," Peter said, darting back and forth between her and the ski-lift shed.

"Brad!" she screamed, waving both arms. "Brad, I'm here! Find him, help him!"

He evidently heard her because he turned

in his double seat. He waved an arm but didn't shout back. Her instinct was to jump into the next chair, but what if Chuck rode back down here while Lauren and Brad were after him up there? Then, too, she had the feeling that the FBI was to be obeyed. But had Lauren done that?

She bit her lower lip and blinked back tears at Chuck's predicament — and at hers, treating him so coldly these last months when she loved him so much, despite his stupidity and his sins.

"That travel writer," Peter called to her from the door of the shed, "he gonna have a lot to write so far."

Dee nodded and kept her face turned away so he wouldn't see her tears.

Lauren moved slowly, deliberately. She rolled Chuck over, facedown, despite what that might do to his hurt arm and shoulder. Then she stood. Bears always tried to roll a prone person onto his back to get at the stomach, the softest spot they could attack. It was good to play dead, and Chuck was doing a fine job of that. Hopefully, he wouldn't regain consciousness right now.

At least this bear wasn't a grizzly, she thought. Still, she averted her eyes and watched the animal sideways. Brown bears considered a direct stare a challenge. She'd seen many around here over the years, but never this close. And never one that looked interested in her. They usually preferred avoidance to attack, but this one must have smelled something.

Unfortunately, her standing stock-still in a nonthreatening posture didn't deflect its curiosity. In addition to not wanting to abandon Chuck, she knew it was not a sane option to turn and flee. Everyone in these parts knew never to run from a bear, since they could go up to forty miles per hour. And to them, flight signaled prey. It was best to talk low or sing in a soft monotone while you backed slowly away. But if she did that, she was leaving Chuck to the bear.

The five-hundred-pound animal reared on its hind legs to its six-foot height and wriggled its nose, trying to identify her and Chuck by smell. Food? A threat? Everyone said bears were very complex, unpredictable animals, but always vicious if cornered.

An errant thought raced through her brain. The arsonist must be like that, complex, unpredictable, and if cornered . . .

Though her voice snagged in her throat, she began to recite a singsong rhyme that came to her, half remembered, half created on the spot: "Bear, bear, go away, come again another day and not where people like to stay. Bear, bear, go away . . ."

But it didn't. It snorted again. ". . . where people like to stay . . ." It could have cubs around, too, though she didn't see any ". . . another day . . ."

She thought of Nicky, how desperate she'd been to protect him after his father's death. Yet she'd endangered herself now. Ross should not have risked his life, but here she was facing down a bear on a mountain.

Brad, where are you? The ski lift was still running. Brad, where are you? ". . . come again another day . . ."

Lauren knew that if the bear came close, she should try to intimidate it, though that had always sounded pointless and stupid. One should shout, hit it with a branch or rock, she'd heard.

She felt slowly through her jeans pockets. She found only a candy-bar wrapper and the key to the fire tower. Most weapons other than a high-caliber rifle would be powerless against this raw power.

Don't panic, she told herself, chanting the silly song aloud again. Keep calm. Brad had told her that very thing just today. The worse the situation, he'd said, the better it is to keep calm.

But she couldn't fight the frenzy filling her.

The bear dropped to all fours and charged. Lauren dropped to her knees beside Chuck and shredded the air with a piercing scream.

When Brad heard Lauren scream, he was still four chairs below the break in the trees where the platform must be. He drew his gun, glad he had it. But would he be in time? And what would he find? Had she come upon Chuck injured or even dead?

It took an eternity for his chair to lift the last, short distance. He was closer now to the other chairs heading down, coming at him empty.

Lauren had come to mean a lot to him in a very short time. And so had Nick, with his wild imagination, his passion for Indians. He'd sensed instantly how much the boy missed his father and felt protective of the little guy. Though Brad had been older when he'd lost his dad, his whole world had shattered. But Nick had a father to be proud of, not one to be ashamed of, not one whose deeds now drove Brad to right wrongs.

Brad heard no other sounds after the scream. In his line of work, he'd never had to rescue anyone directly, hadn't since his stint in the Alexandria, Virginia, Fire Department. He'd saved a woman from the flames there once, but like the BND's victims, she'd died later of burns and smoke inhalation.

Despite the safety bar across his lap, Brad shoved himself up in the chair as it crested the treetops over the platform he would see now. If only this damn safety bar would free him . . .

He didn't see her or Chuck at first. And then he did.

They both lay, facedown, on the grass just beyond the concrete loading ramp, not moving as a huge bear faced them, just a few feet away.

Wishing he had a rifle, Brad lifted his Glock .45. Despite the bar lifting before his face and the chair swinging as he jumped off, he took a shot at the bear.

Still out of breath from his run down the mountain, Evan heard the boy's high voice from here in the ravine beside the Taylor house. Since the kid's mother must still be somewhere up on the mountain, Evan hadn't expected to find anyone home. Maybe Dee Cobern was keeping an eye on Nicky again.

"Can I go out and play in my Indian tent

just in the backyard?" Evan heard him ask. Evan instinctively ducked, though he knew no one could see him except from the balcony or roof.

A young woman's voice he hadn't heard before answered, "Oh, yeah, nice tepee. Sure, but come back in for this PBJ sandwich you asked for, okay? I'm going to turn on a TV show here while I straighten up this kitchen a little for your mom, but I'm right here if you need me."

"Thanks, Gerri," Nicky called to her. Evan heard the back door bang.

Almost immediately, Nicky stuck his head out from under his makeshift tent, just the way Evan had told him to. Yeah, he liked this boy. He followed orders well.

"I was hoping you'd be there, Chief," the kid called to him in a stage whisper. "I'll be right down."

He half slid, half scrambled down the slope and managed to put on the skids before he fell into the stream.

"I got a banana and graham crackers for you," he said, digging things out of the back of his shirt where he tucked its tails in. "But I'll have a peanut butter and jelly sandwich for you soon!" His eyes were huge as he extended the food and studied Evan.

"White Calf not know what those are, but

any food good."

"Oh, yeah, I forgot, those are modern things, but I don't have buffalo and bittersweet root and all that we've been reading about. I saw that in the books about your people at my teacher's place last night."

"Where your teacher live on White Calf's land?" Evan asked, taking the food from the boy. He was careful not to touch his hands, but he could probably explain that ghosts had to have real bodies sometimes, especially when they ate.

"She lives in a 'partment over the Montana Range Gift Shop in town, by the firehouse. Ever since her husband died, she lives alone there 'cause she needed a smaller place."

"Good. That good for her."

"I went with my mom and her new friend, the writer, to visit her there."

"Big, blond man?"

"That's him. He calls me Nick, not Nicky, just like my dad did."

"He write for newspaper?"

"I think he writes travel books. But at Mrs. Gates's, I figured out another reason you appear to me here by this stream."

"What that?"

"Because it runs into the lake at the place where your people used to dig out the clay with the vermillion to make war paint."

"You very wise, boy. I give you name Running Deer, but you tell no one."

"Oh, I won't. Running Deer? That's way cool. I guess I better go up and get your sandwich — that's two pieces of bread with some really good stuff between them. My mom's not here right now 'cause she's taking the writer around town and to the fire tower."

"The fire tower?"

"That's why I'm here with a babysitter. I'm not a baby — it's just the way white people talk. I let her in with this," he said and showed Evan a single key dangling from a coiled neon-orange elastic bracelet around his thin wrist.

"That beautiful with bright color of the sun," Evan said. "You make peace and friendship gift of that to White Calf?"

"Uh, well, I guess so. I can just take the key off."

"But that shiny silver. I not know what key for, but if it that metal charm, I like that, too."

"Oh, okay. We have other keys, even ones just like this, so I guess so," he said, slowly pulling the whole thing off and extending it to Evan.

His dramatic triumph over his kiddie audience made Evan want to break into laughter. He managed to stay in character until the boy scrambled up the ravine and crawled into the back of his tent to emerge out the other side and run into the house.

Ah, what recompense for his performances today! The Smoke Ghost, stage name White Calf, long-dead chief of the Blackfeet, was now the proud owner of the key to the sheriff's house and the key to Lauren Taylor's place. It was just too perfect — kismet!

Evan laughed out loud. He might have lost his familiar *pied-à-terre* in the ski-lift cabin, but he now had a choice of attics in which to make a nest. That is, until he decided to light a mighty big campfire in one place or the other. He was on such a roll, surely he could find a way into Teacher Gates's apartment, too. Then the entire town could search for him high and low outside, but he'd be all cozy and closer to them than they'd ever know. Why, when his vacation was all done here, they'd have to dub him not the Boy Next Door but the Man in the House!

Cursing and shouting at the bear, Brad squeezed the trigger again and again, but the recoil and his rush to get out of the moving chair made him miss. He thought he might have hit him the animal the first time, but maybe the noise scared him more than anything. Thank God the bear turned and lumbered away.

Brad kneeled by Lauren and Chuck. Chuck had blood on his head, but it looked dry. And Lauren . . .

He bent down to her, afraid to move her if she'd been mauled — or worse. He wanted to cover her body with his own, pull her into his arms and race to safety with her. Tears blurred his vision. He was afraid to roll her faceup. Check for blood and injuries first, he told himself.

"Lauren? Lauren, it's Brad. Are you hurt?"

She had her eyes squeezed shut, but they blinked open. She'd been crying; her face was streaked with tears.

"Just terrified. Is it gone?" she whispered. "It charged at us, but it stopped after we didn't run. Still, I was so faint, I thought I'd better play dead. You — did you shoot it?"

"Yeah, but it wasn't like firing at a shooting-range target. It may be back. How's Chuck?" he asked, feeling for the man's carotid artery with his left hand. As he did, Brad realized he, too, was shaking all over.

"He's out cold," she said, getting to her knees, then sitting unsteadily back on her heels. She glanced around and brushed herself off. Damp with sweat, she trembled as if she had a fever. "Let's get him down the slope. I can help you get him in a chair. I'll be all right," she insisted, but her knees buckled when she tried to stand, and she broke into tears. Both kneeling next to Chuck, they hugged hard. She spoke with her mouth against the side of his warm neck.

"I thought it would kill me. That I'd never see Nicky again, that I wouldn't be able to help you find that man so he doesn't hurt others. Brad," she cried, pushing herself back from his hard embrace but gripping both his arms, "I swear to you that Rocky Marston was on the lift just a few chairs ahead of Chuck. I swear he was! You have to believe me."

Frowning, helping her up as he stood, Brad scanned the area again. "Was Marston in sight when you got off the lift?"

"No! No, and neither was the bear. I got off because I saw Chuck lying here. He looked dead. I saw Rocky on the lift but not when he got off. He just disappeared. Brad, I saw him!"

"You can tell me all about it when I get you two back down to the lodge. We're not

160

doing any sweep for Marston here, with bears loose and the sheriff hurt. Let's try to get him into a chair. He's heavy, so I'm gonna need your help. I'll ride down with him so he doesn't roll out. Can you get in the next chair on your own?"

She nodded and swiped at her tears, smearing dirt on her cheeks. "Did you make the chairs stop and shake?" she asked.

"No, but I saw that. I think someone up here was overriding the controls — and it sure as hell wasn't that bear. Of course I believe you about Marston. It opens up all sorts of new possibilities."

It scared him how limp and unsteady she looked. But he and his entire trained-to-the-teeth team would probably be blithering idiots after what she'd just been through. FBI teams didn't do bears.

"You did the right thing, Lauren," he assured her, his voice catching in his throat. "I'm just glad you're not hurt. Now let's get the sheriff back to Dee. Peter called her. She's at the lodge."

Together, they got Chuck on a chair next to Brad, and he held the big man upright until the safety bar came down. Brad craned his neck to look back at Lauren as she made it into the chair right behind. Though the ride was smooth, she held on with both hands as if her life depended on it.

"You've been a great help, pard'ner," Brad called to her. "But I think it's time for you to retire from the posse and just hole up with your boy at the old homestead."

"No way! I'm going to help the FBI get the Fire Phantom before he pulls any other deadly stunts! And I'm not doing it for the reward money but to get him off the streets and off the slopes!"

Brad grinned despite himself as he turned forward and held hard to Chuck Cobern. She was a hell of a woman, and one he absolutely refused to let get hurt again. Somehow he had to get her off the case before anything else exploded in her face.

Dee was so happy to see Chuck, however terrible he looked, that she burst into tears. Peter ran to phone for the town's only EMR vehicle and to alert the health clinic. As Dee knelt to cradle Chuck in her arms and kissed his dirty cheek, he opened his eyes.

"Wha're you all doin' here?" he managed to say as Dee, Brad and Lauren bent over him.

"I guess you have the magic touch, Dee," Lauren said. "Sleeping Beauty awakened by a kiss. He was out cold the whole time we werc with him."

"Am I in heaven?" Chuck said, sounding as if he'd been on an all-night bender.

"His pupils are dilated," Brad said. "He's probably in shock, or he may have a concussion. Sheriff, we think our arson suspect put you on the ski lift." Dee gasped, but Brad went on, "Can you remember anything about how you got knocked out?"

"Did I?" he said, frowning, even as he nestled his head tighter in Dee's lap. "Can't recall."

"Loss of short-term memory's not unusual with a head injury," Brad said. "Just relax, Sheriff. That's okay."

"Las' I 'member," Chuck went on, "I was checking cabins. Yeah, that's it — for him. So maybe I flushed him, huh?"

"Brad," Dee said, "can't this wait until later?"

Brad nodded and went over to the ski-lift shed. Lauren squeezed Dee's shoulder and started to rise, but Dee mouthed, "I can't thank you enough — both of you."

Lauren nodded too and got up to follow Brad into the shed. Through its open door and broken window, their words floated clearly to Dee as she held tight to Chuck.

"What are you looking for?" Dee heard Lauren ask Brad.

"Wish I knew. But if Chuck didn't start

the ski lift, maybe Marston did."

"Because Chuck had him almost cornered?"

"Or we did."

"But he can't know who you are. So what if I'd see him? He can't realize I know who he is."

"Lauren, we can't underestimate this man or even predict what he'll do next. I tell myself I can — I want to, but I don't know. It was tough for me to figure out how to operate this thing. And Marston must have gotten to the top and used the override up there. Now, who would know how to do that?"

"Someone who knew machinery? Someone who'd operated a lift somewhere?"

"Or maybe operated it here?"

"What? No way! I'd never seen him before."

"I'm guessing that no one has run this lift for years, except for the current guy who's not around, and Red Russert. And we know this building was locked. Whoever started the lift got in here without breaking and entering like I did. Dee —" Brad popped his head out and called to her "— did Chuck carry keys to this place?"

"Never have," Chuck answered for her. "There's one under that big rock over there, left of the door," he mumbled and Dee repeated what he'd said to Brad.

"It must be the rock I grabbed to break in," Brad muttered, and she heard him swear under his breath. "Yeah, the key's still here. It doesn't make sense," he said as he tried it in the door to be sure it worked. It did.

"Sweetheart, check to see if I still got my badge," Chuck whispered to Dee. "You got my permission to frisk me."

"You're sounding better," she told him, secretly thrilled he was feeling well enough to tease her. "Yes, he has his sheriff's badge," she called to Brad and Lauren.

"Marston might have seen that and wanted to get rid of Chuck or make a fool of him," she heard Brad say, speaking again to Lauren.

"More proof it could be him," she insisted. Dee held Chuck tighter. He'd either blacked out again or gone to sleep. But if he had a concussion, she needed to try to keep him awake.

"So did Marston accidentally find the key?" Brad asked Lauren. "This whole case has been one big, locked room. I need to find Red Russert, and now."

"I think he's out camping," Lauren told him, "but he comes back now and then. We can check his house, leave him a note."

"I want you to go home and stay with Nick! If we can't find Russert on the ground, could you spot him from the air? Do you know where he might be?"

"Marilyn Gates might."

"I got the distinct idea she detested the guy."

"I can tell you've never read a romance novel. Opposites attract, and bickering is foreplay. Brad, what's this sticky stuff on the floor here? See?"

Dee could finally hear the distant wail of a siren. Like the fire department in town, the EMR paramedics were volunteers who received a call, then reported to the station house. It comforted her to hear the siren and to have Chuck safe — though evidently unconscious again — in her arms.

He could have been killed more than once today. And it hardly calmed her when she heard Brad tell Lauren, "Looks like blood. Maybe Chuck's."

After a long silence, Dee heard Brad say, "I think Chuck cornered Marston, who then used this wrench here on the wall to knock him out. See the hair and blood on the metal? It hasn't quite been wiped clean, so our mastermind's made a mistake for once. There have to be prints on here. We can at least charge him with assault and battery, if we can get him to materialize again."

Dee shuddered and held Chuck even closer as Peter pointed the EMR vehicle their way.

9

Though Brad had insisted she go home and stay there, Lauren could tell he was torn. He had to find Rocky Marston fast, before he could do more harm, especially the kind of harm he specialized in. So, he needed her to find Red Russert. Up on the mountain today, they'd both realized how dry the grass was, how wilted even the big conifers looked from lack of rain. And the wind whipped up through the valleys and howled around the cliffs incessantly.

They had just left their horses at the Fencer place, although the twins were babysitting Nicky and Larson in their homes. In Lauren's SUV, they drove directly into town.

"I hope we don't shock her," Brad muttered as they hurried up the stairs to Marilyn Gates's apartment. "We look like something the cat dragged in."

"Or something the bear did."

Halfway up the enclosed staircase, he put his hand to her elbow and turned her to him. He started to speak, then seemed to choke up. Picking a piece of leaf out of her wild hair, he brushed her tresses back from her face.

"Don't tell me again that I need to go home," she said. "I will tuck Nicky in tonight and be with him as best I can. But I can't really be at home until this is all over, when my son and I and our friends are safe and can sleep at night. I'm running on adrenaline, though I'm so exhausted that I think even I could get a full night's sleep."

"Then I can't ask you to take me up in the plane to look for Red Russert, whether or not Mrs. Gates knows where he is."

"I'm the best sleep-deprived pilot around," she insisted, tapping her finger in the middle of his chest. "Actually, I'm the *only* one in town since Wednesdays are big flight days and the other five planes are probably in Kalispell or in the air right now. Come on, Agent Hale. Let's hope that Mrs. Gates knows as much about Red Russert as I think she does."

Almost the moment they knocked, Marilyn Gates flung the door open, her face alight with expectation. She was prettily dressed in a soft aqua jogging outfit.

"Oh, hello!" she said, sounding startled and looking crestfallen before she composed her expression. "I thought it was someone else. Come in, come in and — whatever happened?"

Lauren shot Brad an I-told-you-so look as they followed her in, but he said only, "We've been searching for the suspect up by the ski lodge and had to help Sheriff Cobern, who was almost attacked by a bear. That's the short version of it, but we need your help again. The suspect is obviously hiding — maybe camping — in the area, and I could really use Red Russert's tracking skills."

When Mrs. Gates only nodded, Lauren put in, "He's such a loner, but I know he sometimes tells you where he's going."

"Yes, he does, and I sometimes tell him where he should go, too," she said, her voice angry but strangely wistful. She led them into the kitchenette and pulled out two bar stools at the high counter. They saw she had been fixing herself a sandwich and had a pitcher of iced tea. Both of them started to sit down.

"No, wash your hands first at this sink, both of you. Your face, too, Lauren. I won't ask you for details and you won't ask me for any, either, but while I feed you, I'll tell you what you need to know."

They obeyed without a word as if they were first-graders in her class, then sat at the bar, while she bustled about her little work area. She cut the chicken sandwich she'd evidently made for herself in two and gave each of them half, then poured some potato chips out of a bag onto their plates. Dill pickles followed. "Eat, I said. I'm making other sandwiches for myself and more for you."

Despite themselves, ravenous and parched, they leaped at the food. They'd had nothing but water and her candy bar since they'd set out for the fire tower. They'd left the ski lodge without the lunch Peter had promised them.

"Yes," Mrs. Gates said as she bent over the counter with her back to them, "Red Russert usually tells me where he's going — just in case something befalls him. This time, he's at the high camp, as he calls it, waiting for me this weekend."

Lauren almost choked on a big bite, then managed to chew and swallow. "For you?" she said, but Brad kneed her leg and she shut up.

"Red and I go way back, but I married someone else. That should have been end of story, but it wasn't — isn't." She heaved a sigh but kept busy. "The thing is, after Glen died, Red tried to, well, to retie our ties, but I said no. First of all, we're as different as night and day. Secondly, he had a knock-down, drag-out fistfight with my husband once at the general store that shamed them both.

"You know," she went on, just staring at her cupboards now, her hands momentarily still, "when I was a girl, I always loved those stories where the armored knights jousted for the affections of their lady love. Well, I digress, and you are in a hurry."

She cut the two sandwiches she'd made in half. "You see, Glen was a conservative, mild-mannered man, and Red is just the opposite. You can imagine who got the best of the other in that fight. I feel I'm honor-ing Glen's memory by keeping clear of Red Russert, tracker and trapper that he is . . .

"I'm sorry," she said, whirling to face them. "You didn't need to hear all that. I'm not going to meet him at the high camp, but I can tell you where it is. It will take you about two hours by foot — it's the only way up to it."

"Red's a tracker?" Brad asked.

"Oh, yes, the best around," she said, her voice swelling with pride. "If you took him to the spot where you said Sheriff Cobern had a problem with a bear, he could track that bear for you."

"Has he ever tracked humans?" Brad asked, the last piece of his sandwich suspended in his big hand halfway to his mouth.

"I'm afraid they leave different calling cards, but I'm certain he could help you there, too," Mrs. Gates said with a decisive nod. "I should have thought of that before. Do you have any sort of trail for him to start with?"

"The top of the bunny slopes," Lauren said to Brad. "I'm not sure which way he ran, but it was probably down — maybe back toward town. Can you tell us where the high camp is?" she asked Mrs. Gates. "Since time is of the essence though, maybe you could draw us some sort of map we could use from the air. We can fly over the camp and either buzz Red or drop a note to meet us at the first stop on the ski lift. That way we'll avoid hiking two hours, only to find that he might not be there."

"That would be great," Brad added. "Whether we spot him or not, we can drop a message out of the plane to his camp."

"I have just the thing," Mrs. Gates said and left them for a moment only to return with a bright red beanbag pillow. "You can attach the note to this. It should be heavy enough not to snag in a conifer. And it will drop all the way to the ground but not hurt anything. I'll stitch a small American flag to it while you write your note, Agent Hale, and I'll tell Lauren exactly where Red is up Mount Jefferson. And if you do find him, just tell him I wasn't coming to the camp anyway, and we'll talk about it all later."

"Yes, ma'am," Brad said, sounding excited when he usually stayed icy calm. "And may I say, Mrs. Gates, *you* get an A for the day."

"Nonsense, though I have decided that one chapter of the memoirs I intend to write someday will be titled, 'Marilyn Gates, Special Counsel to the FBI.' "

Evan used the key in the back door of Lauren's house and stepped inside. Nicky had told Chief White Calf that his mother wasn't coming back for a while and that he was leaving with his babysitter, Gerri. He would spend the evening at her parents' house with his best friend and his babysitter.

"And they have some horses there, and I might get to ride them!" the kid had said. "I might ask if I can ride mine without a saddle, the way your people did."

"You be careful. That not easy," Evan had

told him.

But getting into Lauren Taylor's house was a piece of cake.

As soon as he relocked the door, he went straight to the refrigerator, hoping for some sort of gastronomic indulgence he'd been missing lately. He'd noted from his observation of Vermillion that no one had security systems. Many people didn't even lock their doors. But he wasn't taking this risk just to forage for extra food. That wasn't why he was here at all. He was doing research on what accelerants would be best to torch his three candidates' houses.

Evan drank milk directly from the half-gallon plastic bottle and, without using a knife, piled together a slapdash sandwich of bologna and cheese with a squirt of mustard. The food the kid had brought him helped, but he was hungry and sick of canned tuna. He ate cookies and crackers that he found, and took an apple off the counter that he crunched into. Lauren probably wouldn't even realize she had three instead of four there now, not with a kid and babysitter in the house.

He searched through the cupboards, and turned up a cache of miniature Mr. Goodbar candies, individually wrapped like those given out at Halloween. They were stashed high, not like the jar of M&Ms the kid could reach on the counter. He took handfuls of both kinds of candy and jammed them in his pockets.

Were the Mr. Goodbars Lauren's secret chocolate sin? He remembered a movie called *Looking for Mr. Goodbar,* about a woman who picked up a guy in a bar who killed her. He would have liked to play that part onstage. You could hardly do a realistic drama about an arsonist without the props catching the whole theater on fire. His shoulders shook with silent laughter.

He'd observed that the kid slept upstairs and Lauren down, so he went next to reconnoiter her bedroom. It was a small room with white pine paneling and a single twin bed covered by a yellow and blue quilt. There were four framed drawings of local wildlife on the opposite wall, all signed by an artist named Suze M. The animals were a bison, a bighorn sheep, a moose and a wolf. He liked the wolf best.

Evan bet the boy's bedroom upstairs had once been hers — hers and Ross Taylor's. Too bad the guy had been so nosy about how the wildfire they were fighting had spread so quickly and into virgin areas. He'd asked too many questions and had challenged Evan's answers. It was his own fault

176

he'd had to die. And how fitting, by the very fire he was fighting. Ross's demise had been Evan's inspiration to have each later arson ignited by an accelerant that fit the victim. In a way, he owed Ross Taylor a big debt of gratitude for that.

Unafraid now of leaving fingerprints that he so assiduously avoided leaving at the scenes of his masterpieces, he opened Lauren's closet door.

There weren't many dresses and skirts, but lots of jeans, some nice slacks and matching jackets, blouses and T-shirts. He saw boots and running shoes — and even one pair of red heels. A few extra purses were stacked on the single closet shelf. And there were lots of bulky sweaters there, each in its own plastic zipper bag. It smelled good in here, Evan thought, a sort of fresh-wind scent. No expensive perfumes for Widow Taylor. Did she miss having a man? From the way she'd talked about her husband when she'd flown Evan in, she might still be mourning the guy. Get over it, he'd tell her if he had the chance. Life is short and you just never know when your time is up, so enjoy.

He closed the closet door and suddenly wondered if she kept a gun. Gingerly, he felt beneath her pillow. Nothing there. He wondered if she was sleeping with the blond man — not Mr. Goodbar, but maybe Mr. Goodblond. He'd really like to know more about the travel writer.

Evan knelt and looked under her bed, where he found dust and a couple of scrapbooks. Flipping through the books, he found articles about Ross's career, and one from the Kalispell paper about them being a husband-and-wife pilot team. He hoped he had time to look through them later, as it was best to be very well informed about the chosen ones. He was still undecided if he'd need Lauren to fly him out of here after the inferno or whether she was expendable. At one time, he might have spared her because of her boy, but he'd learned that some young men were much better off without their mothers — or either parent, for that matter.

He went to the white, eight-drawer bureau and pulled open the top left drawer. It was full of lingerie, rather fancy stuff for a woman who went around looking like she was camping out. He fingered the items, letting the silky material slide through his fingers and over the sensitive skin of his inner wrist. Deep aquamarine, fuschia, salmon. Pretty lace, sexy stuff. Maybe this was her other little indulgence, besides the

Mr. Goodbars.

Ha! If he had to choose an accelerant for Lauren's house, wouldn't these hot little items be the perfect fire starter, especially if doused with gasoline from her plane?

Lauren took off into the western wind and circled the lake once, gaining altitude. Brad sat in the copilot seat with the beanbag pillow on one knee. Mrs. Gates had sewn his message to Red inside with the words CUT OPEN TO SEE NOTE on the outside.

The note within read,

To Red Russert. Lauren Taylor and her friend Brad Hale need your help to track a stranger who endangered Sheriff Chuck Cobern's life earlier today. Please meet us at the top of the beginner slope near the ski-lift ramp ASAP. Marilyn Gates suggested you would be excellent to assist us with this task.

Lauren Taylor and Brad Hale.

Poor Red, Lauren thought. He'd probably get his hopes up, thinking he was getting a gift or love note, but at least the mention of Mrs. Gates might encourage him. She had even attached a small American flag to the package. It seemed the woman had flags and patriotic memorabilia stashed everywhere inside her little place.

As they flew back across the lake toward Mount Jefferson, Brad said, "The mountains here are awesome, from both the ground and the air."

"They never change and yet they are never the same, especially with the shifting sun and clouds. The Blackfeet called the Rockies 'the backbone of the world.' This area was sacred to them. The early white settlers said this is 'the land of shimmering mountains.' To me these mean just plain home."

"From this height, what amazes me are all the yellow and gold colors mixed in with the green and brown. I know it's early September, but is the gold all dry terrain, too?"

He was looking out at the far reaches of the Vermillion Valley, which Lauren intended to fly through to approach Red's high camp from the opposite direction. That way they'd be able to spot it, maybe even see him, before they soared beyond the surrounding trees.

Lauren had quickly memorized Mrs. Gates's map. She'd hiked up into the area once with Ross years ago. The stark contrasts in the area were stunning. The Vermillion Valley and the canyon beyond both had an eerie aura about them, one Ross had laughed off as "just the old Indian ghosts of fierce warriors hanging around." Again, she hoped Mrs. Gates hadn't shared with Nicky's class the fact that the Blackfeet left their dead to rot on platforms until nothing was left but bones, which they buried on-site.

"No," she answered Brad, "those colors aren't a sign of autumn or, thank heavens, dry grass or foliage. You can't tell from here, but that's late-summer yellow yarrow and, higher up, glacier lilies along the snow line. The rest is alpine larches, which look like evergreens, but their needles turn yellow-gold by winter. Still, the area is tinder dry."

"Don't I know it. Look, an eagle. We're soaring with eagles!"

He sounded like Nicky, as if his troubles and tension had dropped away for a moment. She wondered if he was picturing that fierce-looking eagle on his FBI badge, but thought not. Despite all they had to worry about, she'd learned long ago that flying lifted you in more ways than one.

She flew *Silver* down the valley. It was not a glacial, U-shaped one like the Lost Lake area. This one looked sculpted from stone. Lost Lake was really a tarn, a small, deep lake that occupied a basin scooped out by the glaciers. But this steeper area was waterfall-cut cliffs with jagged peaks above and timber below. The braided river flashed beneath them and then the small, skinny lake it fed. As they flew farther north from the town, the Vermillion Valley continued to narrow until it became a forested area that ended near the lumber camp.

"We're going pretty far," Brad observed. "Surely this wouldn't be a two-hour hike. How old is Red Russert, anyway?"

"About Marilyn Gates's age is all I know. No, I'm going to swing around and head back, but I can't do a big turn until we're over the lumber camp. Look down at ten o'clock."

He craned his neck as she made a large loop. "That's a big operation," he said.

"Dee and I took the boys there earlier this summer, and Larson's dad, Steve, gave us a great tour of the place. Of course, the kids loved all the massive machinery — tree-harvesting monsters with names like the slasher, the skidder, the feller and the dozer — not to mention the log flume itself, which reminded them of a theme-park ride."

"I can imagine. Yeah, I see that log flume now. At least this area is probably too far for Marston to go. I have a feeling that if

Red can help us, we just might be able to find where he's holed up around Vermillion. Look, there's someone down there on the edge of that rock!"

Lauren tipped her right wing slightly to look. "It's Suze Milliman, painting. That's called Cedar Ridge. As you can see, it overlooks both the canyon and the lumber camp — a panoramic view. At least Suze isn't near town where Marston could find her, though she's always carried a gun."

"I don't think she'd be in any danger from him anyway. He's never assaulted or raped a woman. He obviously likes to kill them from afar."

"In short, the bastard fries them to death. Hang on. I'm going to dip both wings, though Suze will know it's me by the plane."

She waggled the wings. Suze looked up and waved, crisscrossing her arms over her head before she was out of sight again.

"Get ready," Lauren warned. "High camp will come up soon. Your toss will have to be fairly accurate, especially in case Red's not there and has to stumble onto the pillow later. Get ready, just past this waterfall called Weeping Wall. There! In that clearing? You can even see his tent. Do you see him?"

"No!"

"I'm cutting back the speed a bit so we

can coast down, but I'll have to climb before that line of trees. There he is — see?"

"Yeah, and I see where he gets his name Red."

"He used to kid me that we were related," she said as she saw the big man walk out into the clearing and look up, shading his eyes. His coppery hair gleamed in the sun. "Brad, open the window. Ready, set . . ."

She watched as he waved an arm out at Red, then heaved the pillow. With its little, flapping flag, it made a bull's-eye drop on the small clearing near Red Russert's tent.

The Taylors' attic was no more than a crawl space accessed from the second-floor ceiling. It was jumbled, hot and airless up there, so Evan decided he'd still camp outside and just visit when they were away. He left his backpack hidden in some bushes about a half mile behind their house. Wrapping his precious, good-luck drip torch — the one he used to set back blazes while fighting wildfires — in his sleeping bag, he set out with only those two items on the campers' trail toward town. He had all of the sheriff's keys, and hoped their attic would be bigger or cooler, their larder fuller. Those chocolate-chip cookies Dee Cobern had given Nicky yesterday were great.

He trudged along on a narrow hiking trail, just slightly up the rise from the only road into town, making certain he was behind a tree or bush when a car or truck went by. Rush hour in Vermillion, he thought, snickering. Maybe twenty vehicles went by in twenty minutes.

He wedged his bedroll in the crotch of a tree and surveyed the Cobern house and the nearby shop where Dee went from time to time. The sign outside it clearly said, Dee Cobern, Owner, and listed the brief summer hours. She didn't sell ski equipment, the display windows indicated, but ski-weather clothing.

He half expected to find the front door of their house draped with black crepe for the sheriff's sad demise, but cops were just plain mean and that often pulled them through. Just plain mean, like his father the world adored. Lecturer, author, consultant, expert on fighting wildfires — expert on absolutely everything. Hell, if the man couldn't even take care of his own family, he was a complete and utter failure as far as Evan was concerned. Talk about King Lear or Hamlet's uncle being a loser. David Durand was a walking tragedy and didn't even know it. But he would learn that someday, when he too became trapped in a fire, the last inferno in his son's long and illustrious career. Evan vowed to be certain that his father knew who had set it and why.

He had planned to just stroll across the street and try one of the sheriff's keys on the Coberns' back door. But then he saw the lady of the house drive up in a truck, jump out and go in. In five minutes, she came back out, carrying a small suitcase. Then she drove off.

Was she staying somewhere else for the night? Maybe the sheriff was all right and she was taking extra clothes to him at the lodge. He wondered if she'd even locked the door.

Then, looking out across the lake between the Cobern house and the shop, he saw Lauren's plane land and taxi toward the dock. Surely she was flying it. So she'd gotten down from the slopes, he realized. Maybe she'd brought the sheriff down, too — with help from her big, blond friend, no doubt.

Evan swore under his breath. He simply hadn't made enough of an impact around here yet. He didn't like the way life went on after he presented the ski-lift drama for them. Something great and grand was needed soon, something big that would bring in all the tourists and publicity they could possibly want. But the thing was, once everyone came to gawk, there'd be nothing left.

10

Brad knew he should listen to Lauren, but he was anxious to get going. She kept assuring him that they had time to clean up and pack food before they set out. It would take Russert way over two hours to get to the ski-lift terminal.

He took a fast shower at her place while she called the Fencers and talked to Nick. Brad came out and sat at the kitchen table, stuffing the extra backpack she gave him. He'd wear one gun and carry the other with the extra ammo. He could hear her still on the phone, and it was just as well she didn't see all this.

"No," she was saying, "I do not want you to ride bareback. I don't care if that's what the Blackfeet did or not. You need that saddle horn to hold on to because you haven't ridden that much and you're still small on a big horse. Hon, Brad and I rode those horses to the fire tower today, so don't you get them too tired, okay? I will come to pick you up as soon as I can this evening. Now let me talk to Gerri for a minute. Yes, give her the phone. Be safe, my Nicky."

After she hung up, she told Brad, "It won't take me a minute to shower."

"My kind of woman."

"Are you set to go?" she asked. "I've got two walking sticks for us." When he rolled his eyes, she said, "Honestly, they will help steady us going up and coming down. They can even be a bit of protection."

"Not from bears."

"A walking stick saved Dee's daughter, Suze, from a rabid raccoon once."

"I'm carrying protection. I have a real feeling we're going to find out where Marston's been besides the lodge. We may even find Marston himself."

While Lauren showered and changed, Brad called the Denver office for an update. The fingerprint search had turned up nothing, which didn't only depress him but made him mad as hell. When were they going to catch a break on this Fire Phantom–Smoke Ghost case? If they didn't find more evidence than Lauren's distant sighting of him, Brad feared Mike would order him back to Denver, where they were still fielding leads from a panicked population. Mike had even joked about him being on a sabbatical while the rest of them covered for him.

They locked up her place and waded knee deep through confetti-colored alpine flowers in the throes of their final blooms, then cut around about half a mile of the foot of Mount Jefferson on a slight slant upward.

"We'd be nuts to go straight up without climbing gear," she said. "And we'd be cut off by the Trident waterfall, which becomes a couple of small streams, including the one that cuts through my backyard."

"Trident? Not named after the chewing gum, I'll bet."

"It's three-pronged," she said, not relaxing her swift pace. "We'll walk upstream by the Otter River, which eventually feeds into the lake. Then we'll cut up to the ski-lift terminal. It's almost three o'clock. We're lucky it still stays light until late."

He was content to follow her, buoyed by her grace and determination, the swing of her shapely hips under her bouncing backpack. He quickly learned she was right about the walking stick helping. He thought he was in good shape, but keeping up with her was a challenge. They both kept looking off to the sides and behind, especially when they got into the woods. But there was no way Rocky Marston would be camping way up here in these deep forests. They finally hiked out of the trees to the edge of one of the beginner ski slopes and followed it steeply upward, the now unmoving ski lift in sight.

To Brad's amazement, Red Russert was waiting for them, sitting on the ground with his back against the ski-lift pillar near where he'd seen the bear closing in on Lauren and Chuck. That seemed ages ago. It was hard to believe it had happened earlier today. In fact, so much had happened, he could hardly believe he'd been in the Lost Lake area for only twenty-four hours. Yet he had the overwhelming sense that time was running out.

The big, red-haired man had already turned his head their way and stood in one smooth movement as they emerged from the trees that edged the ski slope. He looked the way Brad had always thought the legendary lumberman Paul Bunyan must, black-bearded, tall, broad-shouldered with a red-and-black-checkered flannel shirt rolled up over brawny forearms and big, brown leather–laced hiking boots. All the guy needed was a huge ax and a blue ox named Babe.

"Hey, Lauren my girl!" Red cried and

leaned down to peck a kiss on her cheek. "And Brad Hale," he added, shaking Brad's hand. Very few people made Brad feel small, but this guy did. "Got your air mail message," Red said and grinned, flaunting strong, white teeth that contrasted with his sun-browned skin. Mrs. Gates wasn't that big a woman; the picture in Brad's mind of them together was almost funny. Which reminded him, he'd better clear the air about that.

"Mrs. Gates said to tell you she won't be coming to high camp, but she'd like to talk."

"Oh, she's good at that, all right," Red muttered with a shake of his big head. "So our prey assaulted Chuck Cobern?" he quickly changed the subject as he bent to pick up his backpack. "On top of that broken shoulder, how's he doing?"

"Concussion, we think," Lauren said. "Dee's with him at the clinic."

"Well, that's a start back for them, lucky bums. So we've been deputized to track this guy or what?"

They had decided they would tell him that Chuck's assault was the reason they were after Marston, but since Marilyn Gates knew the whole story and Brad instinctively trusted this man, he said, "That's part of it. I am a friend of Lauren's but I'm also here because I'm law enforcement in pursuit of a serial arsonist we believe is hiding in this area — one and the same with the sheriff's attacker. It's highly possible that our man headed down toward town after he got off the ski lift on this platform. We're hoping you can pick up his trail from this end, maybe find his camp. He prides himself on not being seen or found."

"Yeah, and I pride myself on finding anything that moves. I'll give it my darndest."

"He's going by the name Rocky Marston," Brad added. "Dark, chin-length hair, olive skin, stands about five foot ten, military green-brown camo outfit, bright blue backroll and backpack."

"Got it. Good thing Marston didn't head thataway," Red said, pointing up the slope. " 'Cause I see signs a big brown bear went in that direction, recently, too."

"I told you the man was good," Lauren said, folding her arms across her breasts. "And I mean Red, not Marston."

"One more thing," Brad said as Red donned his backpack and picked up his walking stick. "Marston evidently knew how to run the ski lift or figured it out."

"I ran the thing for years, half-asleep or half-soused," Red admitted with a shrug.

"It doesn't take a genius to figure it out."

Brad winced at that, but he surely would have handled the mechanism if it hadn't been jammed or on override.

"But the interesting thing is," he told Red, "Marston was able to override it at another terminal."

"Well, that does show some know-how."

"Other than you and the current operator, can you think of anyone else who's ever worked the ski lift?"

Red gave another shrug, this time with a shake of his head. "Who knows, especially recently. Well, there was this kid who worked at the lodge one summer, and I taught to use it. I was into the sauce pretty good back then, after a fight I had with a guy. But I can't recall the kid's name. He was a funny kid, a loner, liked to do different voices. Wanted to be an actor, I think."

"Dark-haired?" Lauren asked.

"Bet way more'n half the world's dark-haired," Red said. "Truth is, I can barely recall what he looked like and sure can't call up a name."

"Any idea about when that would have been?" Brad asked.

"Had to be the winter of '91."

"And the kid was how old then?"

"Just outta high school, I think. He had

some sorta sad story about him. I think he'd lost his mother and his dad was on the road a lot, so he got him a summer job to pull his life together. The dad may have been some sort of big shot in protecting the environment," he went on, frowning and scratching his head. "Maybe he wrote books and gave talks or some such, a real Smokey the Bear. I don't recall exactly. Hell, I've probably got bears on the brain, now that I spotted that brown-bear track right over there."

"Maybe we could find lodge records on who was hired to work the ski lift in 1991," Lauren said.

"Naw," Red insisted. "Besides, he wasn't hired *for* that. But I can't recall what else he was doing, bussing tables, maybe. You know how that goes, Lauren." Red walked to the edge of the clearing and lifted his hand to hold them back while he bent to scan the ground. "By the way, I gotta tell you, it's too dry all over this immediate area for good prints in the earth."

Brad exhaled hard. This case was a maze, with a series of wrong turns and dead ends. He needed backup but he had nothing concrete to justify it. He'd be a laughing-stock if he got the team here and nothing happened, nothing was found.

"Okay, got something," Red said, jolting Brad from his agonizing. "Dry grass here will help. I see some scuffed up right by the roots in the shape of maybe a boot tip, heading in a hurry this way — down. And since it's the boot tip without the heel marks, this person might have been hustling. Let's get going," he ordered and headed for the trees.

The Lost Lake Health Clinic had four small private rooms where patients could be tended to or simply held until they could be flown to the Kalispell Regional Medical Center. Dee sat in a chair pushed tight to Chuck's bed while the nurse-practitioner, darting in and out of the room, kept an eye on him.

The doctor said his concussion was mild, but being tossed around had reinjured his shoulder, so he was back on his pain meds. Which meant, Dee realized as she listened to him mumble and rave, that he was out of his head again.

They'd even strapped him down in the bed with buckled ties across his ankles, hips, torso and good arm to keep him from flinging off his covers or pulling out the IV drip. He'd settled down at last, with Dee holding his hand. She talked calmly, quietly, to him. And though it seemed to help, she could tell he still plunged from one disturbing dream to another.

"I'm going to go back to the house. I want to be there when Suze comes for Larson," she told him, though she thought nothing was registering right now. "Larson's at the Fencers' with Nicky. Maybe Suze can stop to see you on her way home. She's been out painting near the lumber camp all day, even planned for Steve to have lunch with her up on Cedar Ridge. Remember how we used to have picnics out there years ago?" she asked, blinking back tears.

Suze would be relieved that this was the beginning of her parents' reconciliation, Dee thought. These last five months had been an eternity. Dee couldn't picture her life without this man. She had to get him back to being healthy, vital, in control — and happy. Dear God, she prayed, let us both be back together and happy again. And please protect this town we both love.

As they walked through the forest, Lauren kept up with the two men, but couldn't quite tap into some wavelength they seemed to be on. Nods, grunts, pointing — Brad and Red had some sort of macho telepathy going.

"Scuffed pine needles," Red muttered.

"Still running, but not as wide strides as before."

"He feels safer at this point," Brad said.

"Or he's not really in good physical shape," Red added.

"What about these tracks?" Lauren asked, seeing other footprints in the carpet of dry needles. "They're far apart, too."

Red glanced over. "Ten-inch-long bear tracks, almost human, but look closer. Bear's big toe is on the outside of the paw."

"Oh, I didn't see the toe marks, just the heel."

"Brad, look. He hunkered down here," Red said as they left the thick trees and came to the bank of the Otter River, with its braided streams and stony islands amidst divided waters. "Maybe he needed a rest or a drink."

Lauren and Brad had skirted this area earlier. Now, despite their rush, she admired the brilliantly hued harlequin ducks that had returned to this ancestral stream just the way the cutthroat trout in it had.

"Ducks the colors of the American flag," Brad remarked as they followed Red along the path. "Very patriotic."

"Very stupid," Red said. "The Otter River's full of their namesake, and those little devils are trouble. Cute as can be, swimming on their backs and all that, but real vicious. Besides diving for fish or grubbing for frogs, otters get ducks underwater and rip them apart."

"The animal version of a criminal undercover," Brad said.

"You're not kidding. Otters even tear beaver dams apart along here —" Red pointed toward a pile of logs and debris a bit upstream "— and when the water level goes down behind their destruction, they snatch up the stranded, flopping fish. Nature giveth and taketh away."

They moved on, slowly, stopping and starting. "You're probably right about Marston heading for town," Red said, bending down. "I hope we can find him this way since he's made himself scarce there."

"To everyone but me, he's been invisible," Lauren put in.

"I've been thinking," Red said to her. "You knew to bring Brad up from town the way you did, but I doubt an outsider would know how to get down to town this way. I've had tenderfoot campers and hunters up here argue with me about going straight down the mountain 'stead of roundabout. Your man could have taken the longer trail blazed clearly on the trees, but he took this shorter, easier way. Maybe this Marston isn't a newbie 'round here after all."

"But I've lived here for years," Lauren protested. "I know everyone and I'd never seen him before two days ago."

"Then maybe," Brad said, "he was just here skiing or hiking once and noted how the ski lift was run."

"He told me he hadn't been here before," Lauren blurted.

"Listen to yourself," Brad said, rounding on her. "Are we believing what he says now?"

"Then why did you want me to tell you everything he said?" she countered, hands on her hips.

"Whoa, you two," Red put in. "Sounds like you been spending lotsa time together, but kinda like a shotgun marriage."

Lauren only gasped and cried, "Look!" She pointed but was stunned when Brad whipped out a gun from under his jacket. She'd finally realized it was his weapons and ammunition he guarded so closely in his duffel bag.

"Where?" he said, pivoting with it lifted in both hands.

"Not Marston," she said. "An elk drinking up there. See?"

Brad swore under his breath, and for the first time since they started down, Red chuckled. He stretched as he and Brad exchanged a look she couldn't read. Brad holstered his gun.

Red said, "Yeah, look at the rack on him. It's a big bull getting ready for the autumn rut. It's usually in August, but this drought's thrown off more'n the vegetation. The moose'll probably mate later than the first frosts this year, and the bighorn rams may miss November, too. Everything's off-kilter. But they'll get to their rough lovemaking, you bet they will."

Brad's laser-blue gaze snagged with Lauren's. She felt a fire arc between them that made her knees weak and her stomach go into freefall as if she'd just jumped off a cliff.

"Cedar Ridge used to be our favorite place to go, Chuck. Do you remember?" Dee went on. "We even made love there one time with the sky so blue and the sun so sweet."

She kept one eye on her wristwatch. She'd better get going if she wanted to catch Suze, but she couldn't bear to leave Chuck. Still, if she and Larson weren't there, Suze might panic — or drive to Lauren's, where no one would be, either.

Chuck began to mumble. Was he waking up? Those darn meds.

"Ridge . . ." he was saying. She held on to his hand but stood and bent over so she could get closer to his face.

"Yes, Cedar Ridge," she prompted, thrilled to think he might remember. "Do you recall what a wonderful time we had there, sweetheart? You proposed on the ridge, and we always . . ."

"—idge . . ."

"Yes, Cedar Ridge."

"Jidge."

Dee gasped and dropped his hand. She straightened. He hadn't said *ridge,* but had clearly said *Jidge.* Here she was pouring out her heart to him, forgiving him, worrying about him, and he said that woman's name. He was dreaming about that woman!

With a sob, Dee grabbed her purse from the table by the bed and ran for the door.

"You seem to know all about the mating seasons," Brad told Red, elbowing the big man as they picked up their pace. Marston had evidently walked closer to the river here. His booted footprints were clearer now since the shore was silt as well as stones.

"All 'cept my own," Red muttered. "Like my pa used to say, I hope I haven't missed the bus I'm interested in catching. Now,

Lauren, don't you dare repeat that to Mari Gates."

Mari Gates, she thought. She'd hardly heard anyone call Mrs. Gates Marilyn, let alone Mari.

But she held her tongue as they started across the alpine meadow just above the town. The roofs of the shops and houses were in sight below. Suddenly, Red stopped in midstride.

"Don't know if others been out walking through this tall-grass meadow," he said.

"Lauren and I —" Brad began.

"No, your paths are over there where the flowers and grass are freshly bent in the direction you walked. But see that other faint pathway over there? It's not heading toward town but southeast, a bit away."

Red and Brad both turned to look at Lauren. "And that," she whispered, "could take him toward my place."

"Let's cut across to that path and see," Red said.

Evan tried the sheriff's set of keys until one fit in the back door of the Cobern house. He let himself in and looked around. The walls held photos and lots of artwork, all signed by Suze M. There was a signed photo of her painting, standing next to her mother.

She must be the sheriff's daughter. If she lived nearby, he had another possible chosen one. After all, she worked with oil paints, and those artists always had turpentine around to clean their brushes. With some paint rags and a canvas or two — *whoosh!*

He turned on the desktop computer in the corner of the living room, hoping he didn't need a password. Why would anyone have a PC in this rinky-dink town? He got online easily but waited impatiently for everything to come up on the screen.

He was tempted to read the *Denver Post*'s report about the BND arsonist's fire and the obit of the woman who had died in it, but he'd already done that at the library in Phoenix and time was of the essence here. Instead, he Googled *Blackfeet Indians* and *northwest Montana sacred burial grounds* just in case Nicky Taylor had any more questions about where Chief White Calf had "flown" in from.

The kid must have been referring to the Vermillion Valley, which the tribe used to call Pis'kun, and which early settlers had claimed was haunted. Heck, he thought as he turned the PC off, people could probably call any site haunted if they knew the entire history of the place.

As he passed an upstairs window of the

bedroom, he noted how close the fire station was, just two doors away, on the other side of the Montana Range Gift Shop. How could he pass this up? The sheriff's own wife was living near the ladder truck that would rush to put out a distant fire while her own house went up in flames. And it would have to be gasoline for this blaze, gasoline he'd siphoned directly from the fire engine itself! What could be more perfect?

And then he saw the omen on the wall, the sign that meant he was making the right choice. In the bedroom office hung a large, framed photograph of Chuck Cobern, sheriff of Vermillion, Montana, in full firefighting gear, one booted foot on the bumper of the bright red ladder truck as if he owned it. Evan squinted closer at the photo. Cobern was not only the sheriff but the fire chief here! That meant Evan had already made the fire chief look like a fool. But it wasn't enough, not nearly enough.

He rifled through the desk drawers until he found what he was looking for — a pistol. He had figured the sheriff would have one around that he could borrow, especially since he hadn't been carrying one up at the ski lodge. Evan hated firearms, but things were getting so dicey here that it was a necessary evil. And it was the kind where you rammed a clip up into the handle. He'd figure it out and just hope that fire did his talking for him so he wouldn't have to resort to this. He was lowering himself by taking it, by needing it. Crazy, trigger-happy Americans with their gun fixations, from the minutemen to cowboys to mobsters to today's mafia and street gangs. Degrading and disgusting!

He opened the door to the attic and hurried up to look around. With one glance, more plans fell into place. There were two big, old trunks he could stretch out behind with his sleeping bag, and two dormer windows through which he could watch everyone who came and went. Best of all, there was a small, railed balcony facing the lake. He could use it to get out onto the rooftop so that he wouldn't be trapped.

Hoping he'd have time to get his sleeping bag and precious drip torch up here before anyone came home, he headed downstairs.

But he heard a car door slam nearby and froze. He hadn't heard a car, but the drone of another plane landing on the lake could have muffled the sound.

The front door slammed. "Mom? Larson?"

Perhaps the painter. Since she didn't live here, it was doubtful she'd come upstairs, but he knew he'd better hide just to be sure he wasn't forced to act prematurely. This young woman had become an artist, so maybe he shouldn't think so poorly of Dee Cobern. If his own mother had let him follow the path less taken, let him follow his heart, she wouldn't now be an incinerated corpse buried in Saint Louis's Bellefontaine Cemetery.

Another car door slammed outside; someone else came in the house.

"Mom! Mom, what is it? What's the matter?"

Maybe the sheriff had died. How frustrating! Evan wanted him alive so that he could suffer. Muffled words, more crying.

"But is he going to be okay?"

"You'll have to find out for yourself! I was going to take him back — I tried."

"What did he do?"

More muffled words, more crying. Stomping around. Slamming cupboards. Evan wanted to risk going to the top of the stairs, but he'd better not. It would be just like a distraught woman to run upstairs to cry on her bed. He'd seen more than one female trapped in a fire who fled up to the supposed safety of her bedroom, not down toward a better chance at escape.

"But you said yourself that the meds screw

up his thoughts," the daughter protested. "And maybe he said *ridge.* I'll go back, but you've got to go with me. He's just hallucinating."

"Which is the same thing as dreaming about her. No!" Dee's voice exploded clearly at last. "You've always been Daddy's girl. You sided with him in this, just like he's always sided with you! 'Let her get married early,' he said. 'Let her go off in the wilds all day, even when her son's so small.' Your father spoiled his only child, and now you're all for him! Did you know about that woman before I did?"

"Mother, of course not!"

"Your father may not have left Vermillion lately, but he would if he could. He still loves her, I swear he does."

The two women went on arguing, but all Evan could think was that, once again, he was going to have to change his mind about Dee Cobern. She wasn't the one who had let her child pursue her dreams. Dee had put herself right back near the top of the list, with Lauren still in first place for the diversion blaze. Dee was a lot like his own mother and needed to be taught a final, fatal lesson.

"Are you sure we're still on his trail?" Lauren asked Red as he tracked Marston closer to the line of aspens above her house.

" 'Fraid so," Red told them. "See the same distinctive design on this boot print — two wedges and the waffled sole? You might have problems getting his fingerprints like you said, Brad, but I'll bet we've got his footprints here."

"Sometimes that doesn't prove a thing," Lauren argued despite the glare Brad shot at her. "They had clear footprints in blood at the scene of Nicole Simpson's murder, which matched a pair of O. J. Simpson's distinctive shoes. Yet he still got off."

"Lauren —" Brad started but she interrupted him.

"But why would he be watching my place? I don't live near a firehouse — or alone. Still, there's a clear view of my property from here." She stated the obvious. Her voice got very small. She felt scared, then angry.

Brad put his arm around her, and she leaned gratefully into his strength.

"There is a trail that parallels the road along here to town," Red said. "He could have gone that way, but it's so well walked, I may not be able to be sure. He may not have been coming here at all, Lauren, but just passing through."

"But to where?" she asked. "Where?"

Though she was perspiring, she felt chilled. She longed to hold on to Brad, with both arms tight around him, and bury her face against him. But she stood stiffly at his side.

"Let's go down and have Red look around your backyard," he said.

They walked down with Red still leading.

"Your boy's footsteps are all over here," Red said, "so I can't be certain about where Marston went now. Let's look in the ravine. Maybe he just drank from that stream en route to the hiking path into town. He may not even know this is your place."

"Though we'll have to take precautions," Brad added.

While the two men went into the ravine, Lauren looked at Nicky's piled stones, then peeked into his little blanket-over-soccer-net tent. She got on her knees and peered inside. It didn't look as if he'd even used it, though he had left his headband with feathers here. And one of the feathers was from the bright harlequin duck's back on the path where they'd just tracked Rocky Marston.

11

After thanking Red — though Lauren was hardly grateful to know that Marston had been anywhere near her house — she and Brad watched him walk toward town on the hiking path, his head still down, looking for signs and clues.

"Whew!" Lauren said. "That makes me want to get Nicky home and turn this place into a fortress until Marston's caught."

"My sentiments exactly, but I need to look around here some more first. You go on in and call about us picking up Nick."

That sounded strange, yet so right to her, as if they were both the boy's parents. Brad made a point of not calling him Nicky like everyone else. Everyone, that is, except Ross, who had always thought it sounded too cutesy, even when he was a darling baby.

"I'll stay out here with you," she insisted. "Four eyes are better than two, even when two of them are trained FBI."

"Red Russert ought to teach a class at Quantico," he muttered and went back down into the ravine.

Lauren poked her head into the tent again and picked up the Indian headdress. Nicky's other drab, common feathers were taped on, but this bright one had been poked through the ribbon headband itself. She carefully put the headdress in her backpack, before placing it by the back door, and went down into the ravine. She almost couldn't stop running and had one foot in the cold stream before Brad grabbed her with an arm around her waist.

"Don't walk around too much down here," he said, pulling her past him, then loosing her. "Nick's been down here, too. Is he allowed?"

"He's never come down before. When he was younger that was a rule. We even had a little chicken-wire fence up there once, but lately — I guess I haven't made a point of it."

"Well, young Blackfeet Indians certainly wouldn't like a fence. Lauren, over here . . ."

"What?"

"Here, by the stream. It's the same boot print we've been tracking from the ski lift."

She edged closer to him. Holding on to his arm, she peeked past him, careful not to disturb anything.

"At that angle," she said, "it looks like he drank from the stream. Hopefully that's all he did around here. Brad, Nicky knows not to talk to strangers when we're in Kalispell. But here in Vermillion, at least off-season, there just aren't any strangers."

"There are now. Come on, let's go call the Fencers and pick him up."

"Why? So that you can question him about being down in the ravine?" she asked. Her voice sounded a bit too sharp, but she couldn't help herself. She stood with her hips canted, her fists on her waist, blocking his way.

"Hardly. But he needs to know more about me — and about the dangers."

Biting her lower lip, she nodded. She was starting to act irrationally, arguing with this man who was here to help her. As she walked toward the back of the ravine, she noted scuff marks under Nicky's tent. After spending so many hours listening to Red Russert, was everything starting to get to her? She was trying to keep calm and be civil, but panic and paranoia kept crashing through her like an avalanche.

"Brad, does it look to you like Nicky's been coming down into the ravine by sliding out the back of this tent? See?" she asked, pointing.

"Looks that way. Typical boy. Fastest, funnest way."

"But he does overdo the imagination stuff."

"Lauren, I used to alternate between being Luke Skywalker and Darth Vader while staging entire intergalactic battles with just two friends. When I was alone, I became both Luke and Darth at once, making light sabers from tinfoil-wrapped yardsticks and having duels with myself. I fell down the basement steps once because I wouldn't take off my Stormtrooper's mask and couldn't see where the heck I was going."

"But that must have been before you lost your father. Nicky's only been that way since his father died."

"We can both talk to him tonight. Let's go in."

But he started to walk around the house, looking at the ground under her windows. After she unlocked the back door, she hesitated, wanting to rush in to phone Nicky but curious and even more unnerved by Brad's actions.

He disappeared around the corner and she hurried after him. "Do you think Marston was trying to lift a window to get in?" she asked.

"See this other waffle-soled print where you've evidently watered these flowers? He was either trying to get in or was looking in. Lauren," he said, frowning as he turned to her and grabbed both of her upper arms, "regardless of what he's been doing here, I want to stay."

Her stomach cartwheeled at his putting it that way, but she knew what he meant. "You mean move in. All night?"

"I'll bunk on your sofa just in case. You — and Nick — could use a bodyguard."

The phone rang before Lauren could call the Fencers. It was Suze, sounding really upset.

"I wanted to be sure you were there before I brought Nicky home," she said. "I'm at the Fencers' getting Larson, so I can pick up both of them if you want."

"Thanks. And Suze, be careful. Are you — You sound out of breath."

"Not out of breath. Temporarily out of tears. Dad evidently blurted out that other woman's name in his drug-induced delirium, and Mother's on an absolute tear. I'll tell you when I get there," she added and punched off.

"Brad," Lauren called to him, "Suze is bringing Nicky home, but she says that

Chuck and Dee are feuding again. Suze is pretty upset. I think we have to tell her more about what's happening and who you are."

"Affirmative, partner. I still don't want to cause mass hysteria, but I'm starting to think we may need all the help we can get."

To give Lauren some time alone with Suze, Brad took Nicky and Larson out in the backyard to play catch. The two women sat at the kitchen table where they could see Brad with the kids. Suze's eyes were red. Her mascara had run and been swiped at so many times it looked as if she'd been finger-painting under her eyes. "It was horrible," she told Lauren, blowing her nose. "Mother turned on me, as well as on him. I think she's getting ready to snap."

"Aren't we all?"

"Lauren, what's really going on with Brad? You know my motto is that Picasso quote, 'Everything you can imagine is real.' I'm imagining too many things. What is he to you? He seems so — in charge."

"He wanted secrecy at first, but I can tell you now. He's with the FBI, a serial arson team member."

"Go on!" she cried, her voice mocking as she smacked her palm down on the table.

"Just listen. I saw an arsonist's Most

Wanted picture in your mother's newspaper and called the FBI hotline on Monday."

"Wow. You called the hotline and got a hottie. But who's the arsonist?"

"I flew him in — obviously, before I knew. He goes by the name Rocky Marston. He's been practically invisible, but we think he's the one who hit your dad over the head. Your parents are both in on this."

"So this Marston guy might start a fire out in the forest?" she demanded, getting up and starting to pace. She kept dabbing at her eyes with a tissue. "Can I warn Steve and the guys cutting timber? You know they have buildings full of logs, and the trees up there are dry."

"Marston might have been staying on lodge property. But in general, it looks as if he's sticking close to town. You'll have to ask Brad about telling others. We don't want to start a panic."

"Oh, great, just great! Are you sure this guy you flew in is the arsonist?"

"Almost sure. He's clever, Suze. At first, when no one else had seen him, I was blaming myself so much."

"Who else has seen him now? My dad?"

"We're not sure. We still have to talk to him to see if he can remember more about the assault. We do have the wrench he was hit with, so that will be checked for prints. And we have some other prints that were checked."

"These other prints . . . Did they turn up who the arsonist was?"

"Not exactly. I'll let Brad tell you what he thinks is best."

"In other words, I'm supposed to trust someone who probably thinks our government can do no wrong?" she cried. "Since that National Parks Service investigation over Ross's death, I had the distinct impression you didn't trust anything any government agency decreed or did."

Suze was right. Lauren had vowed not to trust the government after that, yet now she had a G-man ready to move into her house.

"So what's this guy's M.O.?" Suze was back to her interrogation. She leaned stiff-armed on the kitchen table, as if she were a cop grilling a hostile witness.

Despite how exhausted she felt, Lauren popped up from the table. "I'll feed the boys in the kitchen and let Brad talk to you. Brace yourself, because this arsonist is one really sick, dangerous man. You can't imagine —"

"Oh, yes, I can," she said, seizing Lauren's wrist in a tight grip. "Remember, everything you can imagine, in a way, is real. For an artist that's good. For an arsonist, it's really bad."

When Lauren got Nicky out of the bathtub, she let him go back down to the kitchen for cookies and milk. Brad had called Mrs. Gates and was just getting off the phone.

"Did you convince her to rely on Red for protection?" she asked.

"I didn't, but Red did. She wouldn't let him stay at her place, but she did finally agree to switch places with him for the night. He said she was complaining all the way that his apartment needed cleaning and that she couldn't abide the stuffed animal heads staring at her from his walls."

"Better that than to be staring at Rocky Marston peeking through her window. First thing in the morning, maybe we should check around her place for the telltale prints. And Dee's place, too."

"You know, Lauren, you're starting to read my mind and that scares me. Is it okay if I talk to Nick before you tuck him in?" he asked, nodding his head toward the kitchen.

"Fine. It's probably best if some of the explanation comes from you. I just don't want him so scared that I can't leave him at school or with Dee. It's only recently that he's let me out of his sight without tears.

Mind if I eavesdrop so I know what you told him, or I could come with you —"

"Listen if you want, but I think it should be just us guys for a couple of minutes."

She nodded. For too long, Nicky had not had a man in his life.

"Hey, Nick," she heard Brad say as he went out into the kitchen.

Suddenly feeling sad, Lauren sat down on the staircase.

"Hey, Brad."

"Why'd you smash that cookie all up on your plate, pal?"

"So it would look more like Indian pemmican."

"Oh, yeah. Listen, I just wanted to tell you why I'm staying here tonight. I'm really a police officer, and I'm trying to find a man I need to question. I think he might have come to Lost Lake, so —"

"Which plane flew him in?"

Brad hesitated for a beat. "Your mom's did."

"So she knows what he looks like and is trying to help you find him?"

"Right. We've been looking at the fire tower, the lodge, even around here. We want you to know why you can't go outside for a few days, just in case. He's not a nice person."

"I can't even go to my Indian tent?"

"That would be okay if I go out with you, but we're going to be pretty busy tomorrow and you'll be in school. Nick, I don't want you to tell your buddies there, though Mrs. Gates knows."

"She does? Why?"

"Her friend Red Russert was helping us look for the bad man, so we told her. Can you keep a secret for us?"

"Sure. Brad, if you promise someone you'll keep a secret, that's really what you should do, right? Even if someone asks or you kind of change your mind?"

"Absolutely. That's what I'm asking you to do."

"Okay, then."

Lauren took that as her cue to join them, but Brad passed her in the hall. "You thought that would be easy, didn't you?" she whispered and went in to see Nicky making a mess, trying to eat a smashed cookie with his hands.

"Time to head upstairs to bed, my Nicky."

"Can I ask you a favor, Mom?"

"Of course, if I can do it."

"Could you start calling me Nick like Dad and Brad?"

"Sure, if you want. It might be kind of hard for me to switch over, though."

She walked him upstairs to brush his teeth and then pointed him toward his bed. There, on his pillow, she'd laid out his ribbon Indian headdress with its drab feathers surrounding the one bright one.

"Wow," he exploded when he saw it. "Look at that neat feather! But why is it here in my bed?"

He glanced around the room, then at the windows as if it had floated inside of its own accord.

"I brought it in from your tent since you can't play out there for a while — at least until Brad catches that bad guy he's after. But where did you find that harlequin duck feather? Nicky — Nick — I know you can't have been up by the Otter River where all those bright ducks are."

"I guess they just flew over here and dropped it, that's all," he told her, putting the headdress quickly aside as if it meant nothing to him now. "So where's Brad going to sleep?" he asked.

"On the sofa. And you're not to disturb any of his things — not in the pack he carries around or anything else."

"Sure, I know that. Be safe, Mom," he said and held out his arms for a hug. The moment she kissed him, he turned away from her and covered up his head.

"Be safe, my — Nick," she said. She was on her way downstairs before it hit her how cleverly her little boy had changed the subject from his actions to hers. For the first time since she could recall, she had not read him a bedtime story. He didn't want to be her Nicky anymore.

It really scared her how much he was changing. And how much she was changing, too.

As soon as it got reasonably dark, Evan tiptoed down from Dee Cobern's attic. Taking his flashlight and ever-present, precious drip torch, he first headed for her kitchen. It had been over an hour since she'd stopped pacing in her bedroom, though the house creaked in the breeze. Actually, he liked both sounds. And he liked that the breeze didn't let up after dark around here, either. When he chose to release the flames, the wind would feed them.

By the light of the open refrigerator door, he drank some orange juice from a carton, though he preferred the pulp-free kind. Using his flashlight, he searched her drawers until he found a butcher knife to borrow, an eight-inch one with a serrated blade. He already had the sheriff's gun, but that wouldn't do for what he had in mind right now.

He quietly let himself out the back door and relocked it. The night air smelled fresh and brisk, but he could almost imagine it laced with smoke.

As he had last night, he tiptoed up the steps to Mrs. Gates's large side porch. But this time he did not take one of her tidily stacked E-Z Lite logs, for he'd already taken three from her stash and had them hidden nearby. But he did need something from this neatly kept elevated area with its lovely views.

He took out the butcher knife and cut off a six-foot length of the garden hose the teacher evidently used to water the plants she had lined up in plastic containers. Unfortunately, she would notice this, but perhaps she'd ascribe it to teenage vandalism. He knew how women thought.

He had started down the steps when he realized he could also use the three-gallon plastic container she evidently mixed liquid fertilizer in. Holding it upside down over the railing, he dumped out the small amount that was in there, but cursed the gurgling sound it made.

Then he froze.

The back kitchen curtains were drawn

shut, but someone swept one aside. Evan pressed his back to the house near the balcony railing. If someone looked out or came out, he'd have a long jump from here. Or could the person just be looking out at the aurora borealis? It was aglow in the sky again tonight, as if watching over him.

He recalled the night in Denver when the old woman had been watching him from her window, the night he'd decided to lie low in Vermillion for a while. But how could he ignore the abundance of fire fuels, local accelerants and the perfect conditions here, as well as the signs he must act and soon: Ross Taylor's widow, her son playing a part, the vast stage this area offered for a grand spectacle!

To Evan's amazement, the shadow thrown onto the floorboards of the porch was not that of petite Mrs. Gates. It was a big form, with broad shoulders.

The widowed schoolteacher had a male visitor?

Evan held his breath. Had the man heard him? Whoever he was, he went from kitchen window to window, opening the curtains so more light spilled out.

Then the kitchen went black.

Was the man trying to see out better? Hopefully, he was just trying to watch the northern lights.

Swearing under his breath, Evan heaved the plastic container off the porch and onto the side of the building that had no windows. It almost hit the nearby firehouse, but made very little sound. He hooked his drip torch over the back waist of his jeans, then quickly looped the piece of garden hose around one of the boards that supported the railing. Holding on to both ends of the hose, he scooted over the edge of the porch.

Suspended by the hose, he let more and more of it slide through his hands until he was close enough to drop to the ground. Letting go of the hose with one hand, he pulled it down to him and, keeping low, ran toward the firehouse. He snatched up the plastic container he'd thrown and darted around the back of the building.

From there, peering around the corner, he watched a large, bearded man come out onto the porch and look over all the sides, then go down the stairs with a flashlight to look under the porch. The big brute was looking for more than lights in the sky.

Mrs. Gates had a protector? Why? She'd looked like an old-maid type to Evan when he'd peeked through windows or watched her from the Cobern attic. Was she loaning her place to this man? He had seen her go into the front door of the Bear's Den Restaurant this evening and not come out. But so what?

When the big man went back in and closed the door, Evan darted to the back door of the combination firehouse and sheriff's office. Getting excited now — but not out of control, never out of control — his hand shook as he tried different keys on the sheriff's ring until one fit. He entered slowly, listening, peering into the darkness, then realized a dim light was on somewhere within. Surely no one was here at this hour.

His hand still on the back door in case he had to run, he called out, "Anyone here?"

No sounds. He was home free. His luck held.

Ahead of him loomed the dark silhouettes of the single ladder truck and the boxy, white EMR vehicle. He snapped on his flashlight and stroked the sleek, cold, crimson metal of the truck. Vermillion Fire Department — THE EQUALIZER, it read so pompously that he had to laugh out loud.

"You're no match for the Fire Phantom," he whispered. "In like a ghost, out like a ghost. You'll see."

He set about siphoning gas from the truck, using the garden hose. He sucked on the end of it to get the flow started, then fed it into the plastic container. Ah, the clean, sharp smell of gasoline!

When he had enough accelerant, he decided to take a ladder, too. They would miss it, but probably too late. This ladder truck was small. It probably had only one automatic extension ladder, which would emerge from the back of the truck by pulling a lever. But it had a full array of horizontally stacked, aluminum extension ladders on its side, which could be freed by the turn of a handle. He assumed these were standard-length extension ladders of fourteen-, sixteen-, twenty-four and thirty-five feet. He freed and lifted off the shortest one. That would surely be enough to look in or get in second-story windows at night, including Nicky Taylor's, alias Running Deer's, bedroom.

12

Her nightmare was different this time. A huge bear had her down, pressing into her, mauling her. It had thick brown fur — no, its hair was black and she was bleeding black blood. The bear turned her face-up . . . it was Rocky Marston, and Suze was crying trying to draw his face, but his features were burned beyond recognition . . .

Lauren sat bolt upright in bed. Reality came crashing back. Had she heard something in the house? Was Nicky all right upstairs? Brad was here. Perhaps she'd heard him.

She glanced at her bedside clock — 4:00 a.m. She'd slept almost six hours straight — a miracle! But she still felt tired to the bone.

It was finally pitch-black outside. This time of year nights stayed semilight so long, just the opposite of the lengthy winter ones.

If Marston lit a fire, would he want it to be in the blackest time of night?

She thought she heard another sound, maybe just a floorboard creaking. Even in her utter exhaustion, it had been hard to go to sleep with Brad just down the short hall. He had been too tall for the couch, but when she'd given him a pillow and blanket, he said he'd be fine.

Lauren shoved her feet in her slippers, wrapped her robe around her nightgown and peered out into the living room. Pitch-dark. Maybe he was asleep and she was imagining things.

She shuffled down the hall toward the stairs. She'd just look in on Nicky — Nick — then go back to bed if Brad was asleep.

"Are you okay?" His voice came from the dark. As her eyes adjusted, she could make out his form sitting on the couch. He was in his dark jeans but his white T-shirt showed. "I just peeked in on Nick. He's fine."

That's what she'd heard. Brad on the stairs.

"Thanks. Yeah, I'm all right," she whispered, and sank into the chair facing the couch, curling one leg under her. "In one respect, at least. I just slept six hours straight. I'm going to have to hire you for security after this is all over. Did you sleep?"

"Sure, I'm fine."

"I thought I heard you pacing earlier."

"Just looking around now and then."

"Looking outside, just in case?"

"It's been quiet. I've been trying to lay plans for where to look next around town," he said, rubbing both eyes with one hand. She heard him stifle a yawn. "And to decide whether to call in the troops or not."

"The rest of your team?"

"Yeah. I'm trying to talk myself into risking that."

She sat forward in her chair. "Risking?"

"If we're wrong that Marston's the guy, or if he suspects something and bolts, or makes his move with a fire . . ."

"Then you'd look really bad. And that's one thing he loves to do, make those who could catch him look really bad."

He nodded. "You are a very astute woman, Lauren."

"I don't think so. I've tried to wall myself off these last two years, and that was a mistake. You heard Mrs. Gates — it's not helping my son. It's probably not helping me, either. Brad, I've got to tell you something," she said, jumping up and starting to pace. He turned his head each time she passed; she could feel his gaze riveted on her.

"Since Ross died," she said, "I've been really angry with the government for the shoddy job they did investigating his death. He knew better than to be trapped by that fire. I tried to tell the investigators that, but they said he just panicked and made some very bad choices at the end. But I still can't accept that his death was accidental, because he wasn't stupid. He knew fire rules, he knew fires."

"But he died with a friend, too, so doesn't that make foul play look less probable, if that's what you're implying?"

"Yes, but the thing is, I want you to know you've changed how I feel about the feds."

He rose and took her arm to stop her pacing and make her face him. "You're telling me that a while ago you might have liked the feds to look bad — just like our arsonist?"

"I had never thought of it like that, but yes. I was hurt and furious. But as angry as I've been, I'm trying to help."

"You are helping. A lot."

As he reached for her shoulders, she took his wrists in her hands and held tight to them. It was as if they propped each other up.

"Brad, I realize you have so much on your plate now, but sometime, when all this is over, I'd like to show you the articles and transcripts of the government investigation about the Coyote Canyon Wildfire in northern California two summers ago."

"The Coyote Canyon Wildfire. I've heard of that. By government investigation do you mean the Department of the Interior, the National Park Service or what?"

"Both. I have scrapbooks under my bed that cover the whole thing — court proceedings, witnesses who testified, photos, even some tabloid magazines that did pieces. They brought in some really big guns to prove themselves right and Ross wrong. I kept everything. Though I haven't been able to look at any of it, I'm sure I can now."

He pulled her close and gave her a hard hug before he set her back. "Lauren, something Red said today about that kid who helped him run the ski lift years ago has been bothering me."

She felt deflated, but she couldn't blame him for having a one-track mind. For a moment, she'd been certain he was going to tell her to show him the scrapbooks, or at least vow he'd help her once this nightmare was over. Had he even been listening? Blinking back tears, she turned away.

"What?" she asked. "Red said a lot, none of which he was sure of."

"He said more than he knows, more than I picked up on at first, given how anxious I was to get him tracking. Red thought the boy had lost his mother and had a 'big-shot dad' on the road a lot, who evidently tried to solve the kid's problems by sending him off to an isolated place on his own. All that might fit the profile of an arsonist's parents. But Red also said he thought the dad wrote about the environment, and that *he was a real Smokey the Bear.* What does that last comment mean to you?"

Intrigued, she turned back to him. "That the dad wrote about fire prevention, maybe wildfire prevention?"

"What if that's correct?" he cried, putting both hands atop his head as if his brain was going to explode. "And what if we can track the kid — who would be around thirty now — through his father? You said some big guns testified at the Coyote Canyon hearings. They were probably wildfire-prevention experts, maybe authors. Lauren, go get those scrapbooks and put some coffee on."

They huddled shoulder to shoulder at the kitchen table with the two dusty scrapbooks spread before them. Brad felt jived and not just from their first pot of coffee. He was thrilled he actually had his hands on something concrete that might lead somewhere. He was sick of the specters of Smoke Phantoms and Fire Ghosts. He needed a lead, any lead.

But he stopped flipping pages when he came upon a newspaper photo of two knee-high white crosses in the burned grass and trees in Coyote Canyon.

"Lauren, is this where they fell?"

"Yes, but they're not buried there. It's a memorial the Park Service put up, either because that's tradition or because they felt guilty for the way they handled things. I don't know. The flames raced up that slope and caught them. Kyle's buried in Seattle and Ross in the cemetery of the Community Church on the other end of town. I used to visit a lot, even took Nicky daily for a while, but it wasn't helping either of us. He became more fearful and I stayed mad as hell."

He gazed into her impassioned face. She looked wildly beautiful, with her red hair mussed and free, like some goddess of nature.

"You couldn't help him or his legacy," he told her, his voice breaking, "but you're making up for it now."

"Thanks for understanding."

"How could I not with my own past? I don't need a shrink to tell me that my drive to stop arsonists is caused by what my dad did."

He reached out and cupped her cheek with one hand. They stayed like that for one breathless moment as the wind howled outside and another pot of coffee gurgled on the counter. He wanted more than anything in the world to haul her into his lap and hold her, but with a brief press of her hand to his, she jumped up to get the coffee.

"The information on the trial is in both scrapbooks," she said, "but the newspaper articles will probably be best to list and identify the so-called expert government witnesses."

He forced himself to flip pages, skimming headlines like Fatal Fire Trial Continues and Panic and Distortion Cause Double Death. As she sat back down with two mugs of steaming coffee and — to his surprise — a pile of tiny Mr. Goodbar candies, she pointed to one big article entitled Fire Swept Up Slope, Trapping Fleeing Men. She told him, "More than one witness implied Ross and Kyle not only dropped their protective personal body tents in their headlong flight, but that they would have been smarter racing through the flames or keeping one foot in the black."

"Meaning it was their fault they didn't get to an area already burned out and hunker down there so the flames would go around them?"

"Right. That's a known tactic and has been proven to work. Firefighters should stay near some black, or if there isn't any, make their own. Twelve smoke jumpers died in a fire near Helena years ago, but their crew boss survived because he lit dry grass beneath himself and lay in the burned area while the inferno blazed around him. In that fire, they say the grass had dried to a consistency of hay and the firs were as dry as kindling. It was a lightning-set fire with whirling winds."

"Drought conditions, like here?"

"Yes. It was in rough Montana backcountry, too."

He took a swallow of coffee and bent over the articles, scanning them for witness's names. "Do you have a paper and pen around?"

"Go ahead and dictate," she said, relieved to have something to do as she scrambled for the items. "I'll write everything down. Jenkins and Sterling were two of the witnesses, but I can't recall their first names."

"Right, Marlin Jenkins, longtime environmentalist and wildfire expert. Two others were Andrew Sterling and David Durand."

"And Durand was an author, I think."

"I'm looking. Yeah, he had some input in the *Forest Service Manual,* plus he's the author of *Fighting Fire Without Fear* and a list of other titles. He was also a fire consultant to many western states, a lecturer, etc. Here he's called the 'guru' of wildfire investigation, though Marlin Jenkins and — here's another — Jackson Smith sound like big boys too. Do you recall if there were any photos of these men?"

"One of the Sterling guy, I think, but I can't recall where."

"You didn't attend all this, did you?"

"I couldn't stand to. Besides, Nicky had chicken pox about that time, but even if I had been in court, I would have been arrested for standing up and screaming that they were pompous asses and didn't know Ross at all, that he would never have made the mistakes they implied. *Fighting Fire Without Fear,* my foot!"

"Lauren, I promise you I'll study all this later, but right now I'm going to call these names into Denver to see if any of them had a wife who died shortly before 1991 and would now have a son in his early thirties. As soon as I get off the phone, let's use your good old dial-up computer server and see what we can find online."

"I'll check in on Nicky and be right back."

Evan saw that Lauren was burning the midnight oil in her kitchen. He'd intended to put the ladder up to the kid's bedroom window and knock on it to try to wake him up — just to see if that would work for later, when he really needed him. But from the rise under the line of aspens, Evan could see that she was with Mr. Macho Blond again.

Considering that it was about 5:00 a.m., it was pretty obvious the guy was staying with her. Evan could only glimpse them through the windowpanes of the back door because they had the kitchen curtains closed, but if he moved just right, he could catch glimpses of them at the kitchen table. It was chilly out here tonight, despite how warm it could be during the day. He half wished he'd decided to conserve his strength in Dee Cobern's warm attic, but he had an important agenda.

With his sleeping bag protecting the drip torch strapped to his back, he hid the fire ladder in the bushes where he had left his bulky backpack.

He noticed the pale kaleidoscope of lights in the northern sky, pink, blush, bluish green. The aurora borealis, he thought, arrayed just for him, as if the heavens themselves burned with faint fire. It was a good sign, an omen, lights scooting across the sky for the ghost of Chief White Calf.

He stretched and smiled, forcing his brain back to work. His props were scattered all over, each piece now in place. Gasoline and the quick-start E-Z Lite logs were hidden where he could access them for igniting either the Cobern place or Mrs. Gates's — perhaps both. He had gasoline he'd just siphoned from Lauren's pontoon plane hidden in a metal can he'd borrowed from the gas station. And he had a ladder to get to his pal Running Deer, if he needed the boy as leverage for a ticket out of here.

It was almost time for curtain up on his pièce de résistance. He'd use little Vermillion for his prologue and, hopefully, the dry hills behind it for the rest of the extravaganza, all of which he would watch from Lauren's plane before making an exit from this vast stage. Unlike his impromptu work with his only other large-scale wildfire in Coyote Canyon, this was perfectly scripted, all but for who the tragic heroine would be, and that he would decide by tomorrow night.

Something he couldn't quite name made him feel he'd almost overstayed his welcome here. Flat on his back now, hands behind his head, he peered again at the glow of soft spotlights in the sky. Yes, the stage was set for another opening — tomorrow night.

When Lauren tiptoed in to check on Nick, she saw that he'd pulled his Indian head-dress next to his pillow. Had they woken him up with their talking? She tucked him in again; he always kicked the covers off. As she headed back downstairs, she had another idea.

"Brad, before we get online, let's call Red at Mrs. Gates's to see if any of those men's last names remind him of the boy's name. Something might jog his memory."

He was just hanging up the phone. "That didn't take long. They're on it, but you're right. We could do that, too."

She read him the phone number and he called Red. "Sorry to wake you up," she heard him say. "She's called you four times? Well, sorry but it's Brad. Listen, I have some names for you . . ."

Lauren handed him the list of names she'd written. He explained their relevance, then read them off. "Are you sure? That one rings a bell?"

Brad started to nod as if to encourage Red; he began to bounce on his bare feet as if he heard some silent musical beat. "You think his name might have been Ethan Durand? E-t-h-a-n?" he spelled out. "Look, if we get a photo of the guy, we'll be down to see you. But we'll call first so we don't get our heads taken off, or get swept in the door in a big bear hug. Yeah, I hear you. Later."

"What?" Lauren asked. "He recalled the kid's name who could work the ski lift?"

"And who was such a loner and fit the profile of a possible budding arsonist. He thinks it might have been Ethan Durand."

"We're starting to get somewhere!"

"It's a start. By the way, Mari's called Red more than once to tell him he needs to get rid of the mounted bighorn sheep and moose heads on his walls. And to tell him she'd cleaned his kitchen but wasn't lifting one more finger to help him. I'd put a year's salary on their ending up together."

Lauren smiled grimly, but she was already heading to boot up her desktop computer. Brad was right behind her. She waited for her screen to fill.

"I see you put away the pickax, boots and books," Brad observed, looking at the empty shelf where a shrine of Ross's firefighting things had once been.

"They're in the closet — for Nick some-day. I guess if Mrs. Gates were here, she'd make me dust the shelf, too. Okay, here we go," she added and signed on her server.

As soon as she got online, she Googled Ethan Durand. Nothing hit but family-type Web sites and blogs that didn't appear to be about the man they wanted. Then she Googled David Durand and found a lot of sites, including all of the commercial ones that sold his books.

"See if you can find his bio," Brad said, hovering over her shoulder as she perched on the edge of her chair.

"Here's his own Web site. He's also been an investigator for the Federal Occupational Safety and Health Administration and a consultant to the Bureau of Land Management. You'd better sit down and take notes on this. Yes. Yes!"

"Yes, what?" he demanded, trying to see the screen from the side.

"Wait, I'm still reading."

"Lauren, what?"

"Shh! You'll wake up Nick."

Muttering something under his breath, Brad swung his leg over the back of her chair and sat down tight behind her, pushing her closer to the keyboard and screen. His splayed legs pressed against her hips, almost as if she sat in his lap. His cheek pressed tight to her temple so he could read the screen too, and his hands wrapped around her waist to make her as breathless as what she was reading. She didn't protest, but read aloud, in a tremulous voice.

"In 1965, David Durand married a woman whose maiden name was Jeanette Marston. Marston! Ethan Durand, alias Rocky Marston, is using his mother's maiden name! No, it says here their only son's name is Evan, not Ethan."

"Red almost had it. This has to be him!"

"Jeanette Marston Durand died in a single-car accident when Evan was eighteen. She's buried in Saint Louis where Durand still lives — and where Evan was reared, I guess. There's nothing else about the son, only about David's career, his publications, where he's lectured — and cases where he's testified as an expert witness, including at the Coyote Canyon fatal wildfire investigation. It sounds like the guy's traveled all over, especially in the West."

"And so has his son, I'll bet. Incognito, lighting fires to defy his father in some sort of warped hatred, some kind of power play."

She scrolled farther down David Durand's

bio and gasped. In a color photo of AUTHOR, LECTURER, one with his hand contemplatively lifted to his chin, "Rocky" Marston's father stared at her. Perfectly groomed, black hair going silver at the temples, olive skin and that intense look that reminded her of his son's even though he had sometimes seemed distracted.

"Do you believe it?" Brad said, his mouth so close to her ear that her hair rustled. He'd never seen Rocky Marston, so he obviously wasn't referring to the photo but was reading something else on the screen. "David Durand has been a special agent for the U.S. Forest Service and — get this! — for the International Association of Arson Investigators. That's it — arson investigators! And his kid's been running amok for years fighting battles with a father who has no clue. No clue!"

"Brad, this photo isn't a profile view like the newspaper photo, but Rocky Marston — Evan Durand — looks a lot like his father. It's him! We've found him!"

He hugged her tight, lifting them both out of the chair and spinning her once around so hard her feet left the ground. Then he put her down. His expression changed to a grim, determined look, as if his features were sculpted in stone. "But now that we've found him, we've got to *really* find him," he said. "Before it's all too late."

13

Brad and Lauren knew they had to get off the computer to clear the line. The moment they were off, Lauren started upstairs to check on Nick again. Almost immediately the phone rang, and she heard Brad answer it.

She couldn't hear what he said at first, but it was obviously his boss calling back. Then Brad's voice rose. "No, Mike, it's not a one-horse town." He sounded suddenly annoyed. "I can testify that they've got at least two horses, so what did you find out?"

She paused on the stairs.

"You told him what? Why didn't you detour him to Denver and relay whatever he told you in interviews? No kidding? Evan worked at the ski lodge here? Bingo! But I still don't want David Durand or anyone else coming here to panic BND. No, she's staying here. Get someone else to fly you in if you're set on coming."

Lauren didn't care if Brad knew she'd been listening. She raced back downstairs and into the kitchen where he was pacing from window to window, looking out as he talked.

"What?" she mouthed when he saw her, but he held up his hand.

"Mike, if we get too many people coming in, I'm telling you, it will spook our ghost. I need a little more time. I know, but I've got a gut feeling on this. Okay, yeah, I know who's head of the team. Then bring fishing or hiking gear with you so you don't look obvious. At least give me that."

Muttering to himself, he punched off and skidded the phone down the counter, where it stuck between her flour and sugar canisters. Stiff-armed, head down, he leaned over the sink.

"Your team is coming here?" she asked.

"As fast as they can, on an FBI jet into Kalispell and then to Vermillion on a pontoon plane."

"I don't think it will be on one of ours, unless they manage to commandeer one that's already in Kalispell."

"Which I don't put past him."

"But if Rocky, a.k.a. Evan, sees a lot of action going on here, new people and —"

"I know, but I don't think he'd strike in

the light. That gives us several hours. I was overruled, damn it. But that's not the worst of it."

She pressed her clasped hands against her chest and waited. He turned to her, looking angrier by the minute.

"David Durand threw his weight around when the team phoned him to inquire about his son," Brad said, raking his fingers through his hair, making it stand up on end. "And from questioning, he figured out where sonny boy is, though he claims they're estranged."

"That could be true."

"Durand says he hasn't seen Evan in three years. Expert that he is, Daddy Durand insists the serial arsonist Boy Next Door couldn't be his son, but he's coming to help out anyway. He could even be here soon, since they traced him to a speaking engagement in Seattle, not Saint Louis where he lives. Hell, we get a break, then everything gets broken."

"And out of your control."

"It never was in my control, but that doesn't mean I — we — are going to sit around here waiting for others to take over. As soon as we get Nick safely to school, we'll visit the sheriff to see if he's recalled anything about his assailant. And I need to ask him who to call in for a briefing meeting at the firehouse. It's past time to tell the Vermillion firefighters, even if they are volunteers, what we may be up against." He turned away from her to glare out the window again.

"Brad," she said, laying a hand on his shoulder. "You have done and are still doing everything possible. And you've warned the arson team to give you more time, so if they crash in here and things get out of hand . . ."

She bit her lower lip and sniffed hard.

"Yeah, out of hand . . ." His voice trailed off as he turned toward her and stared into her eyes. He seized her wrist. She was certain he would kiss her. She *wanted* him to kiss her so hard that all this would go away, stay away, and it could just be the three of them here, safe together . . .

"Mom, is it time for breakfast yet?" came a voice from the bottom of the stairs. "I'm hungry and if Brad's eating early, I can eat with him before school."

"Sure," she called to her son, her wide gaze still held by Brad's intense stare. "I think we're all starved."

Brad let her go when she tugged back, but not before he quickly kissed the soft inner skin of her wrist.

■ ■ ■ ■

Brad and Lauren checked in at the school office and applied for visitors' passes to take Nick clear to his classroom.

"But why?" the boy asked as they signed in.

"Because we want to talk to Mrs. Gates," Lauren said.

She wanted to hug Nick goodbye again as she had at the house, but she had to be content just to see him run happily into his classroom. She was grateful for the way he'd changed from clinging to her when she so much as made a move to leave him alone. Mrs. Gates saw them and told her students, "Now, do not let the noise level go up, up, up in here," then joined them in the doorway to her classroom.

"You see I survived the night," she told them, but she looked sparkly eyed and as sprightly as ever.

"Mrs. Gates," Brad said, "we're going to have to ask you to stay at Red's for at least one more night. We believe we've had a break in the case, but we don't have an arrest yet. Others on the team are coming in, so it's likely that they will want to position themselves in or near your house and Dee

Cobern's to keep an eye on things tonight."

"And if they take over my house, that means Red Russert would be where?" she inquired, her voice icing over.

"I'm not certain," Brad admitted, "but I'm hoping, whatever it comes to, that you will still be as cooperative as you have been so far. And if Red does need a place to stay tonight, his own home is obviously the best place."

"I see. Well, for God, country and the FBI, I suppose I could abide him underfoot for one night. And it's fine with me if some of your arson team joins us for dinner, or all night for that matter. No one would recognize Red's kitchen right now — it's immaculate. But one more night in that museum of dead animals and I may turn arsonist to get rid of them!"

"Let's just say," Brad told her, "you're adding more to that chapter in your memoirs."

With a little shake of her head, Mrs. Gates said, "We mustn't make light of all this. And you needn't ask about my keeping a special eye on Nicky until you pick him up this afternoon, Lauren."

"You've been great through all this, Mrs. Gates," Lauren said. "And, I must tell you, Nicky has asked to be called Nick now."

"A good sign, I think," she said with a pert nod. "Now, if we can just keep him from turning into a Blackfeet brave when this Indian unit is over, that will be another step in the right direction!"

They left her and drove to the health clinic to see Chuck. The nurse didn't want to let them in at all, let alone this early, so Brad flashed his badge at her.

"FBI working with the sheriff on an old case," he told the astounded woman. Then as he and Lauren headed down the short hall toward the door she'd pointed out, he whispered, "What the heck. If the arson team and the arsonist's father are crashing this party, I'm not going around undercover anymore. Too many people know, and the volunteer firefighters will soon know. I just hope Evan's staying undercover so he doesn't overhear what is probably about to become great Vermillion gossip."

Lauren was trying to act calm, but his words made her stomach knot even tighter. To their surprise, they found Suze sitting by Chuck's bed. At least he was awake. And alert enough to lift his good hand in a shaky, two-fingered salute to Brad, who stood at the foot of the bed.

"I see some of your short-term memory's back, Sheriff," Brad told him after they inquired how he was doing. "Any recall on the guy who assaulted you?"

"Not a damn thing. But I do remember going into the ski-lift shed to check it before I finished the cabins. And I guess, from what Suze said, that almost finished me. A ride up the ski lift and a bear attack?"

"He didn't attack," Lauren put in, "but he was thinking about it, planning it."

"Like this loony we got loose in our paradise?" Chuck asked with a half-suppressed groan. "You close to an arrest yet, Agent Hale?"

"We think we've got his identity nailed down," Brad said, "but as for the man himself, we're still working on it. The arson team's coming in to — I hope — help."

"Federal Bureaucracy of Investigation?"

"Something like that. Sheriff, is there anything else you can think of that might help us find him before he leaves one of his calling cards around here?"

"First let me just say, since my wife's not speaking to me again," he went on, as Suze patted his hand, "Dee needs to be coerced — forced, whatever — to go stay with Suze and Steve."

"I agree," Brad said.

"She's so stubborn," Suze said with a sniff. "She's mad at me, too, and won't come to stay with us. She'll have to be carted out of there."

"I'll arrest her and lock her in with Lauren, under my guard tonight, if I have to," Brad promised.

"Much obliged," Chuck said, his voice getting weaker. "And what you just said reminds me of something I did think of. Unless Dee has them, and Suze says not, I lost my ring of keys somewhere. I had them on me when I was making the rounds of the lodge cabins. I had Suze call up there and the groundskeeper found only the cabin keys, not my ring of them."

"Which had your house keys?" Brad asked.

"House, office, firehouse and fire engine, our truck, you name it. I should've told you sooner, but I didn't even think of it." He threw off his covers and tried to roll onto his good elbow, but Suze and Brad pushed him back.

"Dad, you're not getting out of bed."

"Dee would let the arsonist in 'fore she'd let me in, but I've got to warn her. Let go now, Suze . . ."

"Lauren," Brad said, helping to hold Chuck down, "please send the nurse in here. Then go call a locksmith and get the locks at Dee's house and the firehouse changed immediately, FBI orders. I'll be right out. And then call Dee and tell her we're stopping by to talk to her."

Lauren nodded, patted Suze's shoulder and ran for the nurses' station.

Because Dee didn't answer her phone, Lauren and Brad headed directly to her house from the health clinic. But as they passed the Montana Range Gift Shop, they saw Red. The big man was hard to miss, although he was just emerging from between the fire station and the gift shop.

Lauren braked, and Brad yelled out the window, "Red! What's happening?"

Red lumbered over to the SUV and rested one forearm on Brad's lowered window. "Thought I heard someone on Mari's elevated side porch last night, and today I see I did. Someone's hacked through her garden hose. Could have been some crazy kid, I guess, but we don't get much of that stuff here and considering what's been happening, figure I got a right to be paranoid."

"Any footprints around?"

"That's what I've been looking for, but don't see any."

"A garden hose. Someone just cut it, or maybe took a piece of it?"

"Didn't think to match up the loose ends,

but guess that's the kind of stuff Uncle Sam pays you for. I'll check it and let you know."

"We're going to be at Dee Cobern's for a few minutes."

"Be right down."

The Cobern truck was in the driveway, which worried Lauren. "First we find Chuck unconscious . . ." she began.

"Don't worry about something that hasn't happened," he said, then shook his head. "As if that's not what we've been doing for the entire time I've been here."

They pounded on Dee's front door. Nothing.

"I'll bet she's in the shop," Lauren said hopefully, then added, "but the house phone rings there, too. Since the truck's here, she must have gone for a walk or on an errand."

Frowning, Brad tried the knob on the front door. At least it was locked. Before Lauren could answer, they heard the latch, then the door swept open.

"What?" Dee cried, standing there in a bathrobe with a towel wrapped around her hair. "I was taking a shower. Is Chuck all right?"

"He's fine but —" Brad got out before Lauren elbowed him and interrupted.

"He's not fine. He's guilt-ridden and sick to death of hurting you, of loving you. The man was out of his mind on those meds when he said whatever he said, Dee, and you know it. And Suze hasn't stopped crying over all this. We're here to tell you that we think the arsonist may strike soon, and you live too near the fire station to be safe. Since you won't let Chuck back home — not that he's in any shape to protect you as he wants so desperately to — you had better spend tonight with Nick and me. Brad may be there, too, but some of his other arson team members are coming in today."

Dee listened to the tirade with wide eyes and an open mouth.

"A couple of other things," Brad put in when the two women just stared at each other. "Because the arsonist may have taken the sheriff's keys after he assaulted him, a man — what's his name, Lauren? — from the general store is coming to change your locks."

"Ken Cecil," Lauren said.

"And if you aren't at Lauren's place by nightfall," Brad went on, pointing a finger at Dee, "I'm going to arrest you and take you there myself. Let's go, Lauren."

Before they could turn away from the dumbstruck Dee, Red came loping around the side of the house.

"Your hunch was right, Brad," he said,

then nodded at Dee before rushing on. "Mari's hose wasn't just cut but had a piece cut out — maybe several feet of it. And I'm pretty sure that at least three of the E-Z Lite fake logs she burns in her fireplace are gone, too, 'cause I bought her a dozen of them last week and she told me she didn't intend to burn any 'til I learned to sweep out my own fireplace. Brad?"

"I heard you. I'll bet our invisible tourist is planning to use those artificial logs to start a fire, but I can't figure out the hose."

"Surely those packaged logs couldn't start a big blaze," Lauren challenged, hands on hips. "They burn slow and clean. He'd need some kind of accelerant."

"Which could be funneled through a hose?" Red asked.

"Those logs only burn slowly and steadily," Brad explained, "when they're not cut into or broken open. Then they burn with a hot, fast flame, about 100,000 BTUs of it. They're oil-treated sawdust with some copper-based coloring and can go up big-time, especially with a liquid accelerant. He might have been using the hose to siphon gas out of cars or trucks parked outside around here. Dee," he said, swinging back around to look at her, "we're not playing games here. Will you be at Lauren's to-night?"

Looking stunned, she nodded. Brad turned back to Lauren. "I'm betting that our boy figures Mrs. Gates's tidy little logs would be perfectly appropriate to set her house on fire — or maybe even Dee's. Can you phone the volunteer firefighters and get them here to meet with me about noon for a quick briefing? The sheriff gave me a list of their names, but we can look up their num—"

"Come in here," Dee spoke at last. "I have all their numbers. You can use my phone."

Evan knew he was fated to succeed with his plans tonight when he saw that men kept showing up at the firehouse. From his vantage point in a clump of spruce trees on the hill above the town, he could see far down the one-sided main street. How he wished he could be a little mouse to eavesdrop inside, or at least get a peek in a firehouse window.

But what really caught his attention was that Macho Blond had gone inside, too. Who was he really? More than Lauren's lover, he'd bet. Or was he one of the volunteer firefighters? If so, Evan could only hope he'd be "lost," as polite people like to put it, fighting the fire tonight. Yes, *Lost at Lost Lake,* a great possible title for this masterpiece.

Watching the firehouse with the pair of binoculars he'd borrowed from the Cobern place, Evan counseled himself to be content waiting where he was. The men — six of them, not counting the blond — came out after about fifteen minutes, still talking to each other as they got back in their separate vehicles. Five of them drove away.

Besides the blond, one man lingered, then walked several doors to the Cobern house, knocked once and was let inside by Dee Cobern. A little later, the daughter showed up and hugged that man in the door of the house, then went inside arm in arm with him.

Evan recalled seeing the guy in the family photos. He was obviously the artist's husband. In one picture, he'd looked like a logger. And in another shot, he'd been dressed as a firefighter, just like his father-in-law.

Ah, the plot thickens, Evan thought.

Suddenly hungry, he wolfed down some barbecue sauce on sourdough bread, both of which he'd taken from the Bear's Den Dumpster last night. He'd started stashing food in case he needed it when he blew this place. He'd found plenty to eat. Restaurants should ask their customers whether they wanted bread, he mused, or how much they wanted, before they served it to them. Some Americans were still on that silly diet that made you swear off carbs. And the amount of food Americans wasted in one day could probably feed a Third World country for a year. What was wrong with people these days?

Evan decided he'd best stay put until nightfall, then ignite everything fast. But he'd have to be sure he had Nicky Taylor in hand and hidden first so that Lauren would cooperate. And so that she'd willingly ditch Macho Blond. No way did Evan want to tangle with him at close range.

Evan had almost nodded off when he heard the drone of a small plane. It had pontoons, but he didn't recognize it as one of the town's fleet. It circled the area once, including the town. So as not to be spotted, he scooted farther under the blue spruce branches and cursed when the dry needles pricked his back through his shirt. The plane finally landed on the lake, though not on the usual trajectory the others did.

It headed for the dock: the pilot seemed to hesitate about where to put in to tie up. Finally, three passengers, two men and a woman, got out on the dock, loaded down with what looked like big, matching tackle boxes and other fishing gear. Then their plane taxied out and took off again, leaving them here.

As the three headed toward shore, something familiar about them struck Evan. A woman with long brown hair was completely common. Two gray-headed men, so what? But that guy with the distinctive limp — where had he seen that? Where had he seen this assortment of people together?

Then he remembered and gasped. Only they'd had a broad-shouldered, blond man with them then — a macho blond.

The FBI team from his last fire, in Denver!

Could it be? Could it really, really be?

Had they found him? No, he'd been too careful, too clever.

No one met them at the end of the dock. Darting from tree to tree with his binocs, sometimes sprawling on the ground, Evan watched them walk to one of the B&Bs at the end of town.

At least they weren't headed for Lauren Taylor's place. Could she have ID'd him? Or had the Taylor boy told his mother or the blond man about Chief White Calf? Could someone in town have spotted his Most Wanted FBI picture that old hag in Denver had described to an FBI artist?

He'd been proud of the publicity but horrified by it, too.

Despite the heat of the day, Evan broke out in goose bumps. The FBI team was here to stop him, but no way he would allow that — ever. To calm himself and stay in control, he began to sing, "The hills are alive with the sound of music," then changed the lyrics to "The hills are so dry they will be a huge fuse . . ."

He chuckled. He was so inventive. And he'd give Vermillion, the state of Montana and the entire country an extravaganza to remember, one definitely entitled *Lost at Lost Lake.*

14

At Lacey's B&B, where Brad had spent his first night in Vermillion, the FBI Serial Arson Team set up its on-site command post. When Brad brought Lauren in, he introduced her to the team, then everyone sat around the dining-room table while Annette Lacey, a friend of Lauren's, served them coffee and sandwiches. Annette was plump, middle-aged and always joked she liked her own cooking too much. Her family went way back in these parts, supposedly descended from French trappers, but Annette was the last of the Laceys around.

"Lauren, sit here by me," Brad said and pulled out a chair for her at the table. "You've been in on locating BND in Vermillion from the start, and we need your local knowledge and input."

Lauren saw the only woman on the team, Jennifer Connors, roll her eyes. Brad didn't seem to notice, but Lauren knew that Jen, as everyone called her, didn't want her around. Maybe she liked being the solo female in on all of this, or maybe she just thought civilians should stay out of the way. The two men, both considerably older than Brad, had thanked her for her initial tip about BND.

"Frankly," Brad told everyone, "I was hoping you could hold off on this a little longer. We've obviously been making progress here."

"Not enough, if you can't produce Evan Durand," Mike put in. "Though now that I see the rugged vastness of this area, I can see why not. I'm tempted to bring in choppers with night-vision capabilities."

"But you've also seen it's dangerous flying this terrain day or night," Brad said, before she could tell them that. "I think tracker dogs might be more useful."

"No way," Clay Smith said. "Once BND lights a fire and moves onto burnt ground, dogs would have one hell of a time following him. At the World Trade towers, the cadaver dogs burned the pads right off their feet days after."

Brad leaned forward and looked down the table at Mike. "We all know this guy has a volatile personality and delusions of grandeur. But I still say, if he finds out he has the vaunted FBI team to impress, which he's already lectured once before — boom!"

"I hear you," Mike said. "But we cannot — I repeat — cannot have this man running loose, not while I'm in charge."

Lauren thought the air shimmered with unspoken tension. Poor Brad. This was his boss, and the team he had to work with in his mission to catch arsonists. She was so grateful for being a self-employed pilot with her own plane. If she could only be soaring alone above the mountains right now, or maybe with her son. Brad, too . . .

"Okay, people," Mike said. "I'm going to take just a few minutes to bring Brad up to speed on what we all know about Evan Marston Durand."

"So," Brad said, narrowing his eyes and leaning his elbows on the table to prop up his chin, "that's his middle name as well as his mother's maiden name. The guy doesn't make many mistakes, but using the Marston alias with Lauren was a big one."

"Yeah, she helped us with that, all right," Jen put in, but she sounded almost sarcastic.

Evidently ignoring her, Mike went on, "Now here's the need-to-know intel we have on Evan Durand so far. Only child, thirty years old, born and reared in Clayton, Missouri, a suburb of Saint Louis. Mother, almost forty when he was born, was once a concert pianist, father you all know about."

"In other words," Clay said, "two high achievers who probably demanded that of their only child."

"Fits so far," Mike agreed. "Mother died the month Evan graduated from high school, when her car engine caught fire and she was evidently trapped in the vehicle —"

"Burned to death? No kidding!" Brad said, hitting both fists on the table. "You don't think —"

"I have no idea at this juncture," Mike interrupted, "because we don't know Evan's relationship with her. Field agents in Saint Louis are trying to interview old neighbors and the like. Car engines do catch fire."

"How has he supported himself?" Brad asked. "His father can't still be picking up his bills if he claims they're estranged."

"As far as we can tell so far, through acting," Mike said and shrugged.

"Acting? Like in what?"

"One report says miming on street corners."

"More or less panhandling?" Brad asked, looking doubtful. "What's that word for performing in public venues with a box of coins nearby?"

"I think it's called busking," Lauren put

in. "Street musicians are called buskers."

"But busking can't be all," Brad insisted. "There has to be more to how BND's moved around, fed himself and kept a low profile — though acting skills could serve him well in changing his appearance and even getting in tight with people. I'm thinking of how he must have conned someone into letting him buy white phosphorus for the Denver arson. Anything else?"

"Only that he's pretty much dropped out of government records since he turned twenty," Mike said. "He's not even paying income tax."

"At least we can arrest him on that," Clay muttered.

"Ten years," Jen said. "For all we know, his serious arsons could have started about ten years ago, though we've only been onto the BND fires for about five. But I think Brad's right that this lunatic must have done more than mime on street corners to support himself. Maybe he's a thief, too, or cons people with his acting background. There have to be more pieces to put together."

"Which reminds me," Mike said, "Jen's going to debrief Lauren again. I know you've already done that, Brad, but it won't hurt for our reports to have it not by word of mouth, so to speak, but officially recorded."

Jen scooted her chair back and reached behind her to rip open the Velcro top on her black case. If that bag was supposed to pass for a fishing-tackle box, Lauren thought, these people were really city slickers. Suddenly she was terrified that Evan Durand would outsmart the lot of them.

She could tell Brad was seething, either with excitement or frustration. And he seemed barely able to keep from trying to take over from Mike, she was sure of it. Somehow, she had learned to read him in these few days, to tap into his feelings and needs. But she would lose him soon. And if these people couldn't somehow stop Evan Durand, she might lose much more than that.

"Sorry about all that — your being interrogated again," Brad said.

Lauren was driving him to her place to pick up some gear he'd left there and to bring back the scrapbook photo of David Durand, partly so the arson team could check his identity when he arrived, and partly, she thought, just to get her — or maybe both her and Brad — out of their strategy meeting. As he talked, he kept fussing with his two-way radio that linked him to the rest of the team. It looked a lot like the walkie-talkies wildfire fighters used.

"It's all right," she assured him. "I only told her what I've already told you."

"If Durand tries anything at your place, Jen's an excellent shot, though I'm sorry that I won't be spending the night with you, Dee and Nick. Mike thinks the men should be deployed at the fire station, Mrs. Gates's and Dee's."

"Maybe Dee's made up with Suze and will go to their house instead of mine."

"You're more likely to get them all there, since Suze's husband will be on call in case a blaze is set. It's weird how I feel as if I know your friends already. I haven't had that kind of thing — neighbors I knew — since we had to sell our place in Denver."

He sighed and hooked the radio to his belt. She noted how wistful he grew each time he mentioned anything to do with the "good old days," before his father's arsons brought everything in his childhood crashing down. She prayed that her own son's loss of his father would not take a toll like this. For the first time since she'd lost Ross, she wished desperately that she could give Nick a good man in his life, someone to be a father.

"Small-town living has a lot of rewards," she told him, "as does escaping the daily-pressure grind of a job like yours."

"I know," he said, turning to her. "Lauren, whatever happens tonight or hereafter, and as difficult as what we've been through together has been so far, I want you to know that I've enjoyed working with you, enjoyed getting to know you. If it hadn't been for you, we wouldn't be this close to finding Durand. And I will look into what happened at the Coyote Canyon fire when this is over, I promise."

She nodded, afraid she'd choke up. "You've been great for Nick," she whispered. "It's helped me to have you here." Her voice snagged. How ridiculous would it look if she cried or tried to cling to him, she scolded herself.

They got out of her car and started for the house. But on the stiff breeze they heard a thwack thwack sound that grew louder and louder.

"A chopper?" Brad shouted over the noise, shading his eyes and looking up. "If Mike's called in choppers, he's really nuts!"

A black helicopter buzzed the lakeshore, and they both ran to the water's edge to watch it. There were no official markings on the side of the big bird, but there were two men in it. It tilted into a turn, then headed for an open piece of ground between the town and Lauren's house. "This ever happen before?" Brad yelled as the descending bird kicked up a whirlwind of dry debris.

"Choppers? Not much," she shouted back. "Sometimes the owners of the lumber camp go in and out like that, but not on this side of the mountain. Every now and then someone wealthy comes to the lodge in the winter this way, but they usually land on the other side of town."

"I'll be back," Brad shouted and ran down the rocky shore of the lake toward the chopper, his shoes throwing the red mud the vermillion pigment made at the water's edge.

Despite what he'd just told her, Lauren ran after him.

Evan had been carefully shifting from tree to tree along the ridge above the town, working his way toward Lauren's place, when he saw a helicopter fly low overhead. Grand Central Station, he thought. More of an audience arriving early for his standing-room-only performance tonight? Perhaps even the director of the FBI or a newspaper reporter? How he wished a television logo had been emblazoned on the sleek skin of the helicopter. CNN, FOX, ABC, NBC,

CBS — he'd like to invite all of them to attend, then to write reviews of his greatest performance, which he had to get going right now.

He wanted to be in place before it got dark so that he could take out his hidden ladder and have Running Deer in the tender care of the ghost of Chief White Calf before he set the fires. With the rising wind, the entire area could be one giant lighted stage when Lauren flew him out of here.

He'd decided to leave the ransom note the old-fashioned way — her son's life for her compliance. In this podunk place where cell phones didn't work, who knew if he could even get to a phone. And even then, one of these FBI lackeys might have tapped it. He'd written the note wearing gloves so he'd leave no prints.

Hunkered down behind a cluster of thick conifers, Evan lifted his binocs to his eyes, pointing them toward the helicopter landing on the shore near Lauren's property. He adjusted the focus dial; the scene leaped large into view and etched itself on his mind. He saw that both Lauren and her blond friend were racing toward the big bird as its rotors slowed. And the man who emerged and jumped down to the rocky shoreline was — was . . .

Evan bucked so hard in shock, he threw himself back and hit his head on a tree branch. He steadied himself and gripped the binocs. The two sides of them came together to pinch his fingers. Then, furious and frenzied, he fell flat on his back to the ground and rolled under the tree, suddenly terrified he'd be spotted, that he'd be stopped. Finally he forced himself to kneel and looked through the binocs again to be sure.

Yes, it was his father. His omnipotent, almighty, perfect father was here! But why?

Evan tried to control his racing pulse and ragged breathing. He was hyperventilating, and blood pounded in his ears. His father turned away, started walking in the opposite direction . . .

No! Oh, no . . . He was a little boy again, shuffled off, left behind, ignored. His father beat him and locked him in for starting the fire in the trash can, told him he'd end up a pyromaniac. Evan could still hear the way he'd said that horrid word, as if his voice echoed from the bottom of a barrel: py-ro-maaa-niii-aaac. Evan didn't know what it meant then, but that word had sounded so dreadful. Did his father mean he was crazy? That he was sick? The word sounded so dirty.

Evan threw himself down again. He pulled his hair and kicked the ground, beating his fists on the dry pine needles until he got control of himself again. After all, wasn't this what he'd always wanted? Although his first impulse was to get close enough to just shoot his father, they'd catch him then. Besides, his father deserved to be engulfed in a fire, just the way his mother had been. In more ways than one, he wanted his father to suffer.

Tonight the master arson investigator David Durand, and all of them, were going to be made into laughing-stocks, the butt of all bad firefighting jokes. As Shakespeare wrote in the last act of *Othello, "Here is my journey's end, here is my butt."* How his fellow thespians used to laugh at that line in high school, though Evan told them that *butt* meant the final target, the final ambition for one's life. Yes, this great tragedy was a comedy, too, and the second-greatest playwright since the Bard would have the last laugh in presenting his drama, *Lost at Lost Lake.*

So why was he curled up in a ball crying? Crying like he had not done since he'd so successfully rigged that fuse and fire in his mother's car?

"David Durand?" Brad called to the man who bent low and hurried away from the circle of wind the chopper blades made.

Brad saw it was definitely him, then noticed that Lauren stood just behind him, gaping at the new arrival. Durand frowned at them, then walked closer.

Lauren kept her arms folded across her chest, but Brad thrust out his hand. "Agent Brad Hale, FBI Serial Arson Team," he introduced himself. "Mike Edwards, the head of the team, told me you were coming in from Seattle. That was quite an entrance."

"I flew from there into Kalispell and at considerable cost to myself," the man said. He had, Brad thought, an upper-class East Coast accent. Boston maybe, shades of the Kennedys. "I had to cut short a speaking tour to set things straight. Obviously mistakes have been made. In my profession, I hardly need such a cock-and-bull story to get out about my son — or, by association, me."

"This is Lauren Taylor. She flew your son Evan into Lost Lake, before she knew who he was, of course. He was going by the name Rocky Marston then."

"Indeed?" Durand said, looking startled.

But rather than admit to recognizing the use of his wife's maiden name, the man plunged on, with a slight, stiff bow in Lauren's direction. "I'm afraid you — as well as that old woman who spotted the Denver BND arsonist in the middle of the night — are sadly mistaken and are causing me a great deal of trouble, my dear."

He was ingratiating and arrogant, Brad thought. And not to be trusted since he hadn't come clean on "Marston" being a major clue that BND was his son. But that fit. It all fit.

"As for trouble," Lauren shot back at Durand, "the arsonist is causing this town a great deal of that, not to mention the tragic deaths of the four women and the firefighter his blazes have caused so far."

"I hardly meant to cast aspersions on anyone, Lauren. My entire life has been spent in the cause of fighting fires and stopping those who start them. And where, Agent Hale," he said turning his back on Lauren, "am I to meet with your team?"

"Back in town," Brad told him. "We can either hike along the lakeshore, though you don't seem dressed for it," he said, pointedly looking at the man's polished wingtip shoes, "or Lauren can take us in her van."

"I'll take you," she said, looking at Brad. "But after that dramatic entrance, most people in town will realize someone who thinks he's important has arrived. Wait here, gentlemen. The chauffeur will bring the limo on the road right up there."

Brad watched her stalk off down the beach. He grinned behind Durand's back. He'd love to be there when Lauren took this guy on about his testimony against Ross during the Coyote Canyon hearings.

But there was one good thing about Durand's arrival. A pompous, self-important and preoccupied father like this was the classic kind to produce an arsonist, and if Durand was too blind to see that, he just might be enlightened soon. The trouble was, it might take flames to do that.

As Lauren drove David Durand and Brad toward town, she knew she should think of herself as Brad's assistant and keep her mouth shut. But she couldn't. She just couldn't. This so-called expert was one of the witnesses who had testified at the trial. And he had made it sound as if Ross's own carelessness had caused his death.

"I have to tell you, Mr. Durand," she began, fighting to keep her voice in check. She intentionally slowed the van, so she'd have time to say her piece. "I can't put much faith in your vehement claim that your son's not an arsonist. Not after the shambles you made of the Coyote Canyon hearings."

From the back seat, she heard Durand gasp. Beside her, Brad shifted in his seat but said nothing.

"And why would you be following those?" the man demanded. "Or think you know enough to question my testimony?"

Brad turned partway toward the man, who sat behind Lauren. "In case you didn't catch our driver's last name, Durand, it's Taylor. Her husband, Ross, was one of the experienced, *expert* firefighters your testimony implied was acting like a novice and partly caused his own fatal entrapment in that fire."

"Uh," Durand choked out, sounding as if he'd been belly-punched. "Sorry, Mrs. Taylor, but the evidence clearly sh—"

"The evidence was flawed," Lauren interrupted. "Maybe even skewed. I've kept a record of every word you said, not just from newspaper articles but from word-by-word accounts taken during the investigation. Brad's seen some of it and is going to look the transcripts over more thoroughly later. There's something wrong with two veteran wildfire fighters being trapped without their protective body tents. There's something wrong with a man who hears that Rocky Marston is the suspect's name and doesn't instantly tell an FBI agent that Marston was his wife's maiden name."

As she approached Lacey's B&B, she hit the brakes hard for emphasis. Brad bounced against his seat belt and braced himself on the dash. As she suspected, Durand hadn't fastened his belt, so he banged into the back of her seat.

"Quite a jolt to realize that you can make serious mistakes, isn't it, Mr. Durand?" Lauren goaded. "Maybe you'll think over the slight possibility that you're human and can be wrong once in a while. And maybe you'll decide to be honest enough to admit it and then get on with helping the FBI find and stop your son."

She hit the gas and jerked the cursing man back into his seat as she pulled up in front of Lacey's and came to a smooth stop.

Sounding shaken now, Durand muttered, "I insist you turn the engine off before I try to get out. Agent Hale, I demand you talk to this woman."

"Good idea. Lauren," Brad said, turning to her again, "I agree with everything you said. And I sure as hell am going to look

281

into the ramifications of this man's testimony about Coyote Canyon as soon as we
get our hands on Evan. Of course, I can
only hope he chooses to — as you so ex-
pertly suggested — cooperate with us now.
Durand, let's go."

Brad winked at her and got out, then
pulled Durand from the back seat and
hustled him inside.

Evan Durand pulled on his old firefighting
gloves and tamped them carefully between
his spread fingers. He made certain the note
to Lauren was in his pocket. He felt again
to be sure he had the long strips of cloth
he'd cut from his extra sweatshirt for ties
and a gag, should the boy not be convinced
to come quietly. This was more than he'd
ever risked before, but the isolation of this
place, the presence of the FBI — and the
brazen arrival of his arson-expert father —
all made this necessary. Though he felt
completely in control, it would be all their
fault if anything went wrong.

From his observations, Evan knew that
Lauren's house was full of women, including the female FBI-team member, but that
might work to his advantage. Dee Cobern
and her artist daughter were there, too, so
they must be speaking again. They might all

keep each other occupied, talking and fretting. At least, as far as Evan could tell, Macho Blond wasn't there tonight to get in the way.

He squinted up at the sky. Racing clouds — scudding clouds, poets always said. It wasn't pitch-black yet, though dark enough for what he intended.

He could tell by when the lights went out in the boy's bedroom that he'd been put to bed about ten minutes ago. Too early for Lauren to check on her son already, Evan reasoned. The boy was upstairs and they were probably all downstairs, feeling safe out of town, safe in numbers, safe in knowing that someone would have to go through them to get to the boy. But since the BND arsonist had shown no interest in harming children, and since fools like the FBI relied on their adversary's previous M.O., he wasn't worried about this part of the plan at all. Besides, Nicky Taylor, with his wild imagination, had played right into his hands.

And since everyone was preoccupied with fires on a large scale, one little boy hardly played into their fears, just as another little boy had hardly been noticed by his parents in their busy, busy lives. At the last minute when the flames devoured her, had his mother known? At least his father would recognize the power and importance of his son on this night.

Evan made certain he leaned the fire-truck ladder against the sharply slanted roof shingles, where it couldn't be seen from a window. Someone would actually have to make an outside circuit of the house to see it. He loved the fact that the ladder was labeled Property VFD. All he had to do now was hope that his little Indian brave would open the upstairs window when he knocked on it.

He climbed quickly and tested the roof with one foot first. Sturdy, not slippery. But then again, why should it be in this drought? That surely was another sign that tonight was meant to happen. He knelt outside the boy's curtained window and rapped as lightly as he could, then a bit louder. Women's voices were discernible from here, not the actual words, but the murmur of them. Didn't they realize they might keep the boy awake? He wondered how much they'd told Nicky about what was going on.

To Evan's delight, the bedroom curtains parted slightly, then swept wider open. The boy's pale face pressed to the window, his eyes wide, his mouth in an O. Maybe he had gone to sleep that quickly, Evan thought, because he looked dazed, half out of it. But that might help, too.

Evan had his arms crossed, Indian style, but now he lifted one palm out in greeting, while he pressed the index finger of his other hand to his lips to signal silence. He gestured to Nicky to open the window. He did. There was a screen behind it.

"I'm not dreaming, right?" the kid asked.

"This no dream, but White Calf want you come out for special campfire. Then you come back before your mother worry."

"A campfire? With other Blackfeet ghosts, too?"

Evan nodded.

"I'm not dressed. Should I get dressed?"

"You have robe? Indians like robes. Or blanket."

"Are we going to fly down or just disappear or what?"

"You take screen from window. You know how? I come in, help you get ready."

The boy began to fumble with the screen. There must be something on the frame inside that held it in place. Evan gave it a shove. When it pushed inward, he grabbed at it so it wouldn't make any noise. He shoved the sill up farther and crouched to step into the bedroom, putting the screen aside.

"I have my feather headdress right here,"

Nicky said, backing away and picking something up from his bedside table.

The bedroom door was slightly ajar, and
the women's voices were more distinct now.
If only he had time to eavesdrop.

"Did you put the bright feather in it?" the
boy asked as Evan grabbed the blanket off
the bed, wrapped it around the kid like a
robe, then dropped the note on the bed pillow.

"Bright feather special gift for you," Evan
whispered, pushing him gently toward the
open window. "More gifts when you come
out with me. You come see northern lights
in sky, like ghost lights."

"Yeah, I've heard them called that before.
Chief, I didn't tell my mom that you gave
me the bright feather, but I thought you
were the one."

This was working so well that Evan again
knew his plans were fated — kismet! He
helped the boy step through the window
onto the roof. Nicky wore long-legged
pajamas and socks, so his footing ought to
be good, though Evan realized he might
have to carry him down the ladder.

When they were both out, Evan lifted the
screen back into place as best he could, then
closed the window from the outside.

When Nicky saw the ladder poking up

above the roof, he asked, "Aren't we just going to fly away, like a ghost would? Or like in *Peter Pan* when they go out the window to Never-Never Land? Indians don't use white man's ladders, 'specially not ghosts."

"Other Indians waiting. We make you honorary member of tribe, have feast."

"I don't want to go down the ladder. Just make us appear on the ground like you do in the ravine."

"White Calf carry Running Deer down," Evan said and reached to pick him up.

"No!" the boy cried and darted back up the roof until his blanket tripped him and he sat down hard. "I'll see you in the ravine tomorrow. And why are you wearing gloves? Blackfeet don't have gloves like th—" he went on, his high-pitched boy's voice rising.

Evan shoved the gag in his mouth. As Nicky started to kick and flail, Evan wrapped the blanket even tighter around him, trapping his arms down at his sides. Using a fireman's carry, he slung the writhing boy over his shoulder and, with more difficulty than he'd imagined, went down the ladder.

Laboring, breathing hard, he ran with his bouncing bundle up into the clumps of aspen. He lay the sobbing boy next to his backpack and carefully tied his feet. Evan also loosely tied him to his big backpack, so that the boy would not roll down the hill where someone could spot him. Then he darted back down the hill for the ladder and stashed it in the foliage above the house.

Even if Lauren did not obey his orders in the note, it would take her quite a while to locate the boy. By then, the town would be on fire, and people she'd need to help her would be in disarray or even endangered, fighting the fire. If she did not meet him at her plane, he might be able to roust out that other pilot. He had a gun and a knife, after all. If worse came to worst, he could try to force his father's chopper pilot to get him out of here.

"You not cry," Evan told the boy, not certain why he kept up with the Indian lingo. "I get your mother here later and we go for airplane trip, see lots of pretty sights. Chief White Calf be back for you soon. You be brave, Indian brave."

Evan smiled grimly at the way he could come up with clever lines even in the busiest of times. He took a deep breath. Yes, he was in control. So far so good.

He removed his drip torch from his bedroll, being careful the butcher knife and gun were still there. He patted the kid on the head, then took off running for town where he had his kindling and accelerants stored.

15

Brad thought Mike's plan would probably work — or would if they were facing a more common criminal. He'd come to believe there was a fine line between genius and insanity. And Evan Durand, alias Rocky Marston, fell somewhere in between.

Although Jen, who hadn't been too happy about her assignment, was stationed out at Lauren's, Mike had deployed the three men to key sites to watch for any activity in town. He'd ordered Clay to spend the night at Dee Cobern's deserted house. Clay had set himself up in the attic with night-vision goggles because, as he'd just said on the radio, "There's a window up here with a perfect view of the Gates place, the edge of the firehouse and the main street."

"As if BND would be coming down the main street," Mike muttered into his two-way from his post in Mrs. Gates's front window. "Clay, just be sure you can get down fast to ground level if you spot anything. And don't be smoking up there. You gotta get off the weed again when this is all over. I'm not having a smoker on a team when cigs start blazes. Brad, you in place?"

"Affirmative, babysitting the fire engine. But I'm worried about David Durand's helicopter entrance. If BND spotted his father, he might try to face him down one way or another at Lacey's B&B. I think I could be better used there, since —"

"Granted, the father's a jerk," Mike interrupted. "We saw that in the meeting with him. But David Durand has enough smarts to keep an eye out at Lacey's. The guy's a survivor. Since he's finally acknowledged it 'could possibly' be his son behind all this, he wants to do everything to stop him. But do you know why? 'Cause it's the only way he can salvage his reputation. He's worried about himself, not his son. I know we're spread thin, Brad, but just sit tight. Jen, you there?"

"Affirmative. Lauren Taylor says I can take her vehicle to the B&B or drive into town if anything goes down."

"The sheriff's wife and daughter staying put there?" Brad asked.

"So far so good," Jen said. "That BND bastard just better pick another place to light his diversion fire, or I'll be all over him. Besides, with her son and the other two women here, Lauren's hardly a woman alone tonight. I've been making interior circuits of the house here and everything looks calm outside. I do think both mother and son are missing you though, Brad."

"Knock off the social commentary," Mike said. "Everybody, just keep your eyes peeled and these lines open. If we get this guy, I'm gonna see that part of the reward money goes to getting a cell-phone tower around here. Man, I feel like I'm back in the twentieth century — or even the nine-teenth."

Brad was tempted to defend Vermillion and its people, but he kept his mouth shut. He'd defend them another way, by stopping the Fire Phantom if it was the last thing he ever did.

He'd tried to keep from missing Lauren and Nick, from wanting not only to protect them but just to be with them. It was hard to believe that four days ago he'd never so much as heard of Vermillion, never laid eyes on the Taylors.

And he couldn't keep from wondering how Red and his Mari were doing at Red's place above the Bear's Den Restaurant. He'd lay odds that Red would take good care of her — and that she really wanted him to. Brad had asked Mike to give Red the extra two-way he'd brought, but Mike had told Red to phone him at Mari's home number if he spotted anything. Or if he saw flames, to phone the number at the firehouse that set off the alarm. The volunteer firefighters were in earshot tonight. After dark, they had sneaked into Dee Cobern's shop and hunkered down in sleeping bags on the floor. By running about fifty yards, they'd be here in the firehouse, ready to roll in a matter of minutes.

Partway up the wooded hill behind the town, Evan uncovered his cache of E-Z Lite logs. He strapped his drip torch to his back, as if it were a small scuba lung.

Nineteen inches of beautiful, bright red stainless steel, the drip torch was his favorite firefighting device, but it could also set amazing arson blazes. He hoped not to have to use it tonight, though it always thrilled him to smell its heady mixture of diesel oil and gasoline. He shivered at the thought of its gobs of accelerant drooling to the ground to produce darts of fire. Yet he wanted to keep that as his best, last weapon; he had plenty else to use before he had to rely on it.

Evan had spent hours trying to figure out exactly how the FBI Serial Arson Team had psyched him out. They'd expect him to act as he always did, which meant starting a diversion fire away from his primary target — a single woman's abode near the fire-house. And though he hated to disappoint them, he had a few special surprises in store tonight.

He knew the FBI team wasn't at Lacey's B&B anymore, but he wasn't quite certain where they were. How excellent it would be if he could trap one or more of them just as they yearned to trap him. He regretted having to get Nicky Taylor under his control tonight. Otherwise, he'd have had time to surveil the town continually and known exactly where all the actors in this drama were waiting in the wings.

Evan carried two of the three E-Z Lite logs down the hill toward the back of the Bear's Den Restaurant. Let them watch the Cobern and Gates places — surely that's what they had under guard. He did regret that the restaurant that had fed him so well would have to be sacrificed, but it was the only building he could get to completely undercover. Not only did its Dumpster provide protection for him to get close to the building, but the long, metal, open-air barbecues were perfect for crawling under between the Dumpster and the building itself.

No way he was going to lower himself to starting a mere Dumpster fire. Drunk college kids did that, gangs in the 'hood did that. No, the Dumpster and barbecue grills were merely his paths in and out, especially in case the FBI team had brought night-vision goggles.

He belly-crawled out of the foliage and around the Dumpster, then under the ten-foot-long, raised barbecue grill, squeezing himself and the two logs between its regularly spaced sets of metal legs. He carefully placed the logs where he wanted them, one at the back corner of the restaurant where the wind whipped through from the lake, the other on the second step of the back entrance to the restaurant and the apartment above. The second story evidently belonged to a single man.

Variety was the spice of life — and death. But it was dark upstairs, so he couldn't tell if anyone was up there or not. He assumed there was a front exit, probably through the restaurant itself. If he did this right, flames and smoke would quickly cover the entire upper floor.

The wooden stairs reached clear to the

second story, and like the teacher's upstairs apartment two doors away, the stairs were covered, perhaps to keep the snow off or the cruel winter winds out. Once this log ignited, anyone trying to go up or down would have to run the gauntlet of fire.

Evan crawled all the way back and darted to the hollow tree where he'd wedged the plastic container full of gasoline siphoned from the fire engine last night. Pushing the container ahead of him, he made it back to the logs.

Pressed tight to the rear exterior wall of the restaurant, he used Dee Cobern's knife to hack into the logs to free their highly inflammable guts. How nice that so many of the western-style Vermillion buildings were made of rustic wood. This one even had a shake-shingle roof.

Evan laid a little trail with gasoline to both logs and backed away, dragging the almost empty container with him. He still had a second metal can of gasoline he'd siphoned from Lauren's plane at the other end of town. The extra log and some of that gasoline was destined for the B&B where his father was. The last of the accelerant would be used to set the dry grass field behind Lauren's house afire before he took the boy and headed for her plane.

A three-act play! This restaurant, the place sheltering his father and the field to provide the lighted backdrop to it all!

His hands shook as he lit a match from a half-used book he'd found in the Dumpster his first night here. *Nothing better than BEAR'S DEN chow,* it read.

"Except a Bear's Den fire," he whispered and struck the match.

Lauren hoped the women's chatter downstairs wasn't keeping Nick awake, but she doubted it. His eyelids had been heavy. He'd been excited to have Dee, Suze and Jen, "a friend of Brad's," here for dinner. To avoid upsetting him, Lauren had asked Jen not to talk arsonist business until she'd put him to bed.

"If BND strikes," Jen had told her in a whisper, "your son's going to know all about it anyway."

"But I'm trusting all of you to stop him," Lauren had countered. "Besides, Nick's father died in a fire. He's been doing so well lately that I don't want him upset."

"Oh. Sorry for your loss," Jen had said, though it sounded as if she was reciting a recorded response.

Lauren pushed open the door to Nick's room and tiptoed in. He'd opened one side of the curtains, probably to look out at his Indian tent again. Would he ever grow out of his wild flights of fancy?

He wasn't in his bed. She turned toward the attached master bathroom. She didn't want to startle him. He had downed a lot of orange soda at dinner, but she gave him credit for not wetting the bed anymore.

Lauren tiptoed over to the bathroom, but before she reached it, she sensed he was not here. "Nick? Nicky?"

She looked inside the bathroom, even pulled back the shower curtain and glanced behind the door. She darted back out into the upstairs hall, half expecting him to be leaning against the guardrails, asleep where he might have been eavesdropping on them downstairs.

But he wasn't there either.

She tried to stay calm. She wanted to scream for him, for help, but she didn't.

He had to be here. No one had come down the stairs. One of them would have seen him. She snapped on the bedroom light and ran to look under his bed.

And saw a folded note on his pillow.

He'd left her a note? What was he thinking? Was this some sort of Indian game? Was he going to tell her he was hiding and she had to find him?

As she opened it, her legs went weak and she collapsed on the empty bed. The handwriting — hardly Nicky's big printing — was small but ornate, with loops and embellishments. The message was laid out on the page like a poem or screenplay.

Lost at Lost Lake Stage Directions.
Epilogue

Dear leading lady, this drama's the place
Wherein to settle the FBI's hash — or
    case.
The Smoke Ghost has spirited your son
    away,
Gone for good, unless you costar in my
    play.
So come <u>alone</u> — no FBI, no friend in tow
To the airplane dock at 1:00 a.m., prepared
    to go.
For the finale, you bring Nicky home. Oh,
    happy days!
Or else, he'll be gone with the wind
In a big, beautiful blaze.

It was unsigned, but Lauren knew who the note was from. Her hands shook so hard as she skimmed it again that the words jumped and trembled. Wrapping her arms around herself, she rocked back and forth on her son's bed, fighting to keep quiet, to stop the moaning, keening sound inside herself.

She struggled to clear her head and control her fears. She had to act coldly, calmly.

How had Evan Durand gotten Nicky out of here? Without a sound, without a struggle? Had he sneaked in somehow?

Her heart thudded so hard she was certain those downstairs could hear. She almost screamed for Jen to get Brad on her two-way radio, but then he'd leave his post to rush here and everyone would know. Besides, it was obvious Evan must be watching.

She grabbed Nicky's pillow to her and hugged it hard, almost smothering herself in its depths — the smell of him, pictures and memories of her baby.

Then she got up slowly, dropped the pillow on the bed and walked to the window with the curtain shoved aside. The window was not locked, when she was certain she had checked it earlier. Had Nicky opened it from the inside? Surely he hadn't gone out via the roof.

The screen had not been slit, but the entire frame was loose. Like the window, it could only be freed from the inside. Had Nicky let that man in?

It didn't make sense. Nothing did. But

she knew she must do whatever this madman said to get her son back. If Brad were here, she'd ask him what to do. She trusted him that much. But the entry to the dock was an open area, and the dock itself long and bare. There was nowhere Brad could hide to get close to them. And if Durand was holding Nicky with a gun or a knife . . .

She even thought about getting David Durand to help her, but that could set Evan off. When he'd so much as mentioned his father that day she'd flown him in, his anger had been explosive.

Lauren could only pray that the arsonist had seen the show of force here and was getting out before anything went up in flames. And then, as the note said, she and Nicky could come home.

Whoosh! went the flames behind Evan as he scrambled into the protection of the foliage behind the Bear's Den. He could see that both logs caught quickly, belching coppery-colored light. Then the dancing flames flared to the wooden exterior of the restaurant. The logs were strategically placed to engulf the back of the building, but in this wind, the flames would vault to the second story and devour the eaves and shake shingles above, catching the front of the building too.

It was soon a roaring good fire, at first hidden from the street until it had a strong start. Then it turned into a thing of beauty as it leaped around the sides and caught the roof.

Taking the path above the town, Evan headed in a dead run toward Lacey's B&B.

Brad noticed that a diffused golden glow seemed to settle on the street. He'd been ordered not to go outside unless he saw the arsonist or flames, or if he smelled smoke. But he didn't care what the hell Mike's orders were. He sensed fire. But it wasn't where they'd all been looking. So where was it? Where?

Brad was unlocking the front door as the call came in to the firehouse. It set off an alarm that sounded like screams in his skull. He nearly jumped through the roof. Then the overhead lights came on. No one had told him to expect that. Backlighted like this, he was a walking target if he went out the front, so he tore to the back door and fumbled with the lock and the knob. This alarm would bring the volunteer force, and they'd be here soon.

The moment he tore out the door, the stench of smoke and gasoline hit him. It was obviously nearby, but where?

As he rounded the corner between the firehouse and Mrs. Gates's place, he saw red-orange flames roaring out the back of the Bear's Den Restaurant on the other side of the fire station.

Mrs. Gates and Red were there! Had they called in the alarm? Why weren't they outside where he could see them?

Keeping back from the impact of the heat, Brad made a jogging circuit of the restaurant. The fire must have started in the back, but the wind had already fanned it to the front. Most of the building was already engulfed. Clear to the roof — shake shingles, damn it — was ablaze, and the wooden-covered entry to the back stairs was a tunnel of flames.

"Red!" he shouted. "Red!"

Out of breath, Clay appeared at Brad's side, his face and form lit crimson by cavorting flames.

"Those two still up there?" Clay bellowed.

"Not sure, but that staircase is an inferno! Red! Mrs. Gates!" he yelled. "Clay, meet the firefighters out front and have them hack in the front door. See if that front escape will work. Go!"

For one split second, Brad feared Clay would balk at taking his orders, but he ran around to the front.

Even over the wild crackle of flames, Brad could hear the fire engine and the firefighters. They could walk to this blaze; BND had not lured them away first. Of his own dire necessity, he had changed his M.O. What else had he changed in his plans?

And then, looking up as he heard a first-floor window shatter from the heat, Brad saw a face appear in the window above — no, two faces half hidden by smoke and fire. Red was waving and shouting, but he knew not to try to open the window. They must be right above the back stairs, near that entrance, checking if they dared to open that door to get out. With this side of the building so engulfed already, the firefighters would never get ladders up to reach them. And there was no escape to the roof. The blaze had been cleverly set; it had spread like a wildfire.

And unless the firefighters could break in the front entrance, Mrs. Gates and Red were trapped in that inferno.

"I'm going to turn in," Lauren told the three other women when she went downstairs. She'd washed her face with cold water and was still drying it with a towel, just in case her tears started again. "I've been trying to keep awake by throwing cold water on my face, but I need some sleep." She faked a yawn. "Dee, you take my bed and Suze can take the couch. Jen said she's pulling an all-nighter. I'm going to put a sleeping bag on Nicky's floor. Let me just get a few things out of my bedroom first."

She got a ring of keys from her drawer and jammed a credit card in her jeans pocket. If *Silver* was out of gas when she let Durand off in Kalispell, she'd need the card for a fill-up or to get to the police there. She fully expected him to just disappear into the crowd and become the Fire Phantom again somewhere else. Maybe he'd leave her and Nicky tied up in the plane. It would mean that she and the FBI team had failed, but at least she would have her son back.

From her closet she took a down-filled, sleeveless vest because she knew it could be cold flying at night in the plane. She already had jeans, a shirt, jacket and shoes for Nicky laid out upstairs, ready to go. As far as she could tell, he'd been taken out the window in his pj's and socks. With Jen on guard down here, going out the upstairs window and chancing a drop to the ground might be her only escape route too.

Lauren thought immediately of the

Lindbergh-baby kidnapping so long ago. Someone had taken the son of the famous flyer, Charles Lindbergh, by using a ladder at his nursery window. The baby had turned up dead. Oh, why did she have to think of such a dreadful thing now?

Nick had become Nicky to her again. Her boy. Her baby, who she would fight to defend with her life. And with Evan Durand, it might come to that.

She went out to the kitchen and pocketed a steak knife. Her kitchen was immaculate; Mrs. Gates would be proud. Dee and Suze had cleaned up all the dishes for her while she'd played Slides & Ladders with Nicky. Lauren went back into her bedroom for a pair of kneesocks, the tight ones she used to keep her legs massaged when she was flying long hours. She'd wear the socks and put the knife in one, just in case. Then she went back into the kitchen and dumped all the candy from Nicky's jar into a small plastic bag. The rest of her Mr. Goodbar candies went in another, and then she wrapped everything in her terry-cloth robe so that no one could see what she had.

" 'Night, best friend," Dee said to her as Lauren started back upstairs. "Thanks for throwing the truth in my face today. I'll go see Chuck tomorrow. And," she added with a rueful laugh, "if he doesn't blurt out that he's leaving me, we can start to rebuild again — I hope."

Dee hugged her as Suze smiled at them. Lauren hugged her back, trying to be responsive but not desperate. She didn't want to give her panic away, yet she wanted to cling to Dee and sob out all of her fears.

Lauren said good-night to Jen and waved to Suze, who had gone back to the table where she'd been sketching a golden eagle. Lauren thought of Brad again. Only three days ago, he'd pushed his eagle badge — his creds, as he'd called them — toward her across the table at the airport coffee shop. So short a time, yet it felt like an eternity ago. Would she ever see him again? Would he understand what she had to do?

As she started up the stairs, Lauren heard the distinctive crackle on Jen's radio that usually meant someone was going to talk.

"Jen!" came Mike's voice clearly over it. "Borrow Ms. Taylor's vehicle and get in here. BND's hit, and we need all the help we can get looking for him. Like last time, I'm hoping he's staying around to watch."

"Did you hear that?" Jen cried, coming to the bottom of the stairs and looking up at Lauren. "That still okay with you?"

"Yeah, anything to help," Lauren told her,

wrenching her SUV key off the ring. "I'll hold down the fort here."

Dee and Suze came out into the living room at the bottom of the stairs just as Lauren tossed her key to Jen, who caught it handily.

"What's on fire?" Dee asked. Lauren chimed in too, just so she didn't stand out, though she was amazed at how little it mattered to her now. Nothing was going to stop her from trying to get her boy back.

"What's on fire?" Jen cried into her radio as she raced for the front door. "The what? He said the Bear's Den," Jen called back over her shoulder, then slammed the door behind her. Soon Lauren heard the engine start and the SUV roar away. She prayed neither Red nor Mrs. Gates were in the apartment above the restaurant tonight.

"It could spread, Mom," Suze was saying. "And where's Red? He must be safe. Why didn't they say? Let's drive in. What if the fire spreads to the health center?"

"Steve and Brad both told us to stay here," Dee argued. "But I guess we could go — if we keep out of the way. Of course, Lauren has to stay here with Nicky. Lauren, we'll leave you one of the cars. Will you be all right here alone with Nicky? I hope we didn't wake him. He'll be scared to death when he hears there's a fire."

"Go ahead, but be careful in town," Lauren told them. If she got rid of them, she could meet Evan easier. She knew she sounded like a robot, speaking slowly, one word at a time, but Dee and Suze were so distraught they didn't notice.

"And don't worry," Lauren added as they rushed for the door. "I'll take good care of Nicky."

She put her hand in her pocket and fingered the note from Evan. Yes, she had to risk meeting him alone. She couldn't wait for Brad, but she had to let him know what had happened.

Lauren raced out to the kitchen, grabbed a pencil and scribbled a few words, then dropped the note on the counter. Brad would be desperate when he found it, but not as desperate as she now felt.

16

The crackle of flames became a roar in Brad's ears as he gestured and shouted up at Red. "Go around! Other side! Front!"

More windows exploded; the two faces disappeared. Two firefighters ran around to the back of the house with ladders, only to take one look and run back to the front.

Brad followed, his lungs pierced by thickening smoke. He hacked and his eyes ran. The wind made cinders shoot aloft and drift down in erratic showers. A crowd had gathered in the street, but Clay and Mike ordered them to stay back.

Brad saw Suze's husband, Steve, take down the heavy wooden restaurant door with an ax. Thank God he was a logger, Brad thought. But only smoke belched out; no people emerged.

Steve and Suze Milliman had a son Nick's age. In another change of plans, the Fencer twins were taking care of Larson tonight.

Steve had a whole life of his own to live, but Brad watched him plunge into the roiling smoke to try to save Red and Mrs. Gates.

Brad's firefighting days came back to him in bright fragments. Hot, heavy gear. Feeling his way in the blackness inside a burning building, lit only by incandescent flames. Stay low. Pray for no falling beams, no collapsing floors. The heat, the stench, the fear in your throat and gut like —

Suddenly Jen was there, pulling on his arm, tugging him away. "You can't help with that, Brad! Get back!" she screamed over the cacophony of noise.

She had David Durand with her. He wore just loafers, slacks and an open shirt, his face, lit by shimmering flames, looked both awestruck and enraged. At least he had a front-row seat for what his son had been doing, Brad thought.

"BND's also lit the B&B!" Jen cried. "Annette Lacey is safe. Mr. Durand insisted on coming with me, but Annette wouldn't leave. The chopper pilot's with her. At least there aren't any buildings close by for the blaze to spread to. But with the fire guys here, there's no help for her place."

"Is everything all right at Lauren's?" Brad demanded. "It sounds like the arsonist could have been heading that way."

"For all I know, he could have lit the B&B first and be heading *this* way," Jen insisted. "But, yeah, everything's fine at Lauren's."

Lauren put her supplies into a backpack, checked that her kneesock was going to hold the knife secure and went out the back door. For the first time, she wished she and Ross had kept guns, or that she had one of Brad's. She knew she had to hurry. Even at a sprint, it would take her ten minutes to get to the dock, and she wanted to be early. Luckily she made a habit of filling *Silver* with fuel each time she returned, so she didn't have to do that now.

Rather than taking the road, she ran along the shore she and Brad had run together toward the helicopter only a few hours ago, the shore they had ridden together on the horses toward the fire tower on the other end of town. Her flying feet didn't make the usual crunching sound on the wet pebbles, but a hissing instead.

She could see the flames from the Bear's Den fire in the sky, but she'd steeled herself for that. She prayed again that Red and Mrs. Gates had escaped safely. Then she realized the fire seemed so close, too nearby.

She gasped and paused a moment to get

her bearings in the dark. Could Annette Lacey's place be on fire, too? That made dreadful sense. That's where the FBI team had met earlier and David Durand was staying. Worried now for Annette and even for the arsonist's father, she began to run toward the dock.

The black helicopter in which David Durand had made his grand entrance sat near the edge of the lake. She'd never piloted a chopper, but if it could help her, then she'd try it.

Lauren ran on until the long dock and its tethered planes popped out in silhouette before the distant flames in town. Finally she slowed her stride. She did not want to be gasping for breath when Evan Durand appeared with Nicky. She had to be in command of her mind and body in case she had an opportunity to push him in the water or use her knife on him. She would do anything to save her son and herself.

Lauren walked out onto the dock. Widely spaced pole lights cast puddles of yellow on the wooden boards. The air here smelled of smoke and was peppered with flecks of floating ash. From the Bear's Den or from the B&B? It didn't matter. She knew what she had to do. If her beloved fellow towns-people blamed and banished her for bringing destruction in, she couldn't help it. With Brad, she'd tried to help stop all this. But now she was doing what mattered most.

She went to her plane and unlocked it, then threw Nicky's clothes onto the copilot seat. When no one appeared, she paced back toward shore. Five minutes passed; her stomach knotted even tighter. What if they weren't coming? What if that note had just been a ruse to get her out of her house so that Evan could burn it, too? What if he knew about her involvement and meant to punish her for bringing in the FBI? And what if he hurt Nicky to get his revenge?

A heavy man emerged from the trees beyond the dock. No, not a heavy man, but one carrying a big bedroll. No, it was Durand, carrying Nicky wrapped up in a blanket.

She had meant to stay in control, but she tore toward them.

"Stay back and do what I say!" Durand commanded. "I have a knife at his throat!"

"Is he all right?" she asked, skidding to a stop at the end of the dock. "Nicky, are you all right?" She saw the gag now dangling under his chin.

"He lied to me, Mom. The Blackfeet ghosts will get him for lying to me about White Calf."

She understood none of that. Had he drugged the boy? But Nicky was all right — alive and feisty.

"Evan," she said, gripping her hands together so hard her fingers went numb, "leave him here on the dock, and I'll fly you anywhere you want to go."

"You'll do what I say," he said, enunciating each word exactly.

Lauren could see part of the bright blue backpack he'd arrived with beneath the bedroll strapped to his back. The knife he held to Nicky's throat glinted in the light.

"Yes, yes, fine," she told him, taking a step back.

"Then let's go. And we'll take Nicky, on his best Blackfeet behavior, with us. Now move! Let's get Heigh Ho Silver in the air!"

Brad's eyes were streaming with tears as Steve staggered out, guiding Red, who had an unconscious Mari Gates in his arms. Both Steve and Red fell to their knees in the street, then were helped up to move farther away from the flames. Brad saw that Steve had been sharing his breathing mask with them, but Mrs. Gates looked limp.

Brad rushed to help Red, but the big man wouldn't let her out of his arms. His face was black, his nose and mouth drooled mucus. His beard and hair were singed. As for Mrs. Gates, Brad couldn't tell if she was actually breathing or if Red's shaking was just jostling her.

"Didn't see it — 'til it got started," Red gasped out to Brad. "We were busy . . ." His words dissolved in his choking.

Did he mean in bed together? Brad thought. Suddenly both Dee and Suze appeared, rushing the security lines toward Steve. Brad recognized the nurse from the health center with them. Red finally laid Mrs. Gates on the ground and the nurse began to give her CPR.

"Dee, Suze," Brad said, catching both of them in his arms and dragging them back. "Give Steve and the nurse room. He's a hero — he saved them. Where are Lauren and Nick?"

"They're back at the house, all locked in," Dee said. "Did you get the arsonist?"

"Not yet. Can I use your truck? I've got to go check on Lauren."

Mike was suddenly at his elbow, looking distressed and distracted. "You'll do nothing of the kind," he ordered. "You, Clay and Jen are going building to building with your guns drawn, then up into the hills at first light, to flush BND out. I swear, he'll be watching this and gloating. He may have a unique — a flexible — M.O., but he's never deviated from it so far."

"Mike, he's not going to get trapped here. This place is like an island. He'll try to disappear again," Brad argued, taking the keys Suze handed him. "He came with hiking gear for a reason, and he knows the area. We need someone to watch the valley toward the mining camp, maybe even look for a hitchhiker on the single road out."

"If we don't bag him tonight, I'll order just that. But right now I'm ordering you to help the team, Agent Hale," Mike insisted, his voice cutting, despite an occasional cough from the smoke. "Chain of command, remember? Now follow orders, or I'll have you off the team so fast it will make your head spin!"

Lauren felt nauseous and dizzy, but adrenaline raged through her as she turned the key to start the airplane's engine. Behind her, Durand had tied Nicky into a seat and took the other one directly in back of her for himself. She felt as if he was breathing down her neck.

"Keep that knife away from his throat," she ordered. "It might be a rough takeoff with this choppy water, and if my son gets hurt, you'll have lost the only bargaining chip you have with me."

"Is that right?" Durand asked, his voice mocking. "What makes you think we're not just going up so we can crash right into the action uptown? I want a smooth takeoff or else."

She was amazed at the command in his voice. He'd seemed so quiet and nervous when she'd flown him into Vermillion. Surely he wanted to escape, not treat her little town the way the 9/11 terrorists had attacked the World Trade Center buildings. A terrorist — that's what Evan Durand was. An arson terrorist.

She glanced at the glowing instrument panel and throttled up, forcing herself to pay attention to her task. Nicky had stopped whimpering, but she'd heard him breathing hard before the propellers started. They bounced a bit on the waves. There would be no smooth, skimming takeoff this time.

"Nicky, hang on, okay?" she said. "You always like to fly."

"Sure, Mom. But aren't you gonna call me Nick like Brad does?"

"Brad," Durand muttered, sitting back away from her for once. She heard him click his seat belt in. "Wondered what Macho Blond FBI's name was. Maybe we can all wave goodbye to him as we fly over. Once you get this thing aloft, I want you to circle the town once. I'm mighty proud of my magnum opus, and I want a last look."

She didn't like the way he'd said *last* look. Still, as they picked up speed across the water, she forced herself to go through her preflight routine, all the things she usually did at the dock. She checked the RPMs monitor, the fuel flow and oil pressure gauges, wishing something would go wrong so they couldn't take off.

But the plane began to climb away from the fire, into the wind. She eased off the throttle. With its lights streaming out ahead into the darkness, *Silver* rose in a long curve and then banked, heading back toward Vermillion. The roar of the engine increased with the speed, then settled into its steady hum. Usually when that sound became a constant, she felt comforted as the world slipped away.

But not now.

As Lauren looked below, a primeval blackness seemed to hover around her little town, pierced by hellish flames. The Bear's Den and perhaps the gift shop, which meant both Red's and Mrs. Gates's places, were on fire. She could see the fire engine, even people. Many had come out of their homes. Vehicles parked haphazardly showed that some had driven in from the hills. And then she saw, for the first time, that the dry grass and flower meadow on the rise behind her house was aflame.

"You lit the meadow, too?" she cried.

"The restaurant, the B&B and the field," he said, sounding so proud. "My three-act drama."

She calculated quickly. At least the wind tonight was blowing east to west off the lake, so perhaps the meadow fire would not spread to her land, her house. Winds generally blew upslope in the day and downslope at night, but tonight was different. Although the meadow fire was already spreading in the grotesque shape of a hand with grasping fingers of flame, she tried to take the wind direction as an encouraging sign. Then, too, maybe the Otter River would stop the growing conflagration before it leaped into the Vermillion Valley and from there to the canyon, lumber camp and dry conifer forests that stretched for miles.

But if she lost Nicky — or Durand killed both of them — what would any of that matter?

She wanted to live, and she swore she would win the struggle this madman had challenged her to.

"You want to waggle the wings at them?"

she asked. "Just to show them you've won?"

"I've only won if the fire at the B&B caught my father there, and if he realized I lit it because I hate him. Because he deserved to die that way," he said, his voice suddenly so loud, so passionate and furious.

"You want your dad to die in a fire?" Nicky piped up. "But —"

"Shut up!" Durand screamed.

"Nicky, be quiet," Lauren said and waggled the wings right over the main street. People looked up and pointed, then the plane was out over the blackness of Lost Lake again.

"I didn't give you permission to do that!" Durand shouted and flashed the knife at her, reaching up between the seats so it caught in her hair and nicked her right earlobe.

She almost went into a steep dive to see if she could shake him or get him to drop the knife, but it was too dangerous. If only Brad had seen *Silver* and guessed what had happened! Meanwhile, she had to stay calm — deadly calm.

"I'm setting a course to get you to Kalispell," she told Durand, ignoring how her earlobe burned. She was certain it was bleeding down the side of her neck.

"Hardly," he said, surprising her again.

"You think I'm really going to risk your putting down there and having the cops or more FBI waiting to arrest me? Come around again and head up the Vermillion Valley toward the logging camp. And no more tricks!"

"But that's a narrow valley, bad enough to fly in during the day. The winds are weird tonight. The up-and-down drafts can almost rip wings off planes near the mountains, so —"

"Just do it — or else. You've got much more to lose than I do, Mrs. Ross Taylor, so just do it!"

"Did you see that?" Brad demanded, pulling Mike's arm and pointing up as the silver plane seemed to disappear into the cloudy darkness after a long loop out over the lake. "Damn it, that's Lauren, and two to one, Durand's forcing her to fly him out."

"We'll alert all the airports within the radius of her gas tank," Mike told him, still squinting up at the sky. "That can't be too many places."

"BND's proved he's no fool, but we are if we rely on that! The plane turned south between Mount Jefferson and Mount Nizitopi, not east toward Kalispell. I'm going after her. None of us would even have a lead on BND if it wasn't for her."

"Going after her how?" Mike demanded, swinging Brad around as, keys in hand, he started for Suze's truck. "In that?"

"I'll get someone who flies one of the other planes. We'll never find them if we wait until daylight."

"I'll help you," David Durand said, stepping up. "It's the least I can do. My chopper pilot said he had extra fuel, though I guess we'd have to pay him overtime. He's back with Mrs. Lacey, trying to comfort her."

Comfort her, Brad thought. There was no comfort in any of this. He didn't care what Mike said or did to him. He didn't care if his entire life's goal to make and help the FBI Arson Team went to hell.

"All right, Durand, let's go," he said, nodding. "The chopper may be able to put down places another pontoon plane wouldn't."

Still, Brad didn't like or trust the man. Even though Evan Durand was ultimately responsible for his own actions, and other kids who'd been ignored by their fathers didn't turn to arson and murder, David Durand was partly to blame for the monster his son had become.

Mike muttered something, but Brad kept

going. As he backed the truck away from the fire, he saw that someone had pulled the EMR vehicle out of the firehouse. Next to it, Red Russert was being cared for, laid out on the ground, breathing oxygen. But Brad didn't see Mrs. Gates's petite form anywhere. Hopefully she was in the EMR being tended to.

He skidded the truck in a half turn, the way he'd been taught to drive at FBI school in case other cars blocked in a vehicle for an abduction. Was that what Lauren was facing? With Nicky or without? He hit the brakes and backed up again, sticking his head out the window.

"Dee! Can you and Suze borrow a car and go to Lauren's house to see if Nicky's there?"

"That was her plane!" Dee shouted, running up to the truck. "You don't think he has her and Nicky?"

"I'm going to take Durand's chopper and find out. But Nicky may be at their house, may be hurt . . ."

"Yes, Suze and I will get a car and go together. We — oh, no!"

She gaped past the truck, toward the other end of town. Brad craned his neck. Sheriff Chuck Cobern walked unsteadily toward them, wearing pants under his flapping hospital gown.

"Take him with you, Dee. Get him away from here," Brad told her and gunned the truck toward the B&B. It would have been easy enough to find from the light in the sky, but the entire area above and beyond seemed to be aglow too. Could the B&B fire have leaped to some parched trees? No, the lights in the sky were too bright, like a thousand aurora borealis. And that couldn't be the reflection from the flames in town.

"Looks like your son's set the meadow on fire, too!" Brad said.

"Then we'll have to call in air tankers and hotshot teams," Durand said. "I can recommend several good crew bosses to assess the extent of it and what else will be needed."

Brad slowed to pass a car coming at him, no doubt other area people drawn to town by the flames and smoke. He tried to get a grip on himself. He could not believe this man. So calculating and calm. If his own son had done this . . . If *he* had a son . . .

Nick. Nick had to be safe.

"And if your son's lit all this," Brad challenged as he sped up again, "and is heading up the Vermillion Valley, what's next to be torched?"

"What's up that valley past the Otter River?" Durand demanded. "More than forests and subalpine meadows? Any problems beyond that?"

"Other than the fact that it's almost too narrow to fly during the daytime, let alone at night? After a narrow canyon, there's a lumber camp on the far side and access to dry virgin timber up to the snow line for miles of mountains."

"Is that the area Annette Lacey told me used to be sacred to the Blackfeet, with burial grounds and all that?"

"Yeah, maybe, but it's not the Blackfeet I'm worried about. We're going to have Mrs. Lacey get in this truck and go back to town to find Mike. He can call in help."

"But I'm the one who's the expert on wildfires, not your FBI boss. It seems to me he's made a mess of things."

Brad gripped the steering wheel so hard he could have wrenched it from its base. "Durand, you can put all this in your next book, or explain your expertise on how to raise a serial arsonist murderer on your next lecture circuit. But right now, you're taking orders from me."

"I'm the one who hired the helicopter, Agent Hale!"

"And I'm going to arrest you for withholding evidence, for not coming forward earlier with everything you knew about your son, so just —"

"I had no idea! I swear it!"

"You know what's sad? I believe you!" Brad yelled as he braked a distance from the still-seething shell of the B&B. Two figures emerged and walked toward them. "Now get out and explain things to the pilot while I tell Annette Lacey, as shaken and grieved as she must be, what she needs to do."

17

It was challenging enough to navigate the Vermillion Valley in the light, but this was a nightmare. Lauren tried to level off, to fly between the cliffs and crags from memory as much as by her headlights and instruments. Above the rock-walled valley in the ricocheting winds, she fought the rudder pedals, fought the wing flaps and the wheel. And fought her fears.

They had left behind the burning meadow and the Otter River. If she had to crash-land, she could only pray that, despite the drought, there would be enough water in the smaller braided river that fed the Otter or in the slender, shallow lake beyond to handle a pontoon-plane landing. But the pontoons could be pierced by rocks or ripped apart by logs; the plane could tip over. It would be dangerous to land, but she had to convince Evan to let her try. She'd tell him that she could show him where to follow the road down from the lumber camp. He could hitchhike or even take a vehicle by force there — anything to make him let her land and let Nicky go.

Her mind raced. She had a CB radio on board, but she couldn't turn it on without static that would give her away. She wished she'd bought that expensive Emergency Locator Transmitter, which would have gone off automatically in a crash or could be manually activated so rescue forces could locate the downed plane. The baggage compartment behind the wing contained survival gear such as flares, mess kits, water and blankets, but you first had to put down safely to get to — or need — any of that.

"If you insist on flying in this direction," she told Evan, trying to keep her voice steady though the plane trembled, "there's no way to land in heavy forests. And our gas won't go far enough to get us to any sort of runway in this direction."

"And I siphoned some of it off," he said with a little laugh. "Great accelerant for the B&B and the grass field."

She was beyond being shocked and only squinted at the gas gauge. About an eighth of a tank less than she had assumed.

"Yeah, we should land soon," he went on, "because I have much more planned."

"Mom, he's got a drip torch just like Dad's that he's unwrapping from his sleeping bag!" Nicky cried out. "He's going to start more fires!"

"Quiet! Evan, there's only one place I can turn near here to circle back and try to land in the small lake and stream that feeds the Otter River," she said. "The turn must come over the logging camp, then I'll have to go lower than I'd like until my headlights reflect off the water."

"Mom, you might hit some otters or beaver. And Brad said you saw an elk when you were walking back from the ski lift."

"Ah," Evan said, "out of the mouths of babes. Brad, Brad, Brad. I see I should have talked a great deal more to Nicky and not just about Blackfeet business."

"You lied to me!" Nicky yelled. "You —"

"Nicky," Lauren shouted, "do not argue or say one more word! I need to concentrate."

"In short," Evan said, "your mother doesn't know the first thing about the bond between Running Deer and Chief White Calf. Always use your imagination, boy, and don't listen to your mother. I learned not to listen to mine. I did better without my father around, too, the SOB."

"What does SOB spell?"

"Nicky, please!" Lauren cried as she began to bank over the lumber camp she could not see below. Her compass and her gut told her she was right, but if not, both Mount Jefferson and Mount Nizitopi could be much too close.

She brought the plane around just as she had the day she and Brad buzzed Red's high camp. How excited Brad had been to fly with eagles, to see the reach of the valley and the beauty of this place. Now the land she loved most had turned terrible and terrifying.

Dee and Chuck sat in the back seat of a borrowed car while Suze drove. "Once we check on Nicky," Suze said, "I'm going to the Fencers' to get Larson. I don't care what time of night it is."

"They live far enough around the mountain that they may not have seen the fires," Chuck said. Dee could tell he was in pain, but he was covering it up. His voice had even regained some of its strength. "He may be sound asleep and best left that way for now, honey," he told Suze.

"I just have to see him, be with him, Dad. You understand."

"Sure. Sure I do."

He scooted closer to Dee. She knew he

longed to put his arms around her but couldn't manage with one shoulder broken and the other wrist sprained. With one arm, she reached around his back and hugged him hard.

He shifted his hand to her knee and squeezed it weakly. They hadn't said the words they needed to yet, but they were together. And Suze, too, all talking, all working in unison.

"Look!" Suze cried. "The lights are on at Lauren's. At least that pyro didn't torch this place, but that meadow fire's too close for comfort."

"We'll check the house for clues — for Nicky," Chuck said, "then hightail it back so I can help coordinate the wildfire teams we've got coming from Kalispell and Missoula."

They climbed out of the truck, Chuck with difficulty, though Dee sensed she should not help him. Suze ran up to the door and tried the knob. "It's locked."

"Here's the key!" Dee cried. She wanted to sob against Chuck's shoulder but she needed to be sure it wasn't just the emotion of this dreadful night affecting her. No, she was sure it wasn't. What had happened in town — and at the B&B they'd passed — had broken her heart, but not as much as how she and Chuck had hurt each other.

Suze took the key and opened the front door. "Nicky?" she shouted as she went in, followed by Dee and Chuck. "Nicky!"

"Mom," she said, turning back to Dee, "I'm scared to look upstairs."

"I'll case the place down here," Chuck said. "You two go upstairs and be careful. At least the arsonist isn't here, we know that much."

Dee and Suze tore through Nicky's room, bathroom. They even looked in the closets. "Nothing!" Dee called to Chuck as the two of them thudded down the stairs. "I'm not sure if that's good or bad, but — What is it?" she asked as she saw Chuck leaning against the kitchen counter, carefully holding something with a torn piece of paper towel to avoid touching it.

As she went closer, she stepped on several spilled M&M candies. They crunched under her feet on the pine-plank floor.

"On the counter," Chuck said, "I found this crazy note that says the arsonist took Nicky, and threatens his life if Lauren didn't help him. The damn thing rhymes like a poem."

"Oh, no. Oh, no!" Suze cried, craning her neck to read it. "Do you think she left it here for us or dropped it?"

"Left it, but not for us — see?" he said, and flipped the note over so they could read the back of it.

BRAD — HELP was scribbled in big but shaky printing.

"Nicky's writing?" Suze asked.

"I think it's Lauren's, written in haste," Dee told them and threw her arms around Chuck's neck.

"Never thought I'd say this," he whispered, his voice rough, "but later for that. We've got to get going."

"But Brad's already gone after her."

"It's too vast out there — and too damn dry if that pyro has so much as a few matches with him. Now, if I could hug both of you to me and never let you go, Dee, I would."

She sniffed hard and pulled herself away, swiping at her tears. "What's happening to Lauren and Nicky makes me realize that I never should have wasted so much time between us."

"Save that thought, sweetheart, 'cause we've got to save this area from an inferno. And Brad and whoever else we send in have got to save Lauren and Nicky."

Determinedly, with more speed than Dee thought he could muster, Chuck started for the front door. Yes, she admired the sheriff as much as she loved him, she realized, and hurried to catch up.

After her half circle over the lumber camp, Lauren headed the plane back into the Vermillion Valley, into the wind. It lifted *Silver* and she had to fight it to descend.

Both Nicky and Evan were silent now. Did he have the knife to her son's throat? If only she could risk grabbing the blade she had in her kneesock under her left pant leg, she might be able to lunge at Evan with it. But he could hurt Nicky before she even got her seat belt loose. And in a struggle, it wouldn't take much for the plane to veer, to crack a wing into the cliffs, to go down.

"The lake will come up before the river." She spoke aloud, mostly to herself. "I'll try to land on the lake, not the river, unless there's no other way. Nicky, put your head between your knees and hug your legs."

She gasped when she saw that she had come down too steep and too fast — too soon! She slammed the flaps down full and backed off the power. Treetops rushed at her before she saw the distant glint of water. Yes, the north end of the lake was almost under her. If she could just miss these trees . . .

One of the pontoons brushed, then

clipped a treetop. Nicky screamed as the plane jerked and shuddered. Lauren struggled to control its path and descent. She was over water now, choppy in the wind funneling down the valley, the waves coming at her with small whitecaps. That was good, she told herself as she flew even lower. Movement on water could help her to judge distance and height. She glanced at her altimeter again. Next to nothing — nothing . . .

She was tempted to shout at Evan to loosen his seat belt, hoping in the trauma of the moment that he'd mindlessly obey and then get knocked around. But Nicky might unlock his, too. And even a small body could go right through the windshield if the plane landed wrong.

The minute they were down, even though the waves made them buck a bit, Evan had the knife to her throat.

"Nothing funny now," he told her.

"Get that away from me," she ordered. "How am I going to lean forward to shut down these engines and coast us in? Or do you want to get out in the middle of this rocky water — Rocky?"

"Very good," he said. "Touché — or 'touchy' as an actor friend of mine used to say. Touchy, touchy, Lauren — knife to throat," he taunted, bouncing the blade widthwise against her skin instead of cutting her with the edge.

"You leave her alone," Nicky said. Lauren could tell from his nasal voice that he'd been crying. If Evan didn't leave them with the plane — if he insisted they continue as his hostages — she was going to have to keep Nicky quiet. Evan's already volatile temper was dangerous, and he'd probably keep that knife on the boy. She prayed he'd leave them here. Rescue efforts might find the plane, but if they set off into the tree cover between here and the lumber camp, they'd never be spotted from the air.

"How much flying time do we have?" Brad asked Len Woodruff, the chopper pilot, as they lifted off and tilted toward the Vermillion Valley. They had to shout to be heard over the rumble of the rotors. Brad had commandeered the copilot's seat and put David Durand in back.

"I'm not sure — hour and a half, maybe," Len told him.

Durand's hired pilot had been more than willing to help. Evidently he thought it was a grand adventure to be chasing one of the FBI's Most Wanted.

At least, Brad thought, a chopper didn't

need to take long turns around the lake or large curves to gain altitude. As late a start as they were getting, maybe they could make up for lost time. This baby had a big sweeplight, too.

Brad had seldom been in choppers, and flying in this one made him nervous as hell, though he was grateful for its ability to turn on a dime or hover. From within the invisible bubble of the cockpit, he had a 180-degree view of the yellow-and-crimson meadow fire before they flew into drifting, blowing smoke and night again. Ahead loomed a vast, blind blackness. Nothing was visible except for what the front lights or sweeping beam beneath the belly of this beast illumined.

"Since you're not used to flying in these mountains, Woodruff," David Durand shouted from the back seat, "no heroics. We can't stop or rescue anyone if we go down. And what if we catch up to them and crack into them in the dark?"

"We're at a much lower altitude and with more control than a prop plane could handle, Mr. Durand. I feel like I'm playing a video game, but a real one with escarpments and narrow passages — as you can see."

Despite the man's bravado, Brad could

see the pilot sometimes struggled to keep the controls steady and to work the directional pedals. The turbulence up here was buffeting them around, not only side to side, but up and down.

"I'm trying not to look," Durand shouted, "except straight ahead. But the smoke's starting to get pushed through here, too. We'll never see a red taillight, never see —"

Brad exploded, "If you don't have anything to contribute but grief and fear, Durand, don't say anything!"

He hadn't been this upset since his father had been declared guilty and was taken out of the courtroom in handcuffs and leg hobbles. Lauren and Nick — they had to spot them, save them from this man's brilliantly crazy son and his lust for fire. He tried to calm himself, to speak more civilly.

"To the best of your knowledge," Brad said to Durand as they kept scanning the sky ahead of them, "could Evan have set wildfires before? He's done a couple of woodlots, so I think the urge is there."

"Absolutely not — just the opposite. I think he's temporarily insane, and I intend for that to be his legal defense. Like me, he's fought fires. He worked for the National Park Service each summer, usually in California. And I'll have you know, he got the jobs himself without my pulling strings. I didn't even know at first, but I was very pleased to learn it later."

"California? Did he work the Coyote Canyon wildfire there?"

"Not that I know of. Besides, that wasn't an arson fire."

"But once it got going, some of it spread as if it was," Brad argued. He hadn't mentioned it to Lauren yet, but he'd picked that much up just from skimming the articles in her scrapbooks. And now he couldn't help wondering if Evan had had something to do with the Coyote Canyon wildfire.

But Brad kept his mouth shut on that for now. All that mattered was finding Lauren and Nick before it was too late.

However, he had learned one other thing from Durand. He now understood where Evan had earned the money to live on the rest of the year, which allowed him to move around, study his victims and torch houses. Lauren had told him that even firefighters at the lowest levels, the grunts who worked with spades and root rippers to fight high-risk wildfires, could take home paychecks of up to thirty-five hundred dollars for two weeks of work, not counting overtime and hazard pay. And those guys went from blaze to blaze during the fire season. Whether or not Evan had been a busker or an actor, his personal arson schedule would have meshed perfectly with wildfire fighting.

"We're above some sort of divided river with islands between its strands," Len told them. "I'm going to have to go up a bit — trees too close ahead."

"There's a little lake beyond, then trees, a narrow canyon and then the logging camp," Brad told him, recalling how it had all looked from the air when he and Lauren had flown over. "After that, forests stretch forever. Lauren's plane has probably gone on, but see if you can slow down and sweep the river and little lake with that beam. I don't know if she could put down there, but we have to keep our options open."

"Will do, but slowing and hovering in these winds will take more fuel."

The minute Lauren opened *Silver*'s door to get out, she thought she could hear the *thwack thwack* of a helicopter's blades somewhere above and beyond them. Surely that's what it was, not just the strange echoes from Weeping Wall Falls. If she could get her lights back on for a signal, or just start talking and make some noise, so that Evan didn't hear the chopper until it was too late . . .

"Nicky, are you all right?" she asked loudly, clicking her seat belt off and turning in her seat. She hit the interior light on. Now to get the wing lights going . . .

But Evan reached forward and grabbed her shoulder. He slammed her back in her seat.

"They're coming," he said, "but they're not going to get me until I've completed my work. I've got the knife you know where, so kill that dome light and start up again — and no exterior lights. I just hope the illustrious firefighter and king of the world, David Durand, is in that helicopter. Lauren, start the plane up again and run it up onto the shore here. Get it under those trees now!"

She clicked off the dome light but tried to stall for more time. "We hit tree limbs before we landed," she said. "I think one of the pontoons is damaged. We may be taking on water, so I don't know if —"

"Do it!" he shrieked.

She blinked back tears. Turning the ignition key, she revved up the engines again. Unable to think of any way out of this but to obey him, she hit the throttle and let the plane coast toward the shore. As she did, she saw a sweeping beam of light zigzagging across the water behind her reflected in her front windshield. This maniac had been right. They were searching for her plane!

She heard Nicky whimper as the pontoons hit several rocks in shallow water. They bumped and crunched while the plane skidded sideways onto the stone-littered shore. The wings and fuselage made it under the aspens untouched, but swept into the lower branches of spruce and pine that swiped at the windshield like brushes in an automated car wash gone mad.

The nose bounced to a stop against a tree trunk, jerking them in their seat belts. Lauren could hear the propeller hacking into the branches as it slowed with a final shudder.

Overhead, the chopper sounded louder. For one second a searchlight blinded them like a strobe, then jumped away as the chopper noise faded.

Lauren sucked in a big breath. To be so close and yet so far from help was almost too much. Tears streamed silently down her cheeks, but she swiped them away with her palms. Nicky's safety — that's what she was living for now.

"I see nothing along the river or lake," Len Woodruff said. "Is there any kind of landing pad at the logging camp?"

Brad's neck ached from craning it to look down. The spotlight from the chopper helped, but its reflection off the water sometimes made him think he'd seen a light or distress signal where there evidently was none.

"Yeah, there must be a landing spot at the camp," he said. "Lauren mentioned that some of the logging company bigwigs fly in on choppers sometimes. Her plane couldn't put down in that small of a space, but maybe in an opening there at the camp."

"Such as a concrete driveway for logging trucks," Len said.

"I saw the camp once briefly from the air, but I can't recall," Brad admitted. He felt disappointed and exhausted — but not defeated. "I think they send most of the logs via an old flume down to trucks waiting below."

"I'm not only thinking of Lauren putting her plane down," Len admitted. "We're lower on gas than I thought, so unless you want to try to make it all the way back to Vermillion, bucking that big wind and the smoke blowing into the valley, I think we'd better land at the camp. First light's only a few hours off, and they'll be looking for her — and us — by then."

"If they can spare men from fighting that

meadow fire," David Durand put in. "The thing is, with these tricky winds and the draft this valley makes, let alone the narrow canyon you mentioned, the meadow fire could possibly leap into it and sweep this way. Canyon fires are notorious for fast spreads."

"And if your son is anywhere around," Brad added, "he could just start another fire."

Maybe Len sensed another shouting match, because he asked again, "You want to try to make it back to Vermillion, Agent Hale? I see the logging camp up ahead, so tell me now. I think I even see a helipad with a big X."

"Let's go back," Durand said.

"Put me down here first," Brad ordered. "Evan didn't make Lauren head into this valley without a plan, and that probably didn't include flying into endless mountains and timber where he couldn't get back on firm ground to do his thing. And take Durand back with you. The arson team thought the mere sight of his father might be enough to set BND off, so maybe I shouldn't be gambling on letting him help me — and his son."

"I resent that!" Durand shouted as the chopper descended toward the helipad. "I had no idea how sick — temporarily insane — Evan is, but I'm probably the only one who could help him, who could talk him out of any more fires. I should be back advising everyone on controlling that meadow fire, but if Woodruff here is willing to refuel and come back for us tomorrow morning, then I'll stay."

Brad was torn. He actually was afraid that, if Evan spotted his father, he'd try to impress him with more fire. On the other hand, he probably wanted his father to suffer more than he did Lauren or Nicky. And getting Evan distracted long enough to jump him could be priceless.

"Then I'm staying too," Len said. He was a big man, a bit too old to be tramping through the brush looking for a plane, but Brad admired his fortitude. "Besides, this bird's right on the borderline of not having enough fuel to get back," he admitted.

"Len," Brad said, "if you can surveil the logging camp and try to contact help on your radio — either from the chopper or from any phones you can find on site — I'll head back up the valley with Durand. I swear, Lauren's plane has to be behind us."

Brad didn't know if David Durand could keep up, but he wasn't going to let him slow him down. He reached under his feet for his duffel bag with his guns and ammunition. Lauren and Nick's safety was what he was working for now.

18

"I think the helicopter's gone. Get out. Get out!" Evan shouted, shoving Lauren's shoulder. She opened the door, pushed some spruce branches back and jumped out onto the ground.

Evan took his time, keeping the knife against Nicky's throat, emerging from the plane while holding the boy tight to him.

"Get back and stay back!" he warned her. "We may be on the ground, but don't think you're safe. No way."

Her insides cartwheeled when she saw Nicky's face glazed with tears. He was biting his lower lip, trying to hold himself together. No way was Evan going to drag her son any farther with that knife to his throat.

"Evan," Lauren said, "just leave us here and go. I've done what you asked. I'll show you the path to get out of this area."

"And you'll go with me on it."

"But Nicky will slow you down. I might, too. You can follow one of the two hiking trails out to the logging camp and its access road."

Months ago she'd heard Red say that there were two trails here. One trail followed the valley and canyon floor, while the other wended its way along a slightly elevated ridge. Surely one or both headed north from this end of the lake, where the valley narrowed to the canyon.

When Evan didn't answer, she thought, so much for the bravado. Now for the begging, which might get her further with this self-centered, volatile man anyway. She gripped her hands so hard together that her fingers went numb.

"Evan," she said, forcing herself to look at him instead of Nicky, "I will be so grateful to you if you leave us here in the safety of the plane."

"You want to make a deal? How about this? I'll leave him, and you can lead me out of here."

"I can't leave him alone."

"Someone will find the plane. You're right, he would slow us down. I'd like to just vanish like a ghost, but —"

"Then get going. I'll point out the path to the logging camp and the access road. And you'll get the Boy Next Door back in business, having made fools of your father and the FBI."

"My, my, very well spoken and quite a fine attempt to manipulate me. I told them I wanted to be called the Fire Phantom or the Smoke Ghost, and after this I will be."

"You told me you were a ghost," Nicky choked out.

"See, it wasn't really a fib at all," Evan said. "And isn't this the area where the Blackfeet ghosts still roam?"

"Y-yes-s," Nicky managed to say, wide-eyed. For the first time, he glanced away from Lauren to skim the spruce branches bowing in the blowing darkness. Beyond, the quaking aspens shivered their leaves.

"Please stop scaring him more than you already have," Lauren said.

"Mom, don't leave me here."

"All right!" Evan shouted, and for one moment Lauren thought she'd won. But he shoved Nicky toward her, pocketed the knife, produced a gun from that same pocket and pointed it at her. When Nicky clung to her, she thrust him away so a bullet couldn't hit him, too.

"Don't use that, don't point it!" she cried. "I'll do what you want."

"You just bet you will," he shrieked, then

seemed to quickly gain control again. "Now, you have been of help to me, so I'll give you five minutes to end this charming soap-opera scene by bidding him goodbye. Then he stays and you go with me."

She gaped at him before she closed her mouth. Survival for Nicky was the goal of this game now.

When Evan lowered the gun, she pulled Nicky to her and hugged him hard. What if she never saw him again, her Nicky who wanted to be a big boy?

"Nick," she said, holding him at arm's length in a crushing grip with both hands, "listen to me. You must not be afraid, because someone will be looking for the plane as soon as it gets light, and that's in just a little while. You are going to have to stay not only with the plane but *in* the plane."

"In case of bears or mountain lions?" he asked, his voice very small. "Or ghosts?"

"There are no ghosts here, that's just stories. But yes, stay in *Silver* to be safe. But if you hear a plane overhead after it gets light, look carefully around for wild animals . . ."

Dear God, she thought in a fragmented, frenzied prayer, a wild animal is here with us now. Please keep my son safe.

". . . and if you don't see any, you could run out and wave your red jacket so they see you. But if they pass overhead, get back in the plane for protection."

"I don't have my red jacket."

"It's in the plane with a pair of shoes and some M&Ms for you. And I'm going to leave you my candy bars, though I know you don't like peanuts and —"

"You know, Nicky," Evan put in, "the Mr. Goodbars from the top shelf to the left of the sink in the kitchen."

Lauren's heart pounded harder. Evan Durand was a ghost; he'd been in her house, in the downstairs as well as in Nicky's room. But she went on, "And whatever happens, honey, I want you to know I love you and think you are the best son ever."

"Cut!" Evan roared, suddenly sounding angry again. He lifted his gun at them. "Great acting job, Mom. Now let's go. If you've got any gear to help us, get it."

Holding Nicky's hand and pulling him along with her, Lauren went over to open the hatch behind the wing. As Evan came closer to watch what she was doing, she took out two canteens she always had filled with water, showed them to him, thrust one at Nicky, then slung the strap of the other one over her shoulder. However pristine the streams and lakes around here looked, they could carry a microscopic germ that messed up your intestines worse than Montezuma's revenge. Blackfeet revenge, Red Russert had called it when he'd warned her and Ross. Maybe Evan didn't know that and she could convince him to drink the crystal-clear water.

The knife pressing against her calf seemed to burn her. What if he discovered she had the weapon before she could use it? She picked up two flashlights and checked both, then held one out to Nicky.

"No," Evan said. "Charity only goes so far. Both of us will need one of those, at least until daylight. As you said, it will be light soon and a brave like Running Deer won't be afraid, will you?"

"I don't want my mom to leave me."

Lauren started to cry. How terrified he'd been after Ross died if she even went into the next room in broad daylight. He'd come so far since then.

"You'll be all right," she told him, fighting to keep her voice steady. "And if the meadow fire should come near here, wade out into the lake until it goes by and —"

"You know, Running Deer," Evan cut in, "for the Blackfeet tribe, rivers and lakes have a special power. I was just reading online the other day that they're inhabited by the sacred underwater people called Suyita-pis and —"

"I don't believe anything you say about them anymore!" Nicky insisted. "I won't believe that unless Mrs. Gates says it's true! Mom, I do smell smoke."

"Yes, but it's just blowing in on the wind. Get up in the plane now. Be safe, my Nicky — my Nick."

"Be safe, Mom," he cried. It broke her heart. She bent to hug him again but, the gun in his hand, Evan dragged him a few steps away and boosted him up into the cockpit, then slammed the door on him.

Lauren almost seized her knife to lunge at him, but he still held the gun, and she didn't want Nicky to see what would happen. Their eyes had greatly adjusted to the darkness under these thick trees. What if Evan shot her and no help came, or Nicky got back out of the plane to help and got hurt . . .

No, she'd lead Evan a little ways off before she tried anything like that. And if she could stop him somehow, she'd run back to be with Nicky. But she had no chance to tell him that. She waved to him and tried to force a smile, but her face felt frozen.

"Let's go," Evan said. She tore her eyes

from the pale circle that was her son's face in the plane's window. Evan swung his big backpack at her, keeping the smaller bedroll for himself to carry. "And no tricks like trying to lead me back toward town. You just get me to the lumber camp fast. Above all, don't get clever or cute. To paraphrase Shakespeare, 'Thus do all things conspire against you.'"

He wagged the gun at her and grinned as they started away. "You see," he rambled on, "as much as I hate guns, I had to borrow this from the sheriff's own desk."

"You've been inside their house, too?"

"Oh, yes. I didn't want to use this in the plane in case I hit some of the controls, but I have no problem using it on terra firma. Now, I may be the best of arsonists," he went on, his voice lighthearted as he clicked his flashlight on and shined it in her face, making her stumble, "but I can't claim to be the best of shots. Still, I assure you, we will be close enough that I would have no trouble hitting you."

She clicked on her flashlight and moved away from him, searching for a sign of the trailhead that must be near. Behind her, as if he didn't have a care in the world, Evan was humming the tune to "Follow the Yellow Brick Road" from *The Wizard of Oz*. To that same melody, he sang, "Follow the trail to the camp. Follow it right through the night. And find me, find me, find me, find me a forest to light."

"Why's this thing moving?" Red Russert asked, startling as if coming out of a trance.

Dee knew the EMR vehicle was bouncing him on his gurney as it pulled up to the dock. She hoped the movement wasn't hurting Mrs. Gates, who was already in a great deal of pain. Dee had volunteered to come along to watch Red while the more seriously hurt woman was tended to. The doctor had a wide-open saline drip going in her arm, and she was swathed in sterile, dry dressings on both legs and one arm. Her hair, like Red's, was singed, including the hair in her nostrils, which indicated — Dee had overheard — severe smoke inhalation. Dee wasn't sure what they had given Mrs. Gates for her pain, but the woman had been moaning.

Red turned his head and stared at Dee. "Are we at the health clinic?" he asked.

"At the dock. Jim Hatfield was going to fly Mrs. Gates into the Kalispell Regional Medical Center, but they're sending their air ambulance for her. We're meeting them on the shore here."

"I'm going with her," he insisted, trying to get off his gurney. Perched in the jump seat at the head of Red's gurney, Dee leaned closer to him, hoping he wouldn't guess how touch-and-go it had been for Mrs. Gates so far.

"The fires out now?" he asked.

"All but the one in the meadow. Because of the prevailing winds, that blaze is spreading upslope and into the Vermillion Valley. You're not as badly burned, so you're going to be admitted to the health clinic here."

"Like hell, if they're sending her to Kalispell."

"Red," Dee whispered and tried in vain to hold him down, "you need to rest. You've inhaled enough smoke to —"

"To be smoking mad!" he finished for her, then started coughing and fell back momentarily. But it didn't stop him from adding in a raspy voice, "That idiot arsonist must have targeted Mari and me, known where we were, maybe 'cause I tracked him back to town. But if they're transporting her, I'm going, too."

Dee was amazed at the man's strength as he firmly pushed off her attempts to hold him and swung his big, bare feet over the side of the gurney.

The doctor and nurse must have heard

him, but they didn't budge from their positions bent over Mrs. Gates. For a moment, Dee was afraid Red would push them away, too. She could glimpse Mrs. Gates's profile, and her usually alert, animated face was almost completely covered by an oxygen mask that hissed softly.

The nurse started to protest, but Red wedged his broad shoulders between them and knelt in the narrow aisle between the gurneys.

"She conscious?" he asked, then didn't wait for an answer. "Mari? Mari, my love."

The nurse and doctor stepped apart and looked at each other but they didn't interfere. Dee sank onto the edge of the gurney that Red had vacated.

"Mari?" he repeated.

Dee leaned closer. She could see the woman open one eye, just above the top of the oxygen mask. Had she and Chuck gone through the years of their marriage like that — with barriers between them, wearing masks?

"Mari, I'm going with you," Red insisted. "And you're gonna be all right. We're gonna finish what we started — you hear?"

She seemed to answer with what little was left of her singed eyebrows, moving them up and down. Then she lifted her unbandaged hand, wagged her index finger at him and tried to speak.

Red lowered his head, right ear down, close to her mask. "What?" he asked. "Who? FBI — oh, Brad? He went after Lauren and Nicky in a chopper, 'cause it looks like the arsonist took them. Mari — Mari, don't you move now, sweetheart."

They heard the *chop chop* of the arriving air ambulance getting louder as it set down on the shore in the halo of its own lights. Mrs. Gates's protruding finger pointed at Red again, then out the door.

"You're not sending me away, Mari, 'cause I'm not going."

He started hacking. She repeated her motions even as the doctor said, "We're going to carry her out to the evac chopper now, Mr. Russert. You'll have to move aside."

"I told you, I'm going with her!" Red insisted as Mrs. Gates made her two jerky motions again: You — out.

"Red," Dee said, jumping up to take his arm and trying to pull him back. "For her own good — for her health — you've got to let them take her."

Red was crying. Whoever thought Red Russert — trapper, hunter and former lumberjack — would cry, and over a woman who hadn't given him the time of day for years? But what was really getting to her was more memories of her and Chuck. He'd been hurt, flown to Kalispell, and she'd intentionally stayed here. Unlike Red, she had said she didn't want to go with him.

When Dee tried again to tug Red back from Mrs. Gates's gurney, he felt like petrified stone. He didn't budge, and Dee feared he might gather the small woman up in his arms and race off with her into the night. She could tell the doctor didn't know what to do.

"You realize," Dee told Red as the thought came to her, "that she asked you first about Brad, and you told her that he, Lauren and Nicky were in trouble. I think she's telling you to go find them, help them, not to stay away from her."

Red sniffed hard as the doctor and a paramedic from the chopper rolled Mrs. Gates's gurney out, then carried it away. He stayed on his knees. "You think that's what she meant?" he asked with a sniff.

"She's the one who said you'd do a great job tracking the arsonist from the ski lift," Dee assured him. "Lauren told me that. I'm going to ride back to town with you, but I promise I will send someone in a plane tomorrow morning to stay with Mrs. Gates in Kalispell. She won't be alone, Red."

"No. If the two of us live through this, Mari Gates won't be alone anymore, I swear it."

"So get a good rest tonight at the clinic. And when the firefighting crews get here tomorrow, you'll be ready to —"

"I'm ready now," he told her. He turned and sat down hard on the narrow platform where Mrs. Gates's gurney had been. "I'll let 'em patch me up, borrow some boots and gear and head out. I know a back way into that valley where it meets the canyon. I'll leave that info with the FBI team and the sheriff. But I'm not waiting around for outside help. Brad Hale didn't, either, 'cause, just like me, he fell fast and hard for a woman, though he might not know it yet."

Since Brad already had a jacket, Len Woodruff gave Durand his. Then with the only flashlight Len had to loan them, shoving back foliage with three-foot tree limbs, they set out on a fairly discernible floor-level canyon path back toward the Vermillion Valley. If Lauren had given this canyon a name when they'd flown over, Brad didn't recall it.

He wondered if this was the path Suze had taken to get up to Cedar Ridge where he and Lauren had seen her painting less than forty-eight hours ago. But if so, she must have cut up on a higher trail somewhere. If he could find Lauren and Nicky and they could make it to that high rock, maybe the flames would pass them, even if they roared this deep into the canyon. If only these damn winds fanning it in his face would let up. He knew sometimes their direction shifted at dawn, but sometimes they kicked the flames up more, too.

Time seemed to have collapsed this week; now it dragged. Though he was exhausted, he forced a quick pace. He was risking everything on his hunch that Evan had ordered the plane put down somewhere so that he could light more fires to impress his father. And he was praying that Evan did not let Lauren fly on where they would have to crash-land into thick forests, mountain peaks or even high altitude glacier fields.

He tried to block out the terrifying images: the plane down and broken, people broken . . . Lauren, Nick . . .

It astounded and scared him how much the two of them had come to mean to him in such a short time. The people of Vermillion, too, and the town itself, set like a jewel in a raw wilderness that could become a fatal, flaming caution.

Brad kept a firm hold on his duffel bag.

He had a single-action .45 automatic in his shoulder holster but carried his Hi-Power Browning 9mm with fourteen rounds and extra ammo for both guns. He wished he'd thought to bring Clay's night-vision goggles.

The terrain was rough and night sounds shook him. Did bears roam at night? What about mountain lions? Surely cats hunted at night, and they had built-in night-vision goggles.

"I ran out of that fire without any socks," Durand said from behind him. All he'd done so far was pant and wheeze, trying to keep up. "I'm going to be crippled from blisters if I don't jam some leaves or something between my heels and these loafers."

Brad was tempted to say, "Too damn bad," but he stopped. "Make it fast. I think we're at least a half hour from that water where she could have put down safely."

"We saw nothing there from the air," Durand said as Brad heard him ripping leaves from a tree. "I just hope none of this is poison oak."

"I've been meaning to ask, how did your wife die so young?" Brad asked, though he knew she'd died in a car wreck.

"Been profiling me as well as my son?" Durand asked, his voice accusing.

"Wise up. Arsonists are made not born.

We always try to figure out what the parents were like."

"As if no one's responsible for his own acts anymore. That's partly what's wrong with this country. We have a victim mentality. Poor me," he went on, his voice mocking. "It was how I was raised. It was just an accident or a mistake but not really my fault. Or, Agent Hale," he continued in his own voice, "let's just crucify the parents for what a wayward child does."

"Be sure to tell Evan's defense lawyer to use all that when you try to pony up an insanity defense for your *wayward* child, especially since the charges will be multiple counts of arson and murder."

"I refuse to let you blame me and his long-dead mother, for heaven's sakes! If you must know," he said, madly stuffing leaves in the back of his shoes, "she died in her car when her engine caught fire. She couldn't get out in time. The St. Louis police investigated it thoroughly — a tragic accident, that's all."

"A fire. Ever have any strange fires around your house when Evan was growing up?"

"It's not uncommon for kids to play with matches."

"And he did. In spades, I'll bet."

"As you just sarcastically mentioned, I intend to get a lawyer for him, Agent Hale.

And right now I'm going to invoke my rights —"

"Miranda rights?"

"First Amendment! No more questions except to my lawyer or I'll have you out of your elite FBI position so fast —"

"You know, Durand, you're the second person to tell me that tonight, so I'm used to the threat. You want to be on your own out here, fine. See you. And if you run into your son, be sure to tell him you're going to get him a lawyer to help prove he was temporarily insane while he cleverly lit separate fires with carefully chosen accelerants on widely separated dates all over the western U.S., and outfoxed, for a while, not only the FBI but his own father. Sounds pretty insane to me."

"No, don't leave me out here!" he shouted as Brad walked away with the flashlight. "I just don't want to be blamed for something I didn't do, that's all. I do want to help you."

Brad shook his head and kept going. Durand thrashed through the foliage behind him and eventually caught up. He was panting, but he said, "I'm so shocked and horrified by what my son may have done that I can't accept it. I — As Mrs. Taylor pointed out, I may have made some mistakes, yet they weren't my fault. But I do want to help

— to atone, as she put it. Don't you understand wanting to make amends for something like that — crimes committed by someone you thought you knew and trusted?"

"Yeah, I do, Durand. I really do."

19

Lauren was grateful to find a hiking path that led north from the end of the lake, climbing over the canyon floor. She thought there was a path that went lower, but she didn't want to act as if she was confused. With her flashlight, she spotted the I-shaped slash on a tree, the sign for a marked trail around here since the days of Lewis and Clark. But this was a seldom-traveled path with no wooden, carved placard at its head. In the dark, facing foliage and underbrush, she prayed it would lead them toward the lumber camp.

Her biggest fear was that, if that meadow fire kept coming this way, the entire area, including what they walked through now on this slightly elevated ridge, could ignite like a pile of dry kindling. True, the canyon didn't have as heavy a ground cover or as many trees as the valley, but it was narrower, which could concentrate smoke and flames. Ross had died in a canyon.

Worse, if the fire approached the plane, Nicky would be afraid to get out and wade into the lake. And what if he did get in the water? She should have told him not to go in too deep. He could swim, but with that heavy coat on, he could get waterlogged. He'd have to duck his head down if the air became superheated. The horror of that scenario kept gnawing at her.

"This trail traverses the entire canyon?" Evan's voice pierced her agonizing.

"Clear to the logging camp," she said, but she had no idea if that was true. Hopefully she could keep him distracted so he didn't light fires on the way with the drip torch as he had hinted he might. Had he actually been a wildfire fighter like Ross? Could he even have known Ross? If so, could she play on his emotions to let her go and to not start a blaze here?

"Should I call you Evan," she asked, "or do you still want to go by Rocky?"

"Evan's fine. My latest stage name is no longer useful."

"I was just wondering about the drip torch Nicky recognized."

"What about it? It's my favorite prop, just waiting for its cue."

"Your possession of it suggests that you

know something about wildfire fighting as well as fire setting."

"Smart girl."

"Could you have known my husband? He used to fight wildfires. He served on a hot-shot crew in the summers, not around here, thank God, but usually on the West Coast."

"Never met him."

"I guess I told you that the day he died he was fighting a fire. Did you always stick to burning buildings, or did you ever set one in the wild?"

"Planning to write a tell-all after this is all over? If so, I really should get part of the royalties. Since your FBI lad Brad has obviously done his homework, he must have learned that my illustrious father is an expert in fighting wildland fires, as they are properly called. So, of course, I would stick to house fires — except for the meadow — because I wouldn't want to make him look bad."

Though he sounded breathless from their hike, he laughed, a strange wheezing sound. Brad had been right, Lauren thought. Evan Durand wanted not only to make himself seem important and brilliant, but to out-smart his father — and everyone else.

"I heard," she went on, though she too was getting out of breath, "that the BND set fire to a woodlot or two, though I guess that wouldn't count as a real forest fire."

"You and Macho Blond spent your time together talking about woodlot fires, did you? I do love sparring with you to pass the time, but since you asked about my drip torch, would you like to see a demonstration of it?"

"No! Ross had one. I know how they work."

"Enough of this little scene, my dear leading lady. Just get us out of this narrow canyon. Should a fire start here, it could be deadly, with the winds funneling through. Can't outrun those once they get going, you know."

"As I told you before, Ross was entrapped in a flare-up in a canyon, the Coyote Canyon in California. Have you ever heard of th—"

"Enough!" he screamed. "Cut the scene, I said, or I'm going to use a prop besides my blowtorch and that's this gun, with real bullets. You'll just have to wait for the epilogue when we get near the lumber camp, my little guide. Now, keep quiet and keep moving!"

Sniffing back tears, Lauren held her flashlight steady, looking for the next blaze on a tree and praying those were the only kind of blazes she would see from now on.

■ ■ ■ ■

Suze made an urn of coffee at Dee's place, then Dee carried a tray of steaming mugs to Chuck, Steve and the FBI team. They had set up a common command center in the fire station. The fire at the Bear's Den had gotten a fast start, but the VFD had put it out before the lower front level was completely destroyed. Sparks had ignited the gift-shop roof, but they'd put that out before it burned more than Mrs. Gates's side porch.

At least the town was safe — unless the winds shifted at dawn and blew the meadow fire this way instead of just north into the Vermillion Valley and canyon beyond it. That would mean the lumber camp and the forests could be threatened too. And then, God forbid, their little town could be engulfed by flames whipping around the far side of Mount Jefferson.

"No, I don't know how many acres are burned yet!" she heard Chuck yell into the phone as she entered the station house. Steve was holding the phone up to his ear. "I said, I need a burn boss, initial attack crew and air support in here pronto."

The FBI team was huddled at the other

end of the long table. Brad's friends had spread out a map, and Red Russert was pointing things out to them.

Dee had thought of telling the nurse to give Red a sedative, but if he heard she'd said that, he'd come looking for her. He was Marilyn Gates's knight in shining armor, and it was better to let him go after the dragon and, hopefully, slay him. She desperately wanted Lauren and Nicky — Brad, too — to be safe.

"Fresh coffee here," she said as she put the tray in the middle of the table.

Jen nodded her thanks and reached for a mug. Mike hardly looked up, but Clay took one too.

"Are you going in after them?" Dee asked.

"I am," Red said.

Under these bright lights, he looked so different with his beard and hair partly singed away. During his stop at the clinic, he'd had both wrists bandaged. He'd borrowed a shirt and jacket that were too small on him. Dee wondered where he'd gotten boots his size so fast, but then she'd noticed that the general store was open. She planned to go down there later and ask Fran if she could fly into Kalispell to stay with Marilyn Gates.

Barely lifting his gaze from the map, Clay

said, "We hope to fly over the valley and canyon at dawn, unless the smoke or flames make a close-to-the-ground search impossible. The fact that neither Lauren's plane nor Brad's chopper have returned . . ." His voice trailed off.

"But that could mean a lot of things," Dee said, trying to argue against her own fears. Suddenly all the coffee she'd been putting away herself made her stomach feel sick — bitter.

She wanted to tell them that Lauren was a good pilot, and that in the few days Dee had known Brad, she'd been impressed with his take-charge attitude and dedication. But she knew her voice would crack, and she might burst into tears.

Nicky's life was at stake, too. How would she explain all this to Larson? Suze had let him stay the night at the Fencers' after all, but she phoned them every hour to be sure they neither saw nor smelled a fire. And she'd told them there would be no school today, let alone in Mrs. Gates's classroom.

Dee moved to the other end of the table near Chuck and his men. Her husband was using Steve as a secretary, writing things down, fielding calls from a phone he couldn't lift on his own.

"More fuel for you," she said, putting

several mugs on their end of the table. Then she added, "I guess I shouldn't have put it that way. Is help coming?"

"Working on it," Chuck told her with a nod and a stiff smile. As distracted as he was, his eyes went briefly over her like a physical caress, and her legs went weaker than they already were.

"Chuck," she said, "I could do the support work for you to free Steve up for other things."

"Good," he said with a nod. "I need you, Dee. Don't think I could even lift a mug of that good coffee without help right now. Feed me like a baby, baby, but I'm gonna roar like a lion into these phones till I get all the help we need in here."

Thrilled she could help, could be close to Chuck, Dee lifted and tilted a mug to her husband's lips.

"I suppose with just one year of college, you've never read Dante's *Inferno*," Evan was saying as they plunged through the leaf-lined path that made Lauren think of a dark tunnel into oblivion.

It surprised her that he'd remembered that tiny detail she'd mentioned about her college years. It showed how sharp he was. Yet, was he crazy? And how was she going to get his gun to turn the tables on him? Talk, keep him talking, she told herself. She'd never known anyone who'd been abducted, but establishing a relationship with the captor was supposedly the thing to do.

"No," she told him, "I haven't read *Inferno.* Is it about a fire?"

"It's about the author's idea of hell," he said, "though, of course, fire plays a part in that." His pleasant, professorial tone unnerved her more than cursing and screaming would have. "You see, according to Dante Alighieri," he went on, "there are nine circles of hell, and evildoers are punished in highly appropriate ways for their sins."

Where was he going with this? He was a man of many moods and bizarre thoughts.

"Well?" he said. "I assume, though you haven't read it, that you can draw some comparisons. What I really like in the *Inferno* is the idea of two souls wandering, seeing the hellish sights, so to speak, just like us. And at the gates of hell, as Virgil leads Dante in, there is a sign which proclaims, *Abandon all hope, ye who enter here.* I rather like the allegory, the symbolism of it all. There will be an inferno, Lauren, and I can't wait."

Despite stuffing his shoes with leaves, Durand kept slowing Brad down. The smell of smoke was getting stronger. What if Lauren had been forced to crash-land the plane and she and Nick were unconscious? What if the flames racing up the valley from the meadow reached them? What if?

"Durand, I'm going to pick up the pace. I've got to get at least as far as the small braided river and narrow lake before I turn back. Light should have filtered down into this canyon by then. If you look straight up, you can see hints of dawn."

"Or the aurora borealis. I can't go any faster, but don't leave me. We only have the one light."

"I'm going to look around, see if I can find where Lauren might have put the plane down. If I find nothing, I'll head back out on this same path, so I'll find you if you stay *on this* path. You could even sit down here and wait if you want to."

"I'm not an outdoorsman!"

"An expert on wildfires should learn to be. Just don't panic. I'll be back ASAP."

"But if you find them injured, you'll need help!"

"Which should be flying over at first light."

"But there could be wild animals, especially fleeing that fire up ahead," Durand cried as Brad took off at a jog.

As much as Brad detested David Durand, he hated to leave the guy. But the thought of Lauren and Nick out here alone — or with that damn arsonist was far worse.

After that spiel about a hellish inferno, Lauren knew she had to change her plans. She needed to get back to Nicky. She somehow had to get away from Evan without being shot or torched with that horrible fire starter he cradled as if it were a child. And she had to do it soon. Daylight was coming, and she'd never escape him then.

Lauren considered different possibilities. She could fall to the ground and fling herself back into him, like a tackle in football, then scramble for the gun. But if it came to a wrestling match, he was stronger.

Or perhaps she could turn on him. Even if he shot at her, she could just jump aside or duck, and hope he didn't shoot to kill. Then she could grab the gun. Or maybe she could find a break in the bushes or the trees and dart away before he could react. Though he might shoot in her direction, she could scramble down this slope they were traversing, hide behind a tree and pray he didn't take the time to look for her in the dark but keep going. She could try to elude him in this thick, dry brush. But what if he started a fire to flush her out? Besides escaping him, she had to keep him from starting a blaze for as long as possible.

Just beyond another slash mark on a thick tree trunk, she noticed an opening through the foliage. Old moose or elk trails, heading down toward the sparse glacier meltwater on the canyon floor, were frequent along here. Nicky would probably say they were Blackfeet trails — ghost paths. The next one she passed, she was going to try it. It made sense that the other trail Red had mentioned would be just a ways below.

She'd have to sit down, skid on her rear and try to keep branches from scratching her eyes. She could click her flashlight off but would have to hold tight to it. Though she had no idea what was in this big backpack he'd forced her to carry, she would drop it behind her or throw it at him to keep him from following her down. Perhaps she could veer to the side as she descended and escape the trajectory his bullets might take.

Yes, here came another opening, not only between trees but one that looked slightly beaten down.

Now or never! she screamed silently to herself.

She swung around and heaved the heavy backpack at him, at the gun. Bending low, she clicked off her light. She leaped into the open space, sitting down to slide, but her legs straddled a sapling partway down, banging her thigh. She thrust herself up away from the snag, then down again. This time she rolled, hitting herself from tree to tree.

"Damn you!" came from Evan above her somewhere. Then the crack of his gun — just one shot.

The sound — or was it the bullet itself? — echoed, zinged off bark, through leaves. Still clutching her flashlight, she lay on her face in a pile of dry leaves.

She stayed still, trying to control her breath. Her head hurt and she felt dizzy. Things were spinning. Had she hit her head on the way down?

Where was Evan? Surely he'd head toward the logging camp, not back toward the plane where they'd left Nicky.

Then a voice, controlled and calm, rang out above her as she gripped the ground to stop the earth from tipping.

"Lauren, call out your position and turn on your light. Right now, or I swear I'll set a fire with this drip torch you will not outrun, an inferno just like in the deepest rings of hell."

She didn't speak. She had to call the bastard's bluff.

"Lau–ren–nn!"

He was furious; he was losing control. Please, dear God, don't let him light a fire.

She kept silent but tried to calculate how far they had come. At least any blaze set here wouldn't buck a breeze this strong to get back to Nicky. And Evan would have to run from the fire; he could be trapped too.

She strained to listen. Was Evan using the drip torch, or had he lied or left? Was he walking away or coming silently closer?

Surely she had blacked out from her tumble. Maybe she'd hit herself with the flashlight she'd been clutching. It would be dawn soon — if the smoke she could smell even from here didn't blot out the sun.

"Hallelujah!" Chuck cried. "If I could clap my hands, I would. We've got a big air-crane helicopter coming in from the National Park Service with on-the-ground support!"

Cheers and applause filled the firehouse. Even, Dee noted, from the solemn FBI team.

"And," Chuck went on, "it's an 88-footer

that can dump water into areas with steep ridges and narrow canyons. Its 300-gallon-per-minute cannon launches water or foam up to 160 feet through the air, and it can draw its supply of water right out of the lake!"

Despite the smiles and relieved looks, Dee thought they still had enough problems to sink an 88-foot chopper.

"Also," Chuck informed them, "they're sending a crew boss to the end of the canyon through the lumber camp entrance. If he determines that the fire could well spread beyond the canyon, we'll also get the use of a foam-dumping air tanker, one of the big babies, so it won't be able to land around here. It'll be flying in from Missoula to Kalispell, then over the fire — estimated arrival time, mid to late morning. Some of you might want to take a break or get some quick shut-eye. We may have a long battle ahead of us. There are still sleeping bags on the floor at Dee's shop, and our daughter, Suze, is serving as chuck-wagon cook at our place — and that's no pun."

Chuck sank back into his chair beside Dee at the table. She was proud of how he'd handled things despite his obvious exhaustion and pain from going off his meds again. He closed his eyes and seemed to waver.

"Chuck," she whispered, putting her hand on his knee, "both of those planes are too big to put down in the valley or canyon, even if Lauren's plane or Brad's chopper was spotted. We'll need another smaller chopper, one that can set down or at least put a rescue basket down."

"That's already on its way. I took care of that before you took over for Steve. Dee," he said, opening his eyes and turning slightly to her, "can you take Suze's truck and drive Jen to the dock to wait for that rescue chopper? It'll be here soon, and she's going up with it."

"Sure. Anything to help."

"I guess Red Russert's loose out there somewhere," Chuck said with a shake of his head. Dee almost told him that she was partly to blame for that. Red had done it for Mrs. Gates's sake, and with a happy heart that would have cracked had he thought his Mari was sending him away. Actually, Dee wasn't sure yet whether the woman had meant for Red to get away from her or to find Brad.

"I'm scared for Lauren and Nicky, Chuck. And for Brad."

"I know. Me, too. But daylight's coming — in more ways than one, I hope."

■ ■ ■ ■

Lauren floated in and out of consciousness, then the horror rushed back, jolting her wide awake. The smell of smoke was so much stronger, more acrid. As she slitted her eyes open, she could see it now, drifting above her. In a burning house, she knew to stay low in the fresher air as long as possible. It was obviously the same way for the open air.

How long had she been out?

She was quite sure it was dawn, but the wan light had a strange, pearly cast to it. And it seemed to be snowing, she thought as she sat up and rubbed the knot on the back of her head. No, the snow was actually drifting ash from the fire.

And worse, through the foliage around her came a skittering sound and beyond her on the rocky canyon floor, other occasional echoing noises. To her amazement, she saw a sporadic animal exodus — mule deer, elk, moose — loping toward the lumber camp, away from the fire. And in the underbrush that she'd evidently fallen through, a few ground squirrels and pikas darted past her.

With her hand against an aspen, she tried to stand. A doe and a large fawn raced by along a trail on the canyon floor not ten feet from her. And by the looks of the panicked parade, even bears wouldn't stop to give her the time of day now.

Nicky — she had to get to Nicky.

Thank God, Evan seemed to be nowhere in sight. How long had she lain there?

She glanced at the wristwatch she'd obviously smashed against something. Despite the flight of frightened beasts, time stood still until she could get to Nicky. Was it her imagination or was the distant fire pumping heat out ahead of it? She shuffled and slid from tree to tree down the rest of the slope to the edge of the canyon floor. Carrying a dead limb and her flashlight for weapons and, avoiding the larger animals heading down the center of the canyon, she began to run in the opposite direction from where she and Evan had been heading.

She was almost to the area where the canyon opened up to the denser growth of the valley. Ahead, she saw a small body partly covered with dried foliage and leaves. Dear heavens, it was all bloody. Surely — no, it couldn't be! Nicky hadn't tried to come after her and . . . and what?

She gasped and shuffled closer. It was the half-eaten body of a small doe. She knew that bears buried the rest of the carcass they couldn't eat. It was mountain lions that covered their kill and came back later. But surely mountain lions would be heading out of here too. She had to get back to Nicky fast.

Just then she heard a hiss and turned to see a big, caramel-colored cat crouched in a tree about five yards away. As she screamed and lifted her stick, it bared its fangs and sprang.

20

Apocalypse now! Brad thought as he saw animals heading down the canyon, from south to north, and smoke roiling in the sky ahead of him. How much could the meadow fire have spread? Maybe he'd never make it back to the small lake and river where he'd hoped to find Lauren's plane or maybe Evan Durand too.

And then he heard a woman's scream.

Or was it? Did wildcats around here sound like that?

Sucking smoky air into his lungs, he broke into a dead run toward the sound. Another scream. Human? Close, very close.

He exploded around a pile of boulders and saw Lauren heave a flashlight at a big, snarling mountain lion. She lifted a limb before her to ward it off, then swung it, clipping the cat across the nose.

Brad dropped his duffel bag and drew his Glock from his shoulder holster. He lifted it and, stiff-armed, steadied it with both hands. Where was Nicky? What was that bloody body between her and the cat?

In the split second it took to fire, all his senses slowed. Sounds stopped, the smell of wood ash settled in his stomach. His Quantico training came back to him: hold breath, sight, shoot!

The bullet hit the animal. He shot again. With a scream of its own, evidently wounded, the big cat backed away from Lauren and vaulted at least twenty feet before it sprinted off, limping and trailing blood.

Brad had barely lowered the gun before Lauren ran and threw herself against him so hard they almost both went down. Her arms tight around his neck, she trembled against him. He was amazed she wasn't sobbing; she looked in shock. They held tight, rocking each other back and forth.

"Where's Nick?"

"With the plane, hidden under trees by the lake. I ditched Evan, and I'm heading back there. Evan has a gun. He made me leave Nicky behind."

She pushed him away. Reluctantly, he let her go. Her face was streaked with dirt, tears and scratches. Her hair was wild, her green eyes wide.

"Thank God," he whispered. "That body over there . . ."

"The cat's kill, I guess. He must have been full but wanted to protect what was left."

"Where's Evan? He's got to be stopped."

"He's heading toward the lumber camp. He says he's going to light fires. How did you get here?"

"I came after you in David Durand's hired chopper. It's over at the lumber camp but with little fuel, not even enough to fly back to check on Nick."

"I have to go to him. With that fire coming this way . . . I never thought it could move so fast."

"It's been light for over an hour. Surely someone's found him, rescued him."

"But if the fire's there already . . ."

"I left David Durand behind me, told him I'd be back."

"You were heading this way from the logging camp but didn't see Evan?"

"No," he said, holstering his gun and retrieving his duffel bag.

"There's another higher trail I came down from. That's the one he's probably still on. I've got to try to get back to the plane!" she said again. "I told Nicky if he saw wild animals not to get out, but if the flames come, he'll have to get in the lake until it passes. There's still some gas in the plane. It could explode. I should have prepared him better. If he sees both animals and flames, I'm not sure what he'll do. I know you have to go after Evan."

She was right. Brad knew he was duty-bound to find and stop the arsonist. And she wasn't begging for his help. She cupped his cheek with her trembling hand, then turned away, running back toward the thickening smoke.

Brad knew he had to head in the opposite direction. The arsonist could burn the entire area. He'd taken an oath to protect the country's interests; that was all he'd worked for and once desired. Besides, one more defiant, maverick move and Mike would dismiss him from his longtime dreams and desires in disgrace.

But he wanted to fight for Nick's life, wanted to protect Lauren. He'd never forgive himself if something happened to them he could have prevented. He had new dreams and desires now, emerging bright and warm through the smoke of the past.

His weapons and ammo bouncing against his body, he broke into a run behind Lauren.

With Agent Jen Connors sitting beside her,

Dee pulled up to the dock in Suze's truck. The rescue chopper landed on the same spot where the air ambulance had picked up Mrs. Gates earlier. Both rescue chopper pilots wore helmets that dangled oxygen masks; she could tell by their silhouettes in the pale light of dawn. One of them got out — he wore a bright blue jumpsuit — and jogged toward the truck as she and Jen got out.

"One of you an FBI agent?" he asked, lifting the opaque visor of his helmet. He was young and clean-cut.

"I am. Jen Connors, special agent to the FBI Serial Arson Team," she yelled over the roar of the rotors. "This is the town sheriff's wife, Mrs. Cobern."

"Change of plans!" he told Jen after a stiff nod at Dee. "We need to take someone up ASAP who knows the area. We can't take two because we'll need the space in the back in case we find evacs. What's the intel for numbers trapped on the ground?"

Jen started to protest, so Dee interrupted, "In the fire area, there are a woman and a boy in a silver pontoon prop plane. Three other men went in a helicopter. We just got word that the chopper made it clear to the lumber camp beyond the fire, but two of the men have gone back into the endangered area. Then there's the firebug."

"Ma'am, I wouldn't call whoever set that raging fire we just saw from the air a firebug or even an arsonist. He's a maniac. The wildland fire's already crowned on the northern mountain slope and is heading way up the valley. Now, I'll take whoever knows the terrain or wait for someone who does — incident commander's orders."

"Listen," Jen said, looking angrier by the minute, "I have a map of the area, and I've gone over it with local experts. And if you find the arsonist, I'll make an arrest on the spot — or stop him if I have to."

"We'd like to borrow that map, Agent Connor," he clipped out, "but we have our orders. Now, if Mrs. Cobern here can't go, please find someone authorized who can, and fast."

"I'll go," Dee heard herself say. "I've hiked the area and seen it from the air. And I know what the plane looks like — and the people."

Jen was sputtering something as Dee pressed the truck keys into her hand and grabbed the map. Bending low, she followed the young man toward the maelstrom of the chopper wash before she turned back and shouted, "Tell Chuck I'll be all right — and that I love him!"

■ ■ ■ ■

Several times as he ran toward the lumber camp, Evan was tempted to use the drip torch. But the winds were at his back so strong he might be caught in the blaze himself. He'd wait until he saw the open spaces of the camp and then light fires within it on all sides — that is, after he figured his escape route. He'd done that when he'd knocked out Ross Taylor and his friend Kyle, then laid their bodies on the hill where the flames would get them. He could only hope that Lauren would get her just desserts by being trapped, just as her husband had been.

Ha! What's good for the goose is good for the gander. Which was maybe one reason the animal kingdom seemed to be vacating en masse in the same direction he was. He laughed low at his continual cleverness and wit, even under duress and stress.

He jogged up over a small rise, then stopped dead in his tracks. Ahead of him, plodding toward the lumber camp, was his father. He recognized him instantly, though he was limping and the usual arrogant set of his shoulders sagged.

Again, kismet! Act four of his magnum opus!

Just in case the wonderful, the marvelous David Durand gave him a hard time, Evan drew his gun. Only one bullet had been shot from it, but he wasn't sure how many he had left. Enough, no doubt, if he needed them.

"Hail, David Durand, guru of wildfire fighters of the world!" Evan shouted. Holding the gun, he crossed his arms, spread his legs in a defiant stance and smiled. Arnold Schwarzenegger, governor of the tinderbox state of California and cinema star of *The Terminator,* could not have done better.

His father's gasp was audible from here. "Evan! What in the — Where did you come from?"

"From your loins and Mother's womb, unfortunately. That kind of makes all this your fault, doesn't it? I won't ask if the FBI and the mediocre American media have poisoned your mind against me, because it was poisoned from the beginning, wasn't it?"

"You're not making sense. And why the gun?"

"Because I wasn't sure I could catch you with a fire, so perhaps firing this will be my new M.O. And may I offer my belated congratulations on your miraculous, phoenix-like resurrection from the blaze I set at the Vermillion B&B."

Pointing the pistol at his father's chest, Evan walked closer.

"Put that down. Aren't you in enough trouble already?"

"You're not talking to a ten-year-old who used to worship at your feet — your absent feet. Why are you even here? Researching a book about moral deviants?" Evan taunted. "Preparing a talk about pyromaniacs, using your own son as exhibit A?"

"Evan, just calm down. I came because I didn't believe what the FBI said. I want to help you. I'll get a good lawyer. I'll —"

"I don't need a lawyer. I just need a little more time and for you to shut up for once. And of course, I need my trusty little drip torch. Just keep away — you've always been good at that," Evan ordered as his father kept coming closer.

"I see you still wear your mother's ring from Grandfather Marston. I've been wondering recently if the fire your mother died in kind of got you started."

"What do you mean?"

"When you lost her in that fire, you got so angry with the world. Maybe you decided that others should have to die the way she had."

"Close but no cigar," Evan told him and laughed. "But I do suddenly have a fierce desire to explain it all to you."

"Good. I can help you, I said. I'll get you professional help. We can get out of this and —"

"*We?* If you had ever wanted to be in my life, this wouldn't have happened, so don't bother trying to climb in with me now. What I do, *I* do, including explaining everything."

"Fine. That's just fine. I want to know, to understand," his father said, holding up both hands as if to ward him off. "Maybe we should start with the past. Would you like to tell me about your mother's death?"

"Yes, let's start with the sacred past. There's a sacred spot right down in the center of this canyon that I want to show you. I read about it online just the other day. It's sacred to the local Blackfeet Indians, now sadly gone from this area but for their ghosts."

"You always were so bright, Evan. Are you still acting?"

"All the time. And don't try to change the subject or manipulate me. Head across the canyon just a little ways, to that flat rock over there," he said, pointing with the gun.

"We can climb it to watch the animals vacate the valley while I explain."

"Let's head for the logging camp instead. I've got a helicopter there. It's almost out of fuel, but we can wait there for help — then I can get *you* help."

"After I show you the sacred spot. Go on."

The animal exodus had almost ended, Evan noticed. With his father walking ahead, they crossed the shallow, dry gully and headed for the rock. He would shoot his father if he balked, just enough to wound him, then do what he had to do. An ingenious idea had been forming in his brain ever since he'd read the Blackfeet beliefs about this area.

"That rock?" his father asked, pointing at it. "What about it? What's the story? Evan, that smoke from the valley fire's funneling down this way, and I don't doubt that the flames will, too. Tell me quickly and then let's get back to safety. What about this area and this rock?"

"Let's climb up for a better view, then I'll tell you."

They scrambled up strewn boulders to reach the fairly flat top of the ten-foot-wide rock, set like a small mesa in the middle of the canyon.

"All right, I'm listening, but make it

quick," his father demanded, crossing his arms and frowning.

"Oh, sure, I'll make it quick. Wouldn't want to hold up your schedule. This area was sacred to the Blackfeet tribe," Evan said, drawing out the words and speaking in a sonorous voice. "It was, Daddy Dearest, where they laid out their dead. And you've been dead to me for years now."

Still holding the gun on him, Evan swung his backpack down and fumbled in it for the strips of torn sweatshirt he had left over from tying Nicky Taylor. He heaved them at his father. "Sit down and tie some of that around your ankles, then put your hands behind your back."

"How ridiculous! I will not!"

Evan fired the gun at his father's feet. Rock fragments splintered and flew. The report echoed. David Durand jumped back and sat down hard. Then he leaned forward, grabbed the strips of cloth and began tying his own ankles together.

Lauren knew she loved Brad Hale when she heard him running behind her. In four days together, they'd lived a lifetime of danger. Now if only they could find Nicky. If only they could save him and then all stay together.

She tried to ignore the stitch in her side as each deep, smoke-laced breath she took bit into her lungs. Where was that narrow lake and that shallow river? They had to be near because the canyon widened to the valley here. But she saw only gray clouds of smoke beyond, and above that, orange-gold, leaping flames that were much higher than those which had swept the meadow grass. Trees must be on fire. But surely not those surrounding the plane! she thought in desperation.

"It's close — too close!" she cried and started to run again.

"Lauren!" Brad shouted, grabbing her arm to swing her back toward him. "Wait! Quiet!"

"No! I have to go — have to find him!"

Brad grappled her backside to him and put a big hand over her mouth. "Listen!" he ordered. "A plane!"

She strained to hear. The terrible crackling of fire was all she heard at first. And the continual, low rumble of Weeping Wall Falls blurred with the other sounds. But then — Yes, he might be right.

A chopper? A rescue chopper. Going or coming? Could it have pulled Nicky out of that inferno and be taking him back to Vermillion — or to a hospital?

When she nodded, Brad loosened his grip. Her eyes streamed tears, not only from the smoke but from hope, even relief. She hugged Brad hard, and they clung together, both looking up, squinting through the pall of thickening smoke. To her dismay, the roar of the chopper didn't seem to stay in one place. It got louder, then sounded as if it passed right over them.

"Maybe they've got him," she cried. "I don't know if they hovered long, but maybe we only heard it when they were taking him away."

"Smoke's too thick here and flames are coming!" Brad gasped out. "We have to retrace our steps, try to beat the wall of it. The animals knew."

"And that wild animal, Evan Durand, knew exactly what he was doing. Let's try to get to him, stop him no matter what. You came with me to be sure Nicky's safe, now I'll go with you to find —"

A big blast jolted them, then echoed down the canyon walls. They threw themselves flat, but no other sound or repercussion followed. There was no falling rock, only a rain of brown pine needles and sifting, silver ash salting the ground and their skin. They shook their heads to get it out of their hair and flicked debris off themselves.

"That chopper didn't go down, did it?" she asked. "It came from the other direction . . ." She saw the stricken, frightened look on his face. "Not my plane's gas tank?" She started to sob. "Dear God, please don't let Nicky have been in it."

Brad threw one arm over her and pressed his face close to hers as they huddled on the ground. "If the chopper didn't pick him up, maybe he was in the lake water like you said. Lauren, we have to go or we're going to be roasted here. We're going to have to run like hell now."

"Evan promised me it would be hell," she said as they staggered to their feet. "And I'm going to help you get him for that. For everything."

"What was that blast?" Dee demanded of the two men who sat in the helicopter seats ahead of her. The impact from it buffeted the aircraft and made more ground smoke mushroom ahead of them.

"Sounded like a fuel explosion," Tony, the one who had asked her to come along, said. "But sometimes big trees get superheated and explode into flames."

Dee hoped and prayed it was the latter. She'd zipped herself into a fireproof, silver jumpsuit and had an oxygen mask she could pull over her face, though when she did, it got in the way of her looking out the window. She gripped the mask in her lap and squinted through the coiling smoke and stabbing flames to see where they were. She had thought she would be able to tell exactly where that little lake and river were, but she hadn't been sure — until now.

"I see a rock formation I recognize!" she shouted to the pilot. "It's called Cedar Ridge. We've gone just a little too far north. Can you turn back? And that blast. Could it have been an airplane's gas tank exploding?"

"Could be!" Tony told her. "But even if we see something below, smoke's too thick to put down. We're gonna have to head for the lumber camp."

"Please just go back for a minute!"

The pilot pivoted the chopper and tilted them back toward the worst of the blaze. "Yes, there!" Dee screamed. "See that little lake? That's where I was thinking she could have landed."

Both men looked down as they hovered.

"Something bright red on the water at four o'clock," Tony shouted.

"A flare or something burning out in the lake?" the pilot asked.

Dee pressed her forehead to the glass

bubble of her window. "I think it's a red coat! Nicky has a coat like that. Do you see him? Maybe he got in the water. But where is he? And Lauren?"

"There's a coat, but there's no body with it, so no boy," the pilot said. "Ma'am, maybe the blast blew it there. But I repeat, we can't set down. If we'd spotted the boy I'd risk it, but there's no telling if he's even still in this area. We'll let the ground teams know though. They can check it out as soon as they can hike in. Sorry, ma'am, but we're gonna have to gain some altitude and sweep the canyon to see how far the fire's spread. We need to report in to Incident Command."

Dee wanted to scream at them to descend over the water. She'd go down in their rescue basket herself, though she knew she'd be baked if she tried. She kept picturing Larson, her own grandson, and how that could have been him down there.

She threw herself back into her seat and sobbed silently. "I'm so sorry, Lauren," she whispered, pressing her face to the window. "I'm so sorry."

Partway into the canyon, Lauren and Brad stopped and gasped for air. They'd heard a chopper fly over again, heading north, but it had sounded higher than the one before. Or maybe it was the same one doing reconnaissance. Brad had only pointed to the sky but not remarked on it this time. They were trying to save their breath and strength. Lauren prayed silently, repeatedly, that the chopper had rescued Nicky.

"We're not going to make it running," she told him, panting between words and holding her side. "That was part of the mistake Ross may have made. The flame wall's got a head start on us, and with this wind . . ."

"Yeah. But it's also burning any vegetation to climb the canyon walls, so we can't go up."

"There's one place that may be safe if we can get there in time," she gasped out.

"Under the waterfall?" he asked as if he'd read her mind. "It's a big one. We'd get battered to pieces and not get a breath there either."

"I think we can get under the cliff behind it, but it's . . . still a climb. And they say never go up. It's better . . . to run through it. I think we've got a little while . . . before it gets us . . . like it must have got to the plane."

"But it didn't get Nick!" he told her, his voice fierce. "He's all right, I feel it."

She nodded but started to cry again. At

least he couldn't tell; her eyes were streaming with tears from the smoke. He hugged her, quick and hard.

"We've got to save ourselves before we can stop Evan. I swear to you we will stop him," he vowed.

She didn't want to let go of Brad. She was desperate for his strength.

"Let's go!" she said. "Next stop Weeping Wall Falls. Follow me."

21

"I really need to be going," Evan told his father as he stood over him. "That was the line I've heard from you over the years, so I've perfected it."

"Evan — son — you can't leave me here. The smoke is bad, and with the wind direction, the flames will follow."

"What a brilliant deduction from the wildland firefighting guru of the nation! But before I ring down the curtain here, let me fill you in on why I've chosen this exit for you. As I said, this land is sacred to the Blackfeet because it was their ancestral burial grounds. They put the corpses on elevated platforms until they had decayed and came back later to collect and bury the bones. I'm afraid, though, I won't be back for that part. Too busy! Onward to new challenges, greener pastures, so to speak."

"Evan, I'm begging you. I'm sorry for whatever I did to make you so angry. I've made mistakes, lots of them, but you cannot leave me here!"

"You left me here!" Evan roared, looking down into his father's panicked face with the pistol pointed at him for effect. "Not exactly here, but you sent me into exile to work at that ski lodge right after mother died. You couldn't even spare time for me then!"

"I had to support you. I had a full schedule I couldn't change without losing fees and honoraria. The alternative would have been to put you in the care of doctors — psychiatrists. And you refused, don't you remember? If you want to know the truth, I was terrified of what they might get out of you!"

"Oh, sure. I might make you look bad. And Mother."

"You — you didn't have anything to do with that engine fire in her car, did you? I wouldn't let myself believe it, and accidents of that type happen. The investigators said such a thing couldn't be rigged so skillfully, even by an expert, so —"

"Granted, it would have taken a brilliant mind to devise that fire with a timer and a fuse. A fire that burned up all the evidence. A mere eighteen-year-old who loved his mommy — no way! Surely it isn't that a mere lad had outsmarted professional investigators and my own genius father!" Evan cried. And then he smiled.

"You — you can't mean it. I — Your mother didn't deserve that, and I don't deserve this. Just let me go. You can take off again, and I won't —"

"Just shut up, David Durand, expert witness, expert human being! This is an honorable death. If you don't like the Blackfeet Indian comparison, let's say your denouement entails a funeral pyre like that of a Viking king going up in flames. Or think of all the great martyrs and saints of the world who shared this fate, like Joan of Arc. Now I really must be going. But I will do you one last favor. I'll pile some brush closer to you so that things will go quicker once the flames get here — and I'd judge that will be in less than a quarter of an hour. Farewell, Father!" he cried with a sweeping gesture. "Farewell, for parting is such sweet sorrow."

He jumped down and started to gather dried branches and underbrush from nearby bushes. He dragged those up onto the flat stone, shoving them against the writhing man. His father continued to beg, jabbering, making promises Evan didn't even listen to, let alone believe. He was done with him now. His unjust, brutal past was over, and there was only a very, very bright future.

At the last moment, before Evan had to flee to get a good enough start on the encroaching flames, he got out his drip torch and waved it over his now-sobbing father in an elaborate flourish.

"We who are about to start more fires salute you!" Evan declared, hacking from the smoke. "I would ignite your pyre with this, Daddy Dearest, but I want to save it for fires today that are much more important."

He could think of nothing to top what he had already said, so he wrapped the drip torch in his sleeping bag, hurried down from the funeral pyre and ran north.

When Brad got close enough to see beyond the trees guarding the foot of the falls, he knew they were in trouble. The trail they'd have to climb to get up and behind the torrents of the wide waterfall was blocked with fallen rock.

"Oh, no!" Lauren cried. "I don't think it used to look like that."

The water pool they'd expected to find below the falls, which they could get into as Lauren had told Nick to do, was nonexistent. Brad knew the thundering water from above did not run into the canyon, where it could have acted as a firebreak. Now he saw that it ran off between the rocks and was swallowed by clefts in the cliff behind it, perhaps becoming an underground river. But even worse, the strands of crashing water had dumped a lot of debris, rocks that ranged in size from boulders to golf ball–size talus.

"An avalanche hit here last winter," Lauren went on, "but I didn't realize . . . When I fly this narrow canyon, I always have to look straight ahead."

"I can see where the cave shelter is higher up, but let's go closer and look for something on a lower level. Can you do it?"

"Yes — go ahead."

They scrambled up, around and over rocks, then started to climb a talus field of broken stones. But the area was wet from the spray of the falls, so it was like trying to climb a pile of slick ball bearings. More than once, Brad rolled down into her. They slammed together, sat down and slid in a rumble of small, round rocks.

Bruised, they got to their feet, still at the foot of the falls. "At least the smoke seems lighter here," Lauren said.

"Airflow from the falls is pushing it back, at least for now. But I can't see any place where the impact of the water is light enough for us to stand in it and survive when the fire wall gets closer. The water would pound us, suffocate or even drown us."

"Maybe we'll have to burn out an area in the canyon, then hunker down in it. You know, stay in the black, while the worst of it sweeps past us," Lauren suggested.

"We don't have anything to set a fire with. And there's no way to get ourselves a blackened area ahead of the flames."

"If we could just get up these rocks a ways, there would be nothing to burn under us and —"

"These trees around the falls could topple into us when they burn, or throw flaming branches or embers," he argued. "I've seen that happen even at house fires, where they end up igniting the next roof. Maybe we could make it to one of the bigger rocks out in the canyon, get on or behind it, be sure there's nothing that could burn near as it roars past. Are you sure there's no other trail around here that goes down the canyon toward the logging camp? Something high? We can't outrun the fire on the canyon floor, but if we could just get some protection . . ." He started hacking again.

"I don't know. I recall some things Red said about this area, but I've never hiked it. I told Evan I did, but I was lying in the hopes that I could get away from him and get back to Nicky."

Brad felt helpless as Lauren put her face in hcr hands and sobbed. He pulled her to him and watched their massive enemy approach, marching with orange and red strides down the canyon, leaping from tree to tree, devouring bushes. As the temperature rose, the fire seemed to suck air from the entire canyon.

Through the scrim of marauding smoke, Brad scanned the area, looking for a rock formation or a boulder that could shelter them. Even hunkered down in the relative shelter of one, they would have to hope that the superheated air or flames didn't make them casualties of Evan's grand-scale arson.

Then he saw what he prayed was the perfect rock: large, flat on top, one they could maybe hide behind or even under. But something moved near it. An animal — no, a man was running toward it.

"Lauren, look. There's a man running toward that flat boulder, closer to the other side of the canyon." He turned her and pointed while she swiped tears and drifting mist from her cheeks. "And there's a pile of something on the boulder."

"I can't tell what," she said, "but that looks like Red Russert running toward it. Is it? Where could he have come from?"

"He knows the area, so we have to get to him. I think something's moving amidst a pile of brush."

"Is it Evan?"

"Can't tell. I hate to leave this cool mist where the air is better, but Red may know a way out and what's happening back in Vermillion."

"Let's go!"

Holding hands like kids, they slid the rest of the way down the slippery slope and ran as fast as they could across the canyon.

"There's the commercial helo, just where Command said it would be!" Tony shouted, pointing as they hovered over the lumber camp.

"My son-in-law's a foreman there," Dee told them. "I know the area well. That chopper is sitting on the only landing pad."

"Doesn't matter," the pilot said, lifting one of his headphones to hear her better. "I see a lot of open area where we can set down. The pilot radioed that he was out of fuel, so we'll take him back with us, or his two passengers if they've turned up yet. So, Mrs. Cobern, where have they been logging?" he asked. "It looks like virgin timber stands for miles."

"That's what everyone's afraid the arsonist will burn, or the fire will spread to next. They try to keep this area looking pristine, partly because it can be seen from the ski runs, but also because they've logged just around the curve of both mountains to the east and west. They send the logs down to the service road at the bottom of Mount Jefferson on that wooden-log flume there," she said, leaning forward and pointing between their shoulders.

"An antique!" Tony said. "It looks like that Disney ride where you get splashed at the end. Could some of that water flow be diverted to fight the fire?"

"I don't know!" she cried. "Look, there's a man waving at us."

They put the rescue chopper down in an open area between massive piles of logs and the huge machines that hauled, delimbed and lifted them into the flume. The man, who Dee didn't recognize despite her desperate prayers it might be Brad, ran up to them as Tony opened the door.

"My two passengers went into the canyon and haven't come back!" he yelled without introduction or preamble. "I don't have enough fuel to get back to town, but I hate to leave the bird!"

"I see heavy equipment here!" the pilot

shouted to him as the man leaned into the cockpit, trying to hear over the wash of the rotors. "There has to be a gas pump around!"

"I don't want to be caught fooling with gas if the fire's coming this way."

"Unless this wind shifts, it's plowing its way right up the canyon," the pilot told him.

"Then I will head back with you."

"Did you spot a silver plane?" Dee demanded as the man scrambled into the back seat.

He gasped, evidently surprised to see her. "No. Agent Hale was determined to find it, and that's why he headed back, but he was dragging my charter with him, David Durand, so I don't know how much headway he made."

As the man buckled himself in and Tony slammed the door, Dee bit her lower lip hard to keep from crying. Worse than Durand out there, somewhere his maniac son was on the loose.

Drifting smoke obscured their view of Red and the rock, while the roar of the falls and cacophony of flames muted their desperate shouts to him. Between clouds of smoke, they saw Red half drag, half carry someone — David Durand, they thought — toward the lumber camp. Lauren knew they'd never catch him now, not exhausted and choking like this.

"He may get safely to the lumber camp, but I'm not sure about us," Brad told her and she nodded grimly. "But let's try to make it — at least as far as that rock."

They had both pulled their T-shirts up over their mouths and noses for smoke masks, though it didn't help much. Despite how parched Lauren felt, she knew they had done the right thing not to soak the shirts in water at the falls. Ross had said that could steam your lungs, which was deadlier than inhaling smoke. And since Brad had been a firefighter, he must have known to fight that instinct, too. She wanted to ask Brad so many things about his life, but now . . .

They pushed on, staying toward the middle of the canyon because it was the shortest distance toward the logging camp — and the smoke was thinner here than along the canyon walls.

The dry canyon floor, which offered the fire less fuel than a thick forest or field might have, brought new problems. Behind them the conflagration seemed to leap from bush to bush, tree to tree, vaulting faster and closer than it might have if it had more fuel to take its energy and time.

At the head of the fire, which they could see now boiling up behind them, flames surged and pulsed in fire fingers grasping at the canyon. Still holding hands, they stared aghast as the wind sucked burning pine needles, cones and branches into a twenty-foot updraft that leaned sideways to spew out embers like a thermal slingshot. But all that became an erect pillar of flame again, roaring and breaking loose from the main body of the fire and roaming the edge of the canyon as if of its own accord.

"A fire whirl," Brad said, his voice raw and awed. "I've only heard of them. It looks like an evil giant. We're going to have to make a stand. Let's get as close to the downwind side of the big rock as we can and hunker down." They began to run again.

"But the brush around it and on top of the rock where we saw Durand . . . It'll catch on fire. We need to have it burned off — gone."

"We have nothing to light it with!"

They stumbled toward the rock with the inferno's hot breath on their backs. Lauren yanked her hair into a knot and tied it back with a dry vine she pulled from a bush. Better not to have the bulk of it loose, to be ignited by an ember or even the huge pieces of ash falling now.

"I'll try to clear the brush," Brad said. "We'll get on the leeward side and maybe the worst of the fire will go by fast."

"If it doesn't devour the oxygen here. But we're not getting caught like Ross was. Evan is not going to do us in!"

Another thought hit her hard. She'd almost said that Evan was not going to do us in, *either.* Could Evan have had something to do with Ross's death? Evan had claimed he'd never heard of him, but he was as skilled an actor as he was an arsonist.

"I'll be right back with a firebrand to ignite whatever you can't clear!" she shouted.

"What? No! Lauren, you can't — don't go . . ."

But she was off at a run toward the nearest burning bush.

Evan was exhausted but exhilarated as he reached the edge of the logging camp and gazed back into the tinderbox canyon with the smoke-filled Vermillion Valley behind it.

Magnificent in its power, the inferno lit the sky with its fury. Tall, blowing columns of gray-black smoke and tongues of golden flame filled his view and his vision for his future. His enemies were sacrifices to the

417

power of the fire and to his own might: his father, Brad of the FBI, and maybe Lauren, too. Sad about Nicky, though. Evan would have considered taking on a boy with that fine an imagination. Yes, he could have taught him all he knew.

He tore his gaze away and forced himself to survey the central open area of the camp behind him. Tall piles of logs lay waiting to be moved and sold — or, in this case, burned. Huge machines that did the bidding of the men who timbered in these mountains were parked nearby. Yes, he'd burn this place, too, sending a blaze into the forested mountains. He would then get down to the service road Lauren had mentioned and hike out to a new life.

He laughed and looked back into the canyon, where he saw two figures struggle from the periphery of smoke, staggering toward the camp, almost on the same path he'd just used. At first he thought it could be Brad and his father, but —

He didn't know the burly man, but whoever he was, he had rescued Evan's father from the flames! Oh well, in many of the great tragic operas, the dying singer came back to life for a swan song before croaking for good. Now he'd simply have to find a way to write the epilogue to his masterpiece tragedy by eliminating — in an appropriate, clever way — anyone who emerged from that glorious conflagration.

Dee was shocked to see Chuck himself meet their chopper when it put down by the dock. And she was even more surprised when, despite his sling and bandages, he held her to him the moment she ran out from under the rotors.

"I couldn't believe it when Agent Connors said you had gone instead of her!" he cried.

She hugged him hard, pressing herself against him as she had not done in months. "I thought I could help find them, but we couldn't. All we saw was Nicky's coat floating in the lake. Chuck, I think her plane was down there. We heard the gas tank explode."

"That doesn't mean they were with the plane. Lauren's a smart woman."

"But who knows what the arsonist did to them. And if that was her plane, he could be on foot out there somewhere, doing his damndest to make things worse."

"Come on back to town," he urged and led her toward a car Steve was driving. "This fire's got a red alert now — all kinds of help being flown in. They were going to set up their command at the lumber camp, but they figure it's in the path of the fire now, so they're hunkering down here for the duration. It's best, Dee, 'cause it'll protect the town if the flames spread around the mountain or come rushing this way. The weather report says the wind should shift soon. Then we'll see what we have on our hands. Meanwhile, you and I've got to make up time — just make up."

She let him put her in the back seat of the car. Slowly, still guarding his shoulder, he got in beside her.

"Suze was really shook when she heard you went in the rescue chopper, Mom," Steve told her. "She went to get Larson, and he keeps asking where his buddy Nicky is."

"And I keep wondering where Lauren is. Chuck, if they're lost out there, I'll just die!"

Stunned by the hot wind that slapped her, Lauren grabbed a two-foot limb that looked to be only half on fire. The unburned part was hot, though, and she had to steel herself to hang on to it. She turned and tore back toward the rock, surprised to see that Brad was coming after her.

But when he saw her returning, he did as she had ordered, and started yanking brush away from the rock, even climbing it to heave off bundles of sticks and grass that someone — Red, or David Durand? — had piled up there. With her flaming brand she quickly lit everything he threw down, then darted from bush to nearby bush, lighting them.

Is this how Evan Durand felt when he burned something? she wondered. It sickened her, but it must thrill him.

Huge silver ashes continued to rain down along with embers. The smoke was thickening. She could see flames that now flanked the canyon on both sides where vegetation, maybe seeking shade, had grown along the paths they had been on earlier.

"Lauren — now!" she heard Brad scream as the winds increased their turbulence and almost lifted her off her feet.

Was this how it had been for Ross in the last minutes of his life? She was grateful her brain no longer bombarded her with the horrible scenes of his death. Even in this hellish inferno Evan had promised, she was not swept back again into her living nightmare.

She ran toward Brad. She wanted to live, wanted to help him stop the man who had done this. She wanted to find her son and to tell Brad how much he meant to her.

She expected he would lead her up on top of the large rock where they could lie flat as the fire passed over and around them, but he grabbed her and pointed at a split in the side of the stone away from the fire. He wedged her in face-first, pushing her into a triangular-shaped cleft, so that she was standing with her back to the opening. Then he shoved in tight behind her.

"This is good," she cried to encourage him. "We're in the black. It's not like having an aluminum survival tent, but —"

"Save air!" he ordered, nuzzling the top of her head with his chin as he fitted close behind her. She could feel his shoulder holster pressing against her back. Where had his precious duffel bag gone? He managed to get one hand between her and the stone at the level of her waist. He held her there firmly, his fingers on her bare flesh under the T-shirt she still had over her mouth and nose. He pressed his thighs against her bottom. It took her back to the day he had protected her as they'd climbed down from the fire tower and she'd felt faint.

She felt faint now. Her head was spinning.

Even in the shelter of the rock, they heard, as well as felt, the conflagration coming. The sound of it was like a freight train with its wheels ripping by right above their heads.

Lauren worked one hand free and took the hand that gripped her shoulder. As they interlocked their fingers tight, she felt so close to him. He had been so good for her in the short time they'd had together.

It was hard to breathe. If they died like this — suffocated or burned — would anyone ever find them? Or would they be wedged here, hidden, their bones like those of the Blackfeet, together in this sacred area for all eternity? Suddenly, strangely, the thought of such horror didn't scare her at all.

But Nicky needed her.

Sweat poured into her eyes, making them sting. She thought she could smell singed hair. Save air, he'd told her, maybe the last words he'd ever say.

Save air, she chanted to herself. Save air, save air, save us.

She tried to breathe slow and shallow. Smoke seeped in, worse, thicker as the temperature rose. Save air.

Lauren tried to picture swimming in Lost Lake, so cold, so good. To remember skiing down the slopes, breathing in the brisk cold, the frosty air in her face.

She felt someone shift behind her, come closer. Brad, taking care of her. From the first moment she'd seen him in the airport coffee shop, coming to help, he had taken her breath away . . . taken her air.

The fireplace was putting out too much smoke and heat as she and Nicky roasted hot dogs and then gooey marshmallows to make s'mores . . . if Brad would only stay with them . . . He knew a lot about fires, and he'd built one inside of her.

She wasn't sure, but she thought he said, "I love you, Lauren," before she stepped into the void of utter blackness.

22

Brad was kissing her and murmuring her name . . . Pressing close over her . . .

Lauren opened her eyes. Was it night? No, the sky was seething gray.

"Lauren, thank God," he gasped, pressing his cheek to hers.

She sucked in a breath of sooty air and started to cough. Was Brad crying? Maybe it was just the smoke, the fire — the fire that might have hurt Nicky.

Brad must not have been kissing her, but using mouth-to-mouth to make her breathe . . .

"Did I faint?"

"I was scared I'd lost you. The winds shifted. The flames went by us, then came back. The fire's turned on itself. It's not out but it's better now."

"Are you burned?" she cried, trying to get up. Her hands were black with charred soil, with soot. Her head spun. He helped her up and she leaned against him, dizzy. She felt so dizzy.

"My jacket roasted right off my back when the winds changed," he said. His voice was a rough whisper. He coughed every few words. "The fire went past us, then came back," he repeated, as if he, too, was dazed. "Behind us it seemed temporarily stalled. I don't know if the shift is permanent, but we have to try to get to the lumber camp. If Red went that way, it's got to be the best way out. Do you think you can walk?"

"If I have to, I can run."

But her legs were wobbly, and they had to walk together at first. He held her hard to his side, as if they were in a three-legged race. Then, up ahead, on both sides of the canyon, she saw green trees and unburned brush edging the lumber camp.

"Out of hell into heaven," she gasped.

"This is where the wind turned it back. There are hot spots, pockets of fire still. Unless we get some planes dropping water or retardant in here, this area might ignite, too. But yeah, it's a paradise compared to what we've been through."

The air was better here, pumping in from the forested mountains beyond the camp. They tried to breathe deeply of it, but her throat felt so raw even that hurt. The stench of smoke and death sat in her stomach.

"We can't just go rushing in," he said as he steered them along the lower path of the canyon's eastern edge, "in case Evan's at the camp."

"If he's there, it's probably only to find the service road and escape. He must know people are after him. If he lights another fire, it will give away his position."

"No, I'd bet all this has only whetted his psychopathic appetite for more. He believes he's invincible. And, I swear, that's why we're gonna get him."

We, he'd said. He must mean his team, but they weren't here. Anger at Evan and strength to help Brad poured back into her. Reluctantly letting go of his hand on the narrow, shaded trail where they had to walk single file, Lauren steadied her legs — and her heart — and went on.

Evan figured he had time to break into the office in the center of the camp. Each building, he'd noted, was clearly identified with a carved, wooden sign. He'd literally held the key to Vermillion — those to Lauren's and the sheriff's houses, at least — and he wanted to see if he could find any here. These big, sleeping monsters, with their shovels and sharp blades entranced him.

427

Before he lit other fires, he could picture himself riding one of these to mow his father down.

He headed for the log cabin–style edifice labeled Main Office. Beside the building, on a post, was a metal State of Montana Historical Landmarks sign, which read in part,

In this area, including the lower reaches of the Nizitopi and Jefferson Mountains, the Blackfeet tribe once buried the bones of their dead. The spirits of these great people, including their powerful Chief White Calf, are said to yet inhabit this sacred area.

"Perfectamente," Evan muttered. "Just like my stage character, White Calf. Once again, I'm in like a ghost, out like a ghost." He laughed, but the thought made him shiver, too. He was fated to burn his father's body near here, not down on that rock in the canyon.

Evan broke the window of the office with a piece of log and smiled as he listened to the crash of the glass. Not quite the same sound as when a roaring house fire shattered windows, but music to his ears anyway. He found the keys hanging on hooks

428

in the office, all nicely labeled: delimber, skidder, dozer, feller, knuckle boom and crane. Now if only someone had been kind enough to identify the big beasts, too. But he was just going to have to guess which was which.

He took the keys labeled skidder and crane and rushed back outside. As he saw the two men staggering over the slight rise to the camp, he found the machine that took the key for the skidder. Boasting massive tires, the dusty, yellow vehicle looked like a huge tractor with a sharp shovel in front. It was something like the dozers he'd seen scrape vegetation from the path of a blaze to help hotshot crews make a firebreak. He climbed into the cab and crouched, peeking out to see what his father and his father's rescuer would do. Then, his hand shaking with excitement, he fumbled to fit the key in the ignition.

Imagine, another chance to kill his father! The man with him looked big and burly, though he was no spring chicken. Could he be someone from this camp? Too late, Evan realized he should have cut the phone lines, but he'd been so intent on the keys. At least he'd made so few mistakes that, hopefully, this one wouldn't matter.

The key slid smoothly into the ignition.

Just to be sure he had all the protection he would need, Evan pulled his gun from the pocket of his camos.

The men were close under him, panting hard, their sentences punctuated by gasps. The lumberjack-looking guy was saying, ". . . call for help . . . tell them what your son did so . . ."

Then he heard his father's voice, one he thought he'd never hear again — never wanted to. "Thank God the wind shifted, or we might not have made it out. We'll tell the FBI, too . . ."

Evan studied the dashboard controls of the skidder: steering wheel, stick shift, pedals. He'd turn it on and roll it right over them. But what if they made it to the safety of the office? He'd hate to waste time trying to knock the building down to get to them. Besides, there could be a back way out.

Damn, he'd left the office door open and one window was shattered, so they'd smell a trick. What was the matter with him? It infuriated him that the winds had indeed shifted to stop the progress of the valley and canyon fires. He had to start new ones here, quickly, before those who would interfere came. Once his father summoned help, he'd have to leave his life's work unfinished here, and he could not allow that.

Instead of using the skidder to chase them, he realized he needed to move stealthily and quietly — especially to get control of that big man. Leaving the key in the ignition, Evan dropped from the cab to the ground and tiptoed after the men, drawing his gun.

If he could just tie them up, it would be much easier, so much quicker. And once their remains were shoveled by this big skidder to the edge of the camp, he'd start the first fire there, right on top of them. He so wanted his father to have his funeral pyre.

Just before Brad and Lauren started up the slight rise that would take them to the lumber camp, he stopped and turned to her. Breathing hard, they leaned together. They both looked like hell, but that hardly mattered. And he knew she was even more exhausted than he.

He'd been terrified she'd actually suffocated, jammed in the rock during the onslaught of the fire. But she'd only fainted and had come right back with mouth-to-mouth. Lauren Taylor was a fighter, but he could not bear for her — or Nick — to be hurt anymore. He needed not only to corner Evan Durand, but to get Lauren in touch with rescue operations so that he could prove to her that her son was safe. He had to be!

"Okay, partner, let's lay some recon plans," he told her. He almost didn't recognize his own raspy voice. "We know Red and David Durand headed here, but we have to assume, from what you said, that Evan might have, too. I'm just hoping Durand's pilot is all right. If he's still here, he'll have a radio that we can use. If not, are there phones here?"

"Yes, in the main office. And they use two-ways when the teams are out harvesting or in the vehicles. Steve gave the boys a tour this summer, so I know the layout of the place pretty well."

He expelled a rush of air through flared nostrils. Then he might do well to take her in with him, he realized, though he wanted to keep her here until he surveilled the area.

"Unfortunately," he told her, "Evan's M.O. has included cutting phone wires, so we can't risk just waltzing into camp and trying to find a phone. For all we know, he could have laid a trap, so —"

They both jumped and instinctively ducked at the sharp crack of a gun. Did it echo off the rocks or had someone shot twice?

"Where was that from?" she asked, gripping his arm.

"The camp. Does Red carry a gun?"

"A hunting rifle sometimes."

"That wasn't a rifle. So much for plans about how we'll recon the place. You stay here. I'll try to sneak up on Evan," he told her and drew his gun.

"Where are your other guns? I could help."

"My bag with them burned up. You stay here."

"Listen! What's that sound?"

"Maybe one of the big vehicles starting. Could he drive out of here in one of those?" Brad asked as he jogged up the slight rise in the path, Lauren right behind him.

"The single, narrow service road out of here twists and turns, so he couldn't go fast and he could plunge over the side. That's why they use the log flume."

He thrust his free arm out to his side to stop her. They peeked up over the rise to the camp.

"Stay back," Brad repeated. Keeping low, darting from tree to tree, then from massive machine to machine, he carefully worked his way closer to the heart of the camp. The chopper he'd arrived in was sitting on the landing pad, but it looked empty. He wondered if the pilot was anywhere around. Maybe he was hiding so he didn't get shot.

When Brad peered around a machine — one with huge blades with SLASHER written on its side — he *finally* got a good look at Evan Durand, alias BND and Rocky Marston. The trouble was, he held a gun on his father and evidently on Red, too, though Brad could only see the Durands. Brad didn't have a clear shot at Evan from this spot, nor could he shift his position without being seen.

But Brad could see that the arsonist was dark-haired with a good tan, just as Lauren had described him. His camo fatigues may have once been green and brown, but they were now smeared by soot and charcoal. He was a villain all in black.

Despite his bad position, Brad was actually tempted to just try to shoot the bastard. But he wanted him alive to stand trial, to be studied so that they could find out what made such a sicko tick. He had to stop Evan before he harmed anyone else or set another fire.

When Evan turned his head slightly away, Brad shuffled slowly to his left. Since Evan controlled Red and David Durand, this had become a hostage situation with new rules. Too bad he'd never taken sniper training at Quantico.

Slowly, Brad sidestepped farther. Holding

a gun on his two prisoners, Evan was evidently forcing his father to pull the big, inert body of Red Russert — shot or dead? — into the lowered, front shovel of a tractor-like machine that was already running. Its glassed-in cab was set high on huge tires, but the wide shovel had been lowered to ground level.

Struggling with his rage, fearful that Evan could have killed Red, Brad pressed himself behind the cab of the crane likely used to lift logs to the flume overhead. Even now, he could hear the rush of water within the elevated wooden trough. Just before he could dart closer, he heard something behind him and spun back.

Damn! Lauren had followed him into the camp and was hunkered down behind one of the tresses supporting the flume.

He gestured broadly and mouthed at her, *I said, stay back!*

Her mouth formed the words *I am!*

Brad glared at her before turning back to assess whether to rush Evan or wait to see what he was up to. If he'd already shot or knocked out Red — and Brad couldn't imagine the guy cooperating — he had to move fast.

But just as Durand bent over to lift and drag Red, Evan hit him on the head with the butt of the gun so that he crumpled into the shovel beside Red. Praying Lauren would stay where she was, holding his gun up with both arms stiff in front of him, Brad rushed Evan's position.

"FBI!" he shouted. "Drop the gun, Durand! Hands in the air!"

But Evan wheeled, ducked and shot as he darted to the other side of the big machine. The shot went wide, pinging off metal somewhere nearby; Brad kept charging.

He saw Evan's head appear in the tall cab of the bulldozer. The machine roared to life, lifting the shovel with the two unconscious men inside, and jerkily started off, away from Brad's position.

His first instinct was to shoot out the glass in the cab. But what if he hit or killed Evan? He wanted him alive. And what if that made the machine, with Red and Durand in the raised shovel, go over the edge of the camp or crush them to death?

The bulldozer wasn't fast, though he supposed Evan had it going full tilt. By jogging, Brad could keep close to it as it rolled on its huge tires toward the Mt. Nizitopi side of the camp. The dozer took out a bush or two and bumped the bottom of a fifteen-foot pile of logs that began to roll.

His gun still raised to keep Evan in his

sights, Brad ran out and around the thudding, bouncing, cut and delimbed tree trunks. He looked back to see where Lauren was, but in the avalanche of logs, he didn't see her anywhere.

"The incident commander's here, Dad!" Steve shouted in the front door of the house. Dee scrambled off Chuck's lap where they'd been sitting half sprawled, half embracing on the sofa.

"Send him in!" Chuck yelled and gave Dee's bottom a quick pat.

"Please," she said as she straightened her shirt, "ask him to send whatever choppers he has in to look for Nicky and Lauren."

"You know I will. We out of coffee yet?"

"I'll get you some."

Their gazes held before she turned away, and he went to greet the man who would coordinate the wildfire-fighting operations. As they'd been praying for, the wind had shifted when the temperatures rose after dawn, sending the fire back upon itself to partly burn out.

As Dee fixed coffee and food in the kitchen, Suze and Larson came down from upstairs. "Are they going in after Lauren and Nicky?" Suze asked.

"The cavalry just rolled in," Dee said.

"Actually, I was trying to overhear what they were saying to your father."

"I can go listen!" Larson volunteered. "I want to know if I can go with them to find Nicky."

"You're not going anywhere near that fire, buddy," Suze told him. "Let's just you and I sit here quietly at the table and make Mrs. Gates a get-well card so your grandma can eavesdrop."

"Does that mean drop on the floor and listen real easy to what people are saying? 'Cause Nicky and me, we've done that."

"I'll bet you have," Dee told him, feeling sick over Nicky and Lauren again. "But I don't plan to drop to the floor," she told him, trying to sound normal, in control. She was shaking so hard inside she might just drop to her knees in desperate prayer that not only Nicky and Lauren, but Brad, too, might be safe out there somewhere.

Lauren gasped as the cascade of piled logs rolled at her. She'd been trying to keep Brad in sight but not stay right behind him. Had Evan intentionally bumped the lower, supporting logs, or had he hit them because he wasn't used to driving that big skidder? They were tumbling like Nicky's Lincoln

Logs, which he used to build forts and castles.

Lauren ran, but they kept coming at her. At least the rumbling pile slowed as it leveled out, but Evan just kept going. And Brad must have been far enough ahead to miss getting crushed.

She fell, but scrambled on all fours until she got to her feet again. She threw herself behind the slasher and let it take the hits of the logs that rolled this far. Against the big vehicle, they bumped and thudded until there was just dust and silence.

To her surprise, Brad came running around the corner.

"You all right?" he asked.

"At least he won't be burning that pile of wood," she told him, trying to sound bold. "Let's go, FBI!"

He nodded and ran around the now-wide pool of logs with her right behind him. "Next time I say stay back," he said, "I mean it."

"Roger that."

But they gasped when they saw that Evan had dumped both Red and his father on another pile of logs, one about six feet tall, under a long wooden shed. Lauren shaded her eyes to see what Evan was going to do next and recognized the shape of what he was holding up in the glass cab of the truck.

"He's got his drip torch out!" she cried. "He's going to start a fire there! Can you shoot at him through that glass?"

She watched as Brad ran closer and pointed his gun at the glass window of the skidder cab. He shot. It shattered around Evan, but he still managed to launch flames into the pile of logs. Then he leaned out to shoot a line of flaming oil and fire at Brad, all the while laughing.

Brad jumped back, then shot at Evan again. Bending low, Evan hunched down in the cab and headed the skidder toward the trees at the foot of Mount Nizitopi. Brad scrambled up the end of the flaming pile of logs to drag first Red, then David Durand down. Lauren rushed to help, pulling Red away from the spreading flames while Brad hauled the screaming Durand to the ground. He looked woozy; he was bleeding from a blow to the head.

"Red's breathing!" she shouted to Brad over Durand's hysteria. "He has a pulse, but he's been shot. He's bleeding from his belly."

"Durand!" Brad yelled in the other man's face. "Durand!" He slapped the man hard to shut him up. "You're safe now and Lauren's going to stay with you. Lauren,

see what you can do for Red. I'll be back
with him soon. And I mean it this time —
stay back."

23

Lauren ignored the trembling, cursing Durand and turned immediately to Red. He was conscious now, obviously racked by pain, but not making half as much noise as the other man.

"Not been shot for years," Red ground out through clenched teeth.

"What can I do to help?" she asked, leaning over him.

"Get me a hospital room with Mari."

She blinked back tears at his grit and devotion. "I think I should try to stop the bleeding, but I don't want to hurt you."

"It already hurts. Do it. Lauren? In more ways than one time counts."

"The only chopper here doesn't have fuel, or, I think, a pilot. But help should come soon. I'm sure it will come soon."

"If we — have to wait — don't know."

"I've got a horrible headache, but I'm hiking out of here down the service road," David Durand interrupted. "I'll send help. Where is that — the road?" He was hunkered down as if to use Lauren for a shield. "Evan's tried to kill me twice, and I've got to protect myself."

"Red can't wait that long for you to send help. Hiking down could take over an hour."

"I'm not staying here where I'm a target!"

"Then shut up," she ordered, "or Evan just might find you again. And don't mind Red here. He only saved your life in the canyon, didn't he? But there is a way to get to the highway fast — though you'll get soaked."

"Fine with me after nearly being roasted twice," he said, glowering at her and holding his head with both hands. "You — you mean down the flume?"

"Yes — with Red. You and I can get him up the service steps to the top. No logs are in it when the men aren't working. The flow of water is cut way back clear down to the holding ponds. Those are just off the highway that connects Vermillion to Kalispell. And firefighting or rescue vehicles should be on the road to give Red help."

"But he's bleeding bad," Durand whined. "You don't mean I should get him down that way by myself, do you? I couldn't hold him all the way down in a flume. Now, if you go with me, Lauren, I —"

"She can't leave Brad, Durand!" Red muttered through clenched teeth. "Just shut up and do it."

Lauren was certain Red would have told the man off if he didn't need him.

"Come on, Mr. Durand," Lauren urged. "You drag Red as carefully as you can to the bottom of the service stairs while I go look for bandages in the office. The door's open there. Wait for me. I'll bandage him and help you get him up top so the two of you can slide down together. Okay?"

"Yeah, sure." Still crouched, Durand alternately glared at her and scanned the area. She too was getting jumpy at the mere thought of new fires Evan could be setting. And she thought she smelled fresh smoke.

"But," Durand went on, pointing a bloody index finger nearly in her face, "I so much as catch a glimpse of my demented son again and I'm running for it, Red or not."

"Brad's gone after Evan. I'm sure he'll have him under arrest soon, but his drip torch is as bad as a flamethrower."

"Don't lecture me about drip torches."

She wanted to tell Durand off again, but, as Red had said, time mattered. She got up to go for bandages but couldn't resist one more comment. "I'm sure you're an expert of the same caliber on drip torches as you were on the Coyote Canyon fire in California."

Leaving him sputtering behind her, she headed for the camp office. She could hear the growl of the skidder even more distant. Worse, she could see fresh flames licking at the sky beyond the burning pile of logs Evan had already set aflame.

Brad saw that Evan had run the bulldozer into a barrier of brush and trees at the foot of Mount Nizitopi, but he'd done worse damage with his drip torch. Fire after new fire flared, then burst into flame, spreading through the parched foliage. Brad could even follow the maniac's path by where new blazes were springing up.

He was tempted to get up into the still-running machine and use it to scrape out a firebreak that would cut off the flames from the logging camp and the mountain itself. With the new wind direction, if the fire got a good start up and around Nizitopi, the conflagration could threaten the ski lodge, then Vermillion itself. But he'd followed his heart once before, in going with Lauren to find Nick, rather than pursue Evan, and he had to stop him now, one way or the other, once and for all.

Still holding his gun, exhausted but with adrenaline and rage rampaging through him, he tore toward the spot where the next blaze was breaking out.

Lauren found a large first-aid kit in the back room of the office. She grabbed tape, bandages and antiseptic and started away, then went back for scissors.

A phone sat on the desk. Undecided whether to take the time to make a call — and terrified she might hear that Nicky was still missing — she hesitated, then grabbed the receiver and punched in Dee's number. To Lauren's relief, Dee's familiar voice came on right away.

"Fire Command."

"Dee, it's Lauren."

"Oh, thank God, thank God! Chuck, it's Lauren! Where are you?"

"Brad and I are at the lumber camp. Red's hurt and Evan's starting more fires, so send help up here. Did the rescue planes get Nicky? He was with my plane on the shore of the little lake where the valley meets the canyon."

Silence. Had the phone gone dead? Was Dee crying?

"Dee!"

"A lot of help has just arrived. They'll be

heading up there and to you, Lauren. I was in a plane that flew over that area, but the smoke . . ."

"What about Nicky? Did you see Nicky? I think my plane exploded! He had on his red coat. He'd be easy to spot. Dee . . ."

"I'm not sure. I'm —"

Lauren's legs gave out; she grabbed the edge of the desk and went to her knees. He had to be all right. Had to.

The phone dangled by its twisted cord. She could hear Dee's voice on the other end, crying her name.

Lauren forced herself to her feet, gathered up the first-aid supplies and staggered out the door. She found Red exactly where she'd asked Durand to deliver him and bent over him quickly, pulling up his blood-soaked shirt. It looked like a single bullet hole but there was very little blood around it. His shirt must have taken most of it. Or was he bleeding internally?

"Wha's matter," Red asked, staring at her strangely. His voice was much more feeble than before and he was slurring his words. "You look bad, Lau'n. He start mo' fires?"

"Yes, but Brad will get him. Red, I'm going to spray your wound with this antiseptic, then pad and wrap it before you have to take that ride down. I talked to Dee. Help

447

is coming but —" she sniffed hard "— just like earlier today, the smoke could hamper rescue efforts. I told them where we are though, so maybe if they get here fast, we won't have to use the flume. Where's Durand?"

"Said go'ng up top — take look . . ."

"Durand!" she shouted, craning her neck to look up the stairs that led to the top of the flume. "Come down here! I need help with Red!"

In a near whisper almost muted by the crackle of increasing flames, Red asked, "Dee say — 'bout Mari?"

"No, but she's as tough as you are. You two deserve each other. Durand should have stayed with you, though I can't blame him for being afraid. Anyone with half a brain would have to be afraid of Ev—"

"You know, dear Lauren," a voice said from behind her. "I think that's the sweetest thing I've ever heard you say."

She jerked her head around to see Evan standing there, the gun still in his hand, his drip torch cradled in the other arm.

"Your father's escaping, Evan," she told him, desperate to keep him from focusing on her and Red. She forced herself not to beg where Brad was, nor to stop wrapping Red's midriff. Keep moving calmly, she told herself. Unless Red was suddenly playing possum, he'd passed out again. But it was just as well, because she must be hurting him terribly.

"Where is he?" Evan demanded.

"He's gone up on the flume to escape to the road below. Maybe you'd better go aft—"

"He left the old man and you? Doesn't that show what a self-centered antihero he is in this drama? Now you see what I've been up against all these years."

His voice was calm but, to her horror, he lifted and pointed the nozzle of the drip torch at them. Then he raised it higher to shoot a spike of flame at the wooden footers of the flume's supporting trestle just a few feet from where Red lay.

Lauren gave a scream that tore at her raw throat. The base of the supporting beams and girders caught fire, and the ladder quickly became a torch.

As she struggled to drag Red back from it, she saw that Evan had managed to nearly encircle the logging camp in flames. Where was Brad? If this was as bad as it looked, Evan had just burned the access to their last way out.

I'm trapped! Brad thought. Evan had enticed him, whether he'd meant to or not, behind a wall of flame outside the camp. He cursed how this whole area was a big tinderbox. And he blamed himself for not shooting Evan the moment he had a bead on his head in the cab of the bulldozer. Lauren was with Durand and Red on the other side of the flames somewhere . . .

His first instinct was to run up the slope of Nizitopi away from the mushrooming fire. But Lauren had told him that might have been Ross's fatal mistake. She'd said it was better to run through a fire than from it.

At that thought, his legs went weak for one moment. Fear of the orange, gold and red monster devouring everything in sight drove him to his knees. He'd tried to fight fire and catch its creators, but he was now reduced to nothing by its power. Please, dear Lord, he didn't want to die. He wanted to live, to help Lauren and Nick, to save Vermillion and stop the murderer who had made this inferno.

From here, the wall of flames looked twice his height. How wide it was he wasn't sure, but he could not afford to give it more time to grow, to be fed by air funneled between the mountains.

Brad kept his shoes and charred jeans on,

but he stripped off his burned jacket and shirt so that the loose cloth wouldn't catch fire. He threw away his gun in case the bullets in it exploded. Scrabbling under a thick pile of dried leaves, he clawed up handfuls of clay soil and smeared it on his forehead, face, chest and arms, praying it might provide some protection.

He knew it was now or never. As he started to run toward the conflagration, pictures paraded through his stunned brain: he was on his horse, Sam, riding with his parents in the forests near Denver; he was flying with Lauren; he was eating dinner with her and Nick . . .

Now or never!

Hands covering his face, holding his breath, praying he didn't run smack into a burning tree through the thick scrim of smoke, Brad ran downhill and vaulted into the fierce face of the flames.

"I hope that stopped him!" Evan shouted as the top section of the flume collapsed and a column of water splattered the ground farther down the slope. "I'm afraid my sire is like a cat, Lauren — nine lives, or at least three so far, no thanks to all of you."

She saw that he was trembling, but whether from excitement or exhaustion she wasn't sure. The hand pointing the gun at her and Red shook as he cradled the drip torch again. She hoped Evan didn't know that Red had saved his father.

"You know, Evan," she said, fighting to keep her voice calm, praying Brad would soon appear from somewhere like an avenging angel. "I understand now why you hated your father. He's pushy and acts superior, and —"

"That's not the half of it."

"I don't think he's much of an expert witness, either," she went on, carefully touching the pulse at the side of Red's neck. She wasn't sure what would be normal for a man of his age and size who was bleeding internally, but his pulse was slowing. Pretending to be smoothing the bandage on Red, while still maintaining eye contact with Evan, she surreptitiously checked Red's pockets for anything she could use against Evan. Somehow, somewhere, she'd lost the knife that was in her sock.

"I think your father did a terrible job testifying at the Coyote Canyon hearings," she went on.

To her amazement, Evan grinned. From this angle, with his face all blackened, his expression reminded her of a gargoyle's with its strange blend of grotesque humor and horror.

A pocketknife? Her hand closed around it and drew it carefully out of Red's pocket. It was closed, but if she could get it open, then get closer to Evan before he used that gun . . .

"You're absolutely right," Evan was saying. "He did a dreadful job at those hearings. Now that you mention it, I wish I'd had time to tell him that and why."

Despite blasts of heat from the encroaching flames, Lauren felt icy chills leap up her spine. "You could tell me now," she said, hoping she didn't do anything to draw him from the near trance he seemed to be in. He was staring at her, but his eyes were not focused on her. He must be seeing other times, other people and places.

"You know," Evan went on, "although that fire didn't begin as an arson fire, I do believe it was further spread that way."

"What do you mean? You said you weren't there, you didn't know my husband," she cried, trying to keep her voice in check.

"Yes, I was there on a hotshot crew and I knew Ross but not well. Like you, he was a meddler, someone I had to simply write out of the script."

"How?" she said, getting off her knees and

slowly standing. She held the pocketknife at her side, just behind her right thigh. It had a thick handle, probably with other items besides the blade recessed there. Which one was the blade? How could she open it with just one hand, especially now that what he was implying about Ross made her shake as hard as Evan was.

"I don't have time for this," he said, focusing on her face again. "And neither do you."

"Tell me, Evan! Tell me what really happened that your father got all wrong."

"All wrong — all right!" he said with a crooked grin. "The expert witness, the all-knowing David Durand, did not know that I had, let's say, encouraged the fire after it was started by other causes. The stupid idiots were using fire to sculpt the forests for safety's sake and things just got out of hand. Ha! But Ross Taylor suspected me of spreading those flames — with this very drip torch, actually. He was going to turn me in, I'm sure of it. And I think he told that friend of his, too."

"You set a fire to trap them?"

"I had to knock them out first with this drip torch. Then I took their personal shelters, and just let nature take its course. But I didn't set the original fire to trap them, I didn't assign them to their posts on the fire line and I didn't do any more than knock each of them over the head. That's hardly murder, so don't look at me that way!"

Stunned, she stared wide-eyed at him, then at the drip torch. Ross's killer and the murder weapon. All this time, her gnawing doubts had been fact. This psychopath had dared to come to Vermillion, somehow befriend their son and get into their home. Then he dared to tell her the horrors he had committed.

"Now, Lauren, I'm going to ask you to run back down the hill into the canyon toward Nicky," he said, aiming the gun at her. "If there's any way still out of here, that may be it. The inferno was too great earlier for you to get to him, wasn't it? And if he's still there, be a good mother and don't nag or try to squelch his fine imagination. If you do, you'll pay dearly. Maybe you should pay dearly now."

Suddenly, she couldn't take any more from this man. He'd killed women, he'd killed Ross and Kyle. His meadow fire now screaming into the valley might have taken Nicky from her. She had no idea where Brad was in this new firestorm that might devour entire forests and her town. If this maniac shot her, that was that, but she had to get her hands on him, get this knife in him if she could, or just claw his eyes out . . .

Though she saw only flames coming closer behind Evan, she cried, "Oh, Brad, thank God you're here!"

Evan spun. She dug out the first two inserted pieces on the knife and ran at him, stabbing, swinging.

He screeched in shock as they went down. His gun flew off somewhere. Cutting his chest and shoulder, she kicked and pulled his hair with her free hand. She was so dizzy, so beside herself with rage, she thought at first that Evan had bested her and was yanking her up off the ground. But it was Brad. Brad, naked to the waist, Brad looking worse than he had before — but Brad!

Evan was screaming and bleeding. Brad set Lauren on the ground near Red, yanked Evan to his feet, then pulled his arms behind him and tied them with the roll of bandages she'd left on the ground. Brad kicked Evan's feet wide apart and started to pat him down.

"I stabbed him," Lauren said. "He told me he killed Ross. He — I had to stop him from killing us . . ." She held out Red's knife toward Brad. "I stabbed him with —" She

456

gapcd at what was in her hand. She had attacked him with only a corkscrew and a bottle opener.

"We've got him now. Any one of the things he's done will put him away for good. But Ross? Lauren, sweetheart, at least you know now. How's Red?"

She felt his pulse again. "I'm shaking so much, I can't tell. Weak, I know that, very weak."

"Hey, FBI agent. Hey, Lauren," Evan said, "I'm really just a Blackfeet spirit — a ghost, that's what I told Nicky. In like a ghost, out like a ghost."

"You can try to convince a judge or jury about that, Durand," Brad muttered. He came up with a key from Evan's pocket and squinted to read what was on it.

"But how are we going to get out?" Lauren said as reality slapped at her like the waves of heat pulsing from the encroaching flames. "Dee said choppers will arrive soon, but they're going to have the same problem here they must have had looking for Nicky with all this drifting smoke. She said they don't have him back yet, Brad."

It terrified her to see how distraught he looked, how suddenly defeated, despite the fact he'd finally caught BND. Tears burned her eyes again as she looked and pointed upward. "Evan burned the steps to the top of the flume when I said that was how his father got out of here."

"Durand left you and Red here?" Brad exploded. "I wondered where he was. I swear, I'll arrest him, too, but now we'll just have to take a page from BND's arson book of tricks."

She could see how that perked Evan up. Though he was bleeding from his chest wounds, his glazed look departed; he quit sniveling and grimacing.

"Backfires will do you no good here, FBI," Evan said, his voice cocky. "It's too late to use these machines to build a firebreak. You could try to survive by staying in the black in the middle of this camp, but I think the log piles and wooden buildings will just plain burn you out and you'll have nowhere to go. What a great finale and —"

Brad jammed some bandages into Evan's mouth and shoved him to his knees. Keeping an eye on him, he took a few steps away and retrieved Evan's gun from the ground, checking its clip to see if it was loaded.

"Hold this gun on the prisoner," he told Lauren, putting it in her hand. "Shoot him if he so much as moves — and I know you'll do it. I'll be watching through the window of the crane cab. I've got to rig our way out of here."

She watched as Brad climbed into the cab. Just beyond, water still spewed to the ground where Evan's drip torch had burned part of the long trough of the elevated flume. For the first time she noticed that the water had also put out some of the newer flames below their position, but not enough to stop the growing inferno on the hillside. She wondered how much water was being fed in from the secondary source a bit farther down the rest of the flume, which still stood.

Then, over the noise of the crane engine, she heard another sound. In the sky? A huge roar, coming closer. Not a chopper, but surely some sort of firefighting plane. Maybe Brad didn't hear it since he was obviously concentrating on moving the boom of the crane up and down.

She realized now what he might intend. He could lift them up in the big clawlike tongs of the crane to the unburned section of the flume, but then how would he get up there himself?

She wanted to tell him about the plane she heard coming, but she had to keep the gun on Evan. Hands tied behind his back, gagged, still on his knees with his legs spread for balance, he too was looking upward, waiting. She waved at Brad and pointed up at the sky, hoping he'd see her and realize what she meant as he lowered the top of the crane to just a few feet off the ground.

"Brad, look up!" she shouted, glancing to see if he saw her. At the last minute, she thought, he understood what she meant.

Half hidden by burgeoning smoke, a big-bellied air tanker appeared, flying low. Coming from the direction of the valley and the canyon, it roared over. In a huge wall of spray, the plane dropped a crimson-colored fire retardant. Lauren screamed and bent over Red, trying to protect him, grasping the gun in both hands to keep it pointed at Evan.

The impact of the spewing scarlet foam smacked her hands to the ground. The gun fired once, then slipped away. The foam blinded her, clinging, smothering everything as the air tanker flew onward, dumping the retardant clear across the camp.

Gasping for air, swiping the slick stuff from her face, Lauren turned back to glance at Brad. The windows of the cab looked like they ran red with blood. Would this save them, put out the flames?

She scrambled for the gun but it was so slippery. Would it shoot now? She pointed it back toward Evan, expecting to see him sprawled on the ground.

But like a vanished ghost, he was gone.

24

Lauren gasped and stared. Evan had disappeared.

She knew Brad couldn't see out the crane cab windows, but he jumped out, pressing his hands to his head. At least he wasn't covered with this goo. Leaving Red where he lay, Lauren scrambled to her feet. Brad looked around, stunned, furious. "Evan?" he rasped out.

"He was here when this stuff hit! I shot once, but I don't know if I hit him. He can't be far!" she added, slipping as she ran to cling to a supporting trestle. She looked down the hill. Under the flume itself, the foam was not so thick. "There!" she cried, pointing. "He's running — limping — down under the flume from trestle to trestle, but there's fire spreading below, even creeping up these support bars. He might be stopped or trapped by flames down there. Oh, Brad, I'm so sorry he got away again."

"Air tanker's fault — and mine," he clipped out, but he looked more angry than she'd ever seen him. "Survival time. If we don't get trapped by flames, we'll get slimed to death if that tanker makes another pass. And we can't let that flume burn out from under us, so we've got to move fast. Help me shove that small log over there into these pinchers, then you get on top of it with Red. The crane will lift it to the spot where the flume starts now. Whether we have to slide or swim down, it's our best — maybe our only — bet. As soon as we make it down, we'll get help and go after Nick — and try to find Evan again."

"But how will you get up to us?" she demanded, grabbing his arm.

"I'll climb the boom of the crane."

"It's got this stuff all over it."

"I'll do it, Lauren," he insisted, seizing both her upper arms and nearly lifting her from her feet. He looked frenzied, fierce. "And if I can't, you'll need to get Red down the flume, back to Mari Gates, then get help and find Nick. If Evan makes it down, we'll get him. If not, the world's a better place."

"I won't leave you here. I can't."

"Do what I say. Help me drag this log."

Side by side, they ended up shoving the four-foot log until the pinchers, as Brad called them, gripped it. Lauren straddled it and held Red, balanced against her. To steady herself, she leaned back against the big metal claws.

And then something went right for the first time today as Brad managed to maneuver the boom up so close to the place on the flume where the drip-torch fire had halted that she could roll Red out and clamber onto it herself. But for slippery red foam, it was dry here now, since the secondary flow of water shot in about twelve feet lower.

Hanging on to Red, she thought that, by comparison, it had been nothing to get the injured Chuck down from the mountain on the ski lift. Her thoughts spun out of control. Ross had been murdered, but Evan might never live to tell the truth. And even if he did, would he admit it to anyone but her? Nicky had to be safe or she'd just as soon throw herself off this flume into the forest burning below.

She peered down to the crane where Brad tried to climb the boom. He had it at a steep angle to reach this far and, as she'd feared, it was slippery with red retardant. But he must have found some footholds. As he inched his way up through thickening smoke, she heard the deep roar of what must be the returning air tanker.

The smoke seemed to devour Brad before he emerged from it. Lauren held out her hand to him, praying his added weight on this end of the burned, curved flume would not make it break.

Coughing, he scrambled behind her, turned her to face downward and put both legs around her almost as if she were sitting in his lap. Together they got Red positioned, feetfirst with his head against Lauren's chest, as if they were ready for a three-man bobsled run.

"We've got to get down where the water starts and fight to keep our heads up in it," Brad told her. "I think it will only be about chest deep. I'm going to hold on tight to you! Besides," he added, his voice breaking, "we could all use a bath."

As Brad had feared, the combination of foam and the gush of water below their entry point on the flume got them going faster than he wanted. He wished Red wasn't unconscious because he was dead weight, but he'd probably be in agony if he was awake. Brad had only been with the guy a few hours on their hike back from the ski lift, but they'd taken to each other well. Like with Lauren, it was as if Brad had known the people in Vermillion for longer than just a few frenzied days.

Although Brad sometimes went to see his dad in prison, he'd missed the camaraderie of an older man. Mike and Clay had never filled that void for him.

In the quick, downward rush of current, they fought to keep their heads up, but at least they were going in the same direction as the flow. The water washed the black soot and red foam from their skin and hair. Brad could feel the burns he'd been trying to ignore, but the cool flow of water still felt good.

Beneath the flume, below them, he saw that they raced the latest fires Evan had set. But that was out of his hands now. That air tanker and other help would surely be here soon to fight that battle.

"Brad — below!" Lauren cried.

He looked around her to see that a couple of logs had jammed in a slight turn in the flume. Water was piling up in little rapids ahead of it, and what couldn't get past the jam or what the flume couldn't hold was spewing over the left side. Brad feared Red and Lauren would take the brunt of the collision and they all might be rocked out, down almost twenty feet to the ground.

"Pull your legs up tight!" he shouted.

"Lean back into me and try to hold on to Red."

As she did, Brad sat straight up, hoping his bulk might slow their descent. He stuck out both legs beyond Lauren's, down to about Red's knees. The tops of trees on both sides of the flume seemed to rotate past him as time stood still. A chopper with rotors *whap-whapping* suddenly appeared to hover over them.

The buffer of water slowed them a bit more, but they hit into the small logjam with a gush. Brad managed to take the brunt of it. The two logs stuck sideways jerked but did not let loose. Water from above smacked them, shot over them and slammed off both sides of the flume.

He could see no way to get into a chopper rescue basket from here, even if they tried to lower one. Not with these logs and all this water below them ready to pop loose.

"Hold on to the side!" he yelled at Lauren. "If you have to let Red go, do it, but hang on!"

He swallowed and spit out water. How crazy would it be if they drowned in the middle of a wildfire, he thought, then remembered what Lauren said she'd told Nicky. If the fire comes, get in the water.

Brad put his arm around Lauren's waist

and clamped her to him. She tried to hold Red between her knees as she gripped the sides of the old wooden flume while Brad kicked at one log then the other.

He pulled Lauren to her knees and, together, they kept Red's face above the deluge. Weeping Wall Falls had failed them earlier, Brad thought, but damned if he was going to be done in by this flume!

Holding Red between them, they knelt against the two jammed logs in the best airspace they could find. It might have taken only a few moments, but it seemed that water battered them for hours, then sloshed over the side, the way they faced. At least it was a great way to get this lower part of the forest ready to resist the fire, he thought.

That must be what Lauren was screaming about as she looked down over the edge of the flume. Or was she having another dizzy spell like that day they'd climbed down from the old fire tower?

And then Brad saw it, too — saw both of them. About twenty feet below the flume, just above where the water cascaded out to splash the ground and run downhill, lay the charred body of Evan Durand, faceup, next to that of his father.

Brad shook his head to clear it and looked again through the rush of water. Yes, it was

Evan, burned and laid out almost formally, as if for his own funeral. The bandages with which Brad had tied his wrists had evidently burned away, for his hands were at his sides, but the gag Brad had stuffed in Evan's mouth partly stuck out, as if Evan were a cartoon character who still had something to say.

And David Durand was definitely also dead. He lay sopping wet, all twisted up as if his neck or back was broken. Evan had run through the flames and gotten this far before he lay down to die. And Durand, trying to get down the flume after deserting Lauren and Red, must have hit this logjam and rocketed out to the ground.

Was it just fate that the Durands had landed side by side? More likely Evan had stumbled across his father's broken body and decided to die there, too. Still, Brad half expected that if he closed his eyes and looked again, Evan would have disappeared.

Through the wash of air the chopper blades made, driving off the smoke right above them, Brad looked up and pointed down at the bodies. But the moment he freed one hand from holding the side of the flume, his weight shifted. The logs shuddered and let loose. The small dam of water around them gushed downward, taking them with it.

It was a thrill ride he didn't want. He reached for Lauren but snagged only her hair. She grabbed at him, gripping his ankle as they shot downward, out of control, until they landed with a flying, jolting splash amid logs in the holding pond.

Lauren spit water, but that was better than smoke. Brad? When they'd hit bottom, she'd lost Brad. And where was Red? Had they really seen Evan and his father dead up on the mountain?

Brad emerged near her in a whoosh of white water and bare skin. He was holding Red up and she staggered over to help him. The chopper must have landed nearby, because two men in jumpsuits splashed into the pond, fighting their way around logs, pushing them out of the way. She could hear another chopper landing.

"Brad Hale, FBI. This man's been shot!" Brad shouted as they sloshed toward him through hip-deep water. He gasped out his words, and his voice was not his own. "He needs . . . hospital. The bodies of the arsonist and his father . . . partway up the mountain under the flume . . . where I pointed. Tree cover's thick there. You see the fire, working its way down? Someone's got to recover the bodies before they're . . . burned beyond recognition."

"Burned beyond recognition." The words revolved in Lauren's stunned brain. Ross and Kyle had been murdered and burned beyond recognition, so was this God's justice now?

The men carried Red to the edge of the pond and handed him over to two others, dressed just as they were, who carried him away. Brad hugged her, leaned on her. Exhausted, they staggered after the men. Lauren let their rescuers help her out of the pond while Brad clambered out. Brad pulled on a nylon jacket one of the men handed him.

"Both of you have visible burns," one man said. "We're going to fly you into Vermillion and see that you're transferred to Kalispell."

"Please, my son may be back in the valley, beyond the canyon," she said, gripping the man's hand. His name on his jumpsuit read Lieutenant Tom Barton.

"We know about the boy."

"You found him?" she cried. "Did you find him?"

"We were going to put down there to search until the air tanker radioed us that there might be people on the ground at the logging camp. We thought the boy might

471

have made it that far."

"No, he didn't make it that far!" she shouted. "Brad, tell them they have to take us there, that —"

Brad scooped her up in his arms and headed for the second chopper as the one with Red took off in a whirl of dust and debris. "That's where we're going, I promise," he said. "That's where we're going if I have to commandeer and fly this thing myself."

The sight of the burned canyon stunned Lauren and Brad into silence. Ahead of them, the once lush valley looked like a bombed-out, blackened war zone. The moment they were over the site where she'd left Nicky, Lauren started to shake so hard that her teeth chattered. All she'd been through and all she'd seen was nothing next to finding her boy.

She saw ragged pieces of the plane on the shore; it had indeed exploded. She was amazed at how little it mattered, yet she began to heave huge sobs. Pulling against his seat belt, Brad leaned over to put a hand on her knee. Then he unsnapped his belt and knelt beside her so that they were both looking out the same window.

She mourned the loss of *Silver,* but that

was nothing next to Nicky's life.

The pilot put the chopper down on the shore not far from where Evan had forced her to run the plane into the trees. No one ran out to greet them. Some places were still smoking; a few tree trunks were gently glowing. The area was thoroughly burned, devastated. Even the little lake seemed to glitter black in the morning sun.

The second they opened the chopper door, Lauren rushed out, ducking under the rotors. Weren't they going to shut them down so she could call his name?

"Nicky!" she screamed, running toward where the plane had been. Not only did she see a fierce circle of fire but there was a hole in the shore under stumps of burned trees that had hidden the plane. Brad put his arm around her shoulders, but she pulled away and ran farther into the charred maze of tree trunks. Bushes and brush were obliterated; there was no place to hide.

"Niii-ck-eee!"

The rotors of the chopper finally ceased, leaving only silence.

"Niii-ck—eeeee!"

Her voice seemed to echo across the lake, or maybe it came back to her from the canyon. Could Nicky have fled into the canyon, trying to follow her? If so, he'd been doomed.

Brad and the others fanned out around the lake, calling his name. She knew Brad was keeping an eye on her, and he didn't go far from where she searched. Finally the pilot lifted a sopping, red jacket from the far edge of the lake.

"Dear God, please let him be safe!" she spoke aloud the mantra she'd been reciting silently as she ran over.

She hugged the sodden jacket to her, sobbing into it, then lifted her head. "I've got to stay here to look for him," she told them. "He might have been in the lake for a little while when the fire passed, but he can swim and knows how to hold his breath. I may have to go back into the canyon too. I'm going to —"

"Ma'am, I know this sounds terrible," Lieutenant Barton said, "but we're going to have to use this chopper for other things right now."

"Fine," she said, turning away from them and wading into the water to stare into its depths. "Fine, I understand. Just leave me here."

"Lauren," Brad said and sloshed in to take her arm.

"No. I know you all have jobs to do. Go

report in. You, too, Brad. I understand that, so —"

"I don't care if I have a job," Brad told her. "All I've done since I've been here is ignore my so-called duty to the masses so that I could try to help individual people — you, Nick, Chuck, Mari and Red. I keep telling myself that one precious life saved now is more important than FBI statistics down the road."

He picked her up as he had back at the holding pond, then strode toward the chopper. "No!" she cried, hitting at his shoulder with her fist. "I'm staying here!"

"We'll get another chopper or hike right back in through the valley with volunteers from Vermillion — and there will be plenty of those."

"He's just wandered off," she said, collapsing against him. "He can't be in that lake, but if he is . . ."

"Lauren, I swear to you, wherever he is, I will help you find him. I will make sure, one way or the other, that he comes home to you."

Back on the chopper, she sank into a stupor, staring out the window, not even blinking. She felt empty, sick to her soul. The chopper lifted up and away. Holding Nicky's wet jacket to her, Lauren felt completely defeated.

The Otter River went by under them, black on both sides. All those lovely flowers burned, she thought, praying she would not need flowers for a funeral. No, he could not be gone . . . not Nicky. He'd been rescued already and no one had told Dee, that was it.

"Ma'am," the pilot said and put the chopper into a tilted turn, "there's someone walking along the river back there, a small man or a boy."

Lauren and Brad pressed their faces to one window, then to the other side. Yes! Yes, it must be. It had to be!

"Please," she cried, "can you put down here?"

But he was already lowering the big bird to the blackened meadow. Where was the boy? She didn't see him now.

When they landed, she pushed past Brad before he could help her down to the ground. She saw tears streaming down his face. She ran with her arms outstretched, shrieking, "Nicky, Nicky, Nicky!"

Nicky started to run toward her, too, his arms wide. "Mom," he shouted just before she reached him, "don't get mad 'cause I didn't stay where you told me. I got in the water when the fire came and lost my jacket, but I'm really hungry, and I knew the way back home. Sorry, but *Silver* blew up and —"

She hit into him so hard that they both went to their knees. Hugging him, kissing him . . . Thank God. Thank you, Lord!

Nicky hugged her back hard, his strong, thin arms tight around her neck. A few moments passed, but they didn't budge. Then she heard him say, "Hi, Brad."

"Hi, Nick, my man."

"Did that bad guy get caught?"

"Yes," Brad said. "Yes, he did."

"He shouldn't tell lies. He told lots of them, but I'm not ever telling them anymore."

Her son's high-pitched little voice reverberated through her, as did Brad's lower, raspy tones. He knelt and put his arms around both of them. How she treasured having them both here, both safe.

"You look pretty messed up," Nicky said as he wriggled from their embrace. "Did you guys have to get in a lake to hide from the fire too?"

As their rescue chopper passed over Vermillion on its way to land, Brad thought the place looked like a busy anthill. Darting here and there, some in clusters, people were in the street and on the shore. He was so glad to be back, to see — but for the burned buildings — the place in one piece. It was almost like coming home.

As the chopper put down on a stretch of shore close to town, Brad could see a huge helicopter hovering over the lake, sucking up water to dump on the fire. Tents had been erected close to the dock. At least two hotshot crews wearing hard hats and fire-resistant yellow shirts and green pants lugged axes, chain saws and, yes, drip torches as they boarded a school bus, evidently heading out to contain the fire.

Brad had rejoiced in Lauren and Nick's reunion. Even now, she held the boy on her lap, hugging him tight while Nick expounded on his ordeal and Lauren made light of hers. She had told Brad how, after Ross died, Nick had hardly let her out of his sight; he wondered if the tables would be turned now. But if Lauren would let him, Brad had plans to be in the boy's life as well as in hers.

Dee met their chopper. And when she saw that they had Nick, she jumped up and down, screaming like a kid.

There were plenty of hugs and tears as they piled out. Exhausted and elated, Brad cried too. Then he saw Mike coming his way with Clay and Jen right behind. He swiped at his cheeks with the palms of his hands.

"You sure he's dead?" Mike greeted him above the hubbub. Suze and Larson were in the mix of people now, hysterical with joy, hugging everyone in sight.

Brad nodded.

"You saw him with your own eyes?" Clay demanded as his team surrounded him.

"Both Durands are dead," Brad told them. "I just wish I could have stopped BND before he started this last blaze — or any of them here."

"They say they'll control the mountain fire," Mike told him. "Damn, I wish we could have gotten him alive, but at least you're okay. We're going to have to debrief you now, while everything's fresh in your mind, then be sure we recover the body. Can you go with a team that hikes up there?"

"I told them where he is."

"It's just — He's been so elusive," Jen said, her eyes widening as she looked Brad over. "It would be just like him to have staged his death and then — *poof.*"

Clay said something else, maybe something about Brad getting his burns tended to. But Dee elbowed her way in, thrusting a mug of coffee at him, and Nick had squirmed between Mike and Clay. The kid was breaking a cookie in half that Larson had given him. He thrust part of it at Brad, then hung on to him. Lauren, looking like a flame-haired pagan goddess, was mouthing, "Thank you. Thank you always," again and again to him over Jen's shoulder.

Brad stuffed the cookie in his mouth and took a swig of the coffee. Then, clamping Nick to his side, Brad turned his back away from the team and headed for Lauren. Eating a chocolate-chip cookie with a boy who had come back from the dead, he walked right into the middle of the townspeople milling around him toward Lauren.

Brad supposed he was a failure in the eyes of the arson team. He hadn't captured BND alive or stopped three structural fires and two massive wildfires. But it was over for Evan and over for the hypocrite who had bred and reared him. If they branded Brad a failure, he still felt his coming here had been worth it. Who knows what Evan would have done if Lauren hadn't helped him fight back.

Mike came after him, repeating his order that he needed to be formally debriefed, but he was pushed back by the nurse who had tended Chuck at the clinic. Grabbing Lauren by the other hand, the nurse hustled them both — with Nick tight to Brad — away from Mike.

"Both of you now — and Nicky, too," she said, "come with me. We're going to the fire-house so I can look at those burns, then you all need a good hot meal. Lauren and Agent Hale, you're both heroes, you know, but even heroes need patching up at times — just ask Sheriff Cobern."

Brad didn't feel like a hero. His long-tended dream of solving arsons and fighting fires might be over, but the fire he felt inside each time he looked at Lauren still burned strong. He guessed the stubborn people of Vermillion thought he was okay because, as the nurse shooed the three of them down the street toward the fire station, people stopped to turn, clap, smile and wave.

Surely they were glad to have Nicky and Lauren back safe. But no, they were looking at him, nodding at him, even calling out his name as if he were a longtime friend.

Mike's voice in his ear muted. For one minute, in his exhaustion, Brad thought the clapping was the crackle of flames, but it went on and on, turning into swelling ap-plause.

He hugged Lauren, then lifted Nick up between them where the boy hooked an arm around each of their necks and pulled them so close to him that their noses and chins bumped.

"I think I just resigned from the FBI," he told her.

"And I don't have a livelihood anymore."

"Finding you and Nick's been worth it."

Lauren nodded and smiled. With Nick screeching, "Way to go!" in his ear, Brad kissed her long and hard.

25

The first snowflakes of the season fell in Vermillion the day Marilyn Gates and Red Russert were married. Mari's sister, in from Omaha, and Chuck Cobern stood up for the couple in the ceremony to which they had extended an open invitation to the community. It seemed the entire town, including Mrs. Gates's first-grade class, had turned out. In a way, two months to the day after the Nizitopi Mountain Wildfire was contained, it was a celebration of Vermillion's survival and recovery as well as a wedding day.

Now, to get the noisy, excited kids out of the reception at Dee's house, Lauren, with the help of the Fencer twins, had twenty hyper, sugar-buzzed first-graders at her house, making Just Married decorations for the inside of the plane that would fly the couple out for their honeymoon. It had been a beautiful day, though the joy of the occasion made Lauren miss Brad even more.

He'd been called to testify again this week in a senate committee in Washington, D.C., about his part in stopping the BND arsonist. It involved FBI funding for a domestic terrorist protection program. Otherwise, he would not have missed Red's wedding. Just as Brad had filled a void in her son's heart, it seemed that Red had become a sort of adopted dad to Brad.

"No," Lauren told Larson, pointing to what he had just printed. She couldn't help herself, but somehow this happy day had made her uptight. "It's not *Just Marred.* That means something else. There's an *i* missing from the word *married.* All of you, listen to me. Copy the sign in the middle of the table. Mrs. Gates is a stickler for spelling, so get the letters right."

"But her name isn't Mrs. Gates anymore, Mom," Nick said. "It's gonna be kinda hard to call her Mrs. Russert."

"I know," Lauren admitted. "Changes are hard but important."

There had been many changes in Lauren's life these last two months. Her insomnia had departed, as had her guilt over not pursuing what had really happened to Ross in the Coyote Canyon fire. It had been in all the newspapers that the arsonist—mass murderer Evan Durand had killed Ross and Kyle and that the ensuing investigation had been a sham.

Posthumously, David Durand's pristine reputation had taken a real hit, so that would have pleased Evan. She wasn't sorry they had found a bullet from the gun she'd been holding in Evan's hip, or the fact that it had probably slowed him down so that he was caught and killed by his own wildfire.

Other changes in her life were more mundane. She tried to help Nick with current events she'd previously ignored. They'd had many discussions about not talking to strangers and telling the truth, but how it was still important to have a good imagination. Lauren could almost hear Evan's voice, telling her not to nag Nick. She and Brad both wondered if the death of Evan's mother in a fiery car crash had been his first death by arson.

And then there was Brad in her life. Brad!

She pulled herself from her reverie as little heads bent over their cutting and coloring, adding stickers and gluing on hearts. Lauren's wedding gift to the Russerts was to fly them into Kalispell, where they would board a jet for Phoenix to soak up the sun and see the sights. It would almost be the inaugural flight for her new Cessna pontoon plane she'd purchased with the reward money for *information which led to the capture and or arrest of Evan Durand, alias the BND serial arsonist,* as the citation, which came with the check Brad had personally delivered, had read.

Both Brad and she had been hailed as heroes and even featured on several nightly newscasts and in an article in *People* magazine. The publicity from all that had worked wonders for ski lodge reservations for this winter. With all the accolades, Brad's boss had not dared to let him go. But Brad had admitted he wasn't happy in his arson-fighting mission anymore. At least he'd made time to visit her and Nick every couple of weeks and called often.

"I know a joke," Susie Parker piped up from down the table where someone had just spilled juice that Ginnie Fencer was mopping up. "Red Russert and Mrs. Gates, sitting in a tree, k-i-s-s-i-n-g! First comes love, then comes marriage, then comes Mrs. Gates with a baby carriage!"

The kids all laughed, but Nick's wide eyes snagged Lauren's gaze. He'd walked in on her and Brad when they were really hot and heavy on the couch in front of the fireplace the last time he was here. They hadn't seen him at first until he'd announced, "I'm not keeping pretend people around or keeping secrets anymore, like you said, Mom. But I can't sleep till I know if you guys are keeping secrets from me."

Startled, they'd scrambled apart, then just sat up to lean shoulder to shoulder, facing him.

"Such as, pal?" Brad had asked, his voice as husky as it had been when they'd inhaled all that smoke.

"I heard where babies come from, and I was wondering if you are trying to get me a brother or sister. I'd rather have a brother, but don't you have to get married first?"

"Nick," Lauren had begun, floundering for words, "you can't just —"

"We're thinking about all that, Nick," Brad had interrupted. "As a matter of fact, we were doing some practice thinking about that just now, so you get on back to bed. Want me to go up with you?"

"No, I'm not afraid of anything anymore, even though I got took out that window by that liar ars'nist. I think he got dead because he was grabbed by a Blackfeet Indian ghost. He lied to me about the Blackfeet, so he got punished. That's what I think. And that's another reason I don't tell lies anymore. It's okay," he'd said, sounding wise and comforting beyond his years as they'd sat there disturbed and disheveled. "You can go back to your thinking now."

After he'd returned to bed, they'd dissolved in laughter, but all that didn't seem funny now. Brad had already won her heart and Nick's, too, but she knew something was holding him back from full commitment. He hadn't asked, but both she and Nick would have given up all they loved here to live in Denver or anywhere else with him — however much leaving would hurt.

"All right, it's almost two o'clock," Lauren announced to the kids, "so you all finish up, and I'll go get changed to fly the newlyweds to Kalispell. I'll decorate the inside of the plane with this beautiful artwork before they get to the dock. I'll tell them what a good job all of you did, but I don't think you should expect any baby carriages. Mrs. Russert has enough on her hands with all of you."

As the plane crested the mountains and descended toward Kalispell, Lauren noted it was snowing halfheartedly here too. Big, lazy flakes spun down from heaven around them.

"We missed Brad today, Lauren," Mari said from where they sat behind her. "But as soon as our new house is finished and

488

you two have a spare evening, you are both to come for dinner."

"We'd love that. I missed him today, too — well, every day."

"Bet he'll be back sooner than you think," Red put in from the back seat where they'd been holding hands the whole way. Lauren heard Mari smack his knee.

"Have you been talking to him again, Red?" Lauren asked. "Sometimes I think he comes to Vermillion to see you as much as me and Nick."

"If you're not kidding, girl, I think you got blinders on," Red told her. "But then, I've known a woman or two in my day who didn't realize how much they were loved 'til it hit them over the head."

"Talk about getting hit over the head," Mari said. "I still wonder about you sometimes, Red Russert. All we've been through might have been worth it to me just to have those staring, glassy-eyed heads of that mounted game in your living room and bedroom go up in smoke."

"Now, Mari."

"Bring one of those into our new house and your head will be stuffed and mounted right beside it, my love."

Lauren could tell they were kissing again as she brought the Cessna down toward the runway. The landing gear on this plane did not come down with a clunk, and the wheels barely bounced as she taxied toward the main gate instead of the storage sheds this time. She and Nick — with Brad voting, too — had named the new plane *Golden* because of a butterscotch-hued stripe down its side.

"Gold is better than silver, right, Mom?" Nicky had asked. "I'm reading a book about skiing in the Olympics, like I want to do someday when I take some more lessons, and gold is better than silver there."

Yes, Lauren thought now, gold was better than silver. And a new life could be better than the old, she was sure of that, if only it could include Brad. She knew somehow, as soon as Mari and Red got out and hurried off to their honeymoon, it was going to be a long, lonely ride back to Vermillion.

"Cessna Bravo Niner Alpha," came the crisp voice on her new radio, answering her earlier call for permission to land, "you are cleared for gate two. And you have a passenger waiting to go back to Vermillion, Lauren."

"Roger that," she said automatically, then recalled that the last time she'd heard something similar, Evan Durand had been waiting for her.

On the tie-down at gate two, she set the parking brake and shut the engines down. "Well, would you look at that," Red said as she opened the door.

"At what?" she asked, then sensed as well as thought what he might mean.

She spun to face the terminal. Striding out through falling flakes came Brad, grinning and waving, pushing a loaded luggage cart. Her insides cartwheeled. He had flowers.

He hugged Lauren and kissed her hard. Her pulse pounded as it always did when he so much as appeared, even from just the next room. If they were ever really together, would she ever get over this permanent heart condition?

"I was hoping to catch you two before you literally took off together," Brad told the newlyweds and kissed Mari's cheek. He stuck out his hand to Red.

"Oh, hell," Red said and hugged Brad, then set him back and smacked his shoulder.

"More flowers for the bride, for your Phoenix hotel room," Brad said and thrust a bouquet of roses into Mari's arms. So this wasn't a special occasion between Brad and her, Lauren thought. That was fine. Anytime he was here was already special.

Brad helped Red get their luggage out of

the plane and put it on his cart, then loaded his gear into *Golden.* The four of them said their goodbyes with more hugs all around. Brad raced ahead to open the terminal door for them, and then they disappeared to start their new life.

"This is way more than you usually bring," Lauren told him as he returned to loading the plane. She tried to sound calm, even businesslike. "Skis? There's not that much snow yet."

"There will be before I leave this time. Dee and Chuck have offered me a room for a while if you don't want me around day and night."

She sucked in a breath. This was starting to sound like a conspiracy — a wonderful one. Because she didn't want to just smother him with kisses or suffocate him with a hug, she blurted, "Nick's going to take ski lessons this winter and —"

"I know. I'm teaching him, with his mother's permission, of course. Besides, I thought you'd have room for skis, but you'd never get six quarter horses into this plane."

"What?"

Still grinning, he piled into the copilot seat and she climbed in the other side. "If you don't tell me what you're talking about," she said, "I'm going to go see if I can pick up some good-looking, macho guy with impressive creds in the coffee shop across the tarmac."

"I hear you. I've been testifying so long under the glares of grim senators and camera lenses, I think I can handle explaining this to one beautiful woman. Lauren, now that the formal, public fallout from the BND case is over and I won't hurt the team or the terrorist funding, I resigned. The lease on my apartment in Denver's up, so I'm looking for a place in Vermillion to buy or build, where I can have a stable for back-country packhorses to start my business there. Man, that place needs more than the Fencer twins' two old mares. Besides, Chuck says he wants more time with Dee, so he'll stick with being sheriff and I'll become Vermillion's fire chief.

"Hey," he went on, sounding ebullient when she just gaped at him, "look at all these great heart decorations in here. Perfect."

"Yes, Mari and Red loved them."

"I mean, perfect for this. I was going to wait until we were soaring over the mountains with eagles today — or should I say snowflakes? — but I'm just like Nick. I cannot wait. I have to barge right in with what I want to say."

From his jacket pocket he produced a small box of dark blue leather. It was a good thing she'd just snapped her seat belt on or she might have taken off without the plane.

"I know this part of it is sudden," he explained, "but I didn't want the intensity of our relationship to stampede you into anything. Since we've both been through so much, and getting everything in order took me a while, you can take your time deciding, if you want. Lauren, I had commitments to my cause, but no more. You and Nick and life in Vermillion are now my cause, if you will have me."

The gold ring was stunning, with a round diamond like a little sun nestled in the blue velvet of its own sky.

"Yes," she said as she stared at it, then him, "I will need some time. About as much time as it takes you to put that on my finger."

His big hands shook as he took the ring out and slid it on her trembling hand. They held tight to each other, then kissed endlessly as snowflakes piled up on the cockpit windows, sealing them in together.

"I'm ready to go home," he whispered.

"Yes, home." She swiped at her tears with the handkerchief he handed her. "And we're going to fly over the Vermillion Valley on the way in because, peeking through the snow and charred grass, you're going to see a hint of green already, new growth, new life."

"I'm betting on it!" he said. "Let's go."

AUTHOR'S NOTE

Readers often ask where I get ideas for my novels. The inspiration for *Inferno* came from a trip my husband and I took to the Rocky Mountains in the summer of 2005. We visited several areas where pontoon planes ferried visitors between smaller mountain towns and larger cities. We visited beautiful valleys and saw pristine waterfalls. Most compelling of all, we took a train through a mountain area that was threatened by a wildfire that we could smell even before we saw it. We also observed what I later learned was a hotshot crew, hiking up the mountain to try to build a firebreak.

Because I live in flatland Ohio and the even flatter Everglades area of south Florida, I was thrilled by the magnificence of the mountains and greatly intrigued by the rugged individuals who live there.

As for the arson investigation information, my thanks to arson investigator Marty

Robinson of the Columbus, Ohio, fire department and arson investigator Craig Hall of the Worthington, Ohio, fire department. And to my nephew, firefighter Aaron Kurtz, for information about fire engines. Thanks to Laurie Kingery, E.R. nurse and author, for advice about treating burns. And to my author friend Karyn Witmer-Gow for advice on St. Louis neighborhoods and cemeteries. Any mistakes in facts are those of the author.

Also, as ever, very special thanks to my wonderful Rotrosen support team, especially Meg Ruley and Annelise Robey. And thanks to Miranda Stecyk, my excellent Mira Books editor, and the entire Mira family. I greatly appreciate all that you do.

ABOUT THE AUTHOR

New York Times bestselling author **Karen Harper** is a former high-school and college English teacher. Winner of the 2005 Mary Higgins Clark Award for her outstanding novel, *Dark Angel,* Karen is the author of twelve romantic suspense novels and two historical novels, as well as a series of historical mysteries. Karen and her husband, who divide their time between Columbus, Ohio, and Naples, Florida, love to travel both in the U.S. and abroad. For additional information about Karen and her novels, please visit www.karenharperauthor.com.